"Is there a relationship between you and Pemberton?"

I delighted in this hint of jealousy. Surely, it was a sign of his sincere interest in me.

"I watched you both tonight, whispering and giggling behind your hands, like schoolchildren."

"I never giggle."

He caught me by the shoulders and pulled me hard against his body. I thought for a moment he was going to shake me.

"You love that puppy? Show me."

I opened my mouth to protest at his violence and he took possession of it, hotly silencing me with his lips. Even as my body betrayed me by its quick, throbbing response, I knew I should resent his furious conquest. No matter. I loved him. I wanted him. He was the only man I had ever wanted quite in this way, with some of his own violence. The heat of his mouth and his male hardness against me evoked a searing response I had not thought myself capable of. I was still in the thrall of this fresh, wondrous passion when he held me away from him, the length of his arms.

"Shall I show you how a true man may love you?" he asked.

☆ ☆ ☆ ☆

Dark Desire

Virginia Coffman

POPULAR LIBRARY

An Imprint of Warner Books, Inc.

A Warner Communications Company

POPULAR LIBRARY EDITION

Cover art by Pino Daeni

Popular Library books are published by
Warner Books, Inc.
666 Fifth Avenue
New York, N.Y. 10103

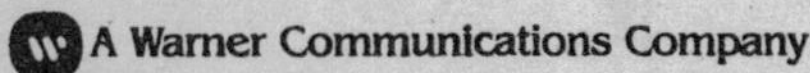
A Warner Communications Company

Printed in the United States of America

First Printing: January, 1987

10 9 8 7 6 5 4 3 2 1

For Donnie always,
in dearest memory of
Johnny Micciche

PROLOGUE

There are memories of passionate love or hate that sear their actions on the brain. And so it was that night before the arrest, before he was taken from me for questioning.

Long afterward, when the autumn air is filled with wood smoke and the great château walls are bright with tenacious red ivy, I remember every detail of our desperate lovemaking on that night.

It began when we argued in an upper hall of the Château Bertold. At all events, Nicolas argued. He had guessed my suspicions and was harsh and bitter.

"You don't really trust me, either, do you? My own nephew has convinced you that I am a murderer. That I poisoned a kind old man who had been my friend since my childhood. Now you believe I would murder that boy, the only blood relation left to me."

"Hush! Someone will hear you."

He seemed to care very little, though the huge old château was filled with dinner guests staying the night and scattered throughout the many rooms around us.

In former days Nicolas must have been just as indifferent

to those who heard his quarrels with my brother William. His eyes burned with the passion of those feelings that had been building all night. He reached for me. I reacted instinctively against that look like burning darkness in his eyes. I backed away.

He caught my arms and pulled me to him.

I feared him and I feared myself. I knew that despite everything, I would never love again as I loved him now when he needed me.

"Come."

"Nicolas, Jeremy is waiting to say good night."

I knew the influence his lovemaking would have on me. Suspicion, certainty, a hundred doubts would fade.

"Come with me."

I found myself propelled across the hall to that bedchamber with its warm, crimson hangings, the Velvet Room in which we had achieved our wildest happiness.

I tried to laugh.

"Look at me . . . darling. A half dozen petticoats, all these yards of taffeta. My jewels—"

His thumbs pressed painfully into the swelling flesh of my bosom above the neckline of my gown.

"That is easily solved. I have always imagined making love to a Venus who let nothing but diamonds intrude upon her beauty. Take off everything but the diamonds. Let me see you as Venus."

"I am no Venus, and you are being nonsensical. There may still be guests wandering about the halls."

He gave me a little shove.

"Take them off. The skirts, the petticoats, all those ridiculous coverings." He bolted the door.

Did he think I would run out screaming, introduce a score of sleeping guests to our domestic crisis?

I began, "Nicolas . . ."

"It was *darling* a moment ago."

"Darling, listen to me."

He laughed. It was not a pleasant sound.

"Please, don't force yourself, my sweet. I sometimes wonder if there ever was a time when you loved me."

I was hurt and indignant at his willful misunderstanding of my nature. I am an English countrywoman. In our family we seldom, if ever, used endearments. I turned away but was startled by his deep, resonant voice. The command came like the crack of a whip.

"Undress."

I was too proud to struggle over his manner. I closed my eyes, so angry that I could scarcely reach the buttons and hooks at the back of my gown. He stood watching me in that nastily amused way, which alarmed, even while it excited, me.

He did not help me.

The gown whose materials and style we had chosen together in Paris spread in a circle around my feet. The stiffened petticoats came after, with my lace-and-satin camisole and the tight lacing.

By the glimmer of two candles, one at either side of his shaving stand, he stared at me, the smile gone, his eyes glowing with that hard light as he studied my unclothed flesh. I tried not to shiver or to laugh nervously, aware of Grandmama's earrings dangling against the flesh of my face.

There was a fire in the grate across the room and I was not cold, but I couldn't hide my quickened breathing or the effect his gaze, his mood, had upon my nakedness. He would notice the rising hardness of my breasts betraying my own desire, the way I moistened my lips without intending to.

But I refused to cover my nakedness coyly with outspread fingers. With the necklace of my grandmother's diamonds heavy against my throat, I stood there trying to look proud and triumphant while he stared at my breasts and then at the curve of my flanks and the red-gold triangle of hair that modesty should have made me ashamed to reveal in the light, even to him.

I got up enough courage finally to challenge him.

"What? Now that you have what you wanted, don't you know what to do with me?"

He was as tense as I, and fully ready. I knew the signs. Extending one hand, he said hoarsely, "Come!"

I could not let that challenge pass. I swallowed hard, managed to exclude all uncertainty. I became greatly daring, for I knew his strength and power; and he looked very forbidding in the stark black and white of evening wear.

"Very well. I am as you want me."

His extended arm was close to me. At my challenge his fingers curled in on his palm. Otherwise he was perfectly still. I thought my heartbeat would stifle me, and I laughed, though I was no more amused than he. But this last taunting sound was too much for him.

He reached for me, pulled me so roughly that my long, dangling earrings lashed my cheeks. At my bare throat, the diamond settings in their intricate, webbed pattern, cut into my flesh as I was pressed against his breast, but neither Nicolas nor I cared for that. His lips, at the hollow between my breasts, further aroused me as he knew they would.

Where we had always been so happy in our lovemaking, on the high bed with its velvet curtains pulled back, I made a struggle for pride's sake, but I knew this only stimulated us further.

In the bed he fell upon me, his mouth like fire, branding my breasts and my thighs so that I would remember forever. Then, as my limbs opened to his invasion, he took possession of me, even as I possessed him, within my body and my heart.

But the end was inevitable. Though I still loved him, my suspicions remained, and minutes later, when we parted, our senses reeling at what we shared, he guessed that nothing had changed.

While I dressed again, tying loops in petticoat cords, lacing myself once more, fastening both buttons and hooks in my gown, he kept watching me, with what bitter thoughts I could well imagine when he spoke.

"My God, I wish I had never met the Daviots, any of them! My loving brother-in-law or that accursed boy or you. You may rot in hell for all it concerns me."

I shot back the bolt of the door and left him. He did not follow me.

It was only a few hours later, on a sunny, autumn morning, that he was quietly charged by his friend, the king's prosecutor, and they rode away together.

How had it all begun, my acquaintance with Nicolas Bertold and murder? And how different my feelings were, before I ever met this dark, embittered French aristocrat!

It was easy to believe him guilty in the days before I knew him, months before that last, fiery night of passion and suspicion.

CHAPTER ONE

In those summer days I knew only what news reached me in rural England. The investigation into my brother's death was still proceeding, but the French judicial system was very slow and very thorough. How sure I was of this unknown Frenchman's guilt!

Each morning I told myself that today the London mail coach would bring news of the aristocratic murderer's trial. During that long wait for the decision of the French courts, it often seemed to me that this bright, flower-scented summer of 1847 was the most harrowing of my life.

It was not until the first beech trees on Ferndene Heath were beginning to turn that we heard the news one August afternoon and the nervous tension was lifted, only to reveal the terror beneath.

The morning rain cleared early that day. I threw on a shawl, got my nephew into a light summer jacket, and we walked into the village to await the mail coach. While we waited, I hoped to free myself, and especially seven-year-old young Jeremy, from anxious thoughts and perhaps show him some of our English ways.

But I should have known we could not escape. There are

helpful gossips in any village, even among the coombes, cliffs, and water meadows of Dorset. Lady Willoughby is the self-appointed social arbiter of our region. She has known me from infancy, and we hold to little formality between us.

Her Ladyship's daughter, Mavis, and I once shared a bedroom at Miss Ponsonby's London School for Genteel Young Females. Though we were still great friends, our school days were far behind us. I was now a spinster of twenty-three, but I daresay that I will never be an adult in Lady Willoughby's eyes.

She called to me from the doorway of the mercer's shop. "My dear Alain, do tell me the latest news."

"What news?" I asked, knowing quite well what she meant.

She shook a finger at me. "The trial, of course. Will there be one? My daughter insists that no one as attractive as Nicolas Bertold can be a villain. There was a sketch of him in the London *Post* last Wednesday week. I daresay, you saw it."

"I did." Indeed, her daughter Mavis had broken all records with her pony cart in bringing the paper to me.

I remembered too well the powerful, dark head of the monster, and the hint of a somber, dangerous nature in those extraordinary black eyes. Mavis claimed his smile might change all that. But for me his looks only added to his crimes against my family. I allowed for my friend Mavis's deeply romantic heart. She would have defended Satan, himself, if she thought him sensual. It could not sway me. I said, "The sketch alone warned me. A villainous fellow if ever I saw one."

Lady Willoughby chided me. "Don't look so serious, child. I am told they still send murderers to the guillotine in France."

"A comforting thought."

"So you need not fear to see that rogue arriving on your doorstep one day to snatch up his sweet little nephew."

Beside me, clutching my hand in a passionate grip, my

nephew reacted. His delicate features hardened, and his lower lip went out belligerently.

"I'm Aunt Alain's nephew."

I squeezed his thin shoulder to acknowledge our warm bond and dismissed Her Ladyship's hint of the threat from that quarter.

"I daresay, the French courts will hold Monsieur Bertold for trial. They are perfectly competent, and Nanny Pemberton has offered Jeremy's testimony. He was an eyewitness."

"It is unfortunate that the boy was too ill to be questioned in his own person, so to speak."

I said stiffly, "The French authorities thought it best. Jeremy has breathing problems when he is nervous or upset."

She held a length of puce-striped barège up in the watery sunlight and nodded to the mercer's wife. "Just so. Nothing elaborate. About eighteen yards. My little seamstress will make it up. . . . Well, Alain, I'm sure we all wish you good fortune with young Jeremy. But they do say this Bertold is one of King Louis-Philippe's bosom friends. And that may save the wretch."

Jeremy was shaken, but he managed to inform her bravely, "I'm to stay with Aunt Alain. He can't make me go back. I won't go!" His voice rose and, with it, the difficulty in catching his breath that always accompanied any excitement. "Will I?" He gaze up at me with that same poignant, wary look I have seen in a vixen I've come upon suddenly in the woods.

I said, "Of course, you shall not go if you don't wish to."

He admitted wistfully, "I'd like to go back. If it wasn't for— But I wouldn't be afraid if you were there."

Between us we had attracted some of the other villagers, who were quite as curious about the fate of Jeremy's French uncle as Lady Willoughby was. Tad Spindler, a man I knew to be a poacher in season, pulled open the door of the one inn our village afforded. I waved to Tad, who grinned back, showering the ground with drops of gin from his rum mug.

"Good day to ye, Miss Alain. Heerd a news o'er the water?"

I often employed Tad at Daviot House for odd jobs when he was sober, and we were old friends.

"Not yet, Tad. Nanny Pemberton and her son will be returning from Paris any day now. But they had many things to do, arranging Jeremy's affairs and presenting Jeremy's testimony."

"They're a bad lot, them Frenchies." His expert opinion received nods from the other villagers within hearing. He was also pleased at my mention of Nanny's son, Richard, who had always befriended him during his scrapes with the game laws. "Aye. Master Richard. He'll do." He finished his gin, and after throwing the mug back through the doorway of the inn, he loped off to Coombe Bower outside the village where he shared a tiny shepherd's hut with his aged father.

To take Jeremy's mind off the subject of his French uncle, I tried to be very cheerful.

"Since we've beaten the London mail, shall we go to the Penny Shop and buy a sweet?"

Jeremy revived like a lamb gamboling through the water meadow. "Oh, may we? And could I have a . . . what you call them? A Banbury cake full of spices?"

I assured him we would both have one, and we walked along the muddy runnel of the street in excellent charity with each other, he in his elegant French boots and I in my country-woman's pattens, to preserve my skirts.

I knew when he bit into Mother Hagar's newly baked spice bun, however, that the delicious aroma brought back memories. He began to look thoughtful and to eat very slowly, preserving each bite in the pocket of his cheek. I tried to tease him out of the sullens.

"What, Jeremy? Spice buns make you sad?"

He shook his head. "It was just the good smell made me think of . . ." He paused, then added in a small voice, ". . . of home."

A little hurt I wanted to remind him, "You are home," but I did not. I knew that Château Bertold, in France's Loire country, was a very grand place, much finer than Daviot House, in which my brother William, Jeremy's father, and I had been born. But I had thought Jeremy's memories of the bloody crime that occurred this January at the château would color his feelings for the place and turn him from it. Evidently not.

"Do you miss the château so much?" I asked him, attempting to make the question casual.

He considered what remained of his spice bun. Having eaten all around the edges, he saved the spicy center for the last.

"Well, I knew the people, you see. And there were Mama and Papa. Of course, Papa hated the big house, and Uncle Nicolas. And he didn't like the pond with all the lily pads. It's a moat for the house, you know, and very old. Papa said he didn't like anything where you couldn't see the bottom. On account of the lily pads, you know." He raised his dark eyes, so like his mother's, I'm told, and looked at me, to see if I understood.

I prompted him matter-of-factly, "But still your father remained at the château. He did not bring you and your mother home to Daviot House."

"He was afraid Uncle Nicolas would take all the land from Mama and me. Uncle Nicolas gets half of everything, you know."

Yes. I knew. It was a divided inheritance that had caused the whole tragedy. Everything I had heard about the death of my brother William, and Yolande, his wife, pointed to that accursed will in which Maréchal Bertold, one of Napoleon's generals, had left his estate equally to his son, Nicolas, and his daughter, Yolande. The estate was all the greater because the wily Maréchal had betrayed his imperial benefactor during the Hundred Days and worked first for the Restoration, then, fifteen years later, had betrayed the Bourbons for the present Orléans king, Louis-Philippe.

A treacherous family, it would seem.

From the moment my good, stubborn brother William went to Paris to sell King Louis-Philippe on the subject of British wool, it had been love at his first sight of the capricious and beautiful Yolande. The Bertolds, as William wrote to me with some amusement, were so proud of their ancient name that they made no effort to acquire spurious titles. But William Andrew Daviot was a foreigner. Worse. He was as opinionated and arrogant as the Bertolds—two black marks against him in Bertold eyes—and there had been some resistance to the marriage, a resistance that galled William. My brother was fully as proud as the Bertolds.

Yolande, however, was determined to have her *Anglais*, and in the end they were married. The son of our Nanny, Richard Pemberton, stood up for William, who had been his boyhood friend. Richard came home to our village delighted with the marriage and describing in detail the elaborate celebration at Château Bertold after a private ceremony in the local village church.

All that was ten years past. Jeremy was born a little more than two years later. William had brought Jeremy here, to meet me in England, when the boy was five. He was a delightful child, if somewhat delicate, and we got on very well, but even then, I could see that William was discontented, more easily angered and more explosive than he had been before he went to France.

I suspected the problem lay in two such different masters ruling over the extensive Bertold estates. I couldn't imagine William living anywhere without loudly asserting his own opinion. I had learned long ago to manage him by quietly ignoring his shouted orders. Eventually he came to see things my way. But it was obvious that this system was not successful with the Bertold family, particularly Yolande's brother.

Jeremy swallowed the last of his spice bun in a great hurry and rushed to the door, rattling off French in his excitement.

"It is the Diligénce, the coach with the mails. I saw it crossing the bridge. There. It passes the church."

I made some attempt at decorum, moving calmly to the door to watch the street over Jeremy's head. The Exeter Coach made connections with the Shaftesbury Mail, thus circuitously bringing both passengers and news of the Great World to our doorstep. I saw the top-heavy coach rolling toward us, over the wagon ruts and cobblestones, the winded team wild-eyed and stirring up dust that made Jeremy cough.

I drew him back, but I was as anxious as he. In order to prevent too great a disappointment I reminded him softly, "Even if the news doesn't come today, there is tomorrow. Remember. Tomorrow."

"You said that yesterday." The accusation was more sad than accusatory. "It's not the news I want. It's—" He broke off.

I ran a hand over the crown of his head in an effort to make him feel less alone, less deserted by all that he loved. I knew now that his real concern was for Nanny Pemberton, whom he had loved quite as much as he loved his father and mother.

Probably Nanny, herself, would bring the news about Nicolas Bertold's approaching trial for the murders of his brother-in-law, William Daviot, and his sister Yolande. I gave him the benefit of the doubt about his sister. According to my correspondence from Nanny's son, Richard, it seemed that Nicolas Bertold had hoped to catch William and Jeremy in the collapse of the moat bridge. On an impulse Yolande had started to the village with her husband instead, and died with him in place of young Jeremy, Bertold's logical target.

Whether Bertold intended to kill his own sister or not, he had certainly planned William's murder, and for that I led the local hatred of the evil Frenchman.

The old coach, which carried a full complement of passengers as well as the mail, lurched to a stop before the inn, and Jeremy pulled hard at my hand.

"Come along, Aunt Alain. We'll be late. They may drive on and take Nanny."

I let myself be tugged along by Jeremy, retracing our steps toward the inn. Three young dandies, who had been imbibing rather too freely on the coach roof, tumbled down, one of them losing his fine silk top hat in the process. Their descent brought them into collision with a lady about to make her way down the coach steps. The lady was wearing the new spreading skirts stiffened with horsehair, and the result was calamitous. The skirts flaired out, revealing petticoats and what may have been a shift, as the lady was pressed hard against the side of the coach.

Behind her, a gentleman was about to assist down an elderly female in a sensible round gown, but he leapt neatly to the ground and managed to set all to rights. It was exactly what one might have expected of Richard Pemberton, looking neat, well-groomed, but far from a dandy in his tan frock coat and pantaloons, his hat firmly in place despite his exertions.

He placated the lady, brushed her off, displayed all the good manners for which he was locally celebrated. The lady, somewhat mollified, was escorted to the inn for a brief refreshment of tea and cakes, while a new team was run out. Richard then turned to assist his mother down.

Nanny Pemberton's round, pleasant face was wreathed in smiles as she caught sight of Jeremy, who jumped up and down crying shrilly, "Nanny! *C'est tu. C'est tu.*"

The plump little woman held her arms out to him.

"Of course, it is, my pet. Come to Nanny and give us a big kiss."

I was a trifle surprised that the boy had behaved in such a grown-up fashion toward me, very reserved in his affections, as I myself was, and then demonstrated such a public devotion to Nanny. He ran to her, let her enfold him, and knocked her bonnet askew while he kissed her on both cheeks in the French fashion.

But why should he not? Nanny had been my own second mother in youth, as she was William's. Indeed, Richard Pemberton often complained in his joking way that his mother was more fond of his friend than of himself. Richard and William often joked about themselves as "brothers."

It was this early companionship between Richard Pemberton and my brother that had several times made me remind Richard, "If I were to marry you, it would be a sin."

"A sin?" Richard was baffled.

"Marrying you would be like marrying one's brother."

Richard saw no humor or irony in that. But humor was one of the rare attributes our childhood companion lacked.

With Jeremy enfolded in Nanny's arms, and myself in a state of apprehension over the result of their trip from France, Richard came to me, holding out his hands, almost as his mother had done to welcome Jeremy. His smile was warm. The afternoon brightened as the clouds dissolved overhead.

"Dearest Alain! Lovelier than ever, I do believe. Those dark Frenchwomen are nothing to you. You are sunlight. They are shadow."

"And you've come home a French gallant," I teased.

Our hands joined as he smiled into my eyes. Still, I could not tell from his manner what news he and Nanny brought, except that he appeared to be his own gently firm self, always capable in an emergency and looking quite as handsome as Mavis Willoughby and I always had considered him.

I turned to Nanny, whom I used to tease because the males were her first priority and I only came second. But today she gave Jeremy over to her son briefly while she welcomed me with a little bobbing curtsy and a pretty blush when I kissed her cheek.

"Nanny, dear, how you were missed! I should hate you. Do you know, I haven't had a day's peace since I welcomed

Jeremy at Dover. He is forever asking when you will be home."

"The dear lamb." She looked around at Jeremy with loving eyes. "Missed his old Nanny, did he?"

Jeremy pulled at the knitted and fringed shawl she invariably wore over her dark, motherly gowns.

"Aunt Alain gave me a kitten, Nanny. And a lamb. A real lamb. And I fell in the brook. It runs through the water meadow. She would have given me a dog, but it jumped on me, and I didn't like that."

Nanny's gaze shifted to me, deeply reproachful. It was Richard who answered with some impatience, "Jeremy can swim, Mother. And Daviot Brook is hardly the English Channel. As to dogs, he should be used to them at his age."

Jeremy looked uneasy, but Nanny softened and patted my arm.

"I know. You did all that a maiden could be expected to do, not having children of your own. But now you may rest, Miss Alain. Old Nanny is home to look out after both of you. I only wish Master William was—"

"Mother," Richard reminded her.

She bit her faintly wrinkled lip, shrugged, and smiled with an effort. "Forgive me, all. Shall we be on our way? It will be good to get home again. Did old John Coachman bring you, Miss Alain?"

"I'm sorry. We walked. You see, we didn't know whether to expect you or not."

Richard looked around the street, frowning. He had become aware of the townspeople's interest in us, and especially in him. He knew very well what they wanted to hear. I shared their burning curiosity but, for some reason, was afraid to ask the all-important question.

He said, "I'll arrange something with the hostler here at the inn. We are old friends."

It was done in a matter of minutes, during which time Jeremy and Nanny chattered with such animation that I had no chance to interrupt them. I found myself trembling with anxiety. This knowledge angered me. I suspected the news was bad, and it would be better to know it now and have done with it. As long as it was not certain, I could still hope.

Finally we were all bundled into Farmer Budleigh's wagon, with Jeremy proudly squeezed between Budleigh and Richard while Nanny and I settled down in a gingerly way near the furze cuttings in the back, which had been collected by the farmer's three sons.

During the ride back through the late-summer meadows, now sparkling with shallow blue pools of rainwater, Nanny spoke of the changes she'd noticed since her departure for France with William and Jeremy after their visit two years ago.

"My dears, Miss Alain, that meadow was ablaze with pretty pink campions. They were so dark, they made me think of—" She cleared her throat. "Well, now, they were positively red, so they were. And that oak. I saw a thrush on the longest branch where William and my Richard used to hang their swings. Light brown it was—the thrush, I mean—with the prettiest spotted bosom. It must be long gone by now. . . ." Her voice trailed off at a memory. "Like so many others."

I hated it when someone aroused all the pain of my loss again. I wanted to be strong, to think of abstract matters, such as justice. Surely, when justice was served in my brother's case, the pain would eventually ease. Finally, I blurted out, "The news is bad."

Nanny reached for my hand. "My dear child."

"It is, then."

"These Frenchies, you know. And the aristocrats are the worst. Monsieur—I mean that man—had such friends! Detestable. They read books like that dreadful George Sand. So shocking! They say he is a woman. And they called Master William *le Sauvage Anglais*. I daresay, it was because of the language. They are so very particular. I must say, my dear, your French was always superior to Master William's. And the accusation is absurd. Monsieur Bertold is much more of a savage than our William."

"What happened?"

Nanny took a long, shuddering breath.

"They freed the m-monster."

CHAPTER TWO

I was stunned, and yet I should not have been. Lady Willoughby had warned me that Monsieur Bertold was closely allied to the present king of France. I did not doubt for a moment that this relationship had shielded the murderer from justice.

Unless, of course, the French courts knew something that we did not, and Nicolas Bertold was actually innocent....

Impossible. Not with the evidence of Jeremy and of Nanny Pemberton.

"Nothing will be done against him, then?"

"Miss Alain, I saw him with these eyes, the great, arrogant creature that he is, walk out of that dreadful castle on the island in Paris. I had no idea people were still taken there for questioning. Exactly like their nasty revolutions, just as Richard says."

"The Conciergerie." I shared her revulsion. Even though I hated the unknown Nicolas Bertold, I remembered all the dreadful stories of victims during the Great Revolution and how they had gone directly from the gloomy, medieval Conciergerie to the guillotine.

That was over fifty years ago, but the dreadful picture

remained in my mind. I could not wish anyone to meet such a fate, unless the evidence of his crimes was overwhelming.

After reordering my thoughts and trying to adapt to the news, I asked her carefully, "Do you know why they dismissed the evidence of Jeremy's own eyes? And yours?"

Nanny picked at her glove, held her hand out before me, the plump, short fingers spread. I remembered how often in my childhood those fingers had been gentle, caressing, sometimes scolding, but never cruel. "It is nice; isn't it? Genuine kid. I never had any before."

"They're very nice, indeed. From Richard?"

She regarded the glove thoughtfully.

"You will not credit it. They came from Monsieur, himself."

That did startle me.

"Nicolas Bertold gave them to you? Handsome of him."

"Perhaps he hoped to buy my friendship. It was last Christmas." Her expression softened. She was recalling happier times. "Monsieur Bertold was always very generous. When I first came to the château, I thought he was abrupt but rather likable. On occasion, when he smiled, he was even—well, that was in his rare moods."

"A strange man," I murmured, conscious of an unwanted ambivalence in my feelings toward him.

"Yes. So strange. At first, nine years ago, when the baby was born, and after, he seemed to like Jeremy. Of course, he never got on with Master William, but who would have thought he would come to hate a harmless little boy?"

"You really think he intended to kill Jeremy as well as William? I know Jeremy saw him with the estate worker on the moat bridge removing the under-supports that morning—if only either you or Jeremy had guessed his purpose!"

"My Richard tried to question the family steward, this Grégoire, but he was one of those creatures with a blind devotion to his master. Oh, Miss Alain, it's all a tangle of

. . . ifs. If we had done this or that. If. Master William would have been saved. And Jeremy's mother too."

Nanny lowered her head, her face anguished as she covered it with her hands. I wished I hadn't mentioned the matter. I could see my brother William now, as clearly as if he sat beside us, a big, athletic man, with his rusty brown hair all awry, his funny, blustering ways silenced as he enjoyed the warm air of a late summer and, truly enough, the company of us women. Dear William!

I felt the bitter stab of loss, those dreadful words *never again*, and cleared my throat. I tried to assume a businesslike voice.

"Then the French authorities took no heed of what Jeremy overheard—when Monsieur Nicolas wished William dead only the night before it all happened?"

"Wished him gone from the château. That was what the monster claimed." She looked at her gloves as if she had never seen them before. Then, to my astonishment, she began to tear them off, her fingers slipping on the leather, frantic to keep them from touching her flesh. "And me with his gift on my hands. It is like a betrayal of them that died."

"No, it isn't, Nanny. They are only gloves. They keep your hands warm. You will need them in the winter." I could see that my argument had no weight with her; so I added, ashamed that my former presents to her of gloves had always been knitted of wool or cotton, "Never you mind. You shall have some fresh ones. And finer than our murderous Monsieur Bertold could produce."

She sniffed and gave me a watery smile. "Dear Miss Alain. You think that matters. It's the giver, not the glove. And the Daviots have given us everything, Richard and me."

I hugged her and cried too. It was a very wet few minutes.

I was relieved when we arrived at the crossroad where a little humped stone bridge crossed Daviot Brook. Farmer Budleigh drew up, eyeing the Pemberton portmanteau and valise with some curiosity as Richard set them on the ground and then lifted Jeremy down. Richard came back to help us, strongly seconded by Jeremy. I was amused to see Budleigh tilt his wide-brimmed black hat back, scratch his grizzled head, and mutter, while he studied the bags, "There'll be some as moves about among the heathen. And there'll be them as stops by their own hearth."

"And you and I are homebodies, are we not?" I called to him.

He did not smile. His gaze was suspicious as he studied the luggage. "Aye. That'll be the way of it."

Richard gave me a hand down in the comradely way we were accustomed to. I had learned very young that if I were to hold my place with my brother William, I must fend for myself. Richard would have scoffed if I let myself be lifted down the way he lifted his mother and set her gently on her feet in the road.

I shook hands with Farmer Budleigh, and the wagon rattled away toward his farm beyond the water meadow, on the outer rim of gloomy Ferndene Heath.

Richard Pemberton hoisted the two cases, and with an excited Jeremy's hand in Nanny's, we started up over the stone bridge.

"How warm the dear place looks when it's coming on sunset," Nanny said. "Not like that dreadful gray monument to Bertold pride in France."

Jeremy surprised us by his quick defense.

"But I like it. It's my very own castle. With turrets and lovely stone steps. And dungeons and tower rooms. Just like Bluebeard's Castle. And the Beast's house."

"The Beast?" Richard repeated, glancing at me. I guessed that he was thinking of Nicolas Bertold.

"You know. Beauty and the Beast."

We were all relieved. We did not want Jeremy to be thinking any more than necessary about his uncle's probable crimes.

We descended the Daviot side of the bridge. Nanny remarked on the shallow state of the brook above whose low bank the cattle of my neighbors, the Willoughbys, grazed contentedly. She had a possessive feeling about the brook and claimed that the Willoughbys were "water thieves." I reminded her of the summer's many showers, and we walked in an easterly direction along the road that wound past the south end of the Daviot barns and other outbuildings.

Daviot House, itself, loomed against the angry, gray-lined clouds on the horizon. As Nanny had said, the time-mellowed, pink-brick main house had a welcoming facade. The original building had been a well-to-do farmer's cottage in the fourteenth century, but much had been added since. It now boasted two and a half stories with the two floors aired and lighted by long casement windows and the Great Hall made over into a comfortable drawing room, a dining room, and modest entry hall. The latter included a straight, single-flight oaken staircase leading to a narrow gallery where the portraits of various Daviot squires and their ladies frowned or simpered down upon new arrivals.

A visitor, Mavis Willoughby, came running out to greet us. She had an instinct about things like the Pembertons' arrival with their all-important news. A pert and charming young woman whose red hair was the exact shade of her sorrel mare, Mavis proudly boasted that she was "a bit coltish" herself. She was an excellent friend, though not a woman in whom one would confide a deadly secret. She was much too outspoken for that.

She embraced her old friend and critic, Nanny, who had often scolded her for impetuosity in her youth but was fond of her. With Richard, Mavis was on even more casual terms. They had been betrothed four years ago for a brief time but broke off the engagement when their natures proved utterly incompatible. I had thought the marriage a wonderful union of my two dearest friends, but perhaps Mavis listened to Lady Willoughby, whose ambitions for her daughter went far higher than a thirty-two-year-old artist whose mother was a governess.

Mavis was not especially fond of children, and she and Jeremy took each other on sufferance. They shook hands now, Jeremy with a stiff, proper little bow, before Mavis pushed aside Richard's outstretched hand and squeezed his upper arms affectionately.

"Welcome home, traveler." She winked at me over his shoulder. "You don't mind my making our Richard welcome in your house, Laney? After all, I'm in and out of here so much, I feel I have a vested right to issue invitations."

It would have been lonely indeed during these last few years if Mavis Willoughby had not treated Daviot House as her second home. I said gravely, "How true! And when Richard makes his delightful sketches, Mavis will be only too happy to sit for hours in absolute silence while he makes her immortal."

She wrinkled her nose at that. She often said that her lively chatter, which had brightened my world and William's, was one of the points on which her relationship to Richard Pemberton had collapsed. I suspected that one of Yolande Bertold's attractions for my brother William was her resemblance in manner to the red-haired minx who had teased him in his youth but flatly refused to marry a man "who shouted as much as she did."

It was Nanny who insisted on climbing the stairs at once with Jeremy and examining his bedchamber to be certain that it was comfortable for a boy with respiratory problems. I did not go with them. I knew Nanny would like to supervise such matters herself, and then there were the several homely tasks necessary to arrange in view of my other guest's arrival.

"With half a dozen bedrooms unused," Mavis began, "Richard shouldn't have to sleep with the cattle." Like her mother, Lady Willoughby, she was always free with advice, often excellent, but before I could hint that propriety was Richard's fetish, not mine, he contradicted her lightly.

"On the contrary, Miss Willoughby, it is my choice. I find the rooms over the haying barn quite satisfactory. There is a sense of privacy, and I may light a pipe at my ease. My mother would never permit me to do so in the house."

I smiled but it was all settled, and I went off to supervise the airing of the bed and the room he chose. I rather hoped to play matchmaker in leaving them alone, but they refused to act upon my hint. When I returned, I started for the kitchen to see if our very late country dinner of roast lamb and fish, and bright new vegetables, was sufficient. Both Mavis and Nanny had a fondness for apple pudding. Nanny had shared our table since time out of mind, so tonight's meal should be festive indeed.

Farmer Budleigh's oldest daughter, Hannah, was our cook. Aside from a taste for spirits that, in my experience has proved endemic in cooks, she was an excellent woman and often relieved the lonely times by her booming good nature. I went across the rear passage to the kitchen where the odor of succulent, roasting lamb and vegetables in the closed stove proved especially inviting.

I was not the only one enticed into the big, light kitchen with its views of the meadow and the distant smudge of darkness that was Ferndene Heath. Mavis had already arrived. She leaned forward in the old ladder-back chair, watching Hannah Budleigh roll out dough for pasties.

Hannah waved a floury hand at me without looking around. "Got to be working fast, so I have. Visitors fresh-come from France where them Frenchies eats fancy tarts and snails and what-all. Mustn't let down the flag, Miss Alain."

"No, indeed. How savory everything looks! You've done wonders, Hannah."

"She's poaching fish the way I like it," Mavis informed me. "And she's promised those honey muffins, haven't you, Hannah?"

"We'll see, miss. We'll just see." But the closemouthed smile that followed was promise enough.

We need not hang our heads in shame at the table before three travelers who had eaten of the best in France.

Unfortunately our travelers were not through with their bad tidings, as I found later that evening.

No one mentioned the actions of the king's prosecutor in the Loire region, or those of the courts in Paris when they refused to hold Nicolas Bertold for the murders of his sister and brother-in-law. Even Mavis seemed reluctant to bring the matter up for discussion, yet I could tell from her suppressed excitement that she would have liked nothing better than a full disclosure of what really happened. She had discussed it often enough with me.

In the first place, Nanny felt that Jeremy was looking pale. "I'm afraid it's our English climate. But he really shouldn't be let to run about so late in the day. He needs bundling, the dear lamb."

Richard looked at me uneasily. Since I felt guilty and was stubborn by nature, I said, "He was in excellent health until this afternoon."

Mavis opened her eyes, looked ceilingward, as if expecting the worst, and Nanny satisfied everyone's expectations by asking in deeply offended tones, "Am I to understand that our arrival brought harm to a child I love better than life?"

"Mother, for heaven's sake! She meant nothing of the sort. Do be sensible."

She gave her son an *et-tu, Bruté* look, and I caught Mavis looking at each of us with intense interest. What a vixen she was! Nothing pleased her better than a rousing quarrel involving others.

It was just before our much postponed dinner and we were in the drawing room at the time. Nanny excused herself, signaling to Jeremy, who did look sleepy.

"If you will forgive me, Miss Alain, I'll just have a tray with Jeremy in the nursery and we will both retire early."

"It's not my nursery anymore, Nanny," my nephew explained as he got up to make his bow to the rest of us. "It's my study now. Just like Papa had."

In spite of our recent excellent relations, he would have

left the room with Nanny at once but she reminded him, "Kiss your Aunt Alain good night. There's a dear."

Though I put my arms out and he touched my cheek with his cool lips, I wished it had not been necessary for her to remind him of this duty.

When they had gone, Mavis and I looked at each other, sharing an unspoken question. We both avoided Richard's eyes, a reaction that told me Mavis, too, wondered what Richard was concealing. He appeared to be far more tense than was natural to him.

Presently, becoming aware of the unaccustomed silence, Richard made some remark about the excellence of Hannah Budleigh's cooking. We both agreed with what must have seemed like startling haste. We held to informality at Daviot House, and his praise caught Hannah just as she was leaving the room with the new, shy kitchen maid she had taken in training. Hannah grinned, pushed the girl out into the passage before stopping to say, "Thank ye. A pleasure, indeed, to serve ye, sir."

She made a vague gesture of curtsying and marched out after the new girl. Mavis exhaled sharply. Her tawny red eyebrows signaled to me, and I knew I must prod Richard into telling us whatever else had been reserved for a more suitable time.

"Nanny had some reason for hurrying upstairs with Jeremy. The failure to charge Monsieur Bertold wasn't the only bad news, was it, Richard?"

He spooned up butter on his muffin, as though his life depended on the care with which he proceeded. Then, as I added nothing to make matters easier, he set the muffin down and looked directly at me.

"No, Alain. I'm afraid not. You see, I spoke with the *juge d'instructions* and several Paris lawyers. The truth is, Nicolas Bertold intends to visit England, claim his nephew, and rear him as the ultimate heir to the entire estate."

I sat paralyzed, wondering how such a thing could happen.

Mavis seemed to get a great deal of satisfaction out of the appalling news. Her eyes shone with excitement as she exclaimed, "But that's wonderful! When Monsieur Bertold dies, Jeremy will inherit not only half, but all of the estate."

"Unless Bertold marries and has children of his own," Richard reminded her. "The man is under forty. He is certain to marry someday. If only to produce an heir . . . I beg pardon, ladies, but this is a time for frank speaking."

I remember staring at my plate before I pushed it away from me. I found my voice at last.

"Mavis, I don't think you understand. Monsieur Bertold very probably murdered my brother. And perhaps, incidentally, his own sister. He hated William and certainly had no love for Jeremy. Now Jeremy owns half the estate. Can't you see what he intends in taking over Jeremy's guardianship? A sick boy?"

Richard nodded, somewhat reluctantly, I thought.

"It is certainly possible. After the boy's testimony there can be no love lost between them."

Mavis gasped. "I don't believe it." She recovered and clung to her absurd misunderstanding of the persons involved. "It would be too obvious. Nicolas Bertold is no fool."

"Far from it," Richard agreed. "In my observation he is anything but a fool. And if the boy should die while in his hands, it will be set down as an accident. A regrettable illness that carried the boy off."

I shuddered, and Mavis echoed my own thoughts. "Heavens, Richard! What an imagination!" But in a peculiar way she seemed to be enjoying the melodrama promised by these events in France.

After that only Mavis continued to eat. Richard and I were too troubled by the possibilities he had suggested.

The evening ended rather flatly. Richard took Mavis home to Willoughby Hall in the pony and trap, and I set about my housekeeping affairs with the grim prospect of displaying our country ways at any time before the elegant and effete Frenchman.

I went through the house snuffing candles and seeing to the usual nightly tasks. I set an oil lamp on the table behind the newel post in the event that Richard wanted to spend an hour or two in William's library before retiring to his rooms over the hay barn.

The house was ordinarily pleasant and well loved at this hour, but tonight, perhaps because of Richard's news, I felt chilled and uncomfortable, intensely aware of shadows and that cold danger reaching out to us from across the Channel.

Setting out through the kitchen garden to see that everything was in order in Richard's little barn rooms, I borrowed the cook's old black shawl from its kitchen peg. The shawl was a fortunate addition. The weather had turned misty, and by the time I returned to the house, my hair was blown across my face in damp wisps, my pattens were muddy, and I was out of sorts.

I left the storm lantern in the pantry, took up an oil lamp with a milky globe, and crossed the passage toward the staircase. It was then that I realized I was not alone on the ground floor. The front door was ajar. Richard must have come into the drawing room. I closed the door tightly, shot the bolt, and called, "Home so soon?"

No one answered.

The four household servants, including our gardener, had rooms in an outbuilding near the barns. There, on a lower floor, the men and boys employed on the fields had their quarters in season. None of these people would be in the house at this hour unless there was illness.

I raised the lamp while, with the other hand, I held the shawl together at my throat against the sudden chill in the house. I went quietly into the drawing room, which was in shadow, lit only by dim shafts from the hall lamp.

A dark, powerful-looking man wearing a traveler's greatcoat and riding boots, stood there by a front casement window.

He was looking out at the road and the humped stone bridge over Daviot Brook. He had pushed aside one of the faded velvet portieres and seemed to be making himself at home in my house. I was about to say so when he glanced at me with insulting indifference and then returned his attention to the scene outside.

"Fetch down the lady of the house, girl. And you might see if you can locate a bottle of wine in this benighted household." He must have noted some reaction in me, because he added, as an afterthought, "If you please."

CHAPTER THREE

I did not hear an accent in his deep, resonant voice, but I knew this arrogant intruder. He had wasted no time. He must be anxious to put his neck under the blade of the guillotine again. Tonight I felt ready to oblige him.

For a minute I stared. It was easy to see that he thought me a dull-witted creature. My first inclination was to challenge him by a flat announcement of my identity. But he deserved what my mother would have called "a severe set-down." I gave him the curtsy I had long reserved in case I should ever meet young Queen Victoria, and promised him in a sickeningly sweet voice, "An it please ye, sir. Seemingly, there may be a wee drop of some'ut."

"Thank you." But he had stared at me long enough. The misty scene of our countryside interested him now. Perhaps he hoped Jeremy would inherit Daviot Farm before he dispatched the boy.

As I left the room I smiled to myself at this truly horrifying thought. Even my vivid imagination did not go far enough to suspect that he had designs on my own life.

On the way up the stairs I promised myself, "I'll show you the mistress of the house, my fine Frenchie! I'll show you a lady so elegant, it's you who will do the curtsying, I promise you."

It was a promise more easily made than kept. I had not worn an elaborate ballgown, or indeed a spectacular day gown, since my last visit to London almost a year ago. But a daring idea occurred to me. In all honesty I was shocked at my own passionate desire to shake this arrogant, satanic Frenchman.

It was not until I reached my bedchamber, a large, airy room with two windows, one looking east to the fields and the other giving a south view of the water meadow and Ferndene Heath, that I made my decision. Monsieur Bertold expected Miss Alain Daviot to descend from her bedchamber to welcome him.

Very well. I possessed a French boudoir robe of quilted velvet and brocade, which was my brother William's notion of an expensive joke, since he could be quite sure I would never wear it. I spent little time in my bedroom sitting around drinking tea or entertaining elegant lovers.

But here, at last, was a purpose for that handsome, useless Christmas present.

I hurried about the room tearing off my plain, green woolen gown with its blond lace collar and cuffs, kicking my wretched mud-crusted pattens into a corner, washing in the now cold basin of water left by Betsy, the upstairs maid, and turning at last to the all-important problem of making my face and hair presentable after my excursion to the hay barn.

When I was very young, I frequently heard myself called "a pretty child." My hair was described as tawny, my eyes referred to, though rarely, as violet. Alas, for age and responsibilities! The tawny hair was now pulled back in a bun on the nape of my neck, and the eyes were busy and sharp, looking after a large farm, including farmers and shepherds who might slacken if not held to a tight rein. Nothing of the pretty child remained.

I still had a fair complexion and symmetrical features, so

I brushed out my wet and tangled hair until it fell about my shoulders, borrowing a gold sparkle from the brocade of the robe. If I had been roused from bed as the Frenchman must suppose at this hour, then my unconfined hair would seem natural. I pinched my cheeks to give them color, and hoping for the best, I descended the staircase in my most regal manner.

The progress of lamplight must have warned him of my arrival, but he didn't look around until I was in the room, and even then it was to complain.

"Be good enough to call your stable boy. My mare needs attending. She is tethered out there. I rubbed her down a bit, but she needs—" He broke off when he got a good look at me. For some reason he seemed taken aback. I tried not to smile, but it seemed likely that he recognized me as the stern-faced moonling who had received him a few minutes ago.

"Miss Daviot?"

He pronounced it correctly, in the British way. I nodded, striving for a polite smile that held more civility than warmth.

"We do not often receive visitors at this hour. I'm afraid the stable boy is fast asleep in one of those buildings near the road."

"I see." Perhaps it was the way he kept studying me with those brilliant, dark eyes or the manner in which he pursed his heavy lips in a fleeting, casual gesture that made me uncomfortable. I set him down in my mind as a sensuous ruffian, exactly the sort to excite a susceptible young woman like Mavis, but I trusted I was more sensible.

I said, "My old governess's son is staying on the estate at the moment, and—"

"Ah, yes. Trust Richard Pemberton to spread the glad tidings."

I could not mistake the malice in that. "And I feel sure he would not want to see a horse neglected."

For the first time I noted the little gleam of humor in his

eyes. "In fact, however much your human visitors may be neglected, you will not permit an animal to suffer."

"I beg your pardon," I said stiffly. "I expressed myself without thinking."

"On the contrary. Animals before people. I subscribe to that theory, myself. If you will show me where I may find feed and water, I will attend to Fleurette myself." To my surprise, he was sincere in his suggestion.

He started past me, to the double doors I had left partially open into the entrance hall. There he stopped to ask me on an amusingly plaintive note, "And dare I suggest a tray of spirits of some kind upon my return? It is damnably wet out there. Living up to its English reputation, I daresay." He pulled up the cape collar of his greatcoat, which protected very little of his unruly black hair.

Ashamed of my own poor hospitality, and angry that he should be in the right, I snapped, "I've no doubt it rains in France as well."

"Prodigiously," he agreed, and unbolted the front door.

I went back to the library where the whiskey decanter was kept, and then took the silver tray out to the stillroom where, by great luck, William had furnished Daviot House with various wines on his last visit. I was not familiar with the great years, but I hurriedly took up a bottle of Madeira and a partially filled bottle of sherry. These, along with the whiskey, would have to do.

If Nicolas Bertold's horse was starving, very likely he, himself, had not eaten. I found myself actually sympathizing with the "poor man." He had been received without the minimum courtesies even a stranger might expect. I looked around but couldn't find any food that might tempt the palate of a Frenchman. The only snails handy were in the garden. He was not likely to accept thick slabs of cold lamb, or the fish, freshly fileted for one of Hannah Budleigh's delicious poached dishes tomorrow.

I put some currant buns and a few tea biscuits in a Limoges

dish sent to me two Christmases ago by William's wife, Yolande. In the drawing room with its worn, comfortable Jacobean furniture, I laid out this spartan repast, on the big, carved oak table beside the case clock. The fire in the basket grate had burned down to mere coals, but there was always the prickly furze common to our region, and after a bit of stirring and poking, I got a creditable, if smoky, fire going.

The portieres where Monsieur Bertold had been looking out at his mare were still open. This concern for his horse was the first decent thing I had heard about him. I saw now that he and Richard Pemberton were returning from the barn. Even at this distance I could see that there was little more than common civility between the trim, neat Richard and our unwanted guest.

Did the Frenchman actually expect to spend the night in my house? Aside from the matter of propriety, he would have a miserable time in such a "plebian" household. He could scarcely find a mouthful of food suited to his tastes, and there wasn't a bedroom in the house that a man of his background wouldn't spurn. I could not forget William's humorously exaggerated stories of the ancient grandeur at the château and the Paris house on the Rue du Faubourg-St. Honoré.

The two men came into the drawing room, having shaken off their wet outer garments in the entry hall. Ushering the tall Frenchman ahead of him as though he, himself, were the host of Daviot House, Richard grimaced at me, revealing all too clearly his own reaction to our unwanted guest.

I was annoyed by what I considered Richard's obvious attempt to warn me of our guest's villainous reputation. It was not necessary. I knew that Nicolas Bertold, this man before me, might have murdered my brother. I was surprised by my own reaction, but truth to tell, I had decided, upon meeting this ill-mannered Frenchman, to make my own decision about his guilt or innocence. By some devious means or other I might even prove his guilt. Or his innocence.

Unfortunately it seemed difficult to make him feel ill at

ease anywhere. He crossed the room toward the table in a couple of strides, rubbing his hands and saying, "Ah, this is more like it. What will you have, Pemberton?"

Richard was angry that Monsieur Bertold had stolen what he considered his prerogative as host in this household.

Neither man was correct in such an assumption.

"I'll remain with the whiskey, thank you. That appears to be the bottle I left in the library tonight."

"Dulls the taste." Nevertheless, Nicolas Bertold poured the Scotch into one of our family Waterford glasses, offered it to Richard, and then, surprisingly, turned to me.

"And for Miss Daviot?"

Richard said stiffly, "Miss Daviot never takes spirits."

That he should speak for me aroused my resentment, and I cut in at once. "A small glass of sherry, I believe."

I saw that I had amused the Frenchman and furthered Richard's pettish mood, but I felt that it was time to assert myself before both men. And the Spanish sherry was excellent, very light and dry. Over the little crystal glass I looked suddenly at Monsieur Bertold, who had been watching me in a disconcerting way.

"Do you remain in England long, sir?"

"Long enough to complete my business."

He was drinking Madeira, without much pleasure. He considered the wine, then took another swallow.

"And we know what that business is," Richard put in.

We both looked at him. Bertold said, "Good. That should make it simpler all around. You may depend on being rid of me almost at once."

"Sir, let us understand this. Am I to be honored by your company in this house until your business is completed?"

"Melodramatic, but essentially correct, Miss Daviot."

I realized too late that he was goading me, amused by my hauteur and perhaps by my absurdly elaborate costume. I felt like some stage doxy, playing a role with which I was unfamiliar. Worst of all, he seemed to see straight through my masquerade with those alarming eyes.

I had to remind myself that this man may have murdered my dear brother, and even more alarming, that he was here to take control of another victim, a helpless child whom I must protect, with my life if necessary. Perhaps if I knew the man better, I could more easily make up my mind about his guilt and act accordingly.

"You must have passed the inn as you rode through the village," Richard reminded him. "They will have a room of some sort. You must realize that it simply would not be possible for you to stay in the house of an unmarried young female."

The Frenchman looked around innocently. "But I've no objection in the world. I have slept in shabby little farmhouses before." I gasped, but he went on, having finished his wine, and touched the spice buns doubtfully. "However, I would appreciate something a little more substantial. I haven't eaten since breakfast."

I was still seething over his insult to my beloved home. Shabby little farm, indeed!

Richard lost his temper as well, and began another somewhat involved warning when I decided to give my self-invited guest exactly what he asked for. Substantial fare. That should discourage him.

"Come, sir. I, myself, will satisfy your appetite."

Monsieur Bertold assured me. "A delightful prospect."

Shocked by the realization that I may have provided him with the chance to insult me, I said, "Very well. You may come to the kitchen and choose your own meal. Though I must warn you, it may be shabby by your high standards."

Richard warned me. "Alain . . . ?"

But Bertold's airy assurance was a new insult. "Oh, I don't mind. I am very democratic. I soldiered in Algeria during its conquest some years ago."

Richard interrupted him again, but I waved him to silence.

I took up the lamp, but the Frenchman reached over my shoulder, his hard knuckles brushing my cheek, his fingers closing over mine as he removed the lamp from me.

"Which direction?"

I said nothing but moved, with what I hoped was dignity, toward the kitchen passage. Richard watched us from the drawing room doorway, drumming his fingers on the wall in a rather obvious way. He must have guessed that I was not leading our enemy around the house from pure pleasure at his company.

Nicolas Bertold examined the stillroom and pantry. He seemed inordinately pleased to find the remains of the roast lamb and brought it out, cutting off a thick slice and placing it on one of the chipped kitchen plates with cold, cooked cubes of turnips. An apple completed this curious dinner for a French aristocrat. He settled down in Cook's big, cane-bottomed chair, which had formerly belonged to my grandfather, and while I watched, openmouthed, he cut up and ate the cold lamb with its accompaniments. He looked up and saw me watching him.

I was heavily ironic. "May I assume that you approve of the work of our chef?"

"You may. A man might be reasonably happy here. I begin to understand your brother's attachment to his farm." He sat back from the table and looked me up and down.

"It is late, Monsieur Bertold. If you mean to stay here, I must see to one of the rooms."

"I certainly intend to stay here. Until my business is concluded, of course." Then he smiled. Nanny Pemberton had been right. His smile lit his face magically, giving his features a kind of somber excitement that made me back away with an instinctive mistrust of my own weakness.

"Very well. Perhaps Nanny Pemberton's son will help me make it ready."

"Rubbish. I'll do it myself. Show me the room."

He simply refused to understand the most common amenities.

We met Richard in the passageway. He lowered his voice to a murmur, but I was sure the Frenchman heard it.

"Will you need me?"

"No thank you. You must be tired after the coach ride. I will say good night and let you get some rest."

"I'll notify Mother. You may need her."

Even without looking his way I could have sworn the Frenchman was amused. As for me, I did not enjoy being made the butt of his humor, and Richard encouraged it by behaving like the hero in a melodrama. Did he honestly think my virtue was endangered by this dark stranger who well could be a murderer! He might more reasonably fear for my life than my honor.

Not that I was entirely convinced of the man's villainy since meeting him. I considered his humorous tendencies, his arrogance, and yet his common touch. None of these added up to the serpentlike, effete French murderer of my imaginings. A highwayman, perhaps. Yes. I could believe that. But nothing so subtle as Jeremy and Nanny seemed to have suspected.

In either case, I did not want Nanny Pemberton involved until morning. I knew I should find trouble there.

I decided to test that sly humor of his. He should have the worst bedchamber in the house. The best to be said for it was that we kept it clean and dusted. It was almost at the head of the stairs, just beyond the short gallery, and through some mischance the sleeper was bombarded with creaking, crackling noises throughout the night. To compound the problem, the one window opened upon a side path where one of our shepherds let his flock amble past every morning at dawn. If the few belled sheep did not trouble the sleeper, the two fierce, barking dogs must.

Long ago my grandmother had given up hope of the room and used it as a catchall for lumpy mattresses, mended sheets, and pillows with their feathers seeping out. It was a room used only in last emergencies and by those young enough to cope with a few ghastly nights. Nicolas Bertold was not young, but I considered him an ideal candidate otherwise.

Let me see you joke this one off, I thought as I led him into the room.

It looked none so bad when seen by the warm, soft light of my lamp. So much the better. The truth would appear gradually throughout the night. With my lamp I lit the candle on the little joint stool below the bed and drew back the bed curtains. Thank heaven they were not dusty, but their faded crimson grandeur certainly would have depressed me.

Monsieur Bertold looked around the room with its Gothic riches and said nothing for a long minute.

"Excellent," he agreed at last. "That armoire is a handsome piece. Has it always been in your family?"

Surprised by his admiration for the clumsy old clothespress at the far end of the room, I could not but be pleased.

"It belonged in my great-grandmother's family. I believe it is very old. The key is beside the shaving mirror on the commode. I will bring you a pitcher of water. We rise early here. Shortly after sunrise someone will bring you tea."

"Tea!" That did startle him. "Dare I bring up the water myself, and perhaps a bottle from your brother's cellar? I must get my luggage, in any case."

"If you like. William did not use the cellar. You will find everything you wish in the stillroom."

"I doubt that."

"I beg your pardon?"

"Never mind."

I was leaving when he spoke again, his voice unexpectedly gentle. "Don't worry. I do not mean to cause you more trouble than is necessary."

I found myself moved by that assurance and smiled at him despite my determination to treat him with chill indifference.

"Thank you. Good night."

Half an hour later I had readied myself for bed in a blue gown and old dressing sacque when the night calm was torn by a shriek of terror. My first fear was that our guest had shown his true colors and tried to murder my nephew. I threw the door open, rushed into the corridor, and saw a sight I shall not soon forget.

Nicolas Bertold had come up the stairs carrying the candlestick in one hand while he held a pewter pitcher in the other, a dusty-looking bottle in the crook of his arm. Facing him at the opposite end of the hall was Nanny Pemberton, obviously caught on her way to our new indoor water closet. She was bundled in a heavy winter cloak, with gray wisps of hair peeping out around her night bonnet.

"For God's sake, tell her I am a guest, not a cutthroat," Monsieur Bertold ordered.

I had never seen Nanny so panic-stricken.

"He—he—that man—he has come to kill little Jeremy!"

"Nonsense," I said sharply. "He is not going to kill anyone tonight. Bolt your door and Jeremy's. And you, Monsieur Bertold—"

"Yes, Miss Daviot."

"I suggest you bolt your door as well."

I had caught him unawares, and he gave me a belated grin. "I certainly shall, Miss Daviot. Your house is not safe for tired, peaceful travelers. I can see that."

"Go to bed."

"Yes, ma'am."

When he had closed his door and shoved the bolt loudly enough to be heard at Willoughby Hall, I turned my attention to Nanny, who stood there trembling so much that I thought she might drop the candle. She must have seen my impatience because she tried to explain.

"I hear Jeremy coughing. I knew it. That dreadful man has awakened him."

Jeremy stuck his tousled head out of his room. He yawned and scratched his head.

"I had a bad dream. I dreamed I heard Uncle Nicolas. Nanny?"

Her attention was all for her charge. "There, there, my poor lamb. Nanny's here. You go to bed. I'll read to you."

He closed the door. He certainly had not looked to me for help or companionship, despite the last two months. No matter. It seemed clear that Nanny knew how to console and comfort him, even if, in my opinion, she encouraged a babyish quality in him. By the age of seven and a half, he should not be running to those who called him a poor, poor lamb.

But then, I had no children of my own and was probably not understanding enough.

I said, "Go to bed, Nanny, for goodness sake. It was your own scream that frightened Jeremy."

She hesitated, but I suppose she was surprised by my insensitivity. She obeyed me after casting at me a hurt look.

I went to bed in much confusion of mind.

CHAPTER FOUR

I awoke to a bright, golden sunrise that glistened on all the wet leaves and late-summer debris in the fields and even on the stone abutments of the humped bridge. I smiled with some satisfaction, picturing myself confounding my impossible guest, as Betsy brought in my tray of tea and the tiny condiment dish of cinnamon with which I laced my tea.

"Betsy, Mrs. Pemberton and my nephew are not awake yet, are they?"

"Not this early, miss. Should I be looking in at the little one?"

I was feeling a bit smug. "No. But I think it is time that one of our other guests was roused. Not Mister Richard. He brews his own tea, but the French gentleman in the gallery chamber."

Irish Betsy's dark eyes rolled. "Poor gentleman, indeed. He'll likely be thanking me for it." She stopped as she was leaving. "Or will he now? The Frenchies, they drink all those wines and that. They hate tea."

"So they do. Yes. On the whole, I think . . . tea."

Somewhat confused but obedient, Betsy went about the task of rousing our unwanted guest.

I had scarcely touched my tea when Betsy came back.

"I can't give the Frenchie his tea, miss."

"Still asleep? Wake him."

"No, ma'am. He's gone off before sunup."

"Gone?" I sat straight up so quickly, I nearly overturned the tray. Could it be possible the Frenchman had been discouraged by his treatment in my house and was on his way back to France without Jeremy?

Or worse. *With* Jeremy.

I leapt out of bed, reaching for my bed robe and, throwing it around me, ran across to Jeremy's room. The door was still bolted, but Nanny's room adjoined it and the door between was very likely open. I roused Nanny, who was understandably confused, but I had only to speak Jeremy's name and she was on her feet, plunging toward my nephew's room.

Jeremy was still in his bed, curled into a ball and apparently enjoying his dreams, though he breathed heavily as he often did when the weather showed its nipping signs of autumn.

Nanny murmured, "He had a troubled night. He woke several times."

"And I suppose you were awake all that time. Nanny . . . Nanny?"

She drew me back into her room, studying my face. "What is it, my dear? Has that man behaved . . . has he threatened you?"

"Heavens, no," I said. "But he seems to have gone. I was afraid— Never mind."

I was wishing I had not upset her. With Nanny's strong suspicions it needed only this additional note to arouse her to panic again.

"Shall I send your tea?" I asked as I went out into the hall.

"Well, my dear, I wonder if I might have chocolate. I'm afraid I've grown quite French in my tastes."

It sounded most unlike the English Nanny Pemberton, and I found it very human. "Of course. I'll see you later, Nanny."

I asked Betsy to give the request to Hannah Budleigh, and then hurriedly washed and dressed. By the time I went downstairs to find out to where the maddening Frenchman had disappeared and why, everyone was busy at the usual tasks. I found Richard Pemberton starting out toward Willoughby Hall with sketching materials under his arm. He was very much on his dignity, and when I asked if he had seen Monsieur Bertold, he dismissed the question with a shrug and the indifferent explanation, "Out surveying the landscape, so I'm told. I make no doubt that he has an eye on Jeremy's English inheritance as well."

Only if I died without leaving a direct heir of my flesh. I resented the insinuation that Jeremy owned any part of the Daviot Farms. William and I had long ago arranged that the property should be mine. In exchange William would receive all the considerable income from Daviot investments in government funds and the surprisingly profitable railway shares. However, I had no time to untangle Richard's mistaken notion.

"He is out walking? Then he hasn't returned to France?"

Richard's fine features softened. "No. I'm sorry. I wish to heaven he had gone. He has already disrupted this household." He patted my hand. "But if we ignore him, treat him with the contempt he deserves, he must leave. It is inevitable."

"Where are you going?"

He indicated his sketch portfolio, adding with justifiable pride, "Lady Willoughby has been good enough to ask if I would make a sketch of her. She was waiting up for Mavis last night." He gave me a sudden, rueful smile. "I think it was gratitude for the fact that I did not become Mavis's husband. The Willoughbys are mighty high sticklers."

"She should have been proud to have you." He was pleased, but I'm afraid I spoiled that by adding on a more urgent note,

"Which path did Monsieur Bertold take? He doesn't know our country at all."

"Old Briggs, the shepherd, said he was following the brook south. Don't concern yourself. He is sure to turn back when he has crossed the water meadow."

But if he did not, it was easy for an outlander to lose himself on rugged Ferndene Heath, which held many tightly grown copses of trees and endless blooming shrubs at this time of year. Then, too, being foreign, he might not understand that our sunny sky overhead could raise a fog off the mist-covered heath, making it even more difficult to find his way. I did not mind giving him rough treatment in assigning him the gallery chamber of my home, but this was a more serious matter.

I did not like to explain my selfish reason for assuring the Frenchman's safety. I was certain that if the Frenchman met with any kind of accident, he would be just clever enough to use this in some legal attempt to obtain custody of his (and my) nephew. It still worried me very much that he boasted friendship with King Louis-Philippe of France. Kings and their ministers often favored each other's causes over a single countrywoman like myself. What if he contrived to break a leg or arm, or received bruises from a fall? Such evidence presented to Her British Majesty's ministers, even in England, might satisfy them that I was a malignant old spinster, anxious to destroy my rival for Jeremy's care.

I dared not think of Jeremy's reaction if he were given back into his uncle's hands. I must see to it that Nicolas Bertold had no grounds for complaint against me.

I let Richard go on to the hall by himself. When I pursued the subject with him, undoubtedly he would remind me that if Nicolas Bertold broke a leg or an arm in some pothole, it would only be what he deserved. This might well be true, but it hardly seemed either a charitable or a realistic attitude.

Besides, there was always the possibility of the man's innocence. Obviously the French courts thought so. A boy

Jeremy's age might be mistaken in what he saw, the conclusions he drew. And what of William's letters to me through the years, his repeated remarks about his brother-in-law's arrogance, his overbearing quality (I had certainly seen the truth of that last night), and, finally, William's persistent remarks that "He and his family lied to me in many ways. Nicolas would like me gone from here. Nothing would please him more than for me to drop dead of an apoplexy tomorrow. Better yet, today!"

To be honest, I also knew that William used to say the same things about everyone who crossed his own stubborn will.

I returned to the house, took up a violet redingote I had worn for at least two years, and went back out along the brook path. An inquisitive cow, wandering down through the grass toward the brook, stuck her big, patient face into my side, and I stopped to disentangle my pocket. At the same time Mavis Willoughby called to me from across the brook.

"Alain! Playing the heroine?"

I pretended not to understand, but she skipped across the brook to me on the log bridge used by herders and farm children. She was wearing a pretty shawl with a paisley design, her red hair a bright, unkempt halo around her face. I tried not to resent the fact that she was so pretty.

"Richard tells me your archenemy is marching off to lose himself in Ferndene Heath. Can it be his conscience driving him to self-destruction?"

I laughed and confessed that I had no idea why the Frenchman would do such a thing. "And I doubt very much if he has a conscience."

"And yet you are going out to rescue him. I came to remind you that Mama expects you Friday for a musicale." She grinned. "I am the musicale. Pianoforte, of course. Luckily she hasn't asked me to sing."

"The difficulty is, I have guests."

Mavis was insouciant about that. I realized that the guests

were one of the features of the invitation. "By all means, invite Richard and the monster."

"I suppose Richard has talked to you."

Mavis wrinkled her nose and stepped along beside me, daintily avoiding puddles from the last night's rain. "Why do you think I'm here? Richard is sketching Mother. I can see her now in all her splendor, seated in Father's great milord chair, posing for posterity."

The Budleigh cow followed us, nosing Mavis along. When Mavis turned to challenge her, the cow remained firm, staring at her with its huge, bovine eyes, its long lashes perfectly still.

I said, "You won't outstare Adelaide. You may as well surrender."

Wisely Mavis lowered her gaze first and pursued the real matter that had brought her out here. Adelaide, too, gave up and began to nibble grass.

"Alain, there is something strange in all this attention to a man you called a monster less than twenty-four hours ago."

"Self-preservation. Nothing more. He may fall off the face of the earth elsewhere, but I don't wish him to come to any harm while he is my guest. You know what the heath is like after a rain, when the sun comes out."

"Fog. Waves of the stuff. At least in London there are things to do, places to go. Shops and the opera and concerts. So you mean to save the monster's life from the dangers of the heath?"

I said, "I hope to keep him from venturing on the heath, getting lost, laying the blame at my door."

"Or he might be kidnapped by gypsies," she teased. "A tinker's wagon stopped at the Hall yesterday. Fierce-looking Honiger family, male and female. They terrified me, and they even cowed my redoubtable Mama into having all the cutlery sharpened by them. I bought a needle case."

"Let us hope Monsieur Bertold can ransom himself with equal success."

She walked a few steps beside me while I looked across the meadow but saw no sign of the Frenchman's dark, tall figure. Mavis guessed my preoccupation and asked confidentially, "What is he really like? Richard says he is a typical Frenchman. Handsome and elegant?"

"This one is inelegant, and I must say, Richard seems to have become quite the chatterbox. Monsieur Bertold is, in a word, unromantic."

"What a pity! I rather fancied this monster in a long black cloak and floating over the heath. Like that wonderful villain in *Varney, the Vampyr*." She sighed. "Well, then, I shan't ruin my London slippers saving the man from the wilds of the heath." She turned back but with the reminder, "Don't forget to bring the monster to Willoughby Hall tonight. Mama will be so disappointed if she fails to meet him."

"Mama?" I echoed, but she merely waved to me and started back toward the Hall.

I was amused at her transparent curiosity, for she was an incurable romantic and I considered myself much too old to be swayed by such storybook notions of life.

After a glance at the sky beyond the thicket of beech trees that marked the border of the valley meadows, I could see layers of white mist above the tangled, gently blowing tree tops. I knew that this was a bad time for a stranger to be wandering over the heath. Surely Bertold ought to have the sense to know it as well.

But perhaps he had gone up there before the piercing blue sky reacted upon the wet heath below. Maddening creature! Couldn't he do anything right?

I strode along to the far end of the meadow where the brook wandered off in several directions. A rabbit dashed across my path, disappearing into the grass, and the beech trees loomed up. Beyond them loomed the heath, which was at a slightly higher elevation than our valley. Beneath the shedding old trees, many rushes and summer grasses provided a soggy carpet.

I climbed the small rise on the south bank where our brook made a semicircular turn eastward, and looked around. Furze cutters had dropped some brush near the wavering brook the previous evening, probably when the mist came down. There had been no footprints on the easterly path since the rain, but a deep indentation that looked like a boot print under the beech trees gave me a clue. He might have gone up on the heath.

I took the narrow path worn by the feet of the furze cutters through the years, and very shortly I was above our valley looking out over the great, desolate heath, which was shadowed by dark patches even on this summer morning. Yellow heath blooms livened the spot, but their stalks grew so tall that it was sometimes difficult to see over the little flowers themselves.

I raised my hands to shield my eyes against the light overhead and frowned at the uninhabited surface that spread out before me like the surface of the moon.

There was something, probably a sheep, moving out of a clump of trees where the shepherd Briggs sometimes set his wagon. But the shy, wild creature proved to be a moorland pony, and he took off at a great pace when a splendid-sized heron flew out of a thicket and then onward over my head, its long beak pointed like a sword blade before the lengthy neck and dappled white body.

The thick summer foliage of a birch grove hid the wilderness from my sight briefly, and when I passed beyond it, the heath spread before me again.

I was out of sorts by this time, partly because I let myself worry about the Frenchman and the possibility of Jeremy being given to his enemy. There were dozens of tracks made across the heath, many by creatures we humans never even saw, and Bertold might have taken any path. In some cases he could wander all day with only the vague chance of coming upon a human inhabitant of these wastes, or possibly a gypsy wagon settling in to make its own private life away from us valley folk.

Even here, some of the gypsies who entertained at our midsummer and autumn fairs did not always welcome strangers. They were a self-sufficient group, very much to themselves, and if they were feared or disliked by some of our moorland farmers, they returned the compliment by despising us. The truth was, we bore each other's presence on sufferance.

The sun was well up now, but this, combined with the mists that lay on the ground and over the wild moorland growth, gradually began to form the inevitable layers of summer fog. I was unlikely to see him now.

"If I walk any farther, I shall find myself practically on the coast." But all around me the sunlight rapidly dimmed, and familiar objects were becoming vague, with no very solid edges. Monsieur Bertold would have even more difficulty finding his way back to our valley.

To salve my conscience I told myself, "He is well served, wandering off into places where he knows nothing of the terrain. And in any case, I don't wish to be accused of trying to do away with him in some sinister fashion. That sounds just like his peculiar humor."

I stood there trying to make up my mind while the shreds of chill, gray fog fingered my cheek softly.

In the eerie silence I began to pick up sounds: the rustle of tiny creatures among the grasses at my feet. The soughing of the wind across the heath, the drop-drop-drop of water from an ancient spring into a hollowed-out stone cup in a nearby abutment. . . .

But I heard more than the splashing water. A peculiar slapping noise followed. Then, unmistakably, the mumbling protests of a human being in anger or distress. I swung around, straining to see through the fog. Failing that, I tried to recall how far to the west I was from the old spring. It often surprised unwary visitors by its presence here in an area that looked much drier than it was.

"Hallo," I called, but this produced no result. My voice dissolved in the thick, moist gloom.

I studied the ground carefully for a path, picking out the worn strip of earth blown free of its evergreen leaves and nettles. The dripping of water was now much more distinct. At the same time I could hear a man's voice swearing in baffled fury. He must have fallen into the muddy debris around the spring. Why he couldn't get himself out, I had no idea. It wasn't as if this place held treacherous potholes like the mired ground in the southeast. There the edge of the heath verged on a meadow of rich, loamy farmland.

The long layers of fog lifted slightly when I reached the spring. I took care not to fall over the abutment or the clods of soggy earth where the overflow trickled away into the ground. A man was certainly trapped here with his right leg knee-deep in the muddy pool below the spring and his body flapping drunkenly as he tried to draw his leg out. But the mud was slippery and his condition such that he could make no headway.

I recognized Tad Spindler's tousled sandy hair. He had long since lost his big-brimmed black hat. His homespun coat, especially the right side, was weighted with mud, making it more difficult to regain his balance in this state.

I was both relieved and impatient.

"Tad, in heaven's name, what are you doing out here in that condition?"

He raised his head, squinted at me, and made an absurd effort to cover his disheveled garments with his even muddier coat.

"Miss Alain . . . missed foot—footing . . . don't look . . ."

"Don't talk nonsense. Give me your hand."

"'S that dirty!" He swiped his left hand repeatedly over his muddy right sleeve and he ignored my pleas, which were becoming sharper.

Balancing my two feet on firm ground, I took his flapping hand and pulled with all my strength. His drunken condition made things worse. He could not coordinate his own efforts with mine. I gritted my teeth and tried again, but this time we only succeeded in sliding his left foot into the mud.

Around us the fog layers settled, one on the other. They seemed to crush us down. Certainly they did not make our efforts any easier. I was already shivering with the cold, and poor Tad Spindler must be frozen. I shifted my position, dug in again, and ordered firmly, "Make the effort. Give me your other hand."

"Need it. For b-balance."

"Give it to me!"

He obeyed very shakily. I was just able to grasp it before he toppled over. He crumpled against the solid ground, but he screamed with pain and I realized that he must have hurt his right leg badly, perhaps broken it. I tried again to drag him out. I had no idea what we would do then. He might use my shoulder as a crutch.

Meanwhile there was Nicolas Bertold. Where had he gone? Was he also in trouble? Working to free Tad Spindler, I saw no way that I could continue my search for the Frenchman. No matter. He looked like a man who could take excellent care of himself. I should have come to this conclusion an hour ago. I wondered why I had not.

My efforts, even with both of Tad's hands, produced another scream. This time the sound was shrill enough to carry across the heath. If Monsieur Bertold had wandered out here, it might well be he who rescued us, rather than the other way around.

Breathing hard, I fell backward against a rocky abutment, and Tad's fingers slipped off mine. He began to scramble madly. One of his hands fell into the little cup of stone that received the water from the spring. More splashing followed. But other sounds intruded on the scene.

I raised my head with an effort, hearing the crackle of twigs and nettles underfoot. Many footsteps.

I guessed at once that a gypsy band must be passing, probably the family of the two boys, Josef and Demian Honiger, who made a precarious living with their tinker's wagon. I was acquainted with the boys, especially Demian, the younger, who had saved one of our mares from a pothole on the heath and brought her home, an act that had surprised the entire village.

We occasionally employed both Josef and Demian to find wandering sheep, but I knew nothing of the other Honigers, beyond the carnival entertainment they provided by their bright, flashing costumes and dances, the stilt-walking and fortune-telling.

They must have passed us on the sheep track I had formerly taken. I called out anxiously, "Hallo!" but got no reply. Tad Spindler was groaning and in no state to help himself.

Scrambling a little, I got to my feet and made my way back to the sheep track, calling Demian's name. He was the one member of the family whose help I thought I might count on. A minute or two later it was as though night had fallen and I was encircled by dark-eyed, unfriendly creatures from some exotic Arabian nightmare.

Unfortunately seventeen-year-old Demian and his slightly older brother, Josef, were not among them. This male was all in black, a big, powerful man wearing one gold hoop earring. He bestowed upon me a toothy smile that did not reach the oblique slant of his vivid black eyes.

He said something in Romany to me that I didn't understand, but the three women with him all grinned in a most unsettling way. Two were girls, pretty, dark, and sloe-eyed. One of them wore a scarf with a gold bangle sewn on the silk over her forehead. Both girls were covered to the elbows with bangled wristlets. Otherwise they looked shabby, like any poor people of the valley.

The older woman, probably the mother, looked the most

malign. In an unexpectedly narrow face, her harsh mouth and high-bridged nose would frighten any hopeful seeker after a vision of the future. One of her canine teeth was missing, and this in no way softened her appearance. Her rasping voice cut into the thick, foggy air. Plainly she was telling her man something unpleasant about me. He shook his head and spoke again in Romany, but this time to me.

I burst out, "Tad Spindler. You've seen him in the village. He is trapped by the spring yonder. Please help me."

The gypsy shrugged. Again came the smile, and I imagine it was meant to be ingratiating. I repeated my plea, raising my voice on the commonly held theory that he must understand if I spoke loudly enough. The girls said something to him with sly glances at me. The mother added a strong order in her guttural voice, obviously urging him to come along with the women.

"Please," I begged. We all heard Tad Spindler cry out, and this time one of the girls hesitated, asking her father something in a word or two.

But the woman won out. He nodded, dismissed me in English. "Bird, eh? Bird?" And he started on with his family.

"No. Not a bird. Tad Spindler."

They ignored me. Desperate, I screamed after him, "Come back. Come back . . . be damned to you!"

Out of the fog at my back there came a definite human chuckle. A well-remembered voice chided me with maddening humor. "What language from a respectable young female!"

Instead of the intense relief I should have felt, Nicolas Bertold had managed to arouse all my annoyance. He came striding toward me, his coat collar pulled up around his throat and his head bare as usual. His coarse black hair looked almost silver in the fog. I remember mentally comparing him once to a highwayman, a breed I had luckily never encountered in life, though I knew one well enough. His body had dangled from the gibbet beyond the village for many months, and my mother actually had touched the wretched fellow once in the superstitious hope of curing her rheumatism of the hands.

I do not recall that the remedy, suggested by a gypsy from the heath, had produced any results as spectacular as the treatment.

"Miss Daviot," the Frenchman said, addressing me politely enough, "you are far from home."

I waved away all this chitchat.

"Don't joke. Tad Spindler is hurt. A villager. Come. Please." I pulled at him, my fingers digging into his wrists. "I need your help, you fool!"

"Since you ask me so charmingly, how can I refuse?"

He let himself be tugged along, but I noted somewhat belatedly that he had been moving faster than I was. By the time we reached the spring, Tad had collapsed against the abutment with his face perilously close to the little stone cup of the spring.

It was not necessary to explain further. Bertold walked around through the muddy clods of earth to a point just behind Tad Spindler's head. While I watched, speechless and impressed, he got Tad under the arms and dragged him out of the mud, along the dry ground. He settled the unconscious man and began to examine the mud-crusted leg.

"Probably a simple break," he told me after washing the mud off with his hands and a large handkerchief he dipped in the spring. "Why the devil couldn't he get his foot out?"

"He drinks."

Bertold looked up at me, examining my skirts, which were almost as mud-encrusted as Tad Spindler was. His gaze rose to my face. There was a curious expression in his gypsy-dark eyes. In another face I might read gentleness. But that seemed foreign to the ruthless, cynical man I had met the previous night.

Perhaps he thought that I would have scorned a fellow human being in trouble because he drank. He had much to learn. Almost every man in the valley drank. The life was not easy, and there were few diversions.

In another moment he was his masterful, abrupt self. "Run back to the sheep track."

"You knew it was a sheep track?"

"Certainly. I've wandered over desolate regions in my time, and I know a sheep track when I see one. Run now and tell the Honiger lads I need them. Their wagon should be along any minute."

I might have known, I thought. *Somehow he has managed an acquaintance with these gypsies that the rest of us have never accomplished.*

He was correct. I scarcely ran two minutes along the sheep track before I heard the rumble and creak of the tinker's wagon. It emerged from the fog with two long-haired young gypsy boys on the box. The wagon was their living quarters when they went peddling. The wooden sides of the wagon were an astonishing sight, with an assortment of kettles, needle pads, cushions, sheep shears, calico lengths, knife-sharpening whetstones, and even a stool for milking a cow. Everything rattled as the wagon reached me, lumbering over the uneven ground.

Both boys greeted me from a distance, a nod from reserved and solemn Josef while good-looking young Demian gave me a wave and leaned down to ask if they could help me.

Thank heaven the boys' English was colloquial and normal! I said, "Oh, yes, if you would. A French gentleman sent me for you. He says he met you this morning."

Demian was pleased, and even the solemn Joseph brightened. Demian leapt down from the wagon.

"Master Nick, he seems like he's home with us. He and Father had such talk. In our tongue. What should we do?"

I said nothing but motioned him to follow me. Josef murmured something to the patient mare and awaited developments. As soon as Demian saw Tad Spindler on the ground, he guessed the real problem.

"Daren't move him without danger, Master Nick?"

"The very truth of it, boy. He is six parts under with Blue Ruin, I don't doubt. But I can't carry him to the village. His leg would never stand it. Feels like a break to me." He had removed his short, dark coat, such as I've seen seamen wear, and had thrown it over Tad, who was snoring now and still shivering. Bertold didn't seem aware that his own white shirt, now somewhat mud-stained, was a poor protection against the wind and fog.

Demian examined Tad's useless leg. "Ye're in the right of it. I'll get some'ut from the wagon. Lift him onto that and into the wagon. We'll get him to the village all right and tight. Tad Spindler. Ay. He's of good heart. When I was a lad and they stoned me, he took the stoning. Threw himself afore me, he did."

I saw the way Nicolas Bertold's lips tightened and suddenly wondered about the "gypsy color" of his eyes, their darkness sometimes warm, sometimes glowing, and once in a while—as now—burning.

I went off to convey their instructions to Josef, who maneuvered the mare into the narrow track between nettles and other furze until the tinker's wagon was close behind the injured man. Demian entered the back of the wagon and came out dragging a rough-hewn door. I was so surprised that I nearly laughed, but the moment was too serious for that, and without being able to help in any way, I watched Bertold and the two boys edge Tad Spindler in through the back of the wagon, laid out stiff and stark on the door.

"Tell Dr. Lauterbourne I'll make myself responsible," I told Josef, and he nodded in his taciturn way. He had his mother's knife-thin face, but his kindness to the animals in our part of the world suggested that his was as compassionate a nature as that of his more popular younger brother.

"Ay." He gave the old mare the signal to circle the area and start downward toward the valley. His brother swung on beside him, waving good-bye to us.

Monsieur Bertold and I were left suddenly with our labor done. I breathed heavily from my earlier exertions, whereas he seemed physically untouched by his own. However, it troubled me to see him in that white shirt, which clung to his flesh in places where the mud and water stains were especially prominent. We surveyed each other, and unexpectedly we both laughed. We must have been an absurd sight to a stranger. He offered his arm.

"Come now, we may walk more easily in this bracing air."

I decided that this rugged man was untouched by the ordinary discomforts of cold and moisture. He must have lived a very active life. In one respect, such a man might find it easier to remove an obstacle like my brother from his path. But there was his concern for a stranger and a drunkard like Tad Spindler. That was compassionate; surely not the act of a ruthless assassin.

"The air is bracing indeed." I turned up the collar of my redingote, conscious of his eyes upon me, watching me in an unsettling way. We started on in the rutted track made by the tinkers' wagon.

After a moment's silence he spoke in the most casual way and without looking at me. "This country air seems to have a salutary effect on the looks of its women."

I felt my face redden and could think of nothing whatever to say. Surely I had never looked worse; my skirts dragged down with mud, and I had no doubt that my face was also spotted with the stuff. He seemed to enjoy putting me out of countenance.

Presently, just before we reached the tangled beech grove and the descent to our Daviot meadows, he stopped and began to examine a bush of yellow heath blooms. He ran the long, slender stem of one flower through his palm, almost seeming to caress it with a gentle finger until he reached the windblown yellow spray of a flower. He cupped it in his palm.

While I stood watching him he snapped the long stem and carried away the flower in his left hand. "It reminds me of someone." I wondered at all this sentimentality, and he seemed to feel that his action called for further explanation. "A lovely thing brightening this desolate heath."

As we made our way down to the wide-spreading water meadow I said, "You must grow many varieties of flowers in the woods around your château."

"Many. Our pond lilies are well-known. Her Majesty asked the head gardener for the secret a year or two ago. I doubt if they did as well in Paris or Compiègne, however. As far as I know, the secret is somewhere in the pond itself. Your brother always called it 'that damned place.' He seemed to think it was bottomless."

I shivered. "Is it?"

He grinned. "If it were bottomless, it would end as a waterspout in China. I imagine the black soil and the lichen and fish that feed on whatever falls into the pond must produce the dark effect. It has been a moat since the twelfth century." He offered his dark hand to help me across a log bridge I had crossed a thousand times. I surprised myself by taking it.

He was still thinking of his home and went on, "It is remarkably rich ground above the Indre River. But your own county here has beauty of a different sort. I like the heath and its inhabitants. I met the entire Honiger family."

I was curious about that. "I'm surprised that the Honigers accepted you. Perhaps it was because you speak their language. You seem to go on very well with gypsies."

"That was inevitable. No doing of mine."

Whatever that meant.

We reached Daviot House just in time to join Nanny Pemberton and Jeremy in the dining room for a late breakfast. Nanny arose at once, still on her dignity.

"I beg pardon, I'm sure, ma'am . . . sir. I wouldn't have sat at table if I'd realized you were coming back so soon."

"Nanny, please," I began.

Monsieur Bertold was impatient but democratic.

"Don't be ridiculous. Sit down, for God's sake! I don't stand on ceremony. You know that."

She settled back into her chair slowly with an uneasy glance at Jeremy. To my chagrin it was Jeremy who caused the difficulty. He set his cup of chocolate down and pushed back his chair. His face was pale but firm.

"I'm not going to sit at table with the man that killed Mama and my father."

There was a dreadful silence.

CHAPTER FIVE

Like Nanny Pemberton, who had been persuaded to sit down but now got up rapidly, I was overcome by shame. Had I allowed myself to be so easily seduced into accepting Nicolas Bertold's innocence? In spite of myself I looked quickly at the Frenchman and saw that even his easy, confident air had been disturbed. If his features had not been so very tough and hardened in some male world of violence, I would have said that he was wounded by Jeremy's childish cry.

Then his heavy lips tightened and he managed a smile. Whether the irony was tinged with sadness I could not say, but I gave him credit for recovering rapidly. Either that or he was a hardened criminal indeed.

"Still at the old song, Jeremy? Is it possible that even the courts have not convinced you?"

But Jeremy was already going out the nearest of the two dining rooms with Nanny trotting, hot-footed, after him.

When we were alone, I tried to frame a question that included the evidence, plus prejudice and common sense. He did not wait for that miraculous eloquence.

"And you, Miss Daviot, do you agree with our nephew

that I am a monster?" He asked it in a quiet, almost whimsical way, but I could not answer in the same vein. I felt too deeply about it.

"I do not know, sir. There seems to be irrefutable evidence. On the other hand, I confess that I should like to believe it was a mistake. A . . . misconception."

He reached for my hand, thought better of the gesture, and moved away, walking slowly around the foot of the table. He seemed to find the tableware of great interest. He no longer looked at me.

I cleared my throat. "The evidence, sir. Why was it disregarded by the French courts?"

He glanced around the room and toward the kitchen passage. "I have had a long walk for the last three hours, and I'm afraid I've developed an appetite. May I order something from your estimable chef? I assure you, I will eat almost anything."

Recalled to common hospitality, I became flustered.

"Of course, I'm sorry. I'll have Hannah Budleigh send in breakfast." I reached for the bellpull, and Hannah burst into the room so promptly that Bertold and I exchanged a quick grin. No doubt our "estimable chef" had been just outside the door listening to every shocking word of our discussion and Jeremy's accusation.

When the order had been given, I went up to see if Jeremy was feeling better, but between them, he and Nanny made me feel so shut out, I came back downstairs with the poor consolation of knowing that Jeremy had won over Nanny Pemberton and both of them considered that I had joined the enemy.

Ultimately I discovered that Monsieur Bertold was right in one respect. The bitter world of suspicion and murder seemed much less sinister when explained over Hannah's Irish potato and onion cakes smothered in lamb gravy, with muffins, slices of ham, and a bowl of fresh apples and one of strawberries. I was too nervous to eat this hearty meal and knew it had been prepared for men, even a man suspected of the Frenchman's crimes, but especially for Hannah's favorite, Richard Pemberton.

Monsieur Bertold enjoyed his meal, behaved with acceptable grace at the table, and suggested finally, "Suppose I answer each piece of so-called evidence in the matter of your brother's death and, I may add, the death of my sister, whom I loved very much."

I sat there fiddling with tea and a lone biscuit on my plate.

"I haven't the reports with me. I can only try to remember. I believe Mr. Pemberton has all the copies of Jeremy's testimony. The originals, of course, are in French hands. I read the copies when Richard Pemberton brought Jeremy to Dover."

"Good." He put aside his knife and a spoon as he spoke. "The boy saw my workman, Jehan-Fidele, and me repairing the moat bridge. He saw it from his bedroom. He claims I returned later to take away the reinforcements. I won't pretend to know why or how he decided that we were trying to destroy . . ." He concentrated on his powerful hands as though they were strangers to him. "Well, no matter. We had put in a log block temporarily, to hold the uprights and supports. It was strong enough. I, myself, intended to take a carriage and team over it an hour later."

"Yes?" I prompted him tensely, seeing that he had forgotten his description and was reliving the incident, trying to understand it, perhaps.

"Suffice it to say, I changed my mind. I went off to get the rocks and fill we would use later. I put them in the cart. It must have been a little more than an hour later that I returned. You know what I found in the pond. Yolande and William drowned in that damned closed carriage. The horses scrambling to climb out, one with a broken leg. Jehan dying, crushed by the collapse of the stone wall. He had been on the box of the carriage. He told me while he lay dying that William had demanded to be driven to our neighbors, the St.

Audens. He and Yolande were quarreling. She insisted on going with him."

I took a long, painful breath.

"That was all."

"All."

"But it is so simple. I can't believe it. William is dead. My brother."

"You can't believe it was an accident, that the log slipped out and everything collapsed?" He nodded at his own question. "I know. At first I didn't want to believe that it was a stupid accident. My sister was so young to die." He looked around at me and then away. "She was barely thirty. I played with some mad idea that someone wanted me to die, someone who knew I had intended to take that carriage. But nothing made sense. They died. That is the only sense."

I said slowly, "It was an accident?"

"The king's prosecutor said so. His Majesty's own investigators said so. But not, it seems, my nephew."

I looked at him. "Why do you think a child his age should be so stubborn in his insistence on your guilt? Can it be that someone did something, loosened the supports you had set up temporarily, and he mistook that person for you? Perhaps someone held a resentment against my brother. William did provoke people occasionally."

His smile was grim. "Yes. I can vouch for that."

I wanted to believe him, and part of me was angered by my own weakness. Yet wasn't this a logical explanation? Rich landowners did not commit monstrous crimes against their own flesh and blood quite as often as the novels would have us believe. "Nanny supports Jeremy's view, and Richard is swayed by Nanny, but I'm afraid that is inevitable."

He admitted, "I was never popular in that quarter. I hold William Daviot to blame, and myself. We never got on. The man was such a narrow, insular, hardheaded Englishman. Nothing was good but what was done by his contrivance."

"Please. I don't want to hear this."

"He wanted to reorganize all our methods. Sell off the land. Invest. A thousand ideas that interfered with our own time-tested ways."

In retrospect I could see William behaving in just that way. The trouble was, the Bertolds had been too impatient and opinionated. They should have managed him differently, as I had done.

I asked, "Why didn't your sister interfere? It was her property too. Surely she could have prevented all these conflicts."

Bertold shook his head, smiling faintly at a memory.

"Not Yolande. She was never happier than when she was the center of controversy and jealousy. What a minx she was! I suspect she enjoyed making Daviot jealous." Seeing my quick reaction, he assured me—or himself. "Not that she ever went beyond the limits of propriety. She was a faithful wife."

I must have looked a bit cynical because he insisted, "Honor would have prevented anything else, even if she wished it. And she remained in love with Daviot. She made that very clear."

Quite out of the blue I asked, "You have never married?"

He shrugged. "There was a betrothal to a childhood sweetheart, but I'm afraid my fatal charm did not make marriage more palatable for Gaby. Gabrielle, that is to say. She subsequently married another neighbor of ours, the Vicomte de St. Auden. Gaby and Pierre and I are still friends. I'm afraid my early experience somewhat soured matrimony for me. Perhaps my manners don't commend themselves to most women. I believe I am considered a hardened bachelor." He looked at me. "Your brother said much the same about you. I must say, he painted you in quite a different light from the girl I've met here in Dorset. Or even that glorious creature who greeted me last night in the rain-soaked finery."

I did not know whether to scowl at his remarks about

William, which I instinctively felt were true, or to thank him for what I assumed was meant to be a dubious compliment.

"Forgive me for greeting you last night in that fashion, but you must remember, I wasn't expecting you."

"No apologies, or you will spoil my first memories of you. You were like a dryad in some forest pool. I had no idea you were the formidable Miss Daviot."

Too embarrassed to proceed along this line, I excused myself, explaining that when one ran a farm as diverse as this, it required all one's attention.

"So I have found on my own farm," he reminded me. I very nearly asked him if he referred to the estate he shared with his nephew, but I knew he would have some flippant excuse.

I knew that if I was not careful, I could accept his story against all my former beliefs about him. I had to learn the story from every angle, to reassure Jeremy. He was probably afraid that I would send him off to France with Monsieur Bertold.

Upon leaving the room, I looked back and saw an odd sight. The Frenchman reached over to the far end of the table where he had been standing when Jeremy made his accusation. The long, slender stem and the daisylike heath flower had been dropped there. He picked up the crushed flower now and sat looking at it. I wondered at this curious hint of gentleness in such a powerful, assertive man. Sensing that he was being watched, he raised his head. He gestured toward me with the cupped flower.

"Remind you of anyone you know?"

I still wasn't quite sure he meant what he seemed to mean. I opened my mouth but could not speak. He smiled. He must know that such a personal remark was unanswerable to me. I went out of the room quickly.

I must visit Dr. Lauterbourne to see if Tad Spindler had recovered, and this might give Jeremy a fresh direction for his thoughts. I found him curled up on the coverlet of his bed with his face to the wall while Nanny held his one exposed hand and caressed it.

"Don't think like that, my lamb. You will see your Mama one day. She is looking down at you from heaven at this very minute, smiling her pretty smile. She hasn't forgotten you. Not she, nor my William."

His voice was muffled by a spasm of coughing. He crushed his other hand into the pillow. "She's gone. She's never coming back. Or Father. He didn't want Uncle Nicolas to stay there in my house. And he wouldn't let Uncle Nicolas try to kill me again. Every time he looks at me, I think . . ."

Nanny became aware that they were not alone. She looked at me pitifully, as if seeking an answer I couldn't give. I had never felt so helpless. The anguish I knew when I heard the news about William seems to pale now before this greater tragedy that had befallen a small, orphaned boy.

I could think of nothing else to ease his mind than to promise him, "You need never go back there. This is your home. We won't let anyone hurt you. Will we, Nanny?"

"Not a one, my dear. Not between Miss Alain and me. And my Richard. We'll stop that monster. Come now, Jeremy, and let's go for a walk. Just to that nice stone bridge. You may wear your blue jacket. The one your mama gave you for your last birthday."

He turned his head. His lips quivered a little with the effort to make us understand.

"I want my house over in France. It's my house now, Aunt Alain, and he shan't have it." He sat up and looked around. "This isn't my house at all. It belongs to Aunt Alain. Nobody likes me here except her. They look at me. They think I'm a Frenchie. I can tell. A foreigner. Well . . ." His young eyes blazed. "I am a foreigner! And Bertold is my home. He can't have it after what he did."

I sighed and looked around in the clothespress for the new blue jacket Nanny had indicated. "Shall we all go for a walk, Jeremy? And maybe have a spice bun at Mother Hagar's?"

He thought about this for a minute and was won over. When Nanny and I each gave him a hand, he got up, and the next minute he was hugging us both together. Quite an armful for a boy his size. I felt a little better and only prayed that young Jeremy did also. His loneliness must be dreadful. In all the world he had only Nanny and me, and I was in many respects a recent acquaintance. I wanted to cry and did not dare to. It would only have accentuated Jeremy's depression. I patted his hand stiffly instead.

"And don't you worry. No one is going to touch you. You are our very own boy, Nanny's and mine. Well, Nanny, what would we do to anyone who tried to hurt him?"

"We'd grind his bones!" Nanny cried, which made Jeremy and me smile.

Jeremy told Nanny, "That's silly," but he liked it. Then he hugged me unexpectedly. "You smell nice, Aunt Alain. You're almost as pretty as Mama." He looked to Nanny for confirmation. "And everybody said Mama was the prettiest lady in the world."

"True enough, my pet," Nanny agreed, but sealed her lips tightly. Afterward I wondered, not for the first time, if Yolande Bertold Daviot had been quite the paragon of honor that her brother made her out to be.

We got Jeremy ready for his walk. He surprised me by producing a muffin Hannah had made for his breakfast and stuffing it in his jacket.

"I'll eat it on the way. Gaby said I should always have my own food, not let others feed me."

"Gaby?" I glanced at Nanny. "The Vicomtesse de St. Auden told you to eat your own food? What had she to say to anything?" And what, precisely, had such an odd comment meant? Did the woman think he might receive tainted food?

Nanny seemed taken aback by his strange remark. She murmured to me, "The young woman Mister William spoke to about our Jeremy's future. Very worried, she was. The boy being the sole heir after the Bertolds are gone."

I was bewildered. "William discussed his son's future and even his . . . safety with a casual neighbor?"

"Not precisely," Nanny explained. "But Mrs. Daviot, Miss Yolande, I mean to say, would flirt a bit. No harm done. The vicomtesse, she was kind and charming, and defended Mister William when her elegant friends called him *sauvage*. She was only a friend, you understand. But most helpful. The vicomte paid little attention to her. I think he had an eye for . . ." She mouthed the words, *Miss Yolande*.

I did not like the idea of all this intrigue. Was it possible that William's marriage had not been as ideal as I was led to suppose? And what of Monsieur Bertold's assurance? Or had he actually been fooled too?

Waiting while Nanny got out a cloak against the bright, chill day, I went to the window to see if the heath fog was spreading to the valley. There seemed to be activity in the kitchen garden involving a gypsy. I opened the window and looked out.

The Honiger woman came through the garden between the feathery green rows after glancing furtively over her shoulder. I think it was her secretive manner that aroused my suspicion. Suspicion of what? I had no idea, except that her attitude toward me and the injured man on the heath was that of an enemy. She wore several layers of clothing like the other gypsy females, the top skirt showing the inner seams. Obviously she had turned the black satin inside out when the other side became soiled. Over her head and shoulders she wore a shawl that looked like delicate black cobwebs.

Hannah Budleigh had seen her from the pantry and came out waving a blackened pan. The woman argued with her. I doubt if Hannah understood the language, but she guessed the meaning and refused brusquely.

Nanny spoke to me. "Are you ready, Miss Alain?"

"Just a minute."

The Honiger woman refused to be cowed. She made a few curious motions in the air, which I assumed might be the components of a curse against our redoubtable cook, and suddenly both women became calm. Hannah disappeared, and Nicolas Bertold stood in her place. He walked out into the pebbled garden path, talking to the gypsy in a friendly, almost confidential way.

What secrets could these two strangers possibly have?

Jeremy called, "Aunt, can you hurry, please? You don't think Mother Hagar's cakes will be all gone?"

"I doubt it. Very well. We'll go."

In any case, I couldn't understand what the Frenchman and the gypsy were talking about.

We went down the stairs and out the front way toward the stone bridge over the creek, but my thoughts were busy on that strange and, to me, slightly sinister business of a friendship between Nicolas Bertold and a gypsy woman who had always shown a malevolent face toward the Daviots.

From the center of the bridge I looked back at the main house, its pink-brick facade looking warm and deceptively soft in the sunlight. From this height I could see the two figures, dark against the surrounding brightness of the house. Then they parted, and the Frenchman returned to the back of the house. The gypsy pulled her spiderweb shawl forward over her forehead. The sunlight gleamed off her big earrings, which had been made from gold coins. She looked up and down. She must have made out the figures of Nanny and Jeremy across the brook as they sauntered along the road. She stared that way a long time, appearing not to notice me on the bridge. Then she went off in the opposite direction toward the easterly farm and sheepflocks of my neighbors. I wondered where her family might be and what she was about.

Presently, by the time we three reached the edge of the village, I had almost forgotten Mrs. Honiger. I was too busy describing for Nanny and Jeremy my earlier encounter with Tad, who Tad was, and how he came to break his leg. I did not expect either of them to react favorably to the sterling work done by Monsieur Bertold, but somewhat to my surprise, Jeremy found the idea of the town drunkard fascinating.

"Father drank when he was angry at the Bertolds. He got loud and funny when he was angry. When I was little, I was scared of Father. But not later, when I knew he didn't mean it."

"Of course, he didn't mean it," Nanny insisted. "Remember how he took you up and hugged you and swung you high until you began to giggle?"

Jeremy looked down at the toe of his boot and kicked a clod of earth. "I wish he was here now. He could shout at people all he wanted to. I wouldn't be scared."

I hugged his shoulders. How deeply I shared his wish!

His spirits raised when he met Tad Spindler, who had been moved from Dr. Lauterbourne's little cottage to a horse barn belonging to the church. We found Tad happily bedded on some hay and nursing a bottle of spirits. His right leg was stiffly lashed to a pair of sticks used to stake beans in season. He showed off the splinted leg to Jeremy.

"An't much hurt if ye've this to nurse, lad," he boasted, stroking the bottle.

Jeremy wondered aloud what it would feel like to go about with bean sticks attached to his leg.

"Like a gypsy at a fair. Walking on stilts. We saw them in Boisville sometimes," Jeremy went on. "That's our village, the town near the château. I love fairs."

I was happy to remind him, "We've a fair of our own right here in the village on Saturday Week."

His eyes opened wide. "Could I walk with stilts? Could I?"

Tad chuckled. "Break a leg an' ye've stilts ready to hand." He slapped one of the bean sticks, winced, and suggested, "The gypsies. Them that walks the sticks. Big sticks."

This unnerved Jeremy a trifle. "Gypsies? Oh, but I thought over here they wouldn't be. I mean . . . others walk too. Felix did. He said he would teach me." He looked around at Nanny and me. "I don't like gypsies anymore. They look like Uncle Nicolas."

I said, "There are good gypsies and bad ones. Like all of us. Maybe at the fair I'll introduce you to a pair of splendid gypsy boys that you are sure to like."

Seeing the beginnings of agitation in him which I missed, Nanny frowned at me and assured him, "There, now, your Aunt Alain doesn't understand about little boys who have been ill. Never you mind. Nanny will protect you."

I did not like this constant stressing of the boy's illness. I thought it a mistake. It would be much better to protect him quietly, subtly, without his constant awareness that he couldn't protect himself. But I said nothing, reflecting that Nanny knew him better than I did.

Nanny took Jeremy into Mother Hagar's shop for spice buns while I walked back to Dr. Lauterbourne's cottage to pay him for his work with Tad Spindler. The doctor was a tired, thin young man who, I suspected, also drank too much, in his discouragement at the conditions of his profession.

In his father's time a physician was despised. I well remember my mother exclaiming when Papa invited Dr. Quilty to dinner, "One doesn't entertain a surgeon socially, much less a man who peddles medical powders."

Father had won out, and Dr. Quilty ate his lamb with our family. This happened before I was born, and I asked Mama if Dr. Quilty "behaved like a gentleman."

Mama thought it over but couldn't remember. Apparently he was never invited back.

I, myself, entertained Dr. and Mrs. Quilty and Dr. Lauterbourne at various times, especially with Lady Willoughby and Mavis. Her Ladyship obligingly overlooked the "antecedents" of the two men. She, herself, was an avid gambler, and Dr. Quilty liked to play the card game of piquet, an old favorite of hers.

The criticism directed against me, a single woman, for

entertaining without a chaperone like Nanny, and indeed, for running a farm, had been tempered lately, since I showed every sign of becoming "the old spinster out at Daviot Farm."

Dr. Lauterbourne was curious about the visitor at the farm.

"Highly efficient, from all accounts," he said. "The Honiger boys are very taken with him. It isn't often that a gentleman gets a kind word from that source."

"I believe him to be a gentleman-born." I made my way carefully in this matter. "His manners are very . . . free."

The doctor was washing knives, especially a wide, flat knife he used to depress the tongue of a little girl from Coombe Bower. He had just examined her for signs of putrid fever and found her free of the contagion. I liked his efforts at cleanliness. I doubt if such notions ever occurred to Dr. Quilty or most of the valley people.

He looked at me in his tired way. His gray eyes always made me sad and uncomfortable.

"Has he troubled you in any way, Miss Daviot? Made advances?"

I laughed such an idea to scorn.

"What? Advances to me? My dear doctor, I would have taken a broom handle to him. You forget. I have sent peddlers, prowlers, and chicken thieves running with a scalding pail of water thrown in their wretched faces."

He smiled. "No, indeed, ma'am, I have not forgotten. But I wish you were a trifle more aware of your own—" He broke off. I wondered if he could be just a trifle drunk. "Foxed," as my father used to say. He held my hand when I insisted on putting two shillings into his palm, and I freed my fingers gently. I changed the subject.

"May we feel free to call upon you if my nephew should come down with a cold or a congestion on the chest?"

"You know you may." He went back to scrubbing his silverware. "Would you accept one bit of advice? From a male?"

Surprised, I could only nod. I hoped he would not bring up the subject of my spinsterhood.

"Then try not to wrap the boy in wool all the time."

"What?"

"I speak figuratively. The boy will never be able to fight his own battles in the world if two well-meaning ladies continually stand between him and life. You will end by making him a weakling."

He was right, but I didn't like him the better for pointing out our errors.

"But he has been ill. And then the shock of losing both his parents; this must have been very heavy to bear."

"All the same, take care." He stared at the pan of soapy water. "I was raised by three devoted aunts who shielded me whenever possible. The result was what you see."

"A man we all trust and admire," I said briskly, but I had a feeling that there was a great deal of truth in his warning.

I soon had the opportunity to test his advice and could not take it.

Throwing Nicolas Bertold's short, heavy coat over my arm to return it, I walked back up the lane toward the street, actually the High Road between Shaftesbury and the South Coast. In front of Mother Hagar's sweetshop I saw a little group. With a sinking feeling I made out Nanny Pemberton's stout, black-caped figure and saw her waving her strong fist as she yelled at someone.

A public brawl involving our very proper Nanny must, indeed, announce a disaster. I rushed forward. There was a good deal of excitement among those, mostly youngsters, who were watching. I pushed my way through and found the protagonists, Jeremy Daviot, cowering away, trembling, two spice buns on the ground at his feet, and the gypsy woman, Mrs. Honiger, pushing against his chest a tambourine that rattled unmusically.

With her earrings flashing and her eyes fierce, the gypsy

woman persisted even after I confronted her, repeating something in her strange language. I guessed she wanted money.

"Go away!" I said. "Leave this child alone."

Several of the youngsters watching volunteered to translate for me. They were all torn between giggles and the excitement of the confrontation. I repeated my command, shoving the tambourine away from Jeremy. To my astonishment the woman pushed the thing against my bosom. Enraged at such effrontery, I pulled the tambourine away from her and tried to hit her on the head. Several coppers and a silver coin rolled away, and she scrambled after them. Some of the boisterous children cheered. It was more than a little embarrassing.

By the time I brushed off Jeremy and pulled myself together, keenly aware that I had provided an unladylike spectacle for the village, the Honiger woman had recovered her property.

Kneeling there in the dirt, she gazed up at me, her slanting black eyes burning like coals in a sudden draft. She raised an arm, pointed one long finger at me, and said clearly in English, "May everything you love turn to evil! May you be destroyed by that you love!"

There was an audible, collective gasp from those around us. Even the redoubtable Nanny flinched. I have my share of superstitions, like all country folk who live by the strange laws of nature, but in this moment there was only one action possible. I said sharply, "Go and join your family and don't come around here again frightening children."

The woman left, looking back at me and grinning.

I kept my countenance, but it was not a very pleasant thing to see the way the children, and even the casual adult passersby, backed away from me momentarily.

I said, "Give me your hand, Jeremy. We are going back to Mother Hagar's to buy another spice bun."

He had burst into tears, perhaps of relief, and Nanny pulled him to her skirts, crooning, "Don't cry, lamb. Aunt Alain won't let the nasty gypsies hurt you."

I tried to be gentle, but a little annoyance crept in. I was nervous, myself, and trying to hide it.

"Jeremy, you must learn to be a big boy now. Dry your eyes and come along."

"My dear, how can you be so cruel?" Nanny scolded as if I was still three years old. "He is only a little boy."

I said no more. We bought the spice bun, and Jeremy was soon smiling again.

But on the way home I began to wonder. Nicolas Bertold had spoken with the gypsy woman an hour or so earlier. Would their conversation have anything to do with this fright she had given Jeremy? Perhaps he hoped to frighten his nephew back to France.

CHAPTER SIX

Most of the household was relieved, sometimes loudly so, when our unwanted French guest absented himself that day, and the next as well. He took a package of meat and cheese, along with a fresh-baked loaf of bread, a bottle of my father's wine, and an apple. Thus suitably armed, he announced to Hannah Budleigh that he was long overdue for a good, stout walk.

As though his journey up on the heath and his return without even a coat had been mere child's play!

When Mavis Willoughby came over to make Monsieur Bertold's acquaintance the following day and caught him as he was leaving, I could see that she did not share the views of Jeremy, Nanny, and Richard about Bertold. I had marshaled up any number of complaints against him myself, including my suspicion about his sudden friendship with the Honigers, but this annoying man behaved charmingly during the brief minutes he spent with Mavis. He even kissed her hand, or at all events, the air above her knuckles.

"Monsieur Bertold has no time for social graces," I explained to Mavis in my blandest voice. "He is much too anxious to be on his way. And with the most excellent company, his own."

"Ah, perfectly true," he agreed, still looking down into Mavis's eyes. "But that was before this lovely little creature came in my way."

So much for his comparing me to rain-washed dryads and yellow flowers!

Mavis was in heaven. Her lashes fluttered.

"What can you mean, monsieur? You are running away from us ladies and you know it. I never thought to meet the son of a Napoleonic general who was a coward."

She seemed to have amused him. Or intrigued him.

"Indeed, Miss . . ."

"Willoughby," I reminded him.

"Mavis," she put in.

Ignoring me he went on. "Miss Mavis, my father served Bourbon, Bonaparte, Bourbon, and finally Orléans. Such talents require a strong stomach for treason, but whether courage is involved, I am not one to say."

She pouted charmingly. I envied her the talent.

"And still you are leaving us. Well, I must say!"

"He is coming to your musicale." After he gave me a look with black brows raised, I added, "I believe he volunteered to turn pages."

"Divine, monsieur. I play the piano." She and I both understood his sigh of relief. He had probably heard enough vocal concerts by young ladies whose mothers were in the market for a son-in-law.

He shook hands with her. "Very well. You may count upon a page turner, thanks to our hostess here."

I walked with him to the front entry. Before leaving, he gave me a grin that made me exceedingly aware of his physical attraction. "Much good it may do you. I suppose you, yourself, will ask Master Pemberton to turn pages for you."

"I do not play the pianoforte."

"You play it very well."

Coming out of the entry hall just after he had gone, Mavis asked, "What on earth did that mean?"

"Heaven knows."

But I was exceedingly pleased.

Mavis spent several minutes discussing Nicolas Bertold, until Richard Pemberton came in with Jeremy. Both of them wore knee boots. They had been over in the water meadow where Jeremy made the acquaintance of various Daviot and Budleigh cows. My nephew was justifiably proud of his courage in approaching these animals, and I wondered if perhaps both his uncle and I had been mistaken in imagining that he was a cowardly child.

Richard showed me the sketch he had made of Jeremy and a milk cow. It was delightful, and I immediately talked of having it framed and hung in the drawing room. Both artist and subject were pleased.

"Uncle Nicolas couldn't do that," Jeremy pointed out. "Father said Uncle Nicolas would do anything to get all the estate, but he couldn't make a picture like Richard can."

"He certainly cannot," I agreed, hoping to end this harping on Monsieur Bertold. "Nor can I."

I could see that Mavis shared my feeling. She had fallen under the Frenchman's spell very readily. I found this surprising. Mavis was pretty and popular, as I remember very well from our two years at the London School for Genteel Young Females, and she could probably entice any man in the county if she chose. But though I, myself, felt his attraction, Nicolas Bertold hardly seemed Mavis's sort at all. He was far from handsome, had few graces, and was not generally well mannered.

Our French guest made more forays into the countryside. What he accomplished I could not imagine, except that he had great curiosity about people and land.

One morning after such a foray he came directly to the kitchen. I was in the stillroom polishing silver when he stuck his head in, looking for Hannah.

I said, "She has gone home to the farm. Her father needed her. She will be back in time for dinner. May I help you? I daresay, you want a lunch made up for later in the day?"

"Nothing so important. I scratched myself. Where does Hannah keep the basilicum powders?"

It was an old remedy, and I hadn't seen any for years, but I did wonder at the seriousness of his injuries. He carried his left arm crooked against his body and made no effort to lower it. I ordered him to sit down at the kitchen table and got out a little pot of salve we had always found highly efficacious. Because there were many injuries on the farm, we always kept handy several rolls of cloth stripped for use as bandages.

I set one of the rolls beside the ointment and touched his arm. I saw at once that the flesh of his arm just below the elbow was mangled in several places, probably by a dog.

Startled and very much concerned, I asked, "Was he mad?"

"Lord love you, no! Just a zealous guardian of his master's farmland. You should have a few dogs with his teeth."

"Thank you. I had rather rely upon Brown Bess, one of William's guns. I am considered something of a shot."

"I don't doubt it. I take it that you prefer a Brown Bess to a tambourine."

I looked up quickly. "Whatever do you mean?" But I remembered the gypsy woman and was angry with myself for having reacted.

"Zilla Honiger tells me you hit her on the top of the head with her own tambourine."

He certainly was having fun with me, though he looked sober enough.

I was matter-of-fact. "She is mistaken. I hit her on the ear. My aim was imperfect." He laughed, then flinched a bit as I washed the wounds and applied the ointment. I waited until I had finished, and I thought he might have forgotten about the gypsy. Then I raised my head, looking into his eyes.

"Mrs. Honiger talked to you earlier that day. You didn't use a tambourine."

"No. But I filled it. A shilling or two. She was persistent. It was the only way to be free of her."

How reasonable it sounded, and how I wanted to believe it!

He pursued the matter. "A single coin, a penny, would have driven her away from the boy. I am surprised that Mrs. Pemberton didn't realize it." Memory gave him second thoughts. "But that woman never had too much common sense. I told Yolande long ago. Nanny Pemberton has made a wreck of my nephew's life. Turned him into an errant, cringing baby. In fact, a child of five might better have handled Zilla Honiger."

"He has been ill. You cannot treat him like an ordinary boy. Besides, Nanny didn't turn William or Richard into a crybaby."

He grunted. "Quite the contrary. The woman seems to have no moderation. And by the by, are we to go on enduring meals full of sulking and petulance? Not that I mind. I am inured to it. But it hardly seems to make you happy."

"I believe the sulking is meant to be pride and the petulance is hauteur. It is Jeremy's defense against the killer of his parents."

His penetrating gaze went suddenly to my own eyes. His flesh felt stiff with tension as I released the bandaged arm.

"And is that how you see me?"

I said honestly, "I do not know. I hope not. I think... perhaps he is mistaken."

He relaxed, and I was again made aware of the power he could exert with that warmth in his eyes. He slapped my hand slightly and got up.

"Thank you for that. And for this. We shall do very well, you and I."

I watched him leave the kitchen and walk out across the kitchen garden between the cabbage rows. I was still watching him when I heard Jeremy's plaintive voice behind me.

"He thinks I'm a coward."

"No. Of course, he doesn't. He only—and I too—think you must stand up to people when they torment you. Like that gypsy woman. She wouldn't dare to have hurt you. Nanny was there. And all the village folk."

He nodded but still looked troubled. "She would have set a curse on me, like she did on you." He went on anxiously. "It won't come true. I love you, Aunt Alain. And I wouldn't ever hate you, like that old witch said." He put his arms around me, squeezing hard until I was breathless. I reassured him warmly.

"I know you won't, dear. Come and sit down and have a cup of milk and one of those apples. They're our first."

"Milk makes me breathe hard," he remarked, but with an indifference that made me wonder how often he had been forced to drink something that brought on his spasms.

Curiously enough, when I gave him a cup of goat's milk, he had no trouble. We were discussing this interesting phenomenon when Nanny and Richard came in from Willoughby Hall where Nanny had properly admired her son's handsome sketch of Lady Willoughby. It could not be expected that Nanny would agree to Jeremy's change of diet without considerable argument, but in this I was abetted by Richard.

"Never liked the stuff, myself. Cow's or goat's. If the goat's milk agrees with the lad and Jeremy likes it, why not?" He hesitated, glanced out the kitchen window and back. "This wasn't his idea, was it?"

"Monsieur Bertold has nothing to do with his nephew's diet. But as a matter of fact, we do agree on one matter about Jeremy."

"Oh?" His hackles were up at once.

"We believe Jeremy should be given a little more initiative. More freedom to make mistakes or defend himself. Or walk out alone, perhaps to the Hall, or just to the bridge."

Jeremy's voice, slightly higher pitched than usual, put in, "I'm not afraid. I mean, I won't be afraid. And if that old witch lady sticks her tambourine into me, I'll take it away and hit her on the head." Apparently he had heard our conversation.

I groaned, Nanny cried, "Mercy on us!" and Richard laughed. It was he who said with enthusiasm, "For once I agree with Bertold. An excellent idea, my boy."

I could only hope a war between the gypsies and the valley folk did not come about as a result of my ill-judged act of temper. On several occasions during the next few days Richard Pemberton hinted that there seemed no point in Bertold "hanging about." On Friday he asked me why I permitted our uninvited guest to remain in my house.

"I know his purpose, but what is yours, Alain? Have you ever asked yourself? Seriously."

I took care to make the most reasonable explanation.

"We must not offend him. He may have all sorts of friends in high places. And these influences sometimes cross borders. Queen Victoria is King Louis-Philippe's friend. What do they call themselves? Fellow sovereigns?"

He interrupted impatiently. "We know that. As a matter of fact, Louis-Philippe's throne is very shaky. Half of France is touting the abilities of Bonaparte's nephew, Louis-Napoléon. Those people revolted in 1789, again in 1814, again in 1815. Once more in 1830. And I've no doubt that by 1850, they will be thinking about cutting off a few more heads. And Louis-Philippe's friend Bertold may be one of those who go."

Richard's excellent features were not suited to all this vengeful talk, and he looked as unpleasant as I had ever seen him. He only succeeded in prejudicing me. He read something of this in my rigid features, and when I turned away, he recovered his friendly manner.

"I'm sorry. No one likes to hear things like that about a member of the family. I only meant to remind you of what we know about him, what your own nephew witnessed."

"Monsieur Bertold has a very sensible explanation for that."

Obviously Richard had been making an effort to understand me, but his grim mood returned.

"Murderers usually do have sensible explanations," he reminded me, and went away to dress for the musicale at Willoughby Hall.

CHAPTER SEVEN

While I dressed that evening I tried to analyze my own feelings and confessed that these personal emotions might have blurred my real view of Nicolas Bertold. I was behaving like one of those silly girls we had all known (and been) at our female academy. An interesting man had only to smile at me or pay me an absurd compliment and I immediately forgot all that I knew about him.

But what did I know as a certainty? Nothing beyond suspicion, and that suspicion came from his enemies.

Perhaps I should simply rely upon what my instincts told me. But that, too, could be dangerous. I had let myself become ridiculously intrigued by Nicolas Bertold. Most of my waking hours were spent thinking about him, speculating about his past, his guilt or innocence. I knew all this but found it the hardest thing in my life to overcome, because somewhere in that experience I knew that he really was sincere in his attentions to me.

Tonight I had determined to wear my lavender silk dinner gown. By wearing this color I might retain my mourning, and yet I would not look like one of our heathland crows, depressing the company in rusty black. I told myself that William would not approve of heavy mourning though only eight months had passed. He had always jeered at such customs privately.

But I still felt guilty. I knew why I was so determined to look my best.

I had secretly pictured myself descending the staircase in all my silken splendor, such as it was, with Monsieur Bertold staring up at me, openmouthed and admiring, from a strategic spot beside the newel post at the foot of the stairs. When I was leaving my bedchamber, however, I realized that I must say good night to Jeremy and Nanny before leaving. Jeremy, in particular, loved to touch silk and satin materials. From his wistful remarks I knew that he was hungry to see the bright colors and materials that were so much a part of his mother's life.

I found Jeremy and Nanny both looking excited as he read *Robinson Crusoe* aloud while she worked at the petit point cover for a footstool. I interrupted what sounded like a spirited discussion of the necessities needed on a desert island. They both looked up in surprise to see me.

Nanny exclaimed, "Heavens, Miss Alain! I hadn't expected—I daresay, I've become so used to you in dark colors."

"But Nanny, isn't she pretty?" Jeremy asked loyally. "I like your hair all curly."

"Poor William." Nanny's complaint was scarcely louder than a whisper, but I resented it and avoided her.

Jeremy caressed my sleeve under my black opera cloak and did much to soften Nanny's words. "Don't mind, Aunt. I'm glad. Have a good time with Richard, won't you?"

"I hope to, dear. It depends on whether Miss Mavis plays well tonight."

He giggled. "It's better than those great, fat ladies singing." He stood on tiptoe and kissed my cheek. I hugged him hard and left the room. I was aware that my spreading skirts made a loud, swishing sound through the silent room, suggesting once more than I had forgotten my dead brother and become a shallow lady of fashion.

By this time I had almost forgotten my original romantic dream of seeing Nicolas Bertold at the foot of the oaken staircase, so I was not too disappointed when he opened the door of the gallery chamber and came out to meet me. I don't know why I should have been surprised to see how gentlemanly he looked in the severe black-and-white evening dress.

I was almost sorry. I needed no word of Mavis Willoughby's to guess how impressed she would be. Thank heaven I had worn a flattering gown and my mother's amethyst jewelry! For the first time in our lifelong friendship I meant to challenge Mavis, whose popularity with our male acquaintances certainly exceeded mine.

But such flirtations had not included a man for whom I felt this vibrant, almost alarming passion.

I expected Nicolas Bertold to bow correctly, perhaps offer his arm, and escort me in a formal fashion down to an ancient carriage, with O'Roarke, our gardener-coachman, on the box. O'Roarke was Farmer Budleigh's brother-in-law and occupied his spare hours driving various farmers and their wives to formal gatherings. Otherwise most of us walked. Tonight he would deposit the Daviot party at the Hall, then drive off to fetch another family. He had probably brought half a dozen other guests to Lady Willoughby's musicale before he pulled up at Daviot House.

Because it seemed impossible for the Frenchman to do what was expected of him, he came to me, took both my hands, and raised them. He must have a great deal of experience. He turned one hand over to reveal my palm above the silk buttons of my glove. He touched his lips to the bared circle of flesh between my palm and wrist. This sensuous touch affected my nerves so thrillingly, it took considerable effort on my part to reveal only a casual pleasure. Perhaps he guessed the truth. Certainly in his eyes I read more than approval.

He made no effort at elaborate compliments but tucked my hand on his arm, with my fingers resting warmly upon his sleeve and the muscular strength beneath. We started down the stairs together.

There at the bottom stood Richard Pemberton, leaning on the newel post and looking up. He straightened at the sight of us, and I remember thinking, *He certainly is the handsomest man of my acquaintance. What a catch he would be for some romantic girl!*

But not Alain Daviot, it seemed. I marveled at my own failure to appreciate his sterling worth.

It took a slight effort to free my hand from Bertold, but I gave it to Richard, who shook it cordially while he gave me the compliment good manners dictated.

"By jove, Alain, you've never looked better. She is a real beauty, isn't she, Bertold?"

The Frenchman considered me. "Very well turned out" was his verdict. Instead of humiliating or disappointing me, this moderate praise made me laugh. I went out between the two men in excellent spirits.

It had piqued my fancy for a moment or two that both the men might flatter me by trying to steal my attention in the old carriage, but I might have guessed that Bertold would not cooperate in such an obvious maneuver.

While we jolted and bounced along the road, over the stone bridge, onward toward Ferndene Heath and turning to the right, onto the Willoughby estate road, Richard and I kept up a volatile discussion about past entertainments in the valley. Not unnaturally, this left Bertold out of the conversation. I was a trifle chagrined when he made no effort to join us.

By the time we reached the Hall and were being ushered up the stairs to the ballroom Lady Willoughby used for her soirees, I wondered if his previous interest in me had evaporated. At the top of the stairs I found new worries. Lady Willoughby stood there looking big and jolly in spite of her tight lacing and an overabundance of diamonds.

Beside her, Mavis was starry-eyed and glorious in deep blue satin and silk gauze. Though she was friendly, as always, to the rest of us, we could not be blind to her overwhelming interest in Nicolas Bertold. I had never been more jealous, but I managed my usual weapon. I pretended to be oblivious.

I confess that this was easier than usual for me. Probably my lavender gown, or even a new excitement in my eyes, attracted more than my share of attention. When Richard took me to the front row of many unmatched chairs in the ballroom, I remembered that the Frenchman would be turning pages for Mavis. But though Richard took the chair on my right, a slightly pompous widower from this side of Lyme Bay settled into the straight, gilt chair on my left, and I felt trapped.

Watching Mavis at her mother's elegant new piano, I realized that her natural grace had never been better displayed. Monsieur Bertold would be blind not to see and admire it. Her fingers danced across the keys. Even her playing was creditable. Richard confided behind his hand, "A waltz. Very popular in Paris. By Frédèric Chopin. Are you familiar with his work?"

I felt that he was patronizing and said, "Certainly." Although I do not have what Mavis Willoughby used to call "a musical ear" I could appreciate the peculiar romantic pathos of the waltz she was playing.

With one of those odd, special senses, I became aware that someone was staring at me. I looked up. Nicholas Bertold, standing beside the piano, had turned to watch us. He must have seen Richard whisper to me behind his hand. He looked somber. When I gave him a tentative smile, he did not return it. Something else was on his mind. Perhaps he didn't even know I was there.

Shortly afterward, however, he bent over Mavis at the end of her particularly good pyrotechnics and congratulated her in a way that made her look up at him with a radiant smile. They seemed unaware that all of us were watching them.

When Mavis completed her little concert, she cried off

from the compliments raining down upon her, and urged another of our neighbors, a gentleman with a powerful baritone, to favor us with a sea chantey. The polite argument began.

Meanwhile, gossips who, like me, had no ear for music, crowded around Lady Willoughby, obviously discussing Nicolas Bertold. Somewhat to my surprise, they behaved very well when he was presented to them. Curiosity, and possibly his own attraction, seemed to make them forget all their old suspicions.

I watched him fend off the excited questions about "The King of the French," as Lady Willoughby said carefully, and I was amused by the curiosity about what Queen Marie Amèlie wore to a musicale and whether Mister Bertold had ever met young Queen Victoria.

The room became stuffy and crowded. It seemed that all the guests and most of the large Willoughby staff were now around the piano. Richard was discussing with two Shaftesbury gentlemen the possibility of a Bonapartist Republic in France, and I walked out into the wide corridor, glad to be alone for a few minutes. I wanted to think about my own unsettling emotions.

A Willoughby parlormaid tapped my shoulder. I looked around.

"A message from Daviot House, ma'am."

Something had happened. It must be Jeremy.

I went downstairs and almost to the big, double front doors before I realized no one was there. I looked back, but the parlormaid, too, had disappeared. If this was someone's humor—Mavis! It sounded like something she might do to keep me out of the Frenchman's orbit.

I hesitated, wondering if I might simply walk home without destroying the last of my reputation for good manners. A hand reached over my shoulder and closed on my arm. I was startled and almost cried out, but I thought I recognized those strong, olive-skinned fingers.

Nicolas Bertold asked, "Are you enjoying this damned affair?"

So Monsieur Bertold was responsible for the message.

"That would depend upon the affair."

Nicolas Bertold laughed shortly, and I turned to face him. He was very close behind me. I marveled that he could have approached so silently . . . stealthily, someone else might say. Why had I thought of that word? The prick of suspicion was always with me, somewhere beneath the surface emotions he aroused. I read that half-humorous, half-sad look in his eyes and relaxed.

"No, I am not enjoying it. I was wishing I might go home. Now. Without apologies."

"Why not go?"

He must know it would not be mannerly, but I suppose "mannerly" notions never entered his head.

"For one thing, if I asked O'Roarke to take me home, Richard would be forced to walk."

"True. And we must give consideration to the Richards of the world. Very well. You and I will walk."

"Impossible." I looked down at my gown, at the low neckline that permitted a display of my mother's amethysts, and the wide hem that came nearly to the top of my best silk evening slippers. But I seldom refuse a dare, and his lively expression certainly challenged me. Why not behave irresponsibly for once in my life?

I shrugged. "Well, why not?" Even so, I looked for an excuse. "Except that I haven't my cloak."

"Now you have it." He must be very sure of me. He took my black velvet opera cloak from a chair behind the staircase and dropped it around my shoulders. Still standing in back of me, he reached around and fastened the clasp under my chin. A second or two later he flipped up the curl at the nape of my neck and kissed the spot he had uncovered. His lips lingered on my flesh, and I was conscious of a wave of ecstasy that coursed through my veins in a way entirely unfamiliar to me.

I managed to recover enough of my usual self-possession to say, after a few seconds, "Is that one of your more successful maneuvers with females?"

It may be that my smile softened the rude question. He seemed more amused than offended.

"You needn't concern yourself with others. I don't."

It was not the quick denial I expected, but then, he was not a man to do the expected. He took possession of my arm, and we walked out onto the wide classic portico of the Hall, then down to the drive and on our way. The night wind brushed my full skirts against his elegant trouser leg, and the tendrils of my hair pressed against my cheeks. I hoped the brisk air would disguise my own glow of excitement.

We walked in the most companionable way. His stride was long and rapid, but I walked in much the same fashion. We said nothing for a few minutes, and yet I felt no effort to make conversation as I might have done with some young men of my acquaintance.

It was he who broke the silence of the starlit night. "I don't trust that puppy."

"Puppy?"

"The Pemberton Adonis. I mistrusted him in France, and I like him even less here. Is there a relationship between you and Pemberton?"

I delighted in this hint of his jealousy. Surely it was a sign of his sincere interest in me. I answered literally.

"A long relationship."

He teased and tantalized me so often, I wanted to give him back a little of his own coin. He looked hard at me. He hadn't expected my answer.

"In fact, you are in love with the puppy." Before I could answer, he went on in a voice that might have alarmed me under other circumstances. "I watched you both tonight, whispering and giggling behind your hands, like schoolchildren."

"I never giggle."

We were somewhere near the crossroad to the Budleigh farm. He stopped suddenly. I wondered if he had lost the way. Before I could point out the correct direction, he caught me by the shoulders and pulled me hard against his body. I thought for an instant that he was going to shake me.

"You love that puppy? Show me."

I opened my mouth to protest at his violence, and he took possession of it, hotly silencing me with his lips. Even as my body betrayed me by its quick, throbbing response, I knew I should resent his furious conquest. No matter. I loved him. I wanted him. He was the only man I had ever wanted in quite this way, with some of his own violence. The heat of his mouth and his male hardness against me evoked a searing response I had not thought myself capable of.

I was still in the thrall of this fresh, wondrous passion when he held me away from him at arm's length.

"Shall I show you how a true man may love you?"

He looked around at our surroundings, the water meadow, the distant beech grove, and the summer fields rapidly turning to autumn in the starlight. Whatever was in his thoughts—and I dared not ask, for it was in mine as well—he decided that this was not the time and certainly not the place.

He laughed abruptly. "Well, the moment doesn't seem right."

He put one arm around my shoulder and began to walk on with me, toward the stone bridge. We might have been an old, settled, married couple. Gradually the frantic desire between us faded to this comfortable nearness.

It was not until we were crossing the dirt drive before Daviot House that I came back to reality. I saw someone at the window of my nephew's room, a boy's dark head, as he rested it on his crossed arms and watched for us. I waved to him, but Nicolas studied him, then said quietly, "He fell asleep waiting for us. Or should I say, for you?"

CHAPTER EIGHT

Apparently Jeremy had not seen me return in such close proximity to the man he regarded as his family's great enemy. I was relieved. Selfishly I wanted to enjoy, alone, a few more hours of that passionate excitement that Nicolas Bertold inspired in me. I thought I loved him, but by some strange contradiction, I still was not sure of his innocence. I was ashamed of my own weakness; yet I could not deny the truth to myself.

It was therefore with mixed emotions that I heard Betsy report the next day, "Mr. Nicolas, he's off to London on business, so he says. It's about the wine the Frenchies grow."

When Jeremy heard this, he poked me in the ribs over the remark about growing wine, but then his young face was suddenly shadowed by what I knew to be his homesickness.

"I should be doing that. It's half my vineyards. I wish I were home." He added quickly, "And that you were there, too, Aunt Alain, with Nanny and me."

"And Richard?" I asked, curious over the omission.

He thought this over. "And Richard."

I pursued the matter. "Richard doesn't like Uncle Nicolas, does he? I mean, even before the . . . accident."

Jeremy said, "It wasn't an accident." Then he fidgeted. "He used to like Uncle Nicolas. He said Father shouldn't get mad all the time."

When Richard himself came in with Nanny, we changed the subject.

Jeremy asked me many eager questions about the musicale, especially what I ate. That posed a problem. I hadn't stayed long enough to enjoy the late supper after the conclusion of the sea chanteys by the baritone guest. While I fumbled for an explanation Richard launched into an eloquent account of what he called the pâtés and pastries served, and the excellent wines.

"Uncle Nicolas sells my wine. And his," Jeremy put in.

Nanny interrupted severely. "Hush, my lamb. You chatter too much."

But Richard looked at me. "He has deserted us so soon after his brisk walk last night? He has great stamina. Or, I wonder if he could have been discouraged in his pursuit of the game."

Jeremy wanted to know, "How could he go hunting at night?"

I ignored Richard's observation, furious that he should come so close to guessing what had happened between Nicolas and me.

It was not until later in the day, when Hannah and I were in the buttery discussing the marketing possibilities, that Richard took it upon himself to chide me for the aftermath of the musicale.

"Lady Willoughby spoke very forcibly on the subject, Alain. I don't wish to scold you. It is not my place, after all."

"Certainly not. Well, Hannah, let us hope prices are higher in the winter."

"Indeed, ma'am. Mr. Nicolas says the market was what he called 'depressed' across the Channel, but it's better now."

I walked back up to the house with Richard walking along beside me, patiently trying to reason with me.

"You know what a gossip Her Ladyship is. If you had no consideration for your reputation, you really might have been kinder to Mavis."

"What did she say?" I asked. He was right. I had been thoughtless and unkind to my friend. "She played remarkably well."

He confessed that Mavis had accepted my departure, and that of her favorite guest, "with her usual high spirits. She is always generous. She only laughed and actually said she would have acted in the same way. A fine young woman, Mavis. But then, I've always thought so."

I agreed. I was ashamed of having been rude to her. She didn't deserve that. If, in my jealousy, I had taken unfair advantage of her, it only proved that I had no confidence in my own ability to hold a sensual and attractive man. It was a relief to know that Mavis accepted my unpleasant trick.

All the same, I had to see her today to make my peace and perhaps explain something of my reasons. I told him I would see my friend and apologize. Then I reminded him, "It's no affair of yours, Richard. My manners, good or bad, are my own." Carried away by my not-so-secret resentment, I brought out several other grievances. "This possessive air of yours has grown worse since you were in France, before William's death. I can only assume that you wish to take William's place in my life."

That shocked him. "No, really, Alain. Not William. I went to visit Mother, and I was on my way home to Paris when the thing occurred. I went down to Bertold to see what could be done."

I ran on. "Let me remind you that William may have dictated to me, but it was all bluster. I did exactly what I chose. And I shall go on doing what I choose for the rest of my life."

He bit his lip and blurted out, "You cannot do as you wish and marry Nicolas Bertold."

I was caught unaware by his frankness. Was this possibility discussed throughout the valley? Did everyone know I was involved with the man I had formerly called "monster" and the murderer of my brother?

I made an emphatic denial. "That is ridiculous. And, I might add, insulting. Especially from you. Wasn't it you who gave me all the details about William's death? And how Jeremy saw his uncle pull away some logs so that William would fall into the moat? Isn't that how it happened?"

He glanced around uneasily, afraid of being overheard. We turned the corner of the house, and he said, after some thought, "More or less. There were differing details, as you can imagine."

"But there may be a dozen reasons why the moat bridge collapsed."

He was distracted by something across the brook on the High Road, but I was wondering, meanwhile, why either Betsy or Hannah Budleigh had moved away so suddenly from the open drawing room window. It had been obvious that one of the women cleaning the sideboard had stopped to listen. Eavesdropping was no civil offense, but it suggested deviousness, and there were enough undercurrents in the house now.

Richard recalled that I had spoken to him.

"Very true. But the motives. I must tell you, Alain, in all honesty, Bertold has one passion in life. To own all of the Bertold land. And then there is his remark the night before the tragedy when he and William argued. Jeremy heard him say, 'I'll see you gone from here forever.' Even Mother heard part of the argument. And when I visited them only days before, they argued in my presence." Before I could remind him that I knew most of these details, except the fact that Richard, himself, had been a witness of sorts, he broke off suddenly. "Did you send for those gypsies? Here they come."

I turned my attention from the house to the High Road. It was as he said. The tinker's wagon rattled up over the bridge and down along the pebble-strewn road to the front of the house. I was relieved to see Demian on the box beside his father, that friendly, big, sinister fellow who had refused to help me when Tad Spindler was in trouble.

Richard Pemberton scowled and warned me. "These gypsies are dangerous. I had best see to them. I understand these people."

No one understood them less. I could see that he was going to be officious, and since I could do that much myself, I said, "Please don't interfere. Your mother just waved to you. Would you see what she wants?" It wasn't true, but he obeyed me after one last menacing glare at the Honigers.

I should have waited on my own doorstep, but I walked along the drive to challenge the gypsies. I addressed Demian, pretending not to recognize Mr. Honiger, who grinned and nodded to me as though we had parted as old friends.

"Thank you, Demian, for helping Tad Spindler. It was good of you and Josef. It may be that you saved his life. He was very cold and his leg had been broken, as Monsieur Bertold thought."

Demian ignored my thanks. He seemed anxious to mend relations between me and his family. "My father wishes to say that he is sorry." He said something to the elder Honiger, who nodded. His grin really was infectious. I almost caught myself returning it.

"Ay. *C'est vrai*. What our Demian says. True. You speak *très vite*. I do not know what you ask."

So the Honigers were French gypsies! At all events, they spoke the language well enough. Small wonder that they got on so well with Nicolas Bertold. I thought the man had understood me very well that day on the heath, but for Demian's sake I pretended to accept his father's explanation.

Demian made a wide, sweeping gesture with one arm

toward the pots, pans, rakes, tubs, everything dangling from the side of the wagon.

"You need anything, Miss Alain?"

"I'll ask Hannah Budleigh." I went into the house, called the cook, and, having sent her out to bargain with Demian and his father, I went to see what had happened to Richard. He might still be looking for his mother, who undoubtedly would be upstairs with Jeremy. It was a trifle alarming to walk into the elder Honiger in the entrance hall. He seemed very much at home and was headed through the house itself. I gave him his due and decided that he might be going to the kitchen garden, but he should have gone around the house, remaining on the path.

"What are you doing in here? Where are you going?"

He replied with the utmost ease in broken English and French. "Come to see Monsieur Bertold. The pony for the cart that is used at Daviot House, he needs a poultice."

"Monsieur Bertold has nothing to do with the Daviot ponies. I give the orders here." However, I felt guilty to think that the pony might need treatment and I had not been told of it. I said after an awkward pause, "Very well. Kindly go back the way you came and march down to the barns. The sheep boy will show you Keeber's stall. You do understand my English now, I see."

Again the elaborate bow and the grin. "*Parfaitement*, Miss Alain." He hesitated, looked up the stairs, apparently saw nothing of interest, and then gazed around him. As far as I knew, he had never been in the house before, and I didn't like the idea of his surveying the situation like a thief preparing for a robbery.

"Monsieur Bertold? I can see?"

"Not today. He has gone up to London. He won't be back for several days."

He found no other excuse for delay, if he sought one, and since I was pointing to the door, he went on out again, shrugging his big shoulders.

He had no difficulty finding his way toward the horse barn.

Hannah Budleigh and the boy, Demian, were haggling in a friendly way over two kitchen pots when I interrupted them.

"Demian, did your family come from France?"

He was a trifle surprised but answered without hesitation. "My father and mother. My brother Josef. He was two when they came to England. My sisters and I, we are born in Sussex."

"Have any of your family been in France recently?"

I think Hannah understood the purpose of my question. She watched Demian with interest.

"No, miss. I have never been in France. Nor my sisters. Nor my parents since many years."

"Yet you all seemed to become great friends of Monsieur Bertold."

"Ay. But he is one of us. He speaks Romany. He has Romany blood. His grandmother, I think."

It explained a great deal about Nicholas. I was not shocked to realize that I had fallen in love with a man of gypsy blood. Perhaps this was one of his attractions. But the knowledge of the connection opened up new fears. Had Nicolas sought them out for some reason? Or were my first groundless suspicions returning, with no better evidence than his natural friendship with a family of people we did not understand and made no effort to include in our lives?

I turned to watch the elder Honiger, who was nearing the barn. With my attention on the man I said, "Demian, would you go down to see that your father applies the poultice correctly?"

"Poultice? Father?" Demian leapt off the wagon and started after Honiger. He caught his father just as they reached the barn. A brief discussion followed. Then Demian went inside, and his father started back across the grassy plot that an occasional vagrant sheep had cropped close.

"There'll be an odd one," Hannah muttered. "Why d'you think the boy did that?"

One rather obvious answer occurred to me. "Because Demian is not a horse thief."

"Ay, but—"

"His father is. And Demian knows it."

"Lord love us! Well, now, should we be a-payin' out good money to folks like that?"

"Do we need the pots and pans?"

"This age, ma'am."

"Then we'll buy them. I do trust Demian."

Hannah added, "And the other lad, him that's called Josef."

But Josef was born in France. He might be closer to his parents with their alien feelings toward us.

"We'll see," I told Hannah, "but meanwhile, trust none of them except Demian. In any way. You understand?"

Hannah didn't, but she agreed politely and took up the pots and a large pan to reexamine them.

By the time Honiger arrived and began to bargain with Hannah, Richard came out demanding to know what I meant by saying that his mother was looking for him.

"She isn't in the house. I've searched her room and Jeremy's. He is gone too."

Hannah stopped arguing with Honiger long enough to explain. "The lad and his nanny, they went out to feed the rabbits. Took one of my cabbages, so they did. The lad was a-saying as how he wanted to ride out today. Maybe in the gig with the mare that takes you and the lad around the valley."

Richard looked at me. He still seemed to be in a bad mood. "You surely don't permit a child and an elderly female to ride about the valley at will, without protection, while these—these gypsies are abroad."

Honiger slapped the bottom of a pan. Its metallic sound rang through the air. While it still rang, he handed it to Hannah Budleigh, who had jumped at the noise.

"See, lady?" Honiger asked her. "Good work. You take?"

While Hannah considered the deal offered her, I answered Richard, who was being very tiresome.

"The gig is safe. Both the mares are safe as well. O'Roarke is here today. He can harness either of the mares. You are trying my patience."

I went into the house, leaving him to complain then that the gypsy was overcharging our cook. Looking out my bedroom window later, I was relieved to see that the gypsies had gone, and so had Richard.

It was a warm day. Knowing how Lady Willoughby was impressed by externals, I dressed as cheerfully as possible, in a blue sprigged white lawn dress and a bright shawl. I walked over to the Hall by the road and found Lady Willoughby just descending from the resplendent Willoughby carriage. I wondered at her smug, self-satisfied expression as she saw me. Her jowls fairly quivered. Something was afoot.

With a regal wave she sent her coachman around to the stable and turned to me, holding on to her bonnet, whose deep straw brim flapped up and down in the breeze.

"My dear Alain, how good of you to give us some of your valuable time! But I am forgetting. Your relative, Monsieur Bertold, has gone up to London. You are not so busy now, I take it."

The woman knew everything. She must have an incredible gossip-gathering organization among our valley folk. I was sure she wanted me to question her about her gossip source and made up my mind to ignore the question of how she had learned about Nicolas.

"I came to apologize for last night's abrupt departure," I explained. "It was so discourteous of me."

Her ladyship ushered me in, sent the supercilious Willoughby butler for tea in the little sitting room at the back of the house, and had her mantelet and bonnet removed by her personal maid. All this done while she made small talk to me on matters of little importance to either of us. Her manner was far too cheerful. I mistrusted it instinctively.

Before tea arrived, I tried to stop this flow of chatter, which took up time but did nothing to mend my bad manners with Mavis, the actual offended party. I said at last, "May we send for Mavis, Lady Willoughby? I did want to explain as soon as possible about the message from home last evening and the reason I left." No need to say that the message had been Nicolas Bertold's little joke.

"You left with Monsieur Bertold."

"He kindly acted as my escort. Jeremy is his nephew, too, you know."

"Indeed, I am not likely to forget. However, the man has interests of his own, aside from the estate he shares with young Jeremy, I understand. Isn't he wealthy in his own right? And, of course, a friend of the French king. One doesn't forget that in a hurry."

"I imagine so." What on earth was she about? Did she hope to bring him into the family? If so, she was making great plans over a simple smile exchanged between her daughter and Nicolas at the keyboard of the pianoforte.

I repeated my request to see Mavis.

"In a moment, dear." She signed to the maid, who brought the tea table over to a point between our chairs on the luxurious maroon Persian carpet. Still there was no sign of Mavis Willoughby. I looked around. Lady Willoughby laughed in her jovial way.

"Oh, but she isn't here. I thought I told you. She went to town." She seemed to be playing with me, cat-and-mouse fashion. "Now, Alain, you musn't feel duty-bound to keep making apologies. Once is quite sufficient, considering . . . but there. I promised not to betray a word, and here I am, gabble-gabble. Before I know it, the story will be spread the length and breadth of the county."

"Then I wouldn't dream of saying another word about it.

Or her." Whatever the story was about, I had some unpleasant clues.

Lady Willoughby chuckled. "Well, considering your closeness to the family, I daresay there is no harm. She is well chaperoned. I saw to that."

I felt a definite sinking at the pit of my stomach.

"Chaperoned to. . ."

"London, of course. I told you she had gone to town. London Town, you know. It was all by merest chance. We saw Monsieur Bertold riding along the High Road, and we were headed in the same direction, in my carriage. I was about to send one of our footmen along with Mavis and the maid. But Monsieur promised faithfully to protect my girl and the maid from any importunities by unsavory young men on the steam cars. Mavis is taking the new steam cars to London. Just like Monsieur Bertold."

The tea was bitter, but I pretended to drink it. Lady Willoughby grew thoughtful.

"Alain, be frank. Do you still suspect your Monsieur Bertold of doing away with Jeremy's parents? I shouldn't like to believe I have entrusted my daughter to a man who murdered our dear William."

"No," I said. "I don't believe he is guilty."

She sighed contentedly. "I thought not. Otherwise you, yourself—but enough of that. My dear, do try the sweet cakes."

I was searching for an excuse to leave as soon as possible, when it was provided for me by Nanny and Jeremy.

I blessed them for their foresight. They had taken out the pony cart and come over to fetch me home. Jeremy insisted that he would walk back.

"It's easier walking beside the pony. And it's my exercise. Father always said so. Are you glad we came for you?"

"You will never know how glad," I told him as I embraced first Jeremy and then Nanny, who beamed and confided, "Even as a girl, Miss Alain, you never got on well with that female. Not true yeoman stock, that one. I shouldn't be surprised if Lady Willoughby had foreign blood somewhere in the line."

I smiled and agreed that this explained all the lady's faults.

With Jeremy trying to take big steps beside us, we started out. Nanny held the reins, and I sat there silently, thinking over what Lady Willoughby had told me. I couldn't believe Nicolas lied to me last night. Our embraces had told me more than any protestations on his part might have.

I did believe, however, that Mavis and her mother were much taken by him. Her Ladyship was already beginning her usual investigation, exactly as she had done on three other occasions when it seemed that Mavis was determined on marriage. My mercurial friend had not reached the altar yet. Her mother claimed, "She fusses about perfection in a male as though there were such a creature."

But I knew Mavis shared my own dream of falling truly and completely in love, and not with some local farmer like those we had known all our lives. What would I do if she felt this very real passion for Nicolas? If he did not love her, I might still pursue my dreams. Otherwise I had lost him.

We were passing the place where we kissed so roughly last night and where I had felt for the first time the violent bodily excitement that Nicolas aroused in me. I was trying to relive that sensation when I saw that Jeremy had dropped behind. I looked back and saw him in the middle of the road, his thin shoulders hunched and his hand pressed hard against his breastbone.

"Stop!" I cried. "Nanny, he's overdone it."

She needed no second command. Dropping the reins as though they were burning, she flung herself out of the cart and hurried back to Jeremy. He looked panicky, with a very bad color as he struggled to breathe. I fumbled for the reins, secured them, and ordered the pony to stay. Then I joined Nanny and my nephew.

Between us, we got him back to the cart. Keeber, the

pony, had wandered on but stopped obligingly at my order, and we got Jeremy in beside Nanny. Looking back at the place where Jeremy's attack had begun, I wondered if the presence of clumps of yellow foliage, including a heath blossom, had caused the trouble. Whatever dust they gave off sometimes made me sneeze. It was reasonable to suppose that it acted more violently upon my sensitive nephew.

Jeremy seemed better in the cart. He calmed down, began to breathe slowly, deeply, and I thought it safe to move on. I walked beside the cart while Nanny took the reins in shaking fingers, hardly able to loop them around her hands.

Seconds later Nanny screamed, cried, "No! Oh, my saints!" I saw one of the reins flutter through the air. It had broken. Scrambling to catch the broken leather, Nanny lost its mate. In a panic she caught Jeremy to her in an effort to shield him from harm. It was a touchy moment, but I knew Keeber. He would never run away. I called to him sharply. He was standing still, his legs trembling a little, when I reached him.

"Good boy," I said, praising him, and rubbed his smooth flank to calm him. I called back, "Are you all safe?"

Nanny gulped "Y-yes" in a high, breathy voice.

Jeremy was trying to wriggle out of her frantic clasp. He coughed at the effort, but when he freed himself, he jumped down to the road. Wheezing badly, he came running to me in spite of my urgent command and Nanny's to "Take care. Easy does it."

He, too, patted Keeber. "He wouldn't run away. Who's afraid of old Keeber? What happened?"

"One of the lines snapped. Worn out, I expect. You go back and sit with Nanny. I'll lead Keeber."

As we moved along, all of us, including a badly shaken Keeber, I suddenly remembered the poultice the gypsy, Honiger, was going to apply to Keeber's leg. But the pony showed no signs of needing a poultice. Nor had one been applied.

True, Honiger hadn't actually gone into the stable. But his son went in to examine Keeber. Demian, whom I trusted.

And the original order for the poultice came from Nicolas Bertold.

There must be an explanation. There had to be. It wasn't as though this had been a deadly threat. It was unlikely that Keeber would have galloped off, killing or badly injuring those in the cart. Any meddling by Honiger or Demian would have been pointless. The accident was a coincidence.

I didn't even want to speculate on the possibilities in the connection between Nicolas and the Honigers.

CHAPTER NINE

Once we reached home, I sent the stable boy to the village to track down the Honigers. I wanted to question Demian in particular. Jeremy had insisted on rubbing down the tired Keeber, and as I started to the stable, having given my order to the stable boy, I met Nanny Pemberton, who said the boy must be put to bed after his exertions.

I argued that Jeremy found it difficult to lie down when he had breathing troubles.

"He would do better to sit up comfortably for a while."

Richard came around the corner of the stable at that minute and agreed with me. Nanny sniffed but took Jeremy up to the house, Jeremy protesting all the way.

"I want to go home. I hate this place. I can't breathe here. And things happen. I'd go home in a minute if Aunt Alain was going."

"Hush, my dear. You know you were unhappy there."

"But that's because of Uncle Nicolas. And now he's here."

They went on to the house, still arguing.

Richard smiled, looking more like the friend I had known all my life.

"Good lad. He's stronger than he looks, poor little devil. What, may I ask, are you doing down in the stables?"

I explained about the rein that had broken. "Worn away, I've no doubt," I added.

He looked thoughtful. "What else is possible?"

We went into Keeber's stall, Richard patting Keeber's haunches while I fed him a little chunk of sugar. Then I reached for the harness and reins on the wall, but they were gone. Concerned and suspicious, I turned quickly to see if anyone had been prowling around the outbuildings but saw Richard holding up the reins. He held them high, to catch the afternoon light, and examined first one, then the other.

"What is it?" I asked. "I've already examined the broken line. It simply wore away and snapped."

He showed me the other in his hand. "Not this one. It is nearly cut through."

"Worn, you mean."

"Cut." He gave it to me. "No mistake about it. A knife did that."

Worried or not, I was also annoyed at this confirmation of my original fears. "You are being ridiculous. Why would anyone do such a thing? What purpose would it serve? It's almost impossible that we could have been hurt."

He considered the leather strip I was running through my fingers. He was right about the cut. It had been very nearly, but not quite, cut through. A little more exertion and it would break. I pointed out to Richard,

"The other line did break. It was worn away. No cut involved. Look at it. And nothing happened to us."

"Except that Jeremy is more anxious than ever to go back to France."

I knew what he insinuated and resented it fiercely.

"According to your theory, he is in danger here too."

"But in France he will be much easier to deal with. It is Bertold's own territory. He is so highly placed, he can literally commit murder and they will look the other way. In fact, they have."

I took the cut rein up to the house, ignoring Richard, who

kept trying to explain, growing a little more upset with every assurance.

"I don't want to upset you, Alain. But I've seen how this creature has made himself attractive to Englishwomen, females one would imagine had more sense."

I gave him what I hoped was a sardonic look. "You astonish me. What females can you mean?"

He hurried on. "I mean women like Lady Willoughby and even Mavis. I've found that he has been successful with villagers as well. I'm learning from the local gossips that Mavis went off to London in his company. Suitably escorted by maids, footmen, and what-not, but in his company all the same. And God knows what his relations with those gypsies may be. Seven of a kind, I'd say."

"Seven!" Then I realized that he included the entire Honiger family, echoing my own private questions. I was no happier and certainly not more pleased with him for having said aloud what I was thinking.

Our dinner was late that day, after darkness fell. Nanny retired early with a bad headache, having taken a roasted onion to hold against her throbbing temples.

Jeremy was long since in bed. When I visited him, he had recovered his breath, his good spirits, and a desire to ride out again in the pony cart as soon as possible.

Just as I was leaving the room, he called to me anxiously. "If I was back home at the château, you wouldn't let Uncle Nicolas do anything to me like he did to Mama and Father, would you?"

"Certainly not." I came back into the room. "Jeremy, when you look into a mirror, you think you see what is actually around you, don't you?" He nodded. He was obviously puzzled by this non sequitur. "But that mirror isn't real. It's a lie. Everything is the opposite way in real life."

"Oh, but I saw—I mean—" He glanced over at the mirror on the highboy. For the first time I think he began to wonder if there was another explanation of what he had seen at the Château Bertold. I kissed his cheek. He crawled down under the covers, smiling at me, offering me a sunny "good night," this time in French, but as I closed the door I saw that a frown wrinkled his forehead. He was giving some thought to what I had said.

I did not get a chance to question the Honigers until midweek, when they came into town to make ready for their part in the Midsummer Fair. One evening between dusk and dark, Demian came walking up to the house with the one member of the family who caused me the most uneasiness. I hadn't forgotten Zilla Honiger's curse upon me. I did not see how it could properly apply to me unless Jeremy and Nanny and Richard were turned against me, and Nicolas Bertold, too, lost all that passion he had hinted at feeling.

Still, like most country folk, I was a repository of superstitions.

The Honiger woman wore one of her fortune-telling dresses, a yellow satin skirt with a pink satin bodice and velvet jerkin. This finery was covered by a black shawl, fragile as a spiderweb, which covered her head and shoulders. Her eyes were heavily rimmed by a black kohl of some kind, which made them look more fierce than ever, as far as I was concerned. In the light from the windows of the drawing room she glittered with polished coins, especially around the forehead and ears.

I knew many valley women who turned their dresses when the material faded. I had done it myself, taking the seams apart and reassembling the garment, but these were the first women who simply turned their garments inside out when they became dirty and wore them, seams and ragged edges showing. The males of the family, especially the two boys, always looked as clean as, or cleaner than, our local farmers.

There was a strong, sweet scent of patchouli about Zilla Honiger, enough so that in spite of myself I stepped back a bit to avoid the overpowering perfume.

Demian put his fingers to his brow in a respectful salute, but I thought his smile was much more subdued than usual.

"They said on the Common that you sent for me, Miss Alain."

"Nice boy. Gets good pay," the gypsy woman reminded me. "I don't like that he works for you."

Demian said something to her in their own language. She shrugged and stood watching us, both hands on her hips and the coins sparkling through the web of the shawl.

I said, "It wasn't about work, Demain. I want to speak to you alone."

He looked uneasily at his mother. "She speaks little English."

"But she understands a great deal." I caught the smirk on her face and motioned him to the far side of the steps. The woman actually would have shuffled her sandals after us, but Demian waved her back.

I pointed to the barn and the stable.

"When your father went to put a poultice on Keeber, you kept him away from the stable."

He lowered his gaze. "My father is not good with horses."

"Did you apply the poultice?" It was a trap, because I knew quite well that Keeber hadn't been touched. Furthermore there had been nothing wrong with the pony.

He shook his head, definitely avoiding my eyes now.

"It was not necessary. The pony's foreleg is not bruised. My father—he misunderstood."

"He misunderstood his instructions? From whom?"

"M'sieur Bertold."

I felt sick. "Did you see them talking?"

"No. But Father said—" He broke off.

Wait, I told myself, Honiger may have lied. But what did he really want in the stable? Probably to steal Keeber and sell him somewhere along Lyme Bay or farther west. Or he may have been responsible for the cut rein.

This was another matter. Demian held the key to it as well.

He had turned away, assuming that I was finished. I stopped him.

"Demian, you examined the pony. Did you happen to see his harness?"

He was puzzled. His answer seemed genuine.

"No, miss." So much for the hope that he might know something about the cutting of the rein. Then he added in the most casual way, "I saw the lines. You know. The leather reins. They had fallen. I put them back."

"Did you examine them?" He shook his head. "Then you didn't see a knife cut across one of the lines."

He stared at me, confused. "Not possible, Miss Alain. It was not necessary to examine them. They were in my hands. I saw them. No cuts. Impossible. I would have seen at once."

Was he lying? If not, what explanation could there be?

I gave up and let him go. Zilla Honiger joined him. I didn't think she had overheard us, but her stare at me was so full of malice that I could believe anything of her.

At the last minute I told Demian, "Good luck at the Fair. Will there be stilt walking? Jeremy loves it. Perhaps you could teach him." I added for Zilla's benefit, "I pay well for honest service."

Demian was pleased, but I think the money was not his only inducement. "I would do that. He is a fine young one, that Master Jeremy." He glanced at his mother. She gave me a sloe-eyed look, accompanied by a toothy smile. Then she nodded.

My meeting with the Honigers, which was meant to solve all my questions one way or another, had only raised more. I decided that when Nicolas Bertold returned, I would be cool and very, very certain of him before letting myself fall in love with him.

But, of course, all those fine resolutions were being made too late.

He returned to Daviot House on the evening of the Midsummer Fair. I had rehearsed my cool, correct reception of him before he arrived, but the minute Nanny came upstairs to inform me, "That man is back," I demonstrated a shocking lack of control by dropping the many taffeta folds of the gown about which Betsy and I were debating. I had ordered it made before William's death and had never worn it. If I wore it to the village celebration, there was likely to be gossip.

Nanny's gaze went from my face to the pool of light green taffeta on the carpet. She blinked. She must have guessed at the depth of my feelings.

To cover this betrayal I laughed, but with a note of asperity.

"For heaven's sake, Nanny, don't rush in with bad news like that! We can deal very well with Nicolas Bertold. I suppose he is *that man*."

"And he only separated from Miss Mavis at the crossroad," Nanny rushed on. Like many people, she got a vicarious enjoyment out of spreading bad news.

I was very matter-of-fact.

"Tell me, Betsy, and you, Nanny, will it be warm enough to wear the taffeta tonight? The sleeves are long and tight."

"Oh, indeed, ma'am," Betsy assured me. "And it's so flattering to your pretty hair, what with the color being reversible and all."

When the light struck it in a certain way, it shone like molten gold. Having helped Betsy pick up all the fifteen yards of it, I held it up against me, gaining some impression of the final result from the reflection in the pier glass.

Betsy went on enthusiastically. "Sure now, Master William would understand. He'd be ordering you to wear it."

I saw at once that Nanny was deeply offended, but I felt younger than I had in years. Nicolas was back. I was determined to show him that I offered as many attractions as Mavis Willoughby.

"It isn't seemly," Nanny pointed out. "It's made too tight by half, there . . . and there." She pointed to the bosom and the waist, which I considered the gown's most flattering assets. Thank heaven Betsy came to my rescue.

"It isn't true. Excusing the liberty. But Miss Alain has such a pretty form, it had ought to be seen, I say."

Flattery or not, I was delighted. I had the hip bath brought up at once, and luxuriated in the warm water poured over my shoulders by Betsy and the kitchen girl, while I wondered just what would be the most successful way to remind Nicolas that I could be quite as sensuous and almost as alluring as my pretty, red-haired rival.

It occurred to me while dressing afterward that I would be handicapped by the presence of both Nicolas and Richard. The ride to Willoughby Hall had been mighty dull as I sat between two men who heartily disliked each other. There was scarcely a word said. On the other hand, since Jeremy and Nanny were going, it was unlikely that I might set up a flirtation with either man.

In the end it became a family group, very correct and even civil. Richard stopped by my room before I joined Nicolas, whom I hadn't seen since his return. I had not finished unwrapping the kid curlers from my hair, and I wore a big pinafore over my gown. Richard was not impressed with what he saw.

"I wanted to explain, Alain. I'm afraid I am engaged tonight and can't escort you as I planned." He smiled on a slightly arch note. "But I daresay I won't be missed."

"Of course you will. You say you are otherwise engaged?"

"Well, you see, Mavis has no escort, and she particularly asked if I would ride in the Willoughby carriage."

It was embarrassing to be so relieved. If Mavis had invited Richard, then it seemed unlikely that she and Nicolas had struck up much of a flirtation on her London visit. I told Richard,

"We will miss you. But I know Mavis is very fond of you."

He was about to go but spoiled everything by hesitating in order to remind me, "Do not be taken in by that rogue. Even if he did not commit two hideous murders, he is a foreigner and—if I'm any judge—a gypsy, besides all else."

"Shocking! I must remember all his sins. But not—I think you said—not murder."

"That's as may be." With this profound statement he left me. I was at least grateful that he hadn't mentioned Keeber's cut rein. In the days since that episode I had recited to myself a dozen ways in which the thing might have happened. It was even possible that the rein had worn away against the harness or the cart's edge in some manner. Demian's evasiveness about his father clearly indicated a doubt that Honiger had ever talked to Monsieur Bertold about a poultice for Keeber.

At all events, this was my reasoning.

The next interruption, of quite a different nature, came just as Betsy was brushing my hair. I knew what to expect as I heard the knock and was in no mood to listen to Nanny's lectures on our evil houseguest. Betsy and I looked at each other.

"She is bound to scold me," I whispered. "Don't leave."

"Ay, Miss. Trust me. The old woman's got a mighty sour tongue."

"She means well. She's just afraid for Jeremy. He has lost so much."

Betsy marched to the door, opened it, and then gave me a quick look, half scared, half amused. I understood when she backed away. Nicolas Bertold passed her, striding into my bedchamber with all the assurance of a husband. He held out both hands in that welcoming gesture I already loved, though I had seen it only once before.

CHAPTER TEN

Apparently Mavis had warned him that he was not expected to dress formally, but he had changed from his riding clothes and boots and looked respectable enough to face an informal evening of pleasure. Considering that much of the male activity would take place in the heavily trampled earth and grass of the Common, he might better have remained in boots and breeches.

Nevertheless, he looked so splendid to me, I was glad he had cared enough to change. I glanced at Betsy, indicating by my raised eyebrows that she might leave, but Betsy nodded and remained. I knew she had a conviction that she was helping me.

Nicolas took my hands, brought first one to his lips, then the other. I looked up into his face, saw the warm, deep light in his eyes, and knew with a delicious certainty that he loved me and had missed me.

He confessed, "I never knew before how long a week could be."

"And for me." But I wouldn't have been a woman if I hadn't added, "Didn't Miss Willoughby shorten the tedium of your week?"

He shook my two hands but would not free them. He seemed to be annoyed at my willful misunderstanding.

"What has that child to do with anything? We met by accident on the High Road. I was too busy to see her in London, and I don't flatter myself that she was interested. I'm not usually the object of pursuit by pretty schoolgirls."

I wondered if he knew I was only months older than Mavis. On a casual note I reminded him, "Flattery or not, she found herself in your company when she returned home."

He scowled, but this time I was certain that he had been amused. "Her footman came to me yesterday saying that they would appreciate my escort on the railway again. I agreed. Does that satisfy you, my darling?" I was extremely conscious of Betsy's presence, but he ignored our fascinated audience. "Your Miss Willoughby is something of a chatterbox, but I heard very little of her chatter. I had some economic reports to consult."

Heavens! Mavis must have found his company far more boring than Richard's. I laughed. Boredom in Nicolas Bertold's company would not trouble me. I did not find incessant conversation a necessity.

I tried to look around the dark barrier of his body to tell Betsy, "I won't need you now, Betsy. I will be leaving shortly for the village with Nanny and Jeremy. My nephew's uncle will escort us."

"Ay, ma'am." Betsy sketched a polite curtsy. I hoped she wasn't offended.

"You are going to the fair tonight, aren't you?" I asked her. "Do have a grand time. And naturally, don't come to work tomorrow until noon."

"Oh, Miss Alain!" Betsy must have had some wonderful plans. She thrilled to the release. "I'll do that. And thank ye."

When she was gone, I complained, "Now I've sent away the only person who can make my hair look neat and respectable."

"Must it?"

"If I am to leave this room."

He had a dangerous sparkle in his eyes that told me he would prefer to remain here, but I said "Nonsense!" with great spirit.

"Very well. Since the fault is mine . . ." He took up the brush where Betsy had dropped it on my dressing table. I pulled away, imagining that with his peculiar humor he meant to leave my hair hopelessly disheveled. Instead he took a length of hair and began to make long strokes through it with the brush.

I knew I must resist this mesmerizing influence. I tried to look sternly into the mirror but felt a little like a thrush under a hawk's eye when he stared back at me. For an instant a thought flashed through my mind. I saw my brother's face at the coach window as the waters rose and he struggled vainly to release the door.

Had Nicolas looked like this while my brother struggled and died?

I closed my eyes to such hideous thoughts. All that I knew against Nicolas Bertold were snatches of gossip, the suspicion of those influenced by my brother's long grudge against him and the testimony of a nine-year-old boy in a room high above the moat bridge.

I clung to the most important evidence in Nicolas Bertold's favor, the fact that a judge and a court of inquiry, working separately, had pronounced him innocent. The scene of the so-called crime would have been investigated by the *juge d'instruction* and one or two of his aides. All had pronounced Nicolas innocent.

Still, the long, delicious stroking of my hair went on. I smiled at his reflection. It seemed to me that he hesitated before his own expression softened. Had he possibly guessed my suspicions? The idea shamed me. I could not bear to lose the passion I had read in his eyes earlier.

Then he leaned over my head, and when I closed my eyes

instinctively at his nearness, he kissed my eyelids, his lips lingering over my flesh with a strongly erotic effect.

Nothing remotely like this had ever happened to me. I loved him. There was no turning back.

Still, I must regain command of myself. When he raised his head, I reminded him, "We must go. There will be great crowds."

He became all business on the instant. "I know. I saw them this afternoon as we came through the village. But you aren't ready." He grinned. "May I help you?"

"Yes. You will wait for me downstairs in the back parlor, if you please."

He agreed politely. "As you wish, Mademoiselle Daviot." He turned to leave but shook his head and complained, as he opened the door, "Daviot. Not the name I would choose for you. It has bad connotations. We must remedy that name. And soon."

He left me speechless.

While I completed preparations for the evening I told myself that his remark was an example of that sardonic humor I must learn to expect. He could select a name for me by only one means, and there were insurmountable obstacles to a marriage between us.

The word *insurmountable* depressed me. It seemed to put an end to all my newly discovered happiness.

I was not as cheerful as I might have been when I went into the comfortable old back parlor that had been the main room of the original cottage. Nanny sat rigidly on the sofa. She wore heavy black with passementerie trimmings and a flat-crowned little black bonnet, its slender ribbons severely knotted under her chin. Jeremy sat beside her in a fawn-colored suit. He was kicking the heels of his second-best boots against the sofa leg and heaving great sighs.

He had reason to sigh. Nicolas stood looking out the long window at one end of the kitchen garden. He drummed his fingers against the window frame, his impatience so evident that he forcibly put me in mind of his nephew.

I should have been flattered by the haste with which all three of them turned to me.

Nanny protested tearfully, "Miss Alain, you surely cannot expect us all to make the trip together."

"Aunt, could I walk on sticks? Uncle Nicolas says I can, but Nanny—"

"Really, Miss Alain." Nanny again. "Will you please tell my lamb that he shouldn't be turning to his—his uncle in such matters."

"Damn it!" Nicolas cut in suddenly, slapping the window frame so hard, we all jumped. "If we are to go, let us, in God's name, go!"

"Master William would never have favored profanity on any occasion." Nanny sniffed.

I couldn't help putting in, "Then you do not know my brother as well as I did, Nanny. Now be quiet."

I pulled myself together, addressed them all in a tone as nearly like a schoolmistress as I had ever managed.

"We are late. All of you, come along. O'Roarke will be waiting."

Nanny bustled up, trying to walk beside me. To my amusement Nicolas firmly, but with great politeness, maneuvered her ahead of us and put Jeremy's hand in hers. "For safekeeping," he told her. She surprised me by giving him a quick, almost pitiful smile of thanks. Then he stepped back and took my arm.

I muttered, "Can there ever be peace between you?"

There was nothing amusing in his hard reply.

"Certainly not. I am your brother's murderer. Haven't you been told that time out of mind?"

"I think Jeremy may be coming around to your side, and even Nanny, if you keep showering her with attentions." I said it with assurance born of nothing but a desperate hope.

"If I could believe that!"

But I thought the muscles of his arm felt less inflexible under my hand.

In the old carriage we were separated. Nanny was beside me, and Nicolas sat opposite with Jeremy on his left. I don't think Nicolas was the great attraction for Jeremy. My nephew stood very tall as he insisted, "Gentlemen always sit backward, facing the ladies."

I touched his hand. "And you are a gentleman, Master—no—Mr. Daviot."

"That's my lamb," Nanny murmured.

We all rode to the village with our spirits raised.

Long before we reached the public Common, Jeremy was jumping up and down with excitement as he looked out at the flaring lights of lamps, lanterns, and candles, which made all the well-known valley people look like fantastic figures, exotic and eerie, scarcely any of them immediately recognizable. Jeremy leapt from side to side, trying to guess who these phantoms were.

Eventually I was pleased to see him climb over his uncle to look out the opposite window of the carriage. What especially pleased me was the way Nicolas lifted him over to get a better view, and Jeremy leaned hard on his shoulder as he stuck his head out of the window. Jeremy hammered the lowered window with his fists in his enthusiasm.

"It's Farmer Budleigh's boy, Aaron. I know how he walks. He's a special friend of mine." He called the boy's name, but our team had already rumbled on past Aaron Budleigh, who seemed to be dressed as a beanstock with legs.

Jeremy turned, not to us women but to Nicolas. He boasted proudly, "He likes me. So does Mother Hagar's grandson. That's Timothy."

"And why not? They should like you."

Jeremy looked gratified by his uncle's words. "Well, at first they didn't like the way I talked in England. But they don't mind anymore. Aaron is teaching me how to hit a fellow."

"Mercy on us!" Nanny murmured, but I could see that Nicolas thought this quite correct for a boy Jeremy's age. Remembering that William and Richard had done their share of fighting, and even more than their share in William's case, I was inclined to agree with Nicolas. In my small world physical courage was not only encouraged but necessary.

O'Roarke pulled up at the edge of the Common, that wide, grassy dirt plot on the wagon road toward Coombe Bower. The fair itself was a strange combination of light and darkness, tents, makeshift stages, flags and banners, a great many pennons, and always the quick juxtaposition of light, then shadows. Wherever the entertainers gathered to perform on improvised stages, torches provided flaring lights almost as bright as the interior of Convent Garden. Lanterns cast a romantic glow over the food stalls and the handicraft work by local farm women.

Personally I was most proud of the boxes of tender green beans and other fresh vegetables and fruits grown by Daviot House, as well as Hannah Budleigh's pork pies and spice buns. I felt great pride in pointing out the first Daviot cabbages, splendid in color and selling well to visitors from Shaftesbury and other cities.

I had thought that Nicolas would be amused at my pride in our garden produce, but he compared our cabbages and beans, not to mention Hannah's pork pies, to his own wines and vegetables. He thought our green apples were not the equal of the Bertolds', though he suspected our cider was superior to his own. He added with a friendly slap across Jeremy's shoulder, "Or I should say, Daviot cider, French-fashion; isn't it so?"

Jeremy was pleased. He reminded us, "Last year I picked apples, didn't I?"

"And then," Nanny reminded him, "you ran away into the woods, naughty boy, and we found you shivering with cold and your mother had to give you laudanum to make you sleep."

Jeremy contradicted her with a casual air. "It was Uncle Nicolas who gave me laudanum."

Nicolas saw me look at him. "Why not add," he said dryly, "that your parents were in Tours at an opera party, and we did not trust the servants to give you the correct dosage."

"But Nanny could have done it."

"Nanny, if I may say so, loves you too much to keep her hand from trembling when she doses you."

Nanny looked utterly confounded, opened her mouth to protest, but thought better of it and stepped aside.

"If you please, sir, I will go back and wait by the Sheepcote Auction. I see I am unwanted here."

"Oh, Nanny, in heaven's name, don't be so sensitive," I scolded, but this did not improve the situation.

She gave me a searingly reproachful look, swung around, and bustled back over the ground without giving a single glance to the troupe of gypsy dancers surrounded by a crowd on her left, or the man on her right who was peddling curative alcoholic nostrums from the back of his wagon.

Jeremy seemed uninterested in Nanny for once. He kept skipping ahead, looking for the stilt-walkers.

"I'm sorry," Nicolas apologized when I sighed over the old nurse's stubborn enjoyment of being put upon. "I suppose she means well, but frankly I would pension her off and put my nephew in the hands of a competent young tutor."

However much she irritated me, this remedy was much too drastic. I could never forget that Nanny was my mother's confidante and, after Mama's death, had served as surrogate mother to William and me. William, of course, could do no wrong in her eyes. If, as often happened, he tripped me or pinched me and I answered back with a sound slap, it was the slap that was reported to Papa.

My father was a busy man in farm affairs in the valley, and he had little time for children's quarrels.

"Settle it between you," he would say, and so neither William nor I was punished, except by each other. William always liked to manage business affairs for our valley in Shaftesbury and Exeter, and when Papa was in his last illness, William speculated in London itself, taking our inheritance and investing in government bonds. At this time I took over the running of the several farms that made up the Daviot estate.

I had the satisfaction of hearing Papa say at the last, as he took my hand, "You'll do, girl. You'll keep it all together."

Indeed I would, and had. But still I felt that as the last mistress of Daviot Farms, I owed Nanny, our early mentor, a place with us for her lifetime. I said something of this aloud and looked at Nicolas to see if his face reflected an understanding of my obligation.

It did not. Marking off the grass square where the Honigers entertained, the smoky torches of oil-soaked brush and rags played over Nicolas Bertold's face, casting it now in glaring red, then in streaked shadows. He looked more saturnine than sympathetic.

"I trust she doesn't expect to return to Bertold with us," he said, showing me how far apart we were in our thoughts.

"She expects to go wherever Jeremy goes," I reminded him. "He is a sick boy, and she acts as his companion-tutor and a kind of personal maid. She has created this role for herself. And I must say, she is irreplaceable."

"Not to me."

I could not resist asking as calmly as possible, "You hope to take Jeremy back to France, then?"

"Certainly. I thought you understood."

"What makes you think I would let him go?"

He said in the most bland way, "I would not dream of separating you from Jeremy. Naturally he goes with you and me. In fact, we will ask him to witness the ceremony. If he plays a part in the wedding, he may accustom himself to the truth."

"The truth." I stared at him, awed by his easy possession of my entire life.

"That I am not the monster of his nightmares."

"There they are," Jeremy cried, running back to pull both Nicolas and me through the crowd that had gathered to watch the Honigers entertain. "Look! I can see the sticks right over their heads."

By this time he could see the senior Honiger's brawny figure as he stepped off the tinker's wagon and balanced on the stilts. Jeremy shrank back, shivering. "They really are gypsies."

Nicolas put an arm around Jeremy's shoulder in the manner of a comrade. "But we cannot let them bully you. We stand up to them. Your friends Aaron Budleigh and Madame Hagar's grandson would do so."

Jeremy looked doubtful, but while I marveled at the influence of pride on us Daviots, Jeremy stiffened his backbone, set his jaw, and said, "*Bien sûr*. They will not bully me."

"Good. Come along."

They circled the crowd with me, following close behind them until we came upon Demian Honiger. He was collecting tuppence here and there, occasionally a sixpence, and even one silver coin from those female customers waiting in line before a many-colored tent.

"Zilla Honiger tells fortunes," I said, answering Nicolas's questioning glance. Annoyed by his pretense of interest in such an occupation, I added, "But I had my fortune told for nothing the other day in the village."

"The witch-woman cursed her," Jeremy put in. "Aunt Alain was brave. You would have been proud of her."

"I am always proud of her." Nicolas continued to gaze at me until I looked away, pretending an interest in Demian's tambourine, which contained the fees for his mother's fortune-telling.

I wondered what fortune fate had in store for me, and if

another fortune-teller would also see the curse that this woman had put upon me.

Demian looked up, saw us, and promised, "Very soon, m'sieu. Miss Alain." Then he got up from the three-legged stool and vanished inside the tent. When he came out, the tamourine was gone, and he announced to the line of waiting women, "One at a time, if you please."

Then he motioned to the three of us, and we followed him behind the gaily striped tent. A dancing performance had ended, and the plank stage was deserted for a few minutes. I was still in a state of confusion, torn between euphoria and the dread of making a decision in the remote case that Nicolas's offhand proposal had been sincere.

I have always found the area behind the stage in such fairs extraordinarily dark, confused, and even dangerous. But I had wandered here alone since I was five, William and Richard and my parents being so busy with the usual booths and entertainment that they totally forgot about me. I had long ago found my way from dangerous darkness to the magic light of the exhibitors at the fair.

This night was very like those scary magic moments of my childhood, the difference being that I was no longer alone.

Demian informed us proudly, "We used to have a dancing bear, but he got very old and died. Father says we may get another one from a French circus. We make twice as much with a dancing bear."

Jeremy's wide-eyed look told me the idea might terrify him, but it also fascinated him.

Meanwhile Demian leapt up onto the stage and began to manipulate a pair of carefully, but amateurishly carved, stilts. I was relieved to find that they were of modest size. Even so, I cautioned Demian, "Don't let him stand by himself."

"No, miss."

"Jeremy will do very well. He is no coward," Nicolas reminded me.

"But even brave men can be hurt."

Demian promised me, "I will not let him fall, Miss Alain."

I watched the gypsy boy and Nicolas try to help Jeremy onto the stage, but Jeremy scrambled up by himself, breathing heavily, yet "game," as my brother would have said. After this there was a good deal of shouting, balancing, and anxious orders punctuated by Jeremy's giggles and shrill cries of excitement. I backed away from this childish business in which the biggest children were seventeen-year-old Demian and the thirty-seven-year-old Frenchman.

It was warm for a night so late in August, and I was just throwing back my dinner cloak when I felt someone tug at my sleeve. By the starlight and a crescent moon I saw one of the little Budleigh girls. She had run so fast, her braids were still swinging.

"Come, miss. The old lady. The gypsies has her."

Anger fought with impatience. "Yes. Just a minute." Nanny ought to stand up to them. But Nanny, strong enough for her age, was a lady. It probably never occurred to her to push them aside, or even to ignore her tormentors. I called to Nicolas, who was chuckling at Jeremy's attempt to balance on the stilts between his two mentors.

"Nanny needs me. The gypsies are apparently annoying her."

Nicolas glanced at Demian. "Keep the balance. As for you, young man, you've had enough fun. We are off to rescue Nanny."

Jeremy elbowed him away. "No! Not yet. Once more. I stood by myself. Just for a second. Look, Demian."

He seemed to be on better terms with this gypsy, at all events. I couldn't wait for the argument to end. If I knew anything about boys Jeremy's age, he would keep this up for half an hour. I went after the Budleigh girl, through a crowd, mostly male, who were bidding on a handsome sorrel mare. At another time I might have joined the bidding, but I made my way around them, past the displays of local produce toward the gypsy dancers, a troupe who came down once a year from their usual habitat on the moors in the west of Yorkshire.

To my horror Nanny was on the ground. She rocked back and forth, moaning and trying to catch her breath.

"Nanny, dear, what happened?"

"Pushed me—awful creature. Fell over a clod of grass."

"Is this true?" I glared at the four dancers, who looked tense, as well they might, but neither the two girls in their spangled, bright clothing, nor the black-clad partners looked threatening. The handsomest and fiercest of those sinuous young men poured out a protest that he emphasized by a balled fist waved in my face. He spoke in his own language, but I had no doubt of his meaning.

I waved the fist away. "Do be quiet, you silly child! Go about your business and stop behaving like spoiled babies."

He looked so surprised, and, I must say, puzzled, that I guessed he understood some English. He was probably used to facing down any of us who accused his people of crimes, often imaginary.

I could well imagine that Nanny's fall had been an accident of sorts. I knew how easily Nanny was panicked by these people whom she seemed to consider the implacable enemies of mankind.

I did my best to make her comfortable until we could get her on her feet. "There, Nanny, try to be calm. Take a long, deep breath. Does it hurt?"

"Of course it hurts." She looked around, demanding querulously, "What are you all looking at? Can't a body trip without being stared at like a fish in a bowl?"

Those around us began to break up into groups and amble away. I resented what I thought were their nasty, leering grins and was relieved when I saw Nicolas holding Jeremy by the hand and approaching with his usual long stride.

I waved him on. "Thank heaven! Nanny has had a bad fall."

"They pushed me," she insisted.

"Well, however it happened," I said to Nicolas, "would you take her to the carriage?"

This produced some fussy twitching on Nanny's part. "No. I can do it myself. Don't touch me. I'm not hurt. Only shaken up."

"Nanny, be quiet."

She caught her breath, raised her chin, and made no further protest. Also, she refused to address me when I asked her where it hurt. Nicolas scooped her up, ignoring her protests.

We had nearly reached the outskirts of the Common, and I was signaling to O'Roarke, who was with some other coachmen, when we met Richard and Mavis Willoughby strolling along, eating fresh apples from the exhibit boxes. At the sight of the fidgeting bundle held so easily in Nicolas's arms, Richard demanded to know what we had done to his mother. At his angry insistence Nicolas dropped Nanny gently into his arms.

"She thinks some gypsies pushed her," I said. "Maybe they did. But still, they've never caused me trouble."

Nicolas gave me a look in which I read gratitude for my defense of his gypsy acquaintances.

Mavis wanted an explanation. She held me back to ask, "Alain, what is this about gypsies? I admit I've always felt odd with them. Those sensual eyes! But to attack that wretched mother of Richard's, well I must say—really!"

I said I had no idea. They seemed to be around ever since Jeremy came to stay with me.

"Ever since Mister Bertold, in fact."

"That is absurd. The Honigers have been in this county for more than a year."

Mavis looked around for Richard, then noticed that Nicolas was watching us. She shrugged.

"Richard tells me that you and Mr. Bertold go on very well. I don't know why I should be surprised. You always had a way with difficult people."

"Jealous?" I asked her with some amusement.

"Me? My dear, he is a dull dog, as you will find."

"How well suited we are, then! Two dull dogs together. Is that what you mean?"

She said, "Don't be sensitive, dear." She drew up the furred collar of her cloak. "Well, then. I had better find Mother. I see that my escort has lost interest in my none-so-fatal charms." I started to say "It was Nanny's fall," but she was philosophical. "It was only a matter of time. I am about to celebrate my twenty-third birthday. Obviously I am too old for him."

I laughed, but my amusement was cut off abruptly when Mavis said, "You were wise not to bring the boy. All this turmoil and darkness. You have enough problems with Nanny Pemberton."

I glanced over my shoulder, suddenly nervous.

"Quite the contrary. Jeremy is here. He has been trying to walk on stilts." At the same time I saw that Nicolas had heard Jeremy's name. He swung around, reaching out as if to take Jeremy's hand again. He had let it go when he scooped Nanny up in his arms.

Jeremy was no longer standing there watching the excitement of Nanny's "rescue," nor was he anywhere around us in the little moonlit clearing.

CHAPTER ELEVEN

Nicolas noticed my panic and tried to give me, and perhaps himself, a plausible explanation. "He has gone back to try his luck with the stilts. I had to pry him away from them." But I could see that he shared my concern, more puzzled, though less worried than I was. He stared around the back of the various wagons, through the darkness toward Demian Honiger and that pair of stilts.

Richard had settled his mother in the carriage and started back to join the search despite Nanny's plaintive reminder, "Don't mind me, dear boy. I shall manage somehow."

"What excitement over a naughty runaway!" Mavis called as I hurried after Nicolas.

It was all nonsense, of course. What could happen to a half-grown boy at a public fairground? He could scarcely get lost. Anyone would tell him how to reach the dozen or so carriages, gigs, and carts with their teams being rubbed down or walked by the gossiping coachmen. At the age of five I had made my own way back to my family after such an event.

But I was a strong child, and this was well-known ground to me. Though I had enjoyed pretending that it was eerie and sinister at night, I had always known in my heart that it was only the familiar Common, which I crossed a hundred times a year, playing games with Mavis and William and Richard.

What would it be like, even today, if I were lost in France, on that great Bertold estate with its unknown black woods and its moat that "reached down to China?" So it might be with Jeremy in this dark place.

I began to call his name, first impatiently, angrily, then with a questioning tone, betraying the fear that had haunted me from the moment I heard that only this one sickly boy stood between Nicolas Bertold and complete control of the huge estate that was the Frenchman's greatest passion. I did not suspect that Nicolas, himself, had spirited the boy away. Indeed, how could he? The boy had been holding his hand only minutes before. But what would others think? Jeremy must be playing some cruel, thoughtless prank, perhaps in an effort to make people wonder about his uncle.

I reached the deserted stage only a few seconds after Nicolas. He was questioning Demian Honiger, who had bound the long stilts and stopped with a leather thong in his hand. I heard what I assumed was his denial. They were talking in the Romany dialect. Demian saw me first and broke off to say in English, "He did not come back here, Miss Alain. Maybe the spice cakes at Mother Hagar's stall. Or the fruit man."

Hopefully I reminded Nicolas, "He loves Mother Hagar's sugary spice buns."

"Yes. Very likely. Thank you, boy." Nicolas took my hand. "Which direction?"

Demian thrust the stilts under the stage.

"I will go too. The young monsieur and I, we are friends now, I think."

This wandering around alone seemed a trifle unlike Jeremy. Still, it was the only possible explanation.

We made our way around the tents, between wagons, and over a wagon tongue where Nicolas surprised both the gypsy boy and me by swinging me over the tongue and setting me securely on my feet. If we had not been on serious business, I would have been angered by such a florid action. It might very well produce some unpleasant gossip after my sudden friendship with the man I had only recently called a "monster."

Mother Hagar's stall was closed. She had gone off to share a late supper with her crony, the Willoughby cook. Nicolas frowned at the lantern lights around Zilla Honiger's fortune-telling tent. The tent flaps were draped open, like portieres in an elegant parlor.

Nicolas said, "Ask your mother if she saw young Jeremy pass here in the last few minutes."

Demian nodded and loped into the tent. He came out in a few seconds, looking around in a surprised way.

"She is not there."

Almost before he got it out of his mouth, the woman came around the corner of the next wagon, her many polished coins jingling over her body as she moved. Even her sandals had copper disks that sparkled in the lantern light. I thought her face looked malign with its big smile that never reached her eyes.

"So, you want the fortune told, isn't it so? I give you fortune, *monsieur français*. This one—she has her fortune. It is written in blood."

Demian snapped something out to her in an adult and somehow sinister way, and she shrugged. Nicolas made a chopping gesture and asked her if she had seen Jeremy. For a small space of time she stared at us from under the heavy lids of her eyes.

"Like a baby, that one," she said in English, dismissing Jeremy. "How do I know where he is? I have not seen him."

Demian moved away from the tent, looking out over the vast darkness beyond the boundaries of the fair. He motioned for us to follow him. When we were beyond the hearing of his mother, he said, "The boy would not go out there. It is impossible. He would not think of that."

"Then where has he gone?" I wanted to know.

Nicolas shook my hand in a playfully scolding way.

"He is around here somewhere, and very close at hand. He is playing some trick. Mark me. The boy is not stupid."

He considered our surroundings, speculating on where Jeremy might hide. I admitted that I did not know my nephew as well as he did. I supposed I must have pictured him as weak and put upon. I hadn't enough confidence in Jeremy's own courage, or in his devious initiative, to believe that he could carry out such a deliberate "joke."

I said, "Why don't we divide the tents and wagons, ask the farmers and the gypsies and whoever else is around to let us look for him?"

He studied me with a curious smile and frown. "I had rather you went with me. I don't want you to vanish as well."

My answer was tart as usual. "Nonsense!" But I warmed to the implication that he cared for me.

We moved rapidly from wagon to tent, from exhibit to entertainers, I on one side of the Common and Nicolas on the other. In other circumstances I would have been amused at how often Nicolas looked across the intervening space to see if I was in sight. I told myself that this was added proof: He loved me.

In my thoughts of Nicolas Bertold I was behaving like a child Jeremy's age, but he was my first passionate love, and passion itself was new to me.

I was invited into the tent of a tinker's family from Ireland. I found nothing suspicious, but they promised to take up the search as well. As I came out and walked around the family wagon I became aware of the thick darkness that enclosed me. A black cat ran across my foot, and I kept remembering Zilla Honiger's chilling prophecy that my fate was written in blood.

Some of the entertainers were already loading up, preparing for the night's long trip to wherever these wanderers called home. I came to the tinker's wagon that belonged to the Honigers. It seemed to be ready for departure. The Honigers were loading their costumes and furniture into their other wagon, which was used as living quarters. This tinker's wagon, as I knew from many purchases, contained only their salable articles. I thought of it as their "shop." If Jeremy had deliberately hidden from us as a kind of juvenile joke, he would use this wagon rather than the wagon in which the gypsies lived. But why would he play such a trick at all?

I didn't believe I would find him inside, and I rather hoped I wouldn't come upon any of the Honigers here. It might seem that I especially suspected them. But since I was making a thorough search, I climbed up the little flight of wooden steps, hoping that the crescent moon would help me make out the interior as easily as I had done with the Irish tinkers. The two narrow wooden doors were ajar, and I pulled them both open.

Unfortunately the wagon was in the shadow of Zilla Honiger's many-colored tent. I barely made out the variety of items for sale in the musty interior. The wagon swayed suddenly, and I clutched at the sheep shears that hung from a hook on the wall. I pulled down the shears, hook and all. At the same instant I realized that the sway of the wagon came from someone mounting the steps behind me.

I called out, "I am Alain Daviot. I am looking—"

I got no further. A dazzling display of tiny lights seemed to explode in my brain. I felt no pain, but I knew I had been struck on top of my head by some blunt, heavy object. While I was still protesting angrily, "Didn't you hear—" I found myself sinking into oblivion.

I recall coming to partial consciousness several times afterwards, but I was not enthusiastic about opening my eyes. I had a raging headache that was partially relieved when I remained half asleep, my eyes closed. Nothing helped my stomach, however. I felt an unfamiliar nausea and gradually realized that the wagon was moving, bumping along over frightful roads, if roads they were. I had no difficulty remembering how I had gotten there. Obviously these damnable gypsies had seen fit to kidnap me. I assumed that their motive was money. They knew the Daviot Farms were worth a great deal.

But where were we now? How far from the village or my home?

I gritted my teeth every time we rumbled over a pothole, a rock, or a clod of grass. It jarred my entire body and especially my head.

We were climbing now. I heard the harness rattle, and the labored snorting of the two horses. We must be headed up onto Ferndene Heath. Had we come so far? It must be late in the night.

I stirred, stretched, was relieved to find that I was unhurt except for an exquisitely painful lump on my head. Thank heaven I had a full head of hair! It may have saved me from a cracked skull.

While I tried to get my wits together I wondered which member of the Honiger family had struck me on the head. Probably the senior Honiger. I couldn't imagine friendly, honest-eyed Demian attacking me. Zilla Honiger was capable of doing it, but it seemed more likely that she would persuade her male relations to carry out her instructions.

I managed to get to my knees but was flung against the side of the wagon. I groaned, a sound that would give my kidnappers great satisfaction, especially Mrs. Honiger. This entire affair was an outrage. I had never been anyone's victim, and once I had risen above childhood, no one had dared to strike me. I was the mistress of Daviot Farms, a woman with certain financial and political powers of my own.

I felt my way through the darkness to the doors at the back of the wagon. I pushed each of them in turn before realizing that they were bolted on the outside. I hammered with my fists, then rattled the doors, but stopped, realizing that the drivers might hear me.

What to do now?

I knelt there with my cheek against the door, wondering if one of the implements for sale in here could break the splintering wood around the bolt. The sheep shears might serve, providing I made very little noise.

I felt for the shears. My fingers closed around them. They were heavy and clumsy to use, but they might prove to be a satisfactory weapon for one of several purposes.

The first purpose proved abortive. The wood around the bolt of the door was too thick. It would take hours and perhaps more strength than I possessed. I scrambled to the front of the wagon and discovered, purely by feeling, that there was a door here. It opened inward upon me, but if I could get it open, I would be directly behind the unprotected back of the gypsy driver.

I knew it was a risky business. Normally Demian and Josef would be driving. I did not like the odds if I encountered Zilla Honiger and the boys' father.

By the time I reached the door at the back of the driver's box, I had winced several times as I knelt upon the sharp edges of other farm and personal implements. But I knew I could not handle another weapon with the sheep shears. These two blades might serve.

"One blade for each of them if they prove violent," I promised myself.

My London friends at the School for Genteel Young Females had confided long ago that they hadn't supposed Dorset produced "ladies." If they could see me now, they would have fuel for their snobbery.

I got my fingernails between the door and the wagon wall. It opened easily. I could see two male figures. The larger of the two was talking in his own language. He was Demian's father. Brawny, cynical, and wily, and no friend of mine. The driver at the reins was Demian. This seemed more promising.

I would threaten Honiger. Demian, being gentler, perhaps

less used to violence, would do as I ordered, out of fear for his father's safety.

I took a deep breath, which further aggravated my headache, and, gripping the sheep shears, I pulled open the door.

CHAPTER TWELVE

As I had expected, Demian and his father were startled. Demian's hands tugged the reins involuntarily, and the horses came to an abrupt halt. We were somewhere out on the heath with nothing in sight under the high crescent moon except straggling heath blooms and unknown vegetation that crept toward us with skeletal fingers at this hour of the night.

Demian tried to look at me over his shoulder. He asked me something and then repeated in English, "We are poor. We have nothing. Who are you?"

I held the shears very close to Honiger, so that he could feel one worn blade just above his ribs. He started and said something to Demian. I tried to make my voice calm, strong, determined.

"Turn about and return to the valley."

They looked at each other. Then Demian reached down beside the seat and raised a storm lantern to see me better. He gasped and set the lantern beside him.

"Miss Alain! Why are you here? You wish us to take you home?"

"Of course, I do. And at once."

"But, miss..." His bewilderment seemed genuine. "You are not comfortable. The pretty gown, all so not tidy. Why did you not tell us? We went past Daviot House half an hour ago and more."

"Turn back." I was a bit confused myself by this time and added, "If you please."

Honiger reached back with one hand and touched the double blades of the shears.

"Not good. We are happy for to take you, Mademoiselle. No need for this."

"Let me judge that. Take me home."

Again the puzzled look between Demian and his father, but already the horses were headed back toward the beech wood and the water meadow beyond.

Demian ventured after a few minutes of uncomfortable silence, "Why are you riding in our wagon, miss? Is your carriage broken down?"

"I think you know why I am here, you and your father."

Demian asked his father a question. I thought Demian sounded harsh, unlike the friendly, harmless boy I had come to know. His father shrugged but kept glancing down at his side. The sheep shears worried him, which was not surprising. I tightened the fingers of both hands around the bulky shears.

Honiger said something to his son that sounded like "*très étrange*," with which I heartily concurred.

The wagon wheels bumped over a rock, and we all jumped. Each of us looked out at the primordial life around us. The night had never seemed more vast.

Honiger turned suddenly. All the muscles in my fingers seemed to have frozen around the shears. Perhaps he was warned by that. His narrow black-rimmed eyes watched me. I felt that he was dangerous, but I promised myself, "So am I."

I asked Demian abruptly, "Why did you do it? Did you think someone would pay money to have me back?"

Again an exchange of glances between father and son

before Demian said, "You will pay if we bring you to Daviot Farms?"

I tried to be sardonic. "Certainly. I will pay each of you a half crown."

I expected anger and a burst of incredulous laughter. The laughter came, but I was surprised at its quality. In other circumstances I would have called their reaction pure pleasure.

Demian turned to me. "That is kind, Miss Alain. We will get you home very fast."

Honiger asked carefully, "A half-crown to me also?"

"Also."

"*C'est bon. Vite, vite*, Demian."

I did not know what to think.

We had nearly come to the beech grove when we heard hoofbeats pounding over the ground toward us. For an instant I had the romantic notion that this must be Nicolas Bertold, mounted on a black stallion, coming to rescue me and carry me home across his saddle like a Walter Scott hero.

The solitary rider came directly toward us, but I knew by this time that the slender rider on the bay horse could never be my Nicolas. The storm lantern glinted off Richard Pemberton's cape and his pale features. He waved a huge, long-barreled pistol at the gypsies, calling fiercely, "You, there, stand and deliver that lady."

It was an unfortunate command. It put me in mind of a play I had seen once in London, all about a highwayman with his eternal "stand and deliver!" uttered on every provocation. I had no doubt that Richard had seen the play as well.

Dear Richard, ready to play the hero at the first opportunity!

Demian pulled up. I could hardly blame him for sounding a little cross.

"We are taking Miss Alain to her home, sir. She found herself in our wagon. We do not know how."

Very likely! I was about to drop the shears and let the

heroic Richard rescue me when Richard said, scoffing, "I can well imagine how she got into your wagon. Get down, both of you."

Demian panicked for the first time. "You will not steal our wagon. You will not do that. It is how we live."

I wanted nothing more to do with this bizarre adventure. All I really wanted was to go home, find Jeremy safely there, and be with Nicolas for at least a few minutes tonight.

"Richard, keep your pistol on them while I get down, and never mind the heroic stand."

I climbed over behind Demian, who asked politely, "May I help you, Miss Alain?"

But I was already down. The final fall was hard on my Moroccan slippers, but I flattered myself that I managed rather well, considering that I was encumbered with yards of wrinkled and torn taffeta skirts, three petticoats, and an opera cloak dangling from one shoulder by its velvet strings. I heard several materials rip and tear, but I was standing on the ground, reasonably free, and that was all-important.

Richard would have helped me, but I waved him back.

"No. Tell them to go."

I am not quite sure he understood, but he waved them away with his gigantic pistol. They swung the team around, and the wagon rattled off into the night. Neither Demian nor Honiger looked back.

Meanwhile Richard leaned down. "Do you mind riding before me? The animal is sturdy, and your slight weight should cause no problems."

I let myself be lifted up before him, and we rode down along the path beside the brook with no difficulty but, I regret to say, with considerable discomfort.

"Here I am, captive across your saddlebow," I remarked, but he didn't see the humor of it. I asked then, "Have you found Jeremy?"

Though his arms were around me in a very compromising way as he held the reins, he was stiff in his reply.

"I believe Bertold had some idea that he would find you and the boy together. He thought the boy might have run away with his friends. It seems that someone saw the boys with their heads together earlier in the evening. Some sort of mischief brewing, very likely. Conceited dog! So sure he was right. At all events, someone had seen a female on the road north and thought it was you, following after the boys; so off he went." Richard added with satisfaction, "I guessed at once where you were when I heard that one of the gypsy wagons had gone south."

"Clever of you."

"Of course, Bertold wouldn't believe that his precious gypsies had anything to do with it."

I felt of my head. The spot was still tender.

"I suppose I only imagined that I was struck on the head, the doors bolted, and myself hauled away across the heath."

He said gloomily, "I don't doubt he will claim that I, or someone else, hit you on the head, and his saintly gypsies had no idea you were there."

"I wish you would not refer to them as *his* gypsies."

Richard was silent for a few minutes. I could see the welcoming lights through the windows of Daviot House across the water meadow, and the dull ache at the crown of my head seemed to fade. This harrowing business was nearly over.

But would I find my nephew at home? The fear for his safety remained.

Richard spoke suddenly. "Alain, you aren't infatuated with that Frenchman, are you?"

He had the fatal gift of making me bristle. However, I owed him a great deal for rescuing me, so I tried to conceal my true feelings with a laugh that even I found repulsive.

"When I become infatuated with anyone, as you so crudely put it, I will confide in you at once. Meanwhile, here we are at home, I am happy to say, and we have something a great deal more important to worry about than my infatuations. I want to know where my nephew is."

I was relieved when Nanny limped out of the house to meet us. She enfolded me in a tense embrace.

"Dear child, I've been so worried. I declare, between you and that poor little lamb, I'm quite distracted. But at least you are safe."

I ached in every bone. My head felt as if it balanced a great load, and my worries were just beginning. Jeremy had not yet been found.

Richard explained briefly, "Those gypsies had her. I'm going to stable this animal. No sign of the Frenchman?"

"Nor of that blessed child." Nanny shook her head and urged me inside. "I hope you will forgive me, Miss Alain, but I still don't trust that Monsieur Bertold, so I sent O'Roarke back with the gig. I thought, if he found Monsieur Bertold with you and Jeremy, he could bring you and my little Jeremy home. The Frenchman can stay in the village tonight."

"I suppose so. I mean, very likely."

We went in together. Nanny kept at me, wanting to know why I had permitted myself to be kidnapped by "some horrid gypsies."

"I had nothing to say in the matter. I was in the tinker wagon when someone tapped me on the head. When I came to consciousness, we were bouncing about up on the heath. Richard told them to let me go, and they did."

Nanny was pleased but a little disappointed too.

"You mean to say that that is the whole of the story? It sounds rather tame to me. Are you sure the gypsies struck you?"

"How else could I have gotten this lump on top of my head?"

Nanny considered the matter and finally gave up. "Probably the gypsies. You are right. One is forever reading romances about gypsies snatching up children and holding them until they are grown, at which time they fall in love with princesses or princes. Such nonsense!"

Even in my present state I had to laugh at the picture she

sketched. At the same time we both heard the rattle of wheels on the gravel in front of the house. We clutched each other.

"He's come!" she said, just as I said, "They're home!"

Before we got out the front doors, Jeremy rushed in, holding his arms out.

"Uncle is putting away the little carriage and the horse. He says he'll be in presently. Nanny, Nanny! Aunt Alain." Then he burst out in French, "I am home. It was so exciting. May I have one of Hannah's spice buns? Uncle promised me."

Holding Nanny's hand and mine, he tramped up the stairs, dragging us with him. Nanny kept protesting. "My lamb, do take care. You will be coughing and choking if you aren't careful."

I didn't dare to look back or to ask about Nicolas. I would betray my overwhelming interest in him, and I ached to know his part in his nephew's disappearance.

Though she was right and he had difficulty breathing by the time we reached his room, he was still so exuberant that I thought his adventure had done him good, however bad it might have been for the rest of us. Other than a brief paroxysm of coughing and hard breathing, which was much aided when we gave him his spice bun and some cocoa made with goat's milk, he seemed in excellent condition.

Nanny coaxed him, "Now, do tell us your adventure. You must have been very brave. What did those horrid gypsies do to you? Or was it your uncle?"

"Gypsies? No!" Jeremy giggled. "Uncle was funny. I ran away with Aaron and Timmy. It was Tim's idea. And then Uncle found us and shook me. But after, he promised to get me my own horse in England. Of course, it's not like having my own pony cart, but still . . . So we came home, and outside he met Richard, who told him about rescuing you from the gypsies." Jeremy licked his finger and pressed it on several vagrant crumbs, which he swallowed quickly.

I prompted him. "Yes? Richard told him?"

Jeremy nodded. “Uncle Nicolas didn’t seem very happy that you were rescued.” He looked at me, his eyes wide. “Doesn’t Uncle Nicolas like you?”

“He likes his gypsy friends better, and they are in great trouble,” Nanny explained dryly.

I had to admit that she was right.

Now and then I still felt the prickle of an ache where the blunt instrument (?) had struck across my head, but aside from that, I seemed to have no ill effects, so I supposed I had not been struck too hard, or possibly the weapon was padded in some way. I wondered if I should be grateful to the Honigers for not killing me.

The one thing uppermost in my thoughts was not the bump on my head but my next meeting with Nicolas Bertold. What would he say about his gypsy friends now? I flattered myself that an injury to me must certainly turn him against them. I gathered Jeremy’s empty plate and cup, set them on the tray, having wished him and Nanny good night, and took the tray down to the pantry.

I had come out of the kitchen passage and into the entry hall when Nicolas opened the front door at the far end of the hall. Understandably he looked tired, older, and I wondered that I should love him more because of this. He stooped there, leaning back against the door. He never took his eyes off me. There was a sadness about him. What was its cause?

“A trifle late but home at last.”

I found it hard to express myself calmly. “An eventful night. Jeremy came in half an hour ago. We all missed you.”

This time his smile broadened. “I doubt it. But may I hope that *you* missed me?” He moved away from the door and toward me, shrugging off his greatcoat, which landed in a heap on the floor instead of the Chippendale hall chair. An apple rolled out of the big coat pocket. He stooped to pick it up. “You were rescued from wicked gypsies by that gallant young Pemberton, as I understand it.”

“So it appears. I beg your pardon, but are you hungry?”

He looked at the rosy little apple in his hand, laughed, and threw it to me. I caught it with what I regard as a deft movement, having learned it from my brother and Richard. He explained as he moved toward me. "Jeremy picked it up somewhere. He made me a present of it."

"And you give it to me. How touching! Luckily I like apples." I raised it to my mouth, only to have him push it rudely out of my hand. He slipped an arm around my waist. "Not quite yet. I do not like to kiss women with apples in their mouths."

"You make me sound like a porker."

"Don't play the tease. It isn't your role. Head up. Lips parted. Excellent. How easily you learn to obey me!"

How little you know me, I thought with a spark of amusement. But I was too excited to pursue the quarrel he seemed to be forcing upon me with his lovemaking.

Though I pretended to back away, not wanting him to think I was quite so easily enslaved, his hands fastened painfully around my arms, his head bent over mine, and his mouth crushed mine so forcefully that I felt for a few flustered seconds as though he would drain me of blood.

It was not so, however. He was in the process of arousing all my desire and a passion that matched his own. His body pressed me hard against the wall, one long leg on either side of me, pinning my body to his as if we were one flesh. I must have been conscious of his body as it enclosed mine, but I remember only the ecstasy I had never experienced before. It coursed through my veins like fire and ice at one and the same time.

Somewhere a sound from our prosaic world of 1847 brought us back to the present. All my passionate senses died away. I was still held tight in his embrace, and somewhere we were being watched.

I heard my protest, a little frantic—"Please, I can't breathe"—and I despised myself for my cowardice. But I could not bear to have anyone in the household see me in

Nicolas Bertold's embrace at such a moment when there were so many suspicions unanswered.

I saw him close his eyes with tired patience, or perhaps irritation, as he shifted his position. He released me from his embrace and looked over his shoulder as I did.

No one was on the stairs, but the area behind the stairs and opposite the kitchen passage was dark. Anyone there or on the short gallery above the staircase might have seen us. Either the Pembertons or Jeremy, I thought. Or someone else, someone we knew nothing about?

But it was clear after a few minutes that whoever had seen us was gone.

It had been an eventful evening. I rubbed my forehead wearily, and he was contrite at once.

"My poor darling! I've given you a rough time of it." He cupped one hand around the back of my head, holding me still while he ran the fingers of his other hand lightly through my hair. "Not too bad. The lump seems to be going down." He drew me to the hall chair. I sat down abruptly while he looked into my face, his eyes searching, studying my features.

"Tell me exactly what happened."

I did, without embellishments. "I looked in Demian's tinker wagon. Somebody hit me on the head. When I opened my eyes, we were on the heath. Then Richard came and took me home."

"Sheep shears. Good Lord!" I thought he suppressed a smile at that. "Did the Honigers object to the shears? Did they fight or hurt you?"

I had to admit that they were unexpectedly mild. "No. They seemed surprised—that I had regained consciousness so fast, I gather. But I've no doubt that Richard has the authorities on their trail. We will have them jailed by tomorrow, I hope. Wait and see."

He said, "Does it seem likely that if they hit you on the head and carried you off, they would be so easily cowed by a pair of sheep shears in the hands of a frail girl?"

"Frail girl!" I had not been so insulted since I was ten years old.

He smiled. "When you have lived as long as I have, you will look at these things differently. Now, you must go to bed, take a drop or two of laudanum, and sleep the night through."

"Dreaming of my handsome rescuer," I snapped, still burning over the frail-girl remark.

He pinched my chin hard but spoiled my excuse for petulance by then touching my lips with his. The feathery touch had a sensual effect upon me that might have surprised him. Though I doubt it.

I got to my feet, ignored his helping hand, and went to the staircase where I looked back.

I was puzzled to see him pick up his greatcoat and start out the front door again.

"Where are you going at this hour?" I asked.

"An errand needs doing. Sleep well, my brave Amazon. And by all means, dream of your hero."

He grinned and went out, leaving me as puzzled about him as ever.

CHAPTER THIRTEEN

Despite everyone's advice, I did not resort to laudanum to sleep. It had always seemed to me rather dangerous, no matter how popular it might be. Naturally Jeremy must take it if the surgeons prescribed it, but it seemed to me a sign of his fragility that this was necessary.

I had much to think about that night. Though I slept well at last, I awoke when Nicolas rode back to the house sometime around dawn. I couldn't guess his direction, whether from the village or Willoughby Hall or the easterly farms in the valley or Ferndene Heath. He dismounted, walked Fleurette to the stable. After some time he came back toward the house but stopped by a stone fence and stood there with one foot resting on a protruding stone while he stared out over the valley.

I wondered what he was thinking, what troubles and problems he considered while he appeared to be looking at the stone bridge, the distant Hall, or even the soft, green water meadow, which seemed to float mysteriously in the dawn light.

Was it his conscience that occupied his gloomy thoughts? I was relieved to realize that I no longer believed this.

Eventually he turned back to the house. Luckily I had been watching him from behind the curtains, for he looked directly up at my windows, studying them for a minute or two. I would have given a good deal to know what he was thinking.

Later in the day I thought I had discovered what he'd been thinking. But then, later in the day, my life changed forever, and there was never any going back.

The entire valley was in an uproar that morning. Lady Willoughby and Mavis arrived for a "pleasant chat," as Her Ladyship called it, but Mavis blurted out at once, "Do tell us what it was like, being a captive of those horrid gypsies. Did they—were they—you know . . . romantic?"

"Romantic, fiddlesticks!" her mother put in.

To which I added, "Precisely."

Lady Willoughby went on. "Your Frenchman will be in serious trouble if those gypsies get away."

"They aren't likely to get away. Besides," I pointed out, "how could he warn them? He has been in the village all morning. I am to testify later."

Mavis told me she was ashamed of my failure to rise to the occasion. "The Honigers didn't hurt you. They politely let you go off in our Richard's arms. Now, don't tell me that wasn't romantic. Where is Richard, by the by? I'll wager he is in the village, being congratulated on his heroism at this very minute."

"Richard's heroism?" I repeated, and added a trifle later, "Oh, yes." I was being ungracious and ungrateful to Richard, after all.

"How wonderful for you!" Mavis's voice sounded brittle, unlike herself.

Ironic that all this time I found myself waiting breathlessly, not for the arrival of my rescuer but for the sound of a door opening; a certain footstep far more firm and decisive than Richard's; a deep, vibrant voice that touched my heart as no other sound would ever touch it.

"I am also grateful to Jeremy's Uncle Nicolas for bringing

him home. It was the boy I was looking for when the Honigers attacked me."

"How odd," Lady Willoughby murmured, "that Monsieur Bertold should so easily have recovered the lad! One would almost imagine that he knew exactly where to find him."

"And the other boys," I reminded her. "It was Aaron Budleigh's idea. Or Timothy's. Something like that."

"Purely fortuitous?"

"Or fortunate, I would say."

Both men were gone that morning, giving their stories to our local magistrate, Lord Rabb, who had come to our village of Ferndene Vale and was hearing the evidence of the attempted crime against me. They had obligingly put off my own appearance, imagining that I must have suffered ill effects after my bump on the head, but I was very much myself, and my worst problem was a fear that Nicolas would be suspected of having connections with the Honigers. How my kidnapping would benefit Nicolas, I couldn't imagine, but my insular neighbors might conjure up their own reasons.

This afternoon I would go to the village and place the blame where it lay, on my onetime friend, Demian, and his father. I rather dreaded that. I had no doubt that the village and His Lordship would condemn the Honiger family for every petty crime that had occurred in the valley during the last year. I did not believe Nicolas would be a party to such charges, but I worried for fear that he might lose his temper and further arouse their suspicions of him.

Much as I resented my bump on the head, I also remembered that neither Demian nor his father had followed up that blow with more violence. Surely a quick movement or two would have gotten those clumsy shears away from me, but they had made no effort to attack me. It was all very puzzling.

Lady Willoughby's visit was something of a failure, since I refused to fall into the trap of betraying some secret knowledge about Nicolas. I was certain that this had been her motive. She disturbed me in parting, however, when she stopped on the steps of her carriage long enough to say with an arch-mysterious air, "I shall not say good-bye, my dear. We may very well meet in the village later today. But hush!" She put one gloved finger over her mouth. "I am forbidden to speak of it. You know how formal Lord Rabb is. A veritable lion of the law. He has given me the strictest instructions to say nothing. . . . Are you coming, Mavis?"

I would have died before I asked her why she had been called to testify and what she could possibly know about the Honigers, but I did look inquiringly at Mavis, who grimaced and rolled her eyes. Either she was ignorant of her mother's evidence or she disapproved of it.

I watched the Willoughby carriage ride away and told myself that the woman knew nothing. She was merely being tiresome, trying to disturb me. She had succeeded.

Neither Richard Pemberton nor Nicolas returned by noon, and Hannah wanted to know what arrangements were to be made for dinner. I had no idea. Nanny suggested that the meal be planned as if they would be here, but as I expected to give Lord Rabb my story by two in the afternoon, I decided that everything must be held in abeyance until late in the day.

I suppose I must have had some premonition and expected the worst to happen, whatever that might be. When the old case clock in the hall reminded me that it was one o'clock and time to be going to that unpleasant business in the village, I was relieved to have Nanny's company and even more relieved when she confided as we got into the gig, "Certainly there can be no connection between Monsieur Bertold and our naughty Jeremy's little prank. I confess, the boy also ran away in France. Not into the woods, of course."

"Why not?"

"Oh, Miss Alain, you are used to Ferndene Heath and these people. But in France such things are strange, less a part of us. They seem more . . . forboding. What with half-pay veterans wandering about without a sou to bless themselves with, and some of them without limbs at all. And I've seen wolves. They run away, of course, when a boy comes by. But there are bears. Well, when the gypsies are about. And so many . . . Frenchies."

"Not unnatural in France," I reminded her.

"Yes, but so different from my William. How often he said so! And from Jeremy. Now and again the lad walked toward Boisville or on the road to St. Auden where the Vicomte and that woman have a town house."

"Is she really beautiful?" I asked, remembering that in her girlhood Gabrielle de St. Auden had been the love of Nicolas Bertold's life. He had not said as much, but clearly she was important to him. There seemed to have been no more serious liaisons until he came to Ferndene Valley. I remembered last night vividly, and that other occasion on the return from Willoughby Hall one starlit evening. I counted the times he had hinted at marriage and told myself that I was the woman he loved today. Unlike his childhood love, I would never let a title or any other obstacle come between us.

How absurd I would sound if anyone guessed my thoughts! But I was blind to everything I had known and practiced in all my twenty-three years. Loyalty ruled me, loyalty to a passion I couldn't control.

I took the reins, and we set out for the village. We passed the church and saw the grassy churchyard crowded with villagers, then rode on to stable the mare, always under the interested stare of our neighbors. I knew that there was trouble ahead. Worse. All these lifelong acquaintances of mine knew something I did not know.

Nanny crowded closer to me, clutching my arm. She looked as pale as I felt.

"My dear, they shouldn't stare like that. It isn't showing proper respect to you."

"Who cares? I'm sure I don't." I smiled and waved Father's old whip as we passed the mercer's wife, then Tad Spindler standing in the open doorway of the inn with his crutch beside him, and a blur of faces outside the cottages that surrounded Mother Hagar's shop.

A bailiff from Shaftesbury owned a handsome thatched cottage between the sweetshop and the Common. Here Nanny and I were met at the gate and ushered across the yard where a belled pet lamb stared at us before jingling off about his business. I did not recognize half the people hanging around the dooryard and the kitchen garden beside the house, but I kept my tight, forced smile.

The main room of the cottage seemed crowded with people. Lord Rabb, a very stout man with pink cheeks, was the center of attention and quite naturally had been given the only armchair, but though Richard Pemberton came over to greet his mother and me, Nicolas Bertold was the most imposing figure in the room.

He looked arrogant, as he had the first time we met. When he saw me, I sensed a question in his eyes, which I tried to answer with a quick, confident smile. After that his expression softened. He returned his attention to the business at hand, looking quite cheerful.

I noticed Lady Willoughby, who, like Lord Rabb, was seated. She gave me a welcoming nod as though we were fellow conspirators, no doubt against the Frenchman.

Nicolas reached over and nudged a frail young man who seemed to be taking down the proceedings for Lord Rabb. The young clerk rose hurriedly and presented me with his chair. The stout bailiff reluctantly offered his stool to Nanny, who took it after a curtsy and an apologetic smile. I would rather stand but didn't want to make a scene, and Richard Pemberton, having seen to his mother's comfort, was already fussing around me.

Lord Rabb settled back, slapping the arm of his chair.

"Well, now. Miss Daviot, isn't it? I had the pleasure of an acquaintance with your parents. Excellent family."

Excellent family. Yeomen, in fact. I understood at once that I had been placed lower than Lady Willoughby in the social scale, though her family had been yeomen like mine. A title bestowed upon Simon Willoughby for his services in procuring females for the Prince Regent's friends went far to raise Her Ladyship in milord's eyes.

I said, "Your Lordship is too kind," but he was moving on rapidly.

"I trust you are feeling more the thing after your adventure last night, Miss Daviot."

"Certainly." What had Nicolas to do with my story? Why was everyone looking so somber? They must know the entire story by now. Richard could have told them my share in the Honiger affair.

"Then, if you will describe the matter..."

I did so, as briefly as possible. I wanted to get to the crucial news that must seriously compromise Nicolas. There might be some way to turn their suspicions. These people disliked Nicolas only because he was foreign. Even as I explained about the Honigers, however, I was remembering all the times Mavis and I discussed "the monster," "that satanic Frenchman," "that murderer."

The silence, when I finished, was complete, but I caught the exchange of looks among them and, worst of all, the quick, furtive glances at Nicolas.

Lord Rabb cleared his throat. "You understood nothing of the conversation between these two gypsies? Were any names mentioned? Could the language have been French?"

I understood that implication right enough.

"Absolutely not. I was taught French in my youth. Mrs. Pemberton, here, is an adept in the language. I might add that I am not seriously injured, and they made no effort to hurt me when they found I had regained consciousness. In fact, they seemed astonished that I was in their wagon at all."

His Lordship's manner was all too patronizing, as though he dealt with an invalid or someone with a weakness he must humor.

"Pardon me, but I shouldn't think an hour's unconsciousness was a minor matter. Indeed, I would say that they did hurt you, and seriously."

Any other time I might have agreed, but his manner and what I considered an effort to entangle Nicolas prejudiced me at the outset.

"Were there any other questions, Your Lordship?"

The little man sighed. I could feel the tension in the room.

"Miss Daviot, there is one question, yes. Are you aware that the Honiger family has left the county, perhaps even the country?"

"I was not aware, though I am not surprised."

"There is reason to believe that they were warned and have fled the country as a result."

We were getting closer to the crux of the problem. I now had no doubt of their next step, but to my surprise Lady Willoughby seemed to be involved. She broke in almost before His Lordship finished speaking.

"Those dreadful gypsies were warned by that Frenchman." She added ominously, "I saw him ride up to the heath last night. He may deny it all he likes, but I used Simon's—my late husband's—spyglass, and I saw him. Past midnight."

Nanny gasped. I said flatly, "Lady Willoughby is mistaken. Monsieur Bertold cannot possibly have been seen last night past midnight." I was conscious of the excitement my statement aroused. I turned, gave Nicolas my warmest look. His eyebrows went up, but he seemed amused.

His Lordship was uneasy. "How can you be so certain, Miss Daviot?"

"Because Monsieur Bertold was with me until he went to the village today. We had matters to discuss concerning my nephew. And his."

Someone tittered, but His Lordship and Lady Willoughby were both shocked by my confession, and Nanny almost fainted. I was well aware that I had placed myself beyond the pale of decent women.

Suddenly we all heard Nicolas saying, "I had only just

returned from London where I arranged for the special license. That is necessary to a marriage, as I am sure you are all aware. Last evening I asked Miss Daviot to pack for herself and my nephew. We are to be married in a matter of twenty-four hours. Naturally this required several hours of persuasion." He gave me the smile that lit his dark eyes. "I am happy to say that she agreed. We leave immediately on the railway cars."

Leave for where? I had no idea. Nor did I care at the moment. There was considerable excitement around me, not all of it flattering, but I was too busy attending to Nanny Pemberton, who had sunk against me in a dead faint.

While Richard and I restored her with a glass of cider furnished by our host, the bailiff, Richard kept whispering, "You can't know what you are saying, Alain. Remember what happened to William. He is marrying you to get closer to Jeremy's half of the estate."

"Do hush!"

"If anything happens to that boy, you will be responsible."

I looked up. "Lord Rabb, you have been so useful today, would you mind doing one more useful thing? Have Mister Pemberton removed."

"Yes—er—certainly." A hand on Richard's shoulder was enough. Richard was a law-abiding man.

With Nanny's head against my arm and her plain bonnet all awry, I got her to drink a few sips of the strong cider. It seemed to revive her. She choked but opened her eyes. What she saw as she looked behind me made her flinch in terror.

When I glanced over my shoulder, I saw Nicolas. He had been staring down at Nanny. For a frozen instant I could almost understand her absurd fear.

CHAPTER FOURTEEN

I had always imagined that my marriage, if any, would be a splendid affair locally, with all my neighbors at hand to wish me well. I certainly did not believe that we would sneak out of the valley in a hired carriage and team, hoping none of the friends of a lifetime could identify us, but so it was. Even the good wishes of Nanny, the unexpected enthusiasm of Jeremy, and the belated apology of Richard Pemberton could not make up for the furtive quality of this, the most important step of my life.

We were married at a county church on the High Road to Portsmouth where we planned to embark the following day on the long cross-Channel voyage to the shores of my husband's country. It was my idea to sail for France as soon as possible. I felt that our future would be shrouded in mystery and uncertainty until I saw Château Bertold and learned to love it for Nicolas's sake.

None of those I loved witnessed the wedding. Nanny and Jeremy would join us at Château Bertold within a few weeks, as soon as I had decided that the most searing memories of the double tragedy had faded. I planned it all so methodically; new hangings here, new furniture there, paint, whitewash, and repairs could do wonders. Meanwhile, until we returned to Daviot Farms on the threshold of winter, Joshua Budleigh would have the care of my land and its produce, profiting as he deserved to but managing it as successfully as he had in the past when I went up to London for the season.

So it was that the persons attending our wedding were the young vicar, a sexton, and a widow just come in from the churchyard where she had laid roses upon her husband's grave. In a poignant gesture she presented me with a tiny, pink, climbing rose from the grave. I was touched and grateful, but I hoped this was not somehow symbolic.

We walked out of the church, my hand in Nicolas's, saying nothing, occupied with our own thoughts. His were very serious, I judged from his somber look.

The ceremony was surprisingly short. Where were the attendants and the lovely gowns, the laughter and embraces, the toasts to our happiness? I wore a taffeta gown and matching bonnet of a deep, rich blue that I hadn't worn since William died, but Nicolas had chosen it for me. He said it brought out the "richness of your honey-colored hair," a compliment I treasured. The many yards in the skirt made it look festive in spite of the very proper tight sleeves that reached my wrists, and the neat lace collar on the high neck.

When we came out into the sunlight after the sepulchral chill of the old church, Nicolas stopped in the dusty road, took both my hands, and studied me with such tenderness as had occasionally filled my dreams.

"I do believe there never was a lovelier bride. Are you really mine, my darling?"

"What nonsense you talk! As though I could ever be anyone else's bride."

He kissed me then, ignoring the little girl walking toward us with a furry white dog and a hoop she rolled ahead of her. I raised my head, ready to answer his kiss with all my heart, but still he managed to tip my bonnet back on my neck like a hoyden and ruin my coiffure with his hands while his heavy, sensuous mouth crushed my own and we were briefly lost to our surroundings.

We were both jolted hard as the child's hoop rolled against my skirts and the girl came rushing after it, hurtling into us. In this ridiculous anticlimax to our wedding kiss, the ring he had just slipped on my finger fell off in the dust. The girl and her hoop rolled on, accompanied by the now wildly cavorting dog.

Nicolas and I both knelt, our fingers closing together on the plain gold ring that he had formerly worn on his little finger. He slipped it on my finger, large as the ring was, then kissed the tips of my fingers and promised, "Once we reach Paris, you will have a decent ring, sweetheart, I promise you."

I wasn't at all sure I wanted a "decent ring." We had made our vows over this gold band with its curious inscription, *ours sombre*. This was my true wedding ring. I said, "I like this one. But I suppose it has been in your family for many years."

"Since the Crusades, probably. The Third, at the least. Almost everything at Château Bertold comes from that gaggle of throat-cutting bandits." He did not seem very impressed by it.

"The inscription is odd. Our sadness? Our shade?"

He dismissed the matter indifferently. "French, of sorts. The symbol of the Bertolds is a bear. The somber bear. Or the sad bear. Something like that."

I confessed to myself that it suited Nicolas somewhat. The first time I saw him in my drawing room, he had looked rather like a black bear. "A snappish black bear," I said, and at once he wanted to know what I could possibly be talking about.

For no reason we began to laugh, and we walked along past the church, sharing a delicious moment of happiness. A woman called to us from the entrance porch of the church.

It was the widow who had given us the tiny rose I now carried in my prayer book.

"Long life and happiness, Mister and Mistress Bertold."

We waved, thanked her, and walked on, but I had a sudden haunting thought: Would I be like her one day, alone, mourning the loss of this man I adored? I clung to his arm and begged him, "Don't die. Don't let anything happen to you. Promise me."

He laughed. Then, unexpectedly, it was as if a shadow crossed his face. "I will never leave you. I wish I could be as certain that you won't leave me."

"Then we've nothing to worry about."

I thought we were in perfect agreement, but of course, I couldn't read his own thoughts. I had long ago discovered that he was a man of secrets. I refused to believe that those secrets involved William's death, or that of Nicolas's sister. But I had good reason to know that Lady Willoughby actually saw him riding to Ferndene Heath. His purpose was clear. He had warned his gypsy friends.

What of it? Did that make him a murderer? It merely made him a loyal friend. Again I banished suspicion.

We spent our wedding night in a waterfront lodging house facing the port so that we might reach our French barkentine at the first light. I did not care that the two-story house smelled of fish and that there were two drunken sailors singing in the public room we passed on our way up to a bedchamber and parlor that overlooked the bare masts of ships from ports in Continental Europe and the New World. I was with the man I loved.

He looked around the parlor with its pathetic effort at homelike furnishings and joked as he closed my eyes gently with two fingers.

"Madame Bertold, you are in a luxurious salon on the Faubourg St. Honoré. Your enchanting satin slippers glide across the parquet floor. To your right a magnificent statue of the Emperor Napoleon—"

"Best make it the Duke of Wellington, Monsieur. I am an Englishwoman."

"No matter, madame. You will soon accustom yourself and become the greatest francophile of us all. . . . Let me see. Gold brocade portieres. Pillars of marble, flecked brown and gold, I think. A gilt chair that was sat in by Marie Antoinette—"

"Before she lost her head, I trust."

"Yes. Well. And an upholstered fauteuil there. A splendid mirror straight ahead so that you may see the loveliest face in the world looking back at you."

Such elaborate compliments always made me nervous. I opened my eyes to say something sharp, but I sensed that he saw me through the eyes of love and possibly even saw me in that remarkable way. I did not snap out the usual "Nonsense!" or "Rubbish!" I kissed him instead.

He seemed to feel that this room was not quite what I was used to. Having opened my eyes, I looked around and saw the hard, straight-backed wooden settle, which had been transformed into a sofa by goose-feather pillows with embroidered cushion covers. The rest of the furnishings were equally primitive, though not, I think, as unpleasant and shocking to me as to Nicolas. He insisted on forgetting that I had grown up in a farming community that frowned on what they considered "Frenchified elegance." Furthermore, the view of the choppy water foaming around the wooden hulls was new to me.

But neither of us had the wonders of travel on our minds.

We walked together into the bedchamber where a huge bed without curtains or tester looked as though its feathery mattress would receive the biggest sailor in the world. I said so aloud, suspecting that he was concerned over introducing a virginal young woman to the sexual embrace.

I added mischievously, "Including any females he might bring to share his bed."

I expected him to laugh, but the look in his eyes excited

me. I trembled, though not from fear, as he may have suspected. His desire communicated itself to me. I was hungry to respond and untied the wide blue ribbons of my bonnet. Then I began to unbutton the tight basque of my jacket while he watched. I wondered if he would think me too bold when I reached out and unbuttoned the golden tan riding coat he wore.

His own hands were soon upon my flesh, caressing my throat and fingering the high curve of my breasts, first one, then the other, as they were revealed to him by the stripping away of my camisole. His dark head bent, and he touched the tips of my breasts with his lips, sending a fiery ecstasy through my body. As I pressed against him I became aware of his hardness against my thighs and marveled that the wildness I felt was so much greater than the erotic dreams I had known since he came into my life.

I would gladly have gone hand in hand with him to that bed, but I found myself picked up and dropped in a heap onto the coverlet. Disheveled, my camisole and petticoat torn, my flesh uncovered to his gaze, I knew I had never wanted him so much. I held my bare arms out. How pale they must have looked in the gray light of dusk!

But the light was blotted out for me by his body as he knelt astride my thighs, lowered his head again, and his mouth lingered over those warm, secret places where his touch made me cry out with wanting him. I touched his head, running my fingers through his thick, black hair, pulling hard as I writhed with a burning pleasure under his assault.

I felt within me the power and strength of his maleness, which I had always sensed would make him a part of me forever. He might have loved many others and might even love another someday, at some time, but tonight he was a part of me, just as I belonged to him. That was the wonder of a sexual embrace, I thought. My limbs shuddered with delight as I felt his driving power take possession of my body and of me.

I had expected that our first lovemaking would be painful. Perhaps it was. I have no recollection of anything but that passionate union, so that the pain was banished by the exquisite joy I felt. I closed my eyes in order to relive each ecstatic moment.

When I opened my eyes, I saw his face so close above me that I blinked, but I was far from objecting. I raised a finger and traced the outline of his lips. He turned his head and kissed the tip of my finger. Before I could say anything, his deep voice sent new chills of excitement along my spine.

"Think back, sweetheart. The first night I saw you. I wanted to make love to you then."

How could I forget the night that changed my life? It was doubly exciting to think that even on that night he had wanted me. I said teasingly, "I am not surprised. I rushed madly up to change into that wondrous robe William and Yolande sent me, and it impressed you."

"What?" He sat up, staring at me in pretended indignation. "Then you don't understand me at all. It was the dryad in the water-soaked condition, the absurd child who looked at me with such haughty condescension. That was the girl I wanted to—"

I laughed and silenced him with my finger.

He kissed me and I, learning quickly, locked my arms around his neck, drawing him closer. Not being of an original mind, I could only repeat, "I love you so much. I do!"

"Do you, my darling?" I was shocked and very much moved by the doubt in his voice. I could prove my love in the way we were both beginning to understand.

We made love again, and in those hours of the night that followed, all our doubts of each other were set aside or burned away by this passion that blazed between us.

We had a brief setback during the interminable hours at sea, day and night. I had never been on a ship before, and all that choppy gray water proved to be far less picturesque than I supposed. I spent more than half the voyage in my bunk, holding fast to anything I could reach that might give me some kind of security against rolling out onto the deck. Worse, my stomach betrayed me on numerous occasions, and I demanded that Nicolas should not see me like this; so when he did make his presence known in order to help me, I was angry enough to quarrel with him. Luckily he was an understanding man and flatly refused to quarrel.

At the time I found this noble forebearance of his extremely annoying!

But our marriage had improved in tempo by the time we took the railway cars to Paris. Nicolas agreed to stop teasing me about my battle with the Channel, and I agreed to forget that he was a magnificent seaman.

I felt familiar enough with my new husband to ask, rather archly, I'm afraid, how many other females he had loved. This did not anger him. To my annoyance he found my question flattering. Worse. He was amused.

"My darling girl, you may think you would like a virginal lover, but I assure you, you wouldn't. At fifteen I was abysmally clumsy."

"Fifteen!"

"Yes. Somewhat overage for such matters in France, but I was no prodigy. However"—he kissed me on the nose to the interest of several other travelers in the noisy, smoky railway car—"I was a boy of rare good sense. I chose only females of impeccable cleanliness and taste."

I was embarrassed by his frankness but couldn't help pursuing the matter. "Were you in love with them?"

With his arm across my shoulder he considered the matter. "For the moment."

He must have sensed my disappointment and discomfort. He squeezed my shoulders, reminding me, "I did not propose marriage to them. The last time I asked a woman to marry me—before you—it was Gaby St. Auden when she was Gaby de Morlaix, nearly fifteen years ago. She was fourteen and something of a beauty, even then."

"You did not ask me to marry you."

"What?" He considered the facts and was forced to agree. He added, "But I thought about it."

"You didn't actually go up to London to get a special license to marry me, then?"

"No. I went to make arrangements for the English importation of Bertold White Bordeaux. But I thought—"

"I know. You thought about it."

"Precisely. How well you read my mind!"

I smiled, but I knew that this was far from true.

By the time we reached the cavernous and overpowering terminal in Paris with its great clouds of white steam that blinded one momentarily, the world seemed to have gathered in order to confuse me. I understood only one word in ten and also began to realize that the man I had married was quite a different and more important person in his own country.

CHAPTER FIFTEEN

At least half a dozen Frenchmen recognized Nicolas from the terminal station to the waiting carriage and team, which looked much more imposing than a London horse and buggy, even though it lacked the social grace of a crest. It all climaxed at the Bertold house in the fashionable Faubourg St. Honoré.

The streets of Paris astonished me. Much of London had been rebuilt after the Great Fire of 1666, but this city, perhaps the center of culture in the civilized world, was a labyrinth of narrow, twisted streets, some few tree-lined, all frantically busy at this hour after sunset on an August day.

Once seated in the small, well-kept coach that was surprisingly free of dust or cobwebs, with the coachman who had so readily recognized his employer in all that crowd, I was fascinated by the fast-moving views of a city that I still remembered from my father's remarks about "The Enemy Capital."

As a young man my father had been among the Allied armies who invaded and occupied the ancient city in 1815 where, according to my brother William, Father confided that all manner of horrors befell the citizens at the hands of the

Russian, Austrian, and Prussian conquerors. "But never from us," William added virtuously. "Father says so."

I looked out now, studying the gray, stone-walled buildings with their curious top floors set back at a cozy slant, and the many chimney pots, and most interesting of all, the cafés set upon the streets themselves.

"Does no rider or team ever collide with those little tables and chairs?" I wanted to know.

Nicolas was surprised by the question. "I don't recall that the matter ever came up. You alarm me. We must take care to watch for wild horses."

I knew he was having fun at my expense, but I was too apprehensive to quarrel with him. We had turned from one narrow, cobbled street to another even more narrow. I could scarcely believe that it was the celebrated "St. Honoré." Our main village street back home was wider than this, and such twists and turns and jogs as we would never dream of in my part of the world.

Nicolas told me with a note of pride, "This is the Rue du Faubourg St. Honoré. You see that imposing house on the left, with the garden behind it? The Hotel Sebastiani, the residence of the Praslin family. Very elegant. The Duc de Praslin is close to His Majesty."

"Your rival, in fact." I looked out at the spacious town house, impressed as I was meant to be.

"Closer than I, in spite of the Bonapartist tinge. The Duchesse de Praslin is the daughter of the Maréchal Sebastiani, a Corsican, but our king is pragmatic. He makes former enemies into friends, as he did my father." He sounded cynical, and I couldn't blame him.

"I will learn to make friends with these aristocrats, I suppose. Must I curtsy very low to dukes and marshals?"

"Good Lord, no. You are my wife. You are anyone's equal." He gave me a glinting side glance. "Except, perhaps, in the case of Their Majesties. . . . You don't, by chance, have some insuperable objection to a curtsy before a mere French king?"

"Indeed not. I shall be happy to recognize him. I am very democratic."

He laughed and began to point out other buildings that he called *hôtels particuliers*, family town houses in which aristocrats lived, all cheek by jowl with the Bertolds. It was as if the two French Revolutions had never happened.

Now that the buildings along the street became richer, yet severe and chaste in their exterior, the street cafés disappeared and the ubiquitous peddlers of firewood, flowers, water, and even sheets of glass became scarce. Before the only facade that lacked a crest over its doors, the coachman pulled up his team. With impressive magic the iron gates opened, the carriage rolled in under the porte-cochère and stopped on the cobbles of a fair-size courtyard around which the four-story house was built on three sides.

The setting struck me as overwhelming in its richness but also in its solid use of the best styles in the past century. It was far from the run-down, ancient castle I expected to find and which William's constant complaints had prepared me for. True. He spoke mostly about the château, but even the Paris house hadn't suited him, though to my eyes, young Queen Victoria herself could not despise this house.

I did not wish the Bertold servants to guess how impressed I was, so I took the arm Nicolas offered as I descended from the coach and remarked for the benefit of the old coachman, "Very nice indeed. But we are to be here so short a time, it seems a pity to have this big house opened just for us."

Nicolas had no interest in servants' gossip. He said indifferently, "I keep it in readiness, since I never know when I may be coming to the city. Yolande and her husband used to stay here in season, of course, though, as I recall, the opera was not his favorite form of entertainment."

"Nor ever was." I laughed at memories of my youth with William, then caught my husband's eye. He changed the subject.

"But the sooner we get down to Château Bertold, the better. I want you to feel at home there."

"For part of the year."

He seemed to like the notion of my loyalty to Daviot Farms and agreed at once to the importance of my properties as he had when we talked with taciturn Farmer Budleigh and arranged for the farmer to take half the profits of the autumn crops.

We walked up the wide steps. Doors opened magically, which made me nervous, and I jumped. Nicolas, however, was completely untroubled. For a man who never paid the slightest attention to manners in Ferndene Valley, he took all this regal splendor with considerable aplomb. He spoke to the young footman in black-and-silver livery, who was so busy staring at me that he barely acknowledged the greetings.

His eyes widened in the most complimentary way, for which I was more than grateful. He returned my smile after a moment's hesitation, and Nicolas remarked, "You have made a convert already." Truth to tell, the young man's smile was the first I had received from a stranger in Paris.

"This is Armand," Nicolas explained. "His father and grandfather and so on were in Paris with the Bertolds. I doubt if this house would stand without them. Has Grégoire arrived from the château? Sweetheart, you will find that there is nothing Grégoire doesn't know about the château. You must learn from him."

This was not reassuring.

Armand said, "Grégoire is in the kitchen, monsieur, giving orders for a late supper. Some problem with the lobsters, I believe. The Praslins are expected. The duchesse has returned from the country with the children, and His Grace wishes to discuss the problem of the workshops in Paris."

"Where the duc is, Fanny de Praslin will surely follow," Nicolas murmured to me. "She hasn't the slightest interest in French affairs, but she has a passion for Theobald de Praslin that borders on the unsavory." He saw me raise my eyebrows and added quickly, "Not quite the passion you and I understand, my darling. No. Not quite." He completely ignored the interest of the footman in this bit of personal information.

Nicolas went on explaining to me as we made our way through this marble Holy of Holies. "You would be interested, darling, in this problem I will be discussing with Praslin. The removal of the slums is merely producing greater problems for the poor. There are no lodgings they can afford. Forty percent of the children born in Paris today are illegitimate."

"Heavens!" But I was sorrier for the fact that they had no place to live their illegitimate lives.

"And you would not believe the unsanitary conditions that—" He looked at me, grinned, and apologized. "Sorry. Come along. I'll show you our bedroom and your boudoir. God knows I had rather spend the evening alone with you. But if His Majesty doesn't do something about our problems, the Republicans will set up Louis-Napoleon Bonaparte in his place. The man has something of his uncle's genius for capturing hearts. He offers them practical help. As we should."

All this went over my head. I was too busy privately marveling at the richness around me, the wide marble steps between breathtaking pillars and the most glorious chandelier I had ever seen, which hung over us as we ascended that staircase. It was one mass of crystal prisms dangling above our heads. When I looked back at the ground floor, I saw that the grand salon opened into endless other pillared chambers.

Everything was so out of balance, thousands homeless, while the Sebastiani and Bertold town houses remained like giant mausoleums. I shook my head at my own preposterous thoughts.

The bedchamber proved to be entirely Nicolas's room. I saw nothing connected with a female, and few signs of the ancient Bertold glory. This suited me excellently well. The bed looked comfortable with four heavy oak posts and no curtains. The leather furniture and the big, double-doored armoire, while rather clumsy to my eyes, reminded me of my father's and brother's bedrooms, which I had often helped the maids clean. I was immediately at home here.

Nicolas watched me with a trace of uneasiness.

"I'm afraid I hadn't counted on a bride when I left in July. If I had, there might have been something a trifle more welcoming in here at least."

I jammed my fist into the mattress, coverlet and all, and said after careful consideration for his benefit, "Yes. Quite satisfactory. And no. I do not wish you had planned this for a female."

He watched me test the bed. I became aware of his eyes and realized that our desires ran along the same track, so to speak. Either that or he had an extraordinary mesmerizing influence on me. I held out my arms to him, then remembered all his servants and reminded him in panic, "Lock the door."

"I've no objection to being seen making love to my own wife." But to oblige me he bolted the tall, paneled door and came back with a purposeful stride. "Now, no more excuses. Get to your place, my love."

"My love," or not, I recognized this as the voice of command. I wanted to resist the voice, but I could not resist the man. When he caught me up and practically tossed me onto the bed, I made only a token resistance. As always, his touch enflamed me. We began to kiss. We tangled in each other's arms, loving with the skill of recent practice.

Thanks to my loving teacher, whose hunger for my body inspired my passion as well as a greater regard for my own person, I was learning to offer him something of the excitement he gave me. We seemed ideally mated.

We lay there much later, enjoying a warm companionship that had little to do with the growing power of our sexual union. With his arm under my head and my face warm against his chest, he obeyed my suggestion and told me something of his country's problems under the "bourgeois" Orléans king.

I tried to be intelligent in my answers, but I also reminded myself that I was far from the first to lie in his arms discussing politics so compassionately. I asked him, very much in the manner of a question about the weather, "You must have enjoyed these conversations with your mistresses in the past?"

He stared at me as if I had somehow shocked him.

"I never discuss politics with females."

"You discuss the subject with me."

"But my dear love, you are my wife."

I was so pleased, I turned my head, brushed his throat with my lips, and saw that my kiss had made him shiver with excitement, just as my own body reacted to his touch.

How well suited we were, I reminded myself.

But eventually I knew we must make ready for his political guest, the Duc de Praslin. I did not mind meeting him, but I was a trifle uncertain about the Duchesse. She would find my wardrobe provincial, my French bad, and my manners "foreign." I mentioned that we must make ourselves presentable for his guests, "especially the Duchess," and he laughed at the importance I attached to such matters, but all the same, I knew he would not like to be disgraced by his country wife's appearance.

He had thought it admirable that I needed no personal maid to dress me, and I soon discovered that this was because he liked to act as my lady's maid, kissing now my bare shoulder, now my bosom, and upon occasion— But enough of that. He was a man of the senses, and I was a woman who had never before known the power of such titillating attentions.

"You must have an entire new wardrobe," he decided. "Made for you in Paris." He told me this as his hands lingered on my bare arms, below the dropped shoulders of the white-brocaded evening gown with black panels in the stiffened skirt. It was my best gown, and he surprised me by remembering that in his exuberance on our wedding night, he had torn my blue taffeta, which I had counted upon for dressy evenings at the château.

I realized that he was right about the new wardrobe, and truth to tell, I was not sorry. All my life I had heard about Paris fashions. I was not sure of the reaction if I wore such clothes at Daviot Farms when we returned for part of the year, but I felt quite certain Lady Willoughby would open her eyes and Mavis would want to know how much had been paid for them.

I found my large black lace-and-ivory fan in the top of my valise and got it out. As I waved it and curtsied low to my husband, I felt confident enough even to meet a duchess. From his expression he thought so too.

He then led me out ceremoniously to show me the house and its beautiful little garden whose rear gate opened upon a narrow street near the copse of trees that he had said was the beginning of the Champs-Elysées. The rigid formal garden with its herbacious border, which I was thrilled to recognize, was lighted like a fairyland with little lanterns hanging from two chestnut trees and a number of bushes. I was horrified.

"Don't tell me you do this every night of the year. What expense! What extravagance!"

He agreed that this might be just a trifle pretentious. "But I did send ahead to have it done for you."

That, of course, put everything in perspective, and I hugged him, causing him to pull a strand of my carefully arranged hair out of its net and dangle it before my eyes. I tucked it back in place at once, not wanting the Duchess de Praslin to see me looking so disreputable. We went around the garden while I admired the borders and the carefully pruned green plants with the beginnings of autumn flowers, which I couldn't even identify, rising up to meet us. Nicolas picked several flowers in assorted shades from lilac to purple to wine color, with deep hearts like the whites of eyes with dark pupils. I recognized anemones, uncommon to my eyes. I was about to say so when we were both startled by a distant series of cries, perhaps those of a great, trapped bird, sounds that floated on the quiet night air and reminded us of the unknown outdoors around us.

"You have loud birds here, louder even than those on Ferndene Heath when I walk alone."

I saw him turn his head, listening. His frown I found disconcerting. Surely, having lived in this house in season for many years, he must be used to the sounds of Paris at night, even here on the outskirts.

"Yes," he said finally. "A bird trapped somewhere."

I was almost glad when a rapier-thin man with silver hair appeared on the veranda behind us. Silhouetted against the lighted hall and music room at his back, he reminded me of a knife blade, gleaming in the starlight.

I was especially curious about him when Nicolas spoke his name aloud, "Grégoire." Knowing his importance to the running of the Paris house and the château, I wanted to discover more about him. He was not unattractive in his thin-lipped, distant way, but there was no warmth about him. He barely indicated my existence by a faint nod before addressing Nicolas.

"Your guest seems to have been delayed, monsieur. It appears unlikely that His Grace will make his call so late tonight. I thought that after your long journey you and madame might care to dine soon. A simple repast but perhaps welcome in the circumstances."

"Give Praslin another hour," Nicolas told him after receiving a shrug from me. "The matter is pressing. According to my informants in London, there have been riots in the provinces and pamphlets flooding Paris, demanding a return to the Republic, and some even asking the return of the Bonapartes. I'm afraid whatever His Majesty does must be done at once. This policy of quietly waiting out the disturbances is not working."

"Yes, monsieur."

Nicolas said to me, "Darling, this is Grégoire, the steward of the estate and my good right hand."

I smiled too enthusiastically, overdoing my effort to win the man's good opinion.

"I am delighted to meet you, Grégoire. My husband has told me so much about you."

The steward bowed. "Very good, madame. Monsieur. Then we wait to serve the little supper."

Nothing produced in me more defensive hauteur than to have my friendly overtures spurned. I made no further effort to win him over, turned my back on him, and moved majestically (I hope) across the wide floor, pretending to examine the elaborate rococco floral chains that ornamented the pale green panels of the wall. I waved my fan in a regal fashion while Nicolas gave the man some last instructions about the possible arrival of the Duc de Praslin in the morning, though this would be far from a social call. I am afraid no one noticed me. No matter. I would learn, I promised myself. After all, I was mistress of this house, ridiculously big as it might be.

Because Nicolas made the tour of inspection entertaining, joking with me, kissing me unexpectedly, tickling me, and in general providing the little tricks that he knew would make me laugh, I recovered from my pique and what may have been at the bottom of my bad disposition: I was homesick in the midst of such splendor. It was a little like being told that one must live in quarters with the queen and Prince Albert . . . something that "gives one to think," as my new French neighbors would say.

Nicolas gave up the wait finally. "I think we had better have that supper Grégoire boasts of, my love, or I'll have you wasting away from hunger."

I was relieved. This meant that the meeting with the all-important friend, the confidant of kings, could be put off until tomorrow.

Nicolas rang for someone or other. Grégoire did not appear, but a stout, heavy-jawed maid in stiff black and white arrived to give orders to Armand. My young friend obligingly brought trays into the charming petite salon, as Nicolas called it. This was my favorite room, and even its size was that of my own drawing room at home. But it was exquisitely furnished in a comfortable Louis Sixteenth style, whose fragile beauty was softened by the crimson velvet draperies and the leather-inlaid desk and chairs at which we ate.

Everyone apologized for the informality of it, but of course, that was what I liked best. I had also looked out the long windows and gotten an excellent view of the lantern-lit garden outside. I was just reflecting that one might grow very fond of this room, and even the house, when Grégoire slipped into the room and stood beside the low-burning fire in the grate of the fireplace. He moved soundlessly, another characteristic about him that I disliked, but this time I was appalled by his pallor which I hadn't noticed before.

"May I have a word with you, monsieur?"

Obviously this was to be in private. My back stiffened, but I said nothing. I knew I was at fault for resenting his interruption and the manner of it.

Nicolas felt my resentment and asked, "Is it something political? Some grave palace secret?"

His sarcasm went unnoticed by the steward.

"No, monsieur. It is the reason your guests did not arrive."

"Then I am sure Madame Bertold, as mistress of the house, may be privy to this grave secret."

Grégoire looked at me, and I could swear that he very nearly smiled. It was not a pleasant look.

"As you say, monsieur. The police have been called to the Hotel Sebastiani. There is a considerable crowd gathering in the street."

Nicolas frowned. "Another robbery in the quarter?"

"I think not, monsieur." Again Grégoire glanced at me. "It seems that Madame la Duchesse has been—is dead."

"Killed in the robbery?"

"That remains to be seen. I believe the magistrates have been sent for as well."

Nicolas and I exchanged glances. I was shocked, but I

could see that something more than an accidental killing in the robbery had occurred to him. He said, "I'll go to His Grace at once."

"I'm afraid that will be impossible, monsieur. His Grace is busy at the moment with the police. It seems that he was found washing clots of blood from his dressing robe when they arrived."

CHAPTER SIXTEEN

I wanted to appear calm before this dreadful news concerning people so well known to my husband, but I must have looked as apprehensive as I felt because Nicolas reached for my hand. He tightened his fingers over mine so hard that I winced. He made the obvious suggestion.

"I take it the Duchesse died in his arms. Have they any clue to the murderer's identity?"

Grégoire said without emphasis, "I believe the police are questioning Monsieur le Duc on the subject at this moment. According to the Sebastiani concierge and madame's maid, the doors were all locked and bolted from the inside."

"Good God!" Nicolas seemed to be considering all the ghastly ramifications. I longed to give him my sympathy, but suddenly, from Grégoire's hints, I began to understand the full impact of this crime.

"Forgive me, monsieur, but His Majesty is being mentioned in the streets in a way little short of treasonous."

I couldn't help interrupting their crucial discussion. "What has the king to do with it?"

Nicolas explained absently, his mind on the problem.

"If Praslin has anything to do with this, His Majesty will

be tainted by his friendship. There have been too many scandals recently, involving the Chamber of Peers. All near the throne."

With a dread that I did not dare to mention, I wondered if Nicolas's earlier trouble was one of those "scandals." I knew that, thanks to Jeremy's testimony and the gossip of the Pembertons, there had been talk about the intervention of King Louis-Philippe, himself, to save Nicolas from prosecution. Tonight there might well be still another case where the most foul murder was suspected.

What had Nicolas said earlier in the evening? The Duchesse de Praslin loved her husband too much.

Too much?

I found a terrible warning in that.

Nicolas apologized to me, but I knew he would have to go to the Hotel Sebastiani and see what might be done, either for the Duc—if he was innocent—or to cut the political ties between Praslin and His Majesty's government if the man should prove to be guilty. Nicolas did not explain in so many words, but I knew why there was so much to be done.

He called in the ancient, stooped concierge with magnificent mustaches left over from his service in the Grand Army. Nicolas ordered rapidly, in French, that all doors and windows be locked and bolted. I understood the conversation very well but pretended to be uninvolved. I thought this would make it easier for him.

The old man looked at me from under shaggy white eyebrows, then asked Nicolas, "Monsieur, you think whoever murdered Madame la Duchesse will try to murder Madame Bertold?"

Nicolas hesitated. I knew from the way he caught himself before a quick no that he believed the Duc was guilty of the Praslin crime.

"There may be trouble of several kinds. The slightest thing can turn that crowd into a mob. And very likely there are thieves in the neighborhood."

The concierge shook his head. "It is not like the Duc, what they say of him. He is not a man of sudden passions. Beaten to death, she was. It is not what one would expect. They do say Her Grace would sell all the nine children to Barbary for one embrace from the Duc. Not maternal, that one."

"Quickly, Old One."

"Yes, monsieur," and he shuffled off.

I had heard everything and wished I had not. Nine children by a man who "had no passion," and apparently the woman's own passion was all for her husband! What of those unwanted children, conceived in such a household?

When Nicolas had taken his greatcoat and hat from Armand and given Grégoire some low-voiced instructions, he kissed me and started out into the street at a fast pace. I watched for a long time through the front windows of the formal dining salon, looking out past the silent, deeply shadowed courtyard to the porte-cochère and the people milling around in the street.

I remembered vividly all the horrors of the Great Revolution, which had occurred before I was born. A smaller repetition of that holocaust in 1830 swept in the present Orléans king. As I considered these events I grew more and more anxious for the safety of my husband. It was true that he did not possess a title, but he was Praslin's friend, a confidant of the king whom the mob now hated, and worst of all, his own past was besmirched by hints and gossip concerning another bloody crime.

Thank God! His imposing form was safely swallowed by the anonymity of the dark street. The scene was only occasionally lighted by lanterns in the hands of running men and boys. These flaring lights illuminated faces that reminded me of fiery painted scenes in Dante's *Inferno*.

Grégoire ignored me, but young Armand came to the window suggesting that I try to get some sleep.

"And when madame awakens, monsieur will be back, safe and sound."

"If I could believe you . . ." I said in my heavily accented French.

"You may, madame. I know monsieur. All the staff agrees that Monsieur Bertold can survive anything. In Algeria once he escaped a Berber trap and saved his men as well. My brother was in his regiment." His eagerness warmed me. Here was one Frenchman who cared about our feelings, I told myself.

"Thank you, Armand. I will hold that firmly in mind."

Nicolas did not return until sometime after dawn. I had gone to the bedchamber he showed me the previous evening but found it impossible to sleep. I made ready, and then, in the elaborate dressing robe sent to me by William and Yolande, I paced the floor, stopped to look out the window at the high hedge enclosing another *hôtel particulier* farther along the street and prayed for my husband's safe return.

I must have made another prayer without expressing it consciously, that Nicolas would always love me as he appeared to love me tonight. I know that I was haunted by the marriage of the Praslins and the monstrous crime that seemed to have been enacted because of those two mismatched and unhappy people.

I heard my husband's brisk, firm tread in the hall, and I ran to the bedroom door to meet him. He had already unbuttoned the coat with its several collars, and his hat was long since discarded. Most overwhelming to me, he seemed tired, tense, and worried. Then he saw me, held out his arms, and I was overjoyed to see how his dark features lightened. We embraced.

"My poor darling," he said, not once but several times, "left alone on what is practically your wedding night. I'm so sorry. Forgive me?"

"How silly you are! There is nothing to forgive. You were needed. But I did miss you so." I squeezed his substantial frame, and he pretended to be crushed. Then we walked arm in arm across the room. He looked at my hair and kissed my head, somewhere near my right ear.

"Always wear your hair like that, hanging down your back and around your face, like streaks of golden honey."

I treasured the compliment but smiled to myself at the naïveté of men. I could imagine his surprise if we gave a ball and I arrived to greet our guests with my hair hanging down my back like a hoyden.

"Can you tell me anything about what you did last night?" I asked as he dropped into the heavy leather wing chair and pulled me onto his lap.

He considered the matter while caressing my hair.

"The Sûreté Nationale is represented, and the *juge d'instruction*. I know a little about that," he added, and pretended to make a mustache from a strand of my hair. I knew he was not being flippant about an intimate tragedy. He merely tried to put the murder in a separate compartment from his life with me. Or perhaps he hoped that sexual byplay would blur painful memories.

I ventured slowly, "How you must have hated those who put you through all that humiliation and pain!"

"Hate?" He thought that over. "How can you hate a child of your own family who merely tells what he saw? And the Pembertons and even the St. Audens reported what they had observed. Not that I hold any brief for that Pemberton fool. William and I were forever quarreling, however. Pigheaded, autocratic, opinionated, impossible fellow that he was!"

"Exactly like someone else I know."

He grinned with some reluctance. "I confess there is a slight resemblance. And one great difference."

"What is that?"

"I was always right, of course."

I laughed at that, even as I felt a painful prick of memory, seeing William in his positive moods, ready to override anyone else's opinion or position. But there was William also, so easily handled when you let him think he'd gotten his way, and you pursued your own way until he came to believe it was his. Dear William! Not murdered but still suffering that hideous death. . . .

I closed my eyes and Nicolas, misunderstanding, kissed my eyelids.

"What a way to begin your life as chatelaine of the Bertold Estates! You need rest. I have a busy day planned for you. Come to bed."

"To rest?" I murmured. "When I have waited up all night for you? I can clearly see it. The first fine rapture of our marriage is over. You've tired of me."

He got up, almost spilling me, and gave me a swat across the back of my anatomy as he strode after me toward the bed.

How good it was to love him and be loved, to be lost in this brief happiness without thinking of the moment when he might decide, like the Duc de Praslin, "She loves me too much!" There were more ways to destroy a fading marriage than to beat a woman to death. But how long would he love me? And what could ever make me turn against him? Nothing, of course.

Late in the day we drove around the city, and Nicolas surprised me by pointing out an alley here, a cul-de-sac there, and an impasse somewhere else, all the haunts of the medieval poet, Francois Villon. He even recited certain lines whose beauty eluded me in the original French, but when he reminded me in English of the best-known rhymes, I found an unexpected poignance in the familiar *l'envoi:*

> The young and yare,
> the fond and fair,
> where are the snows of yesteryare?

"It makes life so sad, so quickly over," I complained.

"It means that we must enjoy ourselves while we may."

True. I must always remember that.

I shook off the somber mood, looking out to express my appreciation of the great, gray towers of Notre Dame. It was difficult to get a true perspective on the cathedral because of the picturesque, appalling slums that huddled at its base. I could find no streets here in the heart of the Seine, only alleys that began between houses tumbling together overhead and ended in some horrid cellar where, according to Nicolas, a dozen people might live.

"All this must change," he pointed out. "But there is such damnable graft in the government. And it isn't among His Majesty's priorities. 'Keep things as they are. Do not rock the boat,' seems to be his motto. It has served for seventeen years, but something will have to be done. The entire city must change." He grimaced. "Especially now, with this latest cancer eating at the royal vitals."

"Heavens!" I approached the subject uneasily. "Is it certain that the Duc murdered his wife?"

Nicolas hesitated, then said, "He hasn't confessed. Poor Fanny! What a fool she was! Of course, it was a marriage of convenience. Her money and his title." He hugged me suddenly. "Well, we can never say that was our reason, can we, sweetheart?"

After the horrible implications of the Praslin story, I told myself that our own marriage looked much more companionable and secure. How good it was to be alive on this August day in 1847 with our lives before us!

The old coachman drove us across the Seine to the Left Bank, and again we found ourselves in winding, twisting little streets that looked exactly as they had in the thirteenth century: dank, ominously dark even at midday, but atmospheric in the extreme. I thought it might be exciting sometime to walk those ancient streets, though not until I knew Paris a good deal better.

We came back by the Tuileries Palace, which shut off one end of the overpowering bulk of the Louvre Palace and museum. I craned my neck to look out at the Parisians sauntering through the geometric formality of the Tuileries Gardens and was pleased when Nicolas, looking out over my shoulder, gave orders to stop the carriage.

"We are going to walk home, Franz. Let the steps down." And to me, "There is someone you must meet."

The old guardsman stood smoothing his white mustache as he watched me descend with my skirts billowing out in the afternoon breeze. I rather hoped we might encounter one of the celebrities said to be gracing Paris these days. I would love to have met that jovial mulatto giant, Alexandre Dumas, whose swashbuckling tales delighted both Jeremy and me, or the great playwright, Victor Hugo, but most of all, what a thrill to encounter the delicate Polish pianist, Frédèric Chopin and his mistress, George Sand! Perhaps I was about to meet one of them, or any of a dozen other geniuses, now thronging the salons of Paris!

We walked up a step and then down a step or two into the garden where I raised the violet silk parasol that matched my gown, and I strolled along beside my husband, feeling very *Parisienne*. Ahead of us in the path a stoutish, elderly gentleman was watching five children chase fallen leaves and stamp on them. The stamp and "crackle" were audible to us and made me think of a similar game played in autumn by my brother and Richard and me.

The old gentleman carried a cane that he plunged absently into dried yellow leaves as they fell. Though he watched the children, he listened, more or less with one ear, to a pair of somber-faced gentlemen all in black with old-fashioned black cravats and their frock coats buttoned up tight to their throats.

None of these men looked like any of the distinguished artists I hoped to meet, but who knew? The gentleman in their midst might be the celebrated writer Honoré Balzac. "De Balzac, as he styles himself," according to Lady Willoughby. In Paris there were so many distinguished men. He might be any of them.

As we reached the homely man with the cane I thought

his face looked familiar, with that amiable smile from a stubborn mouth and eyes that were cautious, watchful. Suddenly I understood. I saw two ladies pass by, resplendent in luxuriant taffetas, their Italian straw hats adorned by late roses. Both ladies paused a second or two near the three gentlemen, curtsied in a perfunctory way, and swept on over the gravel path.

Nicolas glanced at me and nodded. I could scarcely believe it. As often as I had been in London, I never saw Queen Victoria pausing in the public gardens to exchange the time of day with her subjects, yet this plain fellow in civilian dress must be the King of the French, as they called him.

His celebrated bonhomie and his democratic gestures spoiled my illusions of how sovereigns should appear, but for Nicolas's sake I reacted with a fine pretense of awe and pleasure. After all, one could not expect to meet a real celebrity every day, even in Paris; so this king would have to do.

I should not have been surprised that His Majesty saw and greeted Nicolas even before Nicolas could bow respectfully.

"My dear fellow," he said to Nicolas with the enthusiasm of a fellow freemason, "this must be the lovely *Anglaise* we have heard so much about. And what a happy change she will be for that grim old château of yours!"

While Nicolas presented me I made my curtsy, undoubtedly flushing an unbecoming red at the compliment, which I understood without effort. When I arose, it was with the help of the king's own extended hand. He went on to say in very good English that he hoped I would learn to love Paris as he loved London, "A fine old city, to be sure."

To call London "old" after residing in Paris seemed amusing to me, but I agreed that I found Paris fascinating. I was relieved and touched that he should be thoughtful enough to address me in my own tongue. It reminded me of Prince Louis-Napoleon Bonaparte, whom I had met in London. Doubtless the prince was waiting, as this Orléans king had done, for the moment when the volatile French would call him to the throne, or the Republic, whichever proved to be the most practical seat of power.

There was no denying, however, that the king's friendliness appealed to me. I found myself hoping that he would get out of his present political difficulties with throne intact.

One of the gentlemen who had been deep in conference with the king when we first saw them now took over the conversation with me and began in accented English to ask my opinion of the people I had encountered, the servants at the Château Bertold, and those I had seen near the house and gardens.

I was puzzled by his interest in a stranger's opinion until I realized that His Majesty was speaking confidentially and in French, to my husband. This explained my own sudden popularity with the man who, I decided, was a member of the French national police, the Sûreté. This alarmed and yet intrigued me.

CHAPTER SEVENTEEN

I knew the Sûreté Nationale was considered the finest of its kind in the world, with the most modern equipment and a record of solving crimes that struck terror into the hearts of law-abiding citizens. But I never supposed I should be called to give evidence, even unofficially.

I explained that the servants seemed to know only what the gossip in the street told them.

"No possibility that there could have been movements from the Bertold Gardens to the Sebastiani Gardens in the evening by bandits? Thieves?"

"I would hardly know, monsieur. I was only in the gardens briefly with my husband. He pointed out various flowers and plants. The herbaceous border."

"You heard nothing?"

"Possibly mice rustling in the grass, and the screech of some night bird."

"Screech?"

I felt tension in the breezy air of the gardens. "Yes. Something like a peacock or a parrot. Several screeches." As I said it, I felt sickened by a thought. Surely we had not heard the unfortunate woman's death cries!

The inspector asked me what time we had heard this, but I could not say. I had no idea. The whole subject conjured up dreadful pictures that became more and more vivid when I caught snatches of Nicolas's conversation in French with the king.

". . . very little doubt, sir. He seems to have done it."

The king's next question was spoken so low, I did not understand it, but I heard my husband's answer.

"Yes. Bludgeoned to death. With several weapons. Her Grace was a large woman. The struggle must have lasted some time. The greatest fear now is of suicide. The public will demand the guillotine for him. If he is permitted to commit suicide and escapes the guillotine, they will blame—"

"Yes. Yes. They will lay the blame at my door. It is always so." The king sighed. "A pity. The Praslins are loyal friends to the throne. But so is the Maréchal Sébastiani. These Corsicans, you know. I'm afraid Praslin must suffer. I see no way out."

"The Duchesse suffered as well, sir. I am told the police had never seen so much blood."

I shuddered. The king responded in a noncommittal way, and my inquisitor, guessing that he had lost my attention, repeated his own question loudly.

"What is your opinion of the character of the Duchesse de Praslin, Madame? What have you heard of the relations between His Grace and the Duchesse? Motives. It is what we wish to ascertain."

They were asking me to betray remarks made to me in confidence by my husband. Nicolas would tell them what they must know. I said coldly, "I am not acquainted with the family. I have never met them, and I know nothing of either the Duke or the Duchess."

I was relieved when this royal audience ended. The king very kindly waved away the importance of my deep curtsy, but I was sure that if I hadn't shown him the respect his position deserved, I would be despised as a gauche Englishwoman.

Nicolas and I crossed the Rue de Rivoli, quite a wide street in the narrow, centralized environs of Paris. We sauntered past shop after shop of "feminine caprices," as one shop called all those luxury items: the gloves, mittens, the lace, the fragile undergarments, the ribbons and shawls, the jewelry. Nicolas showed a delicious absurdity in front of these shops. He insisted that I would be practically nude without all these additions to my wardrobe.

Being of a practical mind, I couldn't permit him to weigh me down with trinkets, valuable or otherwise, which would serve no purpose. On the other hand, I was determined that my wardrobe should not be outdone by that of his beautiful first love, the present Vicomtesse de St. Auden. I suggested that I should have several gowns made instead, two for evenings and one dress and mantelet or a pélerine for outdoor wear.

"A dozen. For any purpose." He seemed delighted.

I realized that he wanted to think of light, shallow matters, the more frivolous the better. They would take his mind off his friend and the horror of the guillotine yet to come.

By the time we had visited two dressmakers and returned home to the Bertold town house, my head was whirling with memories of crêpes, watered silks, satin and muslins, gauze overskirts and shawls, a length of maroon wool for an afternoon dress, a remarkable green-gold velvet whose style would reveal far too much of my bosom, and an assortment of linen and lace underthings, including flesh-colored hosiery and stiffened petticoats.

I regret to say that I was so excited by all these unexpected riches, I forgot that personal tragedy was close by and that a greater tragedy might be brewing in the streets of Paris.

During the next few hours the gloomy atmosphere in the great houses of the Faubourg was made more noticeable by the constant visits of the police, the highly dignified representatives of the Court of Peers, the Sûreté, and various witnesses. That evening a flurry of excitement warned me even before Nicolas told me, "He may be dying, they say. I should imagine he got hold of some arsenic and has taken it."

I remembered the exchange between the king and Nicolas, in which they discussed the political danger of permitting Praslin's suicide. At the same time I could see that Nicolas was relieved to know that his friend would not face the guillotine. Though he would not tell me the whole of it, I began to suspect that the Duchesse had been murdered for many reasons, some having to do with her treatment of the nine children. I did not understand, and Nicolas seemed to feel that it was not a subject for discussion, but I made no further judgments after that.

In the circumstances it was awkward that the Bertold town house soon became the rendezvous for half the scandal-mongering aristocrats who still found themselves in the city at the end of August. I guessed at once why we were so popular and could only be relieved at the rapidity with which my new wardrobe was fitted, put together, and delivered in time for me to stand with my husband, welcoming two by two, a score of cool, arrogant strangers at one time.

On the first such occasion Nicolas surveyed me in that new golden velvet with its fanciful greenish sheen and stylish décolleté. He announced, "What you need is the final touch. Close your eyes." I did so, expecting a pretty brooch or even earrings to match the far too ostentatious wedding and betrothal rings he had purchased for me on our second day of Paris shopping.

When I felt the chill, heavy weight around my throat, I groaned inwardly, wishing that he had not been quite so obvious in his taste. I could well imagine all his titled friends saying that I had married him for just such jewels.

"May I look?"

"Not yet." He was fastening drop earrings around the lobes

of my ears, the touch of his knuckles bringing a sudden flush of pleasure to my cheeks. He tried to rearrange the loops of my hair he had displaced. Then he nudged me over the black-and-white mosaic squares in the floor until he stopped me suddenly, and my heavy skirts with their four petticoats and stiffened French crinoline swayed against him.

Standing behind me with his hands on my shoulders, he ordered me to open my eyes.

What I saw took my breath away. The heavy topaz necklace that had worried me so much glowed with a deep, golden warmth that no diamonds could match. The topaz earrings were a perfect accompaniment. The stones in the necklace might be too large, but I felt like a queen when I wore them. I said so. He kissed my bare neck, further upsetting the heavy gold-threaded net in which my hair was confined, a matter I did not take too seriously.

"Not a queen," he told me. "There are scores of queens." He considered my reflection. "Scores of empresses, when it comes to that. My darling, you are the only one of your kind."

I kissed one of his hands, and we both stood there before the long, beveled mirror admiring ourselves as a couple.

"The stones are the color of your eyes," Nicolas decided, more poetically than accurately.

I felt his excitement, which equaled my own, but before we could proceed from such a promising beginning, our first guests were announced by an imperious Grégoire. Far more imperious than his employers, I thought.

Among our first score of visitors I had been told that seventeen understood English, but there was no English spoken to me. This seemed reasonable, but I did become annoyed when so many of them pretended that they could not understand my French.

They were mistaken if they imagined I did not understand them. Between a duchesse and a baronne, I received what was probably the most dubious compliment of the evening. First they pretended to show me the beauties of our grand salon as we strolled between all those brown-flecked marble pillars, which, as every female reminded me, had seen the grandeur of the Bourbons and the glory of Napoleon.

In spite of their intentions, I found that I did not feel my inferiority, because the mirrors of the salon told me, when we passed them, that for once I looked quite the equal of these aristocrats. I felt as imperious as Grégoire. Far more important, I knew that I was loved by one man with a passion they could only dream of. I had but to glance across the formal green dining salon with its gold-cloth wallpaper and see Nicolas looking over at me with that glow in his eyes while he pretended to discuss politics with his friends.

I had never seen so much food as that displayed along the splendid side tables and down the center of the room as well. There were so many towering artistic creations, most of them chilly by now, with mounted piles of cream whipped up, plus pâtés and pastries and tarts, even broths and potages, that I could not see the beautiful Louis Quinze tables beneath. I was much too nervous inwardly to eat much, and I feared to drink very many glasses of champagne, which was not a beverage in daily use at home.

Then the elegant Duchesse du Chevreuil et La Roche and her stout little appendage, the Baronne de Vaubraye, turned to accept fresh glasses of champagne, and I moved away, hoping to do my duty by other guests.

"These English," the Duchesse remarked in French, to which the Baronne murmured, rolling her round little eyes, "Always they are so tiresomely regal. Is it certain that she is not of their aristocracy? One would never believe she is a common farmer's daughter."

I did not trouble to conceal my smile.

I regret to say that when I told Nicolas about the absurd compliment, his reaction in our bedroom disappointed me. It also hurt my feelings.

He said, "It was your first attempt, sweetheart. You must

not let them shame you into behaving unlike yourself. If it's any comfort to you, several of the males, including a maréchal and a count, told me I was the luckiest dog in the world to have won such a lovely creature."

I had removed my beautiful topaz set and unfastened my hair. I waved the supercilious Bertold ladies' maid out of the room and then looked at what I saw in the dainty dressing-table mirror, my face framed in a cloud of untidy, disheveled hair.

"But you think I was not myself."

"Whatever self it is, I love all of it."

I said abruptly, "Why do they think you married me?"

He chucked me under the chin with a forefinger bent. "I married you for your riches, your farmland, naturally. They know that you are an heiress."

I laughed, but I was not amused.

The next night was informal, which meant long, tight, brocaded maroon sleeves instead of bared arms and far less food on the long sideboards. In fact, we went nowhere near the formal dining salon. But though I asked the stout, heavy-jawed male cook what was to be served, I knew less than anyone how these foods differed from the fantastic offerings of the previous night. I did learn one thing. In his nicest way, the footman, Armand, reminded me that the cooks in the Bertold employ were called "chefs."

This night I was only slightly luckier in my conduct. I found myself referred to, not as "too regal" but as "so commonplace. One would think we were old comrades in arms . . . Still, one can see, she is trying."

Odious thought!

The comment about my commonplace qualities issued from an acid little female whose antecedents had followed the Bertolds on the abortive Third Crusade. A Crusade in which my own yeoman ancestors fought for the True Cross while her ancestors wrangled over international profits.

Nevertheless, all of this became insignificant when a

gentleman wearing the tiny red ribbon of the Legion of Honor in his lapel arrived late while we were all enjoying a string quartet in the richly decorated music room. After being presented to me, he went to Nicolas at once, and they spoke in low tones. I tried to keep everyone's mind on the music and away from what was obviously an important national problem. I dared not look toward my husband, because if I had, everyone else would have done the same.

The two men left the room quietly, and half an hour later, when the concert ended, the empty champagne glasses were set down in every conceivable place, and our guests began to depart while the two footmen retrieved the glasses.

It was then we learned that our neighbor, the Duc de Praslin, had died a suicide in the prison quarter of the Luxembourg Palace. The news was not surprising, though everyone speculated on why His Grace had not been prevented from taking the arsenic. Evidently the most gruesome methods were taken to make him disgorge the poison, but now, at last, many women thought, the wretched scandal was at an end.

From what I had heard Nicolas say, and from the king's concern, I knew that for France the trouble had only begun. Already the press clamored to know how "the murderer" had gotten hold of the arsenic.

"One law for the peers and another for the people," they charged, and all laid the blame with the complaisant king, whose murderous friends appeared to be above the law.

I was haunted by that charge. The press came perilously close to naming Nicolas Bertold in their indictment. I was sure it had occurred to Nicolas that he, himself, might have gone to the guillotine but for the intervention of His Majesty. The thought was terrible to me.

I was somewhat relieved when I received a letter from Nanny Pemberton and I could concentrate on a subject that had troubled me since the day I left Daviot House on what was virtually a flight from scandal.

Nanny wanted me to know that I was forgiven by my neighbors, who seemed to feel that "the Frenchman" had some sinister hold over me, "which I was in haste to deny," she assured me.

She told me that she and Jeremy were anxious to join "Monsieur and Madame Bertold" at the château whenever it was thought suitable.

> Jeremy is persuaded that with you at the château all will go well and his health will improve. You know I do not approve of his taking laudanum to sleep after his breathing problems, but he claims that he was healthier at "his château," and I do not know what to think. Perhaps Monsieur Bertold does know best and the child should take the wretched stuff. I do not like to make a judgment on such a matter.
>
> Jeremy longs to see the changes you will make, the comforts you will install in that old pile of stones. His reading, you will note, is enormously improved, which is due in no small part to his anxiety to understand your communications. Upon occasion, your writing, if you will pardon my saying so, runs together in your excitement and exuberance, but I have explained all this to my poor lamb, who is as well as we may expect in the circumstances.
>
> He agrees that you must be enjoying yourself prodigiously. He knows, for I have carefully assured him, that your concern for him will return when the wedding journey is over and that your infatuation with his uncle does not diminish your affection for him.

I felt that there was a sting in our good Nanny's reassurance, a hint that I was not carrying out my obligations to my nephew, and only by inviting him to join us at Château Bertold would I satisfy the conventions Nanny expected, as well as my own conscience.

Still, I was very glad to receive the letter. It was also my excuse for bringing up the subject of moving down to the château.

Luckily I had surprising cooperation from the king, himself. When I broached the subject of going on to the château, Nicolas was pleased but reluctant.

"Things are uncertain in Paris now. You heard that yelling and screaming in the street last night. This discontent may spread to the provinces. It seems like the cowardly way if I desert now. Praslin died so recently, and they are blaming His Majesty. It is an awkward time to abandon ship."

"Good heavens! The king didn't give him the arsenic."

All the same, I understood how the public would believe that royalty was thwarting justice. Then the king, himself, suggested that Nicolas leave Paris. Nicolas pretended that this was out of consideration:

"He says I have been away from home too long. He needs my influence at Bertold."

Another explanation was plain to me, but I did not express it aloud: He wants you out of Paris. Your presence here reminds the people of how he interfered in your own detention.

I never let him guess that I had heard many cries against "the murderer Bertold!" Last night at the wrought-iron gates before the porte-cochère of this house.

I ventured, "What do you think of Nanny's letter? Shall we invite Jeremy to join us at the château?"

He grinned ruefully. "It must be done sooner or later, I suppose. It may as well be soon."

"I know you don't like him, darling, but it seems from this letter that he may be softening a bit. Try and remember, he is only a child."

He studied the letter in his hand. He was not as cheerful or optimistic as I had hoped.

"That may be, but there are times when I think he is the nemesis of my life."

It wasn't the answer I had hoped for.

CHAPTER EIGHTEEN

No shadows marred our life together on the ride to the château until we reached the Loire and Indre region, within a day of the château. Nicolas had thought I would enjoy the rough coach trip better if we retained the same Bertold four-horse team and, of course, our Old Guard hero as coachman. I did refuse to take the Paris ladies' maid Nicolas had assigned to me from the staff at the Paris house, which meant that for a brief time I was treated with considerable disdain by the innkeepers and hotel concierges when we stopped each night. However, in his imposing way, Nicolas soon managed to straighten out such matters.

Then we pulled into the coach yard of a fourteenth-century inn, complete with ivy-covered timber walls leaning over the street and unwashed casement windows. Nicolas laughed at my enchantment over living in the fourteenth century, but he was more than pleased.

"If you find this place charming, you will love the château," he promised me.

I found the taproom an historic curiosity as we passed it. Two of the patrons smoking pipes and sipping a dark liquid, perhaps cognac, looked up indifferently, then recognized

Nicolas and put their heads together, gossiping in their low-pitched local patois. A burly man suddenly coming out into the passage stopped in our way, scowled at Nicolas, and then put his fingers to his cap in respectful recognition, but I was shocked when we passed him and I heard his remark to the landlord in French.

"It is the assassin."

I felt the muscles of Nicolas's arm tighten as he hooked my own arm in his and we went up the rickety old stairs. I pretended not to understand the man's French. After a slight movement of his head, as if to gauge my reaction, Nicolas ignored it too.

Our bedchamber, "the best in the house," according to the innkeeper, was just under the steep, sloping roof. In fully half the room near the little casement window, Nicolas was unable to stand up straight. He shook his head at me when I laughed.

"Madame, you are clearly a sadist."

This traveling in the company of a man I adored was such a new experience to me that I treasured every moment. I was also completely unused to having anyone consult my wishes and preferences. I found myself even more in love with my husband. He must be used to going his way, consulting only his wishes. I said so on one or two occasions, but he only hugged me or pinched my ear and told me not to talk rubbish. Sometimes I did think it strange that he and Jeremy hadn't gotten on well, since he could be so considerate and often showed surprising knowledge of matters that one would imagine were far outside his range.

On this day of our arrival at the little Loire town he unlatched and threw open the casement window, looked out for a minute or two, then called to me. I was brushing the travel dust out of my new maroon mantle. I came over to the window caressing the thin edge of sable fur on the collar, curious to see what had attracted him. Two boys about Jeremy's age were tossing a ball to each other. They were sturdy young fellows. I almost grudged them their health.

I said so aloud. Nicolas agreed, adding in a voice that surprised me by its hint of wistfulness, "Yolande liked to see the boy playing ball with me."

"But I thought—" What had I thought, that Jeremy was born hating his uncle?

He caught the implication, and all the regret vanished in a cynical shrug. "You thought he loathed me. I hope you don't think it was mutual. The Monster Bertold, some have called me."

"Never! What a thing to say! As if I would ever call you a monster." Was it possible that I had once thought such a thing? To salve my conscience I asked him, "Why couldn't you play ball with Jeremy? Or go for walks with him?"

"God knows. Pierre St. Auden used to say it was a matter of jealousy only. William always resented seeing us together." He hesitated, then went on, after a glance at me, "I think your brother was used to being the center of attention. Wasn't that the case?"

I remembered all too well how true that had been. I agreed.

He drummed on the window frame. "And there was Yolande. My sister and I were always good friends. Actually, I was her confidant, I suppose. William disliked that." He stopped drumming and added reflectively, "I can appreciate the situation. I'm sure I would have felt exactly as he did if you were my wife and your brother was always underfoot. When this ghastly business occurred, I remembered that the only one who had foreseen the seriousness of the trouble was Pierre St. Auden."

Whenever he mentioned the St. Audens, I thought of the enchanting Gabrielle.

"And did your Gaby share her husband's omniscience?"

He found this amusing. He disarmed me by a kiss and the perfectly true accusation, "You are jealous, my love?"

"Not at all. I simply don't see how your neighbors, on an

estate half a day or more away from Bertold, should know so much about my brother's mind. Not to mention yours."

"I hope you won't let that interfere with your friendship. I promise you that they can be very helpful."

All too helpful. I was rapidly learning to dislike his helpful friends. There seemed to be more of William's qualities in me than our common blood. I had best take care when I reached the château, I told myself. It was a sour joke, but I closed my eyes suddenly. I had a flashing image of my poor William struggling to free himself and his wife from the interior of that carriage beneath the waters of the moat stream. I imagined his agony, the last desperate breath that cost him his life....

Nicolas felt the panic sweep through my body. He pulled me to him.

"Sweetheart, are you afraid you won't fit into the life here? Because you will be superb, exactly what we need. So direct, so honest and straightforward. They will all love you."

"They didn't love William, and he was honest and direct."

"But he didn't have your charm or that piquant sweetness of yours."

This brought a laugh. No one in my life had ever called me piquant or sweet. A few other compliments. I was not without admirers. But—sweet?

I broached the subject of the château itself, shortly afterward. I wanted to be prepared. I knew the general aspect of the château and its surroundings from William's letters. These facts I mentally combined with Jeremy's stories and, later, those of Nanny and Richard, but these bits and pieces did not make me feel that I was approaching my new home. I explained to Nicolas, "It's as though I were on my way to a national monument. Like a visit to Notre Dame or the Tuileries Palace."

His smile told me that my view of the château was far from accurate. He described the place briefly while we went down to the coffee room for our late-afternoon dinner.

"Very old, darling. More or less up and down. Four towers."

"Pepper pots, William called them. Surrounded by the moat. I know." I wanted to move off the subject of the moat. "I mean, the furnishings. How many rooms are there?"

He was puzzled. "I don't think they've ever been counted. So many have been cut up into servants' quarters. Or enlarged for use as guardrooms."

"Guardrooms?"

"For the Bertold troops, the soldiers who kept the peace in the area. Don't worry. We no longer need them."

We had reached the ground floor and the delicious smell of roasts, savory stews, and aromatic herbs. These were promising, but I did not like the manner of the local diners who kept staring at us, especially my husband, and then putting their heads together to gossip.

They were rough-country types, exactly the sort I had grown up with, and I would have felt at home with them, except for their manner toward Nicolas, which was respectful but wary. One man and woman whispered about him in a most hostile way. I could well imagine the woman seated beneath the guillotine watching heads roll, as I have heard they did during what they call their Great Revolution.

I was very much prejudiced against them at the outset. I didn't like to remember that I had once shared their suspicions. What weighty evidence had changed me? Why was I now so sure of his innocence? In my heart I accepted the answer: because I knew him so much better than anyone else in the world knew him. And after all, the French courts had not found enough evidence to hold him. Why should I be more severe?

All these thoughts passed through my head while we were being seated at a table in the bright, modern coffee room, and both of us ordered "what smelled so good," as I put it. This turned out to be a beef stew of sorts and the most delicious I have ever eaten. I remember looking across the worn, patched, and wine-stained tablecloth, bringing my glass of a dry, dark Chinon wine to meet his, and toasting our happiness a little defiantly, very much aware that the pair at the table by the window were watching us in a furtive way.

It would be absurd to say that I felt any fear of my husband at such a moment, but I was aware of a certain pride in the fact that I alone thought him innocent.

Did I say "thought"? How stupid of me! I knew him to be innocent, and I was his only real friend.

Then I looked up and saw an elegant, very aristocratic pair enter the room. The gentleman was tall, slender, noticeably handsome, about thirty-five, perhaps, with a light, teasing manner that made him easy to like. The lady was brunette, generously curved, beautiful in a voluptuous way, wearing a riding habit whose stock was in disarray as was her hat, which had settled back on the net that held her heavy black hair. Plainly she had no interest in appearances. She was laughing at something her husband had said.

They both saw Nicolas at the same time and had been warned of his presence. They came across the room to our table, the lady saying in her loud, not unmusical voice, "There you are, Nico. We saw your old coachman. He is dining on game birds, if you please, so we sent my groom to join him. May we be rude and join you?"

"*Chérie,*" her husband said while he eyed me in a flattering way, "you were born rude. We would hardly know you any other way. And this is your lovely bride, Nicolas, old man? Well, then, let me say you are shot with luck."

"Pierre, in heaven's name do not begin your flirtation beneath my very nose," his wife begged. "At least wait until I have turned my back. Nico, how did you capture the *Anglaise*? I can imagine how furious her brother would have been. Don't tell me it was all to avenge yourself on poor William."

A haughty glaze began to creep over my own manners, and Nicolas saw it. He clasped my hand, smiling as though such jokes were common to him.

"Ignore Gaby's crudeness, darling. She is no lady."

"Never was," the Vicomtesse de St. Auden agreed complacently. She had great self-confidence. She sat down at the table without even glancing back, to be certain that her husband had pushed the chair forward. The innkeeper, a stout, harassed-looking man with unclipped side whiskers, had also hastened to oblige her but lost the race to the vicomte, whose effortless movements were impressive.

Nicolas explained. He looked happy, unshadowed.

"You must have guessed who these addlepates are, darling. The Vicomte and Vicomtesse de St. Auden. I have known them since time out of mind as Pierre and Gaby. My wife, Alain."

The vicomte had seated himself close to me. He observed with interest, "It is a French name. You have French blood, then? That would explain your *je-ne-sais-quoi*, your—"

"Pierre, you will stop flirting with my wife."

"You were ever a selfish beast, Nicolas."

Luckily I had enough "town bronze," as my mother called it, to know when I must accept a compliment lightly.

I said, "Nicolas, you did not do justice to Monsieur le Vicomte. Not by half."

"Never mind," Nicolas assured me. "He will do that. None better. What are you doing here in this village, giving the natives something better than me to gossip about?"

I bit my lip and could not help looking around in embarrassment. It seemed extraordinary to me that he should joke about the horrible suspicions of these people. I hated the villagers already for daring to voice their feelings.

"Talk of crudeness," the Vicomtesse put in, rolling her splendid green eyes. "You know quite well that we came to protect you from being tarred, feathered, and probably hanged by our good peasantry. My dear Madame Bertold, they are all convinced that our Nicolas deliberately drowned his own sister. Not to mention your brother. I must say, I think it was very broad-minded of you to marry him."

"Gaby," her husband warned, but she went rattling on.

"You have courage. I once had the dubious opportunity to marry him, you know. But I preferred this silly fribble. Probably because I didn't want to be murdered in my bed."

While I reacted to this with shock, Nicolas said dryly, "Which you would have been if you chattered as much as you do now. How do you stand it, Pierre?"

The Vicomte broke off a chunk of my bread and began to chew.

"The secret is to appear to be listening while you let your thoughts roam. At times this proves surprisingly pleasant." He was watching me, smiling.

"What a beast you are!" The Vicomtesse reached across the table and slapped his hand, causing him to drop the bread.

I felt very much out of this camaraderie. I had always been of a serious disposition, with little opportunity to practice what even I could see was a refreshing lightness of conversation or manner. Then, too, they were speaking naturally in French, and sometimes I missed a nuance or turn of phrase.

I envied the Vicomtesse her ease and cleverness, but I did not hate her as I thought I would, and her husband, besides being one of the most personable men I've ever seen, was charming. So long as one did not take him seriously, I reminded myself. I began to wish with all my heart that I could entertain and perhaps dazzle my husband as these two did.

The three of them seemed to have an endless repertoire of subjects to discuss. I felt totally inadequate, a boring appendage in this volatile, talkative group. Nicolas included me frequently. He put an arm around me, explaining every few minutes, "Gaby means . . ."

"Pierre is speaking of . . ."

"Grégoire would tell you that . . ."

They were full of all these tales involving people and events I had never known. For one of the first times since my marriage, I felt desperately homesick.

The interminable dinner ended long after dark, and the St.

Audens suggested that they show me the glories of the countryside by moonlight. The Vicomtesse explained.

"The moon will be up at any minute. The Indre River is the most enchanting waterway in the world for romance. You will be fascinated, I assure you, Alain."

With a forced smile I agreed. I was more formal, more old-fashioned than the Vicomtesse. It always made me flinch when strangers addressed me by my baptismal name.

I blessed Nicolas for preferring my company, even when he insinuated a very private concern. He said, "Another time, Gaby. You forget. I am newly married to this beautiful creature."

The Vicomte reminded his wife, "You are being your insensitive self, *chérie*. You were young and newly wed once, long ago."

She wrinkled her nose at the Vicomte, but she did not succeed in overriding my husband's objections. We said good night. The Vicomtesse added, "Until tomorrow."

It was late in the evening when Nicolas and I parted from the St. Audens in the dark lower passage. Flickers of light came from the huge old taproom fireplace, and I caught a glimpse of the High Road outside the open front door. Across the road the trees and some woodland underbrush reminded me of the copse of beeches up on Ferndene Heath.

Nicolas must have seen me blink and understood at once. "Thinking of home? I promise you, sweetheart, we won't neglect your precious farm."

Arm in arm we strolled along the gloomy passage to the front door. Gabrielle de St. Audens had been right. The scene along this branch of the Indre River was like a painting from a fairy tale, with leaves and branches faintly outlined by the rising moon.

"That tangle of trees and undergrowth," I pointed out. "I wouldn't be surprised if Beauty and the Beast walked out of there at any minute. Or Hansel and Gretel. But where is the Old Witch?"

He grinned. "Beauty and the Beast, hand in hand." We kissed and moved out into the dusty road together. We crossed the road. Nothing was in sight. All traffic had ceased with darkness. The scene around us, however, was beginning to brighten as the moon rose over the trees.

Suddenly it seemed exciting to us to make love out here in the wilderness. Since that would prove impractical, we did the next best thing. We embraced passionately, our bodies pressed hard against each other, in a pulse-pounding excitement that made him whisper with his lips at my ear, "Back to our room?"

"Soon!"

I was still in the throes of our obsession when I heard a faint rustle in the underbrush and drew away from him nervously. I suddenly recalled that night in the gypsy tinkers' wagon. Seconds went by. I realized that Nicolas had swung away from me. My instinct was to call out for Nicolas, but I had sense enough to remain silent.

Then two things happened simultaneously. I heard a snap like the breaking of a twig, and Nicolas pushed me. At least, I supposed it was Nicolas. I stumbled backward, found space beneath my feet, and lost my balance. I heard myself scream as I slipped two or three feet into a little ravine.

It was a ridiculous accident, not even bad enough to crack my head, though I felt badly shaken and I knew my right arm and leg were scratched by broken twigs.

Most of all, I was furious with Nicolas. Whatever the problem or the danger, there must have been an easier way to handle the matter than to push me into a ravine!

CHAPTER NINETEEN

Having picked myself up and discovered that I was virtually unhurt, I called to Nicolas but not with any helpless, feminine plea. I had not been pushed so hard since I was a child and played some fairly rough games with my brother, and I resented this.

I fumbled for the bank of earth above me. I found my hands grasped by Nicolas. I saw his face looking down into mine, but his eyes were unreadable in the darkness. Before I could make another furious remark, he muttered, "Quiet!"

My common sense soon told me that he would not knock me down, except to protect me in some way. I let him lift me out of the shallow ravine created by rains and runoff. He held me to him with my face half smothered against his breast and throat. It did not soothe my feelings or my sorely tried body. I wriggled once to remind him of my presence, but I understood what he was doing.

Someone, whether deliberate or not, had fired at us. This explained the snap, like a stick breaking. He must be afraid now that our assailant was waiting for us somewhere out there in the darkness.

He let me breathe finally. "Whoever it was, he's gone now

or we would have ended it. They are cowards, these righteous little men."

"Thank God they are," I managed, breathing fast. "And may I ask, who are these righteous little men?"

He said nothing until we had crossed the road in the shadow of two cedar trees that sheltered a roadside café. I marveled at the little table with the two rickety chairs piled on top, and all within a hoofbeat of the dusty road.

Our room at the medieval inn was a welcome sight. Nicolas had hurried me up the stairs and thrust me into the room and then seemed ready to leave me there alone. I have always been fully able to defend myself, but after the episode of the gypsy wagon, and now this senseless danger, I felt an unaccustomed fear. These were all unseen, unsuspected calamities. I had not consciously brought them onto myself, and worst of all, these enemies were faceless.

Unless, of course, Demian and his gypsy family were behind everything. That made me smile rather sourly. We were a week's travel from them by this time.

No. The two episodes had nothing in common except a general unpleasantness. There were no other common denominators, were there?

I was ashamed to hear my own voice demand, "Where are you going? Please don't."

He looked back over his shoulder. "I thought I would have Gaby stay with you while Pierre and I look for this ambitious night hunter."

I didn't like that at all. I reached for his arm.

"No. Don't." Then, for some idiotic reason, I reminded him, "The Vicomtesse wanted us to walk out there tonight."

He stared at me and then, as he understood the implication, he frowned. "Good God, Alain! Do you think Gaby was out there, shooting at us in the moonlight? Why, in God's name?"

"I didn't mean that. I don't know what I meant."

He was angry, but inwardly my own resentment was building. When he opened the door, I reminded him firmly, "Anyway, did you find the bullet? The shot? Any signs?"

"You know I didn't."

"Well, then, it was probably all your imagination. You heard a twig snap in the breeze. You panicked and knocked me down."

"I was six years in the army and in a few rather exciting skirmishes. I do know the action of a rifle when I hear it."

He went out.

I heard him knocking on the door at the head of the stairs, but he received no answer. I slipped out in the hall and watched him go downstairs. Evidently the St. Audens were in the taproom enjoying the fire and perhaps a glass of spirits. Curious about them and about whether my husband would join them, I closed the door and went to the front window.

A minute or two later I saw Nicolas's unmistakable figure as he walked out into the road, looking around carefully.

So the St. Audens had not been in the taproom. Where were they?

After our quarrel and his abrupt departure, I was obsessed by a fear that something would happen to him. I pushed the window open a few inches to satisfy myself that I heard no sounds of gunshots. Presently I heard voices under the window. I looked out and saw Nicolas with the St. Audens coming around from the back of the inn yard, all of them talking in the most companionable way. Evidently Nicolas had started out on the road, then circled back some distance from the inn and met his friends.

Night walking seemed to be a curious form of pleasure for these people. In my valley everyone was much too busy for such luxurious squandering of time.

Nicolas returned within a short time. I was feeling angry, put upon, and worried over the mood between us. This had been our first major quarrel, if quarrel it was. On my part, unfortunately, resentment was rising.

When he came in, I asked, "Did you find the man you were looking for?"

"We can sleep easily, sweetheart. Pierre and Gaby saw the fellow running off beyond the riverbank with a pack of hunting dogs after him. They say he was drunk."

"I see. He shoots at strangers, thinking they are beasts of prey, no doubt."

He was patient, though he gave me a doubtful glance as he took off his greatcoat.

"Not quite. He knew who I was, and being drunk, he shot at me."

"We must take care how much your neighbors have to drink if they try to kill you every time they overimbibe."

His patience frayed a little. "You know very well why he shot at me."

I knew, and it was not something I wanted to know. Also, I found it annoying that the St. Audens had managed to talk him back into good spirits again. I resented the source of his good spirits more than the change of mood itself.

I said, "If this would-be murderer has run back home to sober up, I suppose we must be grateful. Of course, I can't help recalling that where I come from, he would have gotten ten years in the hulks. Or at least been transported for trying to kill us." I paused, then remarked too pleasantly, "How lucky that the St. Audens should be wandering around at this hour, watching these night shooters racing along with dogs at their heels! It just shows you the many uses of a moonlight walk at midnight."

I expected him to go into a moody silence, but to my chagrin he burst out laughing.

"Sweetheart, you are jealous. Admit it."

"Jealousy has nothing to do with it." It was doubly annoying to be cajoled out of the sullens by his lovemaking and his obvious strength. He had his hands around my waist, and I tried to pry his fingers away from their hard grip. "Confess," he ordered me, still playful as he switched my body first one way, then the other, between his hands.

"It is merely because I don't trust—" I almost said "Your friends" but changed that to ". . . your enemies, who will very likely shoot you at their first opportunity."

"Let me worry about that. I sent a stable boy to Tours to notify the prefect. The fellow will be charged if the St. Audens identify him. Come. Time for bed. We leave this godforsaken place at an ungodly hour."

"An ungodly hour? I thought your friends preferred midnight."

"Don't argue. Bed it is."

"No. Not yet. I happen to—"

"You happen to love it, as you know very well. Come."

We argued another minute or two, partly because I did not like the appearance of yielding. It was too much like surrender, and no Daviot ever surrendered.

But ultimately he won, as I knew he would.

We made love because our bodies craved that sensuous joy, and every touch, every sensation, was still a matter for wonder between us. I learned new ways of teasing him into still another climax of love with me. Even he, I think, was experimenting with various ways to excite me again. And then again.

But though my flesh and my senses were repeatedly satisfied, a part of my practical, suspicious mind busied itself over the story told by the St. Audens. Only they had seen the man running with a rifle. They might not even be able to identify him. What if the man escaped punishment or if there were others who shared his conviction that Nicolas murdered his sister and brother-in-law?

How they must despise me for marrying the man who, in their eyes, had killed my brother!

I banished that horrible little stab of doubt and twisted my fingers into his heavy, disordered black hair, creating new desires in myself and in him.

In spite of our concern about ungodly hours, we were all up at sunrise, fortifying ourselves with hot brandy for my husband and the St. Audens, and some vile weak tea for myself. Having set the trays aside, Nicolas shaved himself as he often did. I had been relieved by this and the fact that Perpigny, his valet in Paris, did not travel with us.

Perpigny was a slippery little man with a perpetual, subservient grin. He seemed unaware that I existed. I had been friendly, humble, cool, dignified, and simply myself, but nothing could make him acknowledge my presence beyond a respectful nod. I almost preferred the frigid courtesy and contempt registered by Grégoire, the Bertold steward, to being ignored entirely.

In spite of our early rising, however, the St. Audens were delayed until the sun was well above the trees. We all met at the coach, which was drawn up before the inn with the splendid black team fretting a little, anxious to be gone. The St. Audens constantly surprised me by their easy behavior, their tolerance for what often sounded like cutting jokes, and by Gabrielle de St. Auden's curious indifference to her appearance.

Her untidy and only half-confined black hair and her riding habit with the same creased and soiled stock she had worn last night were amusing and as likable as her friendly informality. But she did make me feel overdressed and rather like a country girl meeting an aristocrat who was so confident that she had no need to follow the rules of polite society.

This indeed proved to be true. The Vicomtesse traced her mother's ancestral line back to a supporter of Charlemagne himself.

I was still a trifle suspicious of her intentions toward my husband and me, probably because I couldn't imagine any woman willingly refusing to marry Nicolas. And then, she had been so insistent that we go walking together on that deserted road, near the tree-lined riverbank. To cap it all, she and her husband were the only witnesses who could identify the man with the rifle.

The handsome Vicomte also made matters easy with his charm and light conversation, and I began to look forward to the arrival at the château with a little less apprehension.

Secretly I still found myself wondering how Nicolas could have chosen me as mistress of a house that was virtually a palace, so large that he couldn't guess at the number of its rooms, but I resolved not to let anyone see my uncertainty. If I kept to my resolution, I would soon have the household running as successfully (I hoped) as I had organized Daviot House. It was simply a matter of doubling and tripling the methods I had used for many years.

We had barely set out before I found myself once more troubled by that stray shot last night.

The Vicomte told Nicolas as they sat facing us, "It appears that the rogue we identified was not the fellow who fired at you. We were visited by two men from the prefecture before we had dressed this morning. Our lad was a poacher. He is in their hands now."

"Well, then?" Nicolas asked. I could see that the matter troubled him. He was not quite as easy as he pretended to be.

"A poacher. No more. Has half a dozen witnesses, though, of course, he pretends they strayed off their own ground by merest accident."

I said, "But surely poaching is a serious crime. Won't he go to prison?"

The Vicomtesse laughed off such "barbaric" notions.

"My dear! You English! Five witnesses to say he strayed accidentally? And none placing him near you and Nicolas. I'm afraid it's a fine and freedom."

"Probably just as well. It may all have been an accident. A coincidence." Nicolas reached for my hand and squeezed it.

Naturally the Vicomtesse noticed this and teased us as newlyweds.

"I never thought to see our Nicolas being demonstrative with a woman. Pierre, you must take notice. I shall expect a great deal more attention from this day onward. If not—well, Nico, I must win you back." She pursed her full lips and considered Nicolas. "Let me see. I refused you once, but that was such a long time ago. Shall I begin by reminding you that a lady may change her mind?"

I sat with a fixed smile, noting the woman's beauty, even in her present dishevelment, but Nicolas seemed undisturbed, ironic.

"A *lady,* Gaby? I think you said a *lady* may change her mind."

I must have reacted to this insulting remark. I would have been humiliated and unforgiving if it had been addressed to me, but both Gaby and Nicolas laughed at my shock.

"Sweetheart, I don't tell her something she has not heard before."

Gaby was just as quick. "And one must face the truth. I am no lady. I am all female, eh, my angel?" This was addressed to her husband, who nodded in his amiable way.

"Quite true. And, madame, one must learn to expect the outrageous from these two."

I put the best face I could on this relationship, which was far more intimate than I dared to be with my husband, except in bed. There were so many things I would have to remember, ways in which I must adapt. Perhaps Nicolas found it difficult to adapt his ways and thinking at Daviot House. I hadn't considered that.

I tried to relax. The ride was interesting in many ways. We entered the wooded upcountry soon after we turned off the High Road, and I marveled at the thick, dark growth that bordered our road. The trees were slender and less rugged than those I was used to, but they grew so close-packed that they shut out most of the cloudy light overhead.

I forgot sophistication and cool indifference. More than half the time I was leaning out the lowered window, admiring the primeval scene around us. It was the kind of world with which I could associate, a world of growing things, seasonal changes, rooted in the earth. And alive.

How different from the gray stone monuments that represented the ground and the "trees" of cities like London and Paris.

"Enchanting!" I exclaimed, and then, feeling foolish over my exuberance, I said defensively, "I've spent my life growing things and living somewhat retired. So I read a great deal. When I was young, I devoured fairy tales. And this is certainly a fairy-tale forest."

Nicolas said, "Beauty and the Beast." They looked at him, not quite understanding, and he gestured to his chest. "The Beast."

"No. I never said such a thing, darling, never."

They all found my indignation amusing.

There were breaks in the rolling, wooded landscape, green fields in the distance where herds of milk cows ambled along with the hours of the day until, at dusk, they would arrive back at the barns where they began their odyssey. The big gray, inquisitive geese nearer the road looked far too personable to be killed and eaten.

After we had pulled up before a tiny auberge to water and refresh the team, I discovered that this unprepossessing village of a dozen houses and a little church was Boisville, the château's main contact with civilization. Except for some magnificent flowers, especially roses in profusion, it had little else to recommend it to me. I had heard its name many times in Nanny's letters and in an occasional communications from William, but I supposed it to be at least as large as our Dorset village. It was not.

I could hardly complain, however. For hours I had been admiring the primitive, living beauty of the countryside. In the heart of Boisville, I realized just how isolated the château must be.

From this, the last touch of a community life with which I might have something in common, we moved on into wooded country so heavily forested, I wondered how the ancient Bertolds had ever found space to erect their fabled château. The dusty road climbed, slowly winding its way beneath rows of interlaced trees that cast a green glow upon the carriage horses and the Old Guard coachman.

The sun vanished entirely by the time we were well away from Boisville, and the first drops of rain began to spatter the carriage windows. I tried not to be disappointed. Heaven knows the rain is no stranger to Ferndene Heath!

I did not dare to express any of the pessimism I felt. Nicolas and the St. Audens appeared to find a dozen reasons why rain would be a splendid bit of luck if it came now and not a month later. I was not cruel enough to ask what would happen if it rained both times.

About the hour we began a short journey through carefully tended hillside vineyards, the rain ceased, and the world I saw out of the streaked carriage window seemed to be separated from us by a curtain of gray mist under heavy, lowering skies.

We were once more enclosed by the tightly packed woods, and suddenly I made out a great, dark mass moving among the trees. I pressed my hands against the now closed window excitedly.

"I think I see a bear. Or perhaps a wolf."

Across from me, Nicolas looked out. The Vicomtesse sat up.

"Probably a gypsy bear. Bands of gypsies are given refuge in these woods. Some of them have dancing bears that they exhibit at carnivals."

Nicolas agreed with her, to my discomfort. I felt that I was being mocked when he remarked, "They aren't so popular elsewhere."

"Confess it, Nico. They are your friends, these gypsies," the Vicomte put in. He added to me, "They wander through here heading back toward Spain with their wagons and dogs and trained animals."

I raised my head and looked at Nicolas, but he was not self-conscious over this talk of gypsies.

"Are they ever dangerous?" I asked.

Both the St. Audens laughed, although the Vicomtesse said, "I do not advise walking in the woods with one who drinks heavily. They are human, after all, and they resent some of us who live well."

Shortly after midday we came to a little crossroad shrine with a wooden sign beside it lettered ST. AUDEN, and waiting for the Vicomte and Gabrielle were two splendid horses, a black and a bay, their reins held by a mounted groom.

"Here we are at last, Berto," the Vicomtesse called to her groom. "You did not spend as long in Boisville as we did. . . .Well, my dear"—she turned to me, astonishing me by an embrace during which she touched her cheek to each of mine—"until we meet again. Undoubtedly within the week."

Nicolas would have helped her down the steps, but she dropped to the ground after embracing him quickly and ran across the road to the excitable black stallion. I was so busy marveling at the careless ease with which she swung into the saddle that I was startled when the Vicomte kissed my hand, wished me well, and followed his wife.

Our coachman waited until the St. Auden pair galloped off before he gave the signal and our team pulled away from the crossroad in the opposite direction. I noted that when I looked into the woods now, the needle-covered ground was nearly as dark as it would be at dusk. Even the long, green shadows were swallowed in a gray miasma like a thick moor fog back home.

I must have shivered. Nicolas took the seat vacated by the Vicomtesse and put an arm around me.

"Cold?"

"Heavens, no!" I said brightly. "I was only wishing the sun would come out, so I could see the woods. They look fascinating."

I was puzzled by his somber expression as he remembered past moments in these woods. "But you must take care. It's difficult to find your bearings if you don't know the area well. Jeremy used to plead to go berrying alone. Nanny Pemberton wasn't too fond of that. Said he came back with his clothes stained."

"Did you go with him?"

"On occasion. Until a year or so ago. Then your brother decided that the boy was getting on too well with me. He accused me of trying to win the boy to my side. I believe he thought I would force a seven-year-old child to sign over his half of the estate when Yolande was gone. How he expected me to survive Yolande, who was five years younger, is more than I know."

I knew William was possessive, but this seemed a strange jealousy, even for him. "Did Yolande have nothing to say?"

"Yolande? Well, she enjoyed a certain amount of turmoil. I'm afraid she even began a flirtation with Pierre out of revenge. And God knows they have been like brother and sister since their childhood."

He leaned over me and lowered the window. I heard the note of excitement and pride in his voice.

"We are coming to the château. Look. We swung abruptly out of the woods, you notice. Beyond is the moat bridge. My ancestors dammed the stream at the south end to form a pond. The château faces the northeast shore of the pond. There!"

I looked out. Tendrils of misty fog clawed at my face. Beyond the last thick copse of trees, the darkness of the woods lifted with startling suddenness, making me blink. I saw open sky, clouded and gloomy, but I was overwhelmed by my first glimpse of Château Bertold, its four black-capped towers looming up against that sky, the great gray walls looking for all the world like those of the Paris Conciergerie, that last outpost on the bloody road to the guillotine.

"Remarkable, isn't it?" Nicolas asked with that note of pride and deep affection.

"All of that," was the only comment I could think of.

Before I was ready, I heard the coach's wheels rattle onto the wooden planks of the moat bridge, and I thought of William. It was here that he had died. I looked down. Nanny and Nicolas had been right. Those pond waters were the blackest I ever saw. I kept my gloved hands tightly locked together. I was afraid that Nicolas would see my tension and guess the dread with which I faced the prospect of living here, even a few months a year.

The carriage stopped with a jerk forward and back. The steps were let down. Nicolas leapt out, doubtless thrilled to be home. As he offered me his arm I stepped out. Then, humiliatingly, I caught my heel on the bottom step. But for my husband's hand I would have fallen on one knee. It was a maddening and embarrassing accident.

"Damned steps are slippery," Nicolas said, setting me securely on my feet.

It did not relieve my feelings that several of the household staff had gathered around the carriage steps to greet us, and the steward, Grégoire, had apparently rushed down ahead of us from Paris in order to murmur helpfully at this minute, "Let us not regard it as a bad omen, madame."

I did not need that comment in the least.

CHAPTER TWENTY

The carriage and team maneuvered carefully in the narrow, cobbled space between the moat bridge and the ironbound entry doors, which looked to me as impressive as those of Notre Dame Cathedral. The carriage rattled on around the building in the narrow space between the château and the wall that kept out the waters of the pond and the faintly swaying lily pads that looked to me almost like living creatures with animal sensations. They were everywhere in the deeper waters, some of them now covered by blowing yellow leaves from the willows that ringed the pond. Beyond those willows, however, crowded the woods in which ancient cedars gave an occasional black punctuation mark to the horizon.

I asked Nicolas, "Where does the carriage go? Is there a carriage house here on the pond?"

"At the northwest corner of the ground floor. The northwest tower steps lead down to the carriage house." He waved toward the entry doors, which were ajar.

"Welcome to your new home, Madame Bertold."

Everyone stood aside. No effort was made to present the staff members to me. I decided that this was because Nicolas wanted to spare me as much formality as possible in these first minutes. He must have guessed how very much I wanted to make a good impression. If anything, I suspect I exaggerated my coolly confident manner, but I was determined not to enter like a country peasant, or whatever that wretched woman in Paris had called me.

I sensed also, amid my insecurities, that we were now on a stone island in the middle of a bottomless pond, that there was no way off this ancient prison except by the moat bridge.

No matter how much I wanted to be alone with my husband, in a place where we could feel "at home," Grégoire slipped in before us through the doors, calling my attention to the points of interest within the huge entry hall, which he called "the old guardroom." The great hollow room was large enough to be used as a medieval banquet hall, and I did not doubt that was its original purpose. I imagined without enthusiasm the life of that medieval day when every meal involved the entire fifty or a hundred estate serfs and yeomen, besides the family.

Thick Persian-designed carpets covered the center of the hall, but beneath the windows that were set deep in the outside wall, the floor was bare and cold. It would be a sturdy lover of the outdoors who sat down in one of those high-backed chairs against the walls.

Nicolas reassured me cheerfully, "Don't worry, sweetheart. We don't spend our cozy evenings here."

"Only our cozy dinners," I pointed to the long, baronial table in the center of the hall.

He shook his head and reminded me of the three magnificent chandeliers hanging from the high, blackened beams overhead.

"When we entertain, there is a considerable difference. Every luster around those elephantine candles will shine."

Perhaps, but from my vantage point the lusters badly needed soap and water. I did not say so, however.

I looked around, wondering where the grand staircase could

be. If I judged by the Bertold town house in Paris, this one must be even more splendid.

Then the ubiquitous Grégoire said, "Will madame see the master's apartments next?"

Without waiting for our agreement he strode off to one corner of the Great Hall, behind two marble pillars that looked far older than the glorious, polished pillars in the Paris house. More and more astonished, I was ushered over to a niche on the southwest corner of the building. Obviously the interior of one of the towers was nothing but a series of steps leading upward. I had pictured the towers as forming delightful turret rooms.

I remembered very well that Jeremy had been up in a room above these steps when he saw his uncle and the workmen busy at the moat bridge. It was disappointing that such a Gothic tower should be wasted on a series of chill, stone steps winding upward. I pictured myself, as well as our female guests, trying to make our way down those drafty steps to dinner in bare-shouldered evening gowns with their complicated layers of skirts, and our shoes with high, jeweled heels.

Well, so be it. Luckily Nicolas and I would spend most of the year in England.

I saw him watching me as we climbed the steps round and round upward, and I made a great effort to show my pleasure in his ancestral home. I loved him so much that I didn't want to hurt him by displaying any doubts or criticisms, but my effort was bound to have its awkward moments in spite of my good intentions.

When we reached the first-story landing above the ground floor, I noted that the window in the deep-set embrasure was open an inch or so. If this was true of the windows in the second-story landing and on the turret or attic floor above, it was small wonder that the wind moaned down the length of the tower steps.

I took my hand out of my muff, reaching automatically

to shut and latch the window. Grégoire's rapier-thin, black-clad figure paused above us. He looked back.

"The window does not catch, madame. I believe the latch is broken."

I was about to say the natural thing. "Why in heaven's name hasn't it been repaired?" But fortunately Nicolas said at once, "Have it repaired immediately."

"As you say, monsieur. It would have been repaired months ago if the building had been occupied. But with only the servants here to work for the boy and his nurse-governess, these things go unnoticed."

"See that they are noticed," Nicolas said in the voice of command like the lash of a whip. I remembered it painfully well from our first meeting.

I wished I had not been a third party to this. I felt all the discomfort of an eavesdropper. I would far rather have mentioned it quietly, perhaps between Grégoire and me. Then I saw Grégoire's pale eyes as his gaze shifted my way. No. I could not anticipate a pleasant mistress-to-servant discussion between the steward and me.

We moved on up to the next story and out of the tower steps into a narrow corridor whose time-darkened wooden beams overhead made the place look rather like a dungeon. I was thus prepared for the same ghastly dungeon look of the master's bedchamber.

It was not quite a dungeon. I found it to be a large room with considerable light from two windows. Fortunately they were not set deep in damp, drafty embrasures. The furnishings were even more masculine than in his bedroom at the Paris house, but less attractive and certainly less warm. A big, snapping fire in the grate of that enormous fireplace would be an improvement. The carpet was worn and frayed. I was surprised to see several shelves of books against a side wall, almost within reach of the big four-poster bed with its elegant but faded crimson canopy and curtains. This gave the room a more personal look.

I glanced at my husband, read that slight unsureness in his manner, a quality so alien to his normal behavior that I realized I had never loved him so much as I loved him at this moment. I reached around his waist, hugging him with enthusiasm.

"It will be wonderful, our own small haven, where we can be ourselves."

"Small?" His arm crossed over mine as he looked around the room. "I've thought it was a great many things but not small. Grégoire, this place needs airing." He ran his free hand over a bedpost. "And dusting. Where is that housekeeper, Madame . . . Simeon? Sevres? The one who drank." He broke off to assure me, "Only when she wasn't otherwise occupied, of course."

I laughed, hoping for the best.

The steward, however, gave a negative with every appearance of satisfaction.

"Madame Servier died some months ago. A misstep on a cloudy night. As you observed, monsieur, she drank. I was of the impression that I mentioned the matter to you while you were . . . detained."

I had no interest in the dead housekeeper-who-drank. She was not the first person who drank, whether servant or employer. But I knew that the sudden mention of his recent inquisition must have caused Nicolas to relive those terrible weeks. He stiffened and then became the brusque man I first knew.

"Very likely you did. A pity I was otherwise occupied. Well, sweetheart, it looks as though your first task as chatelaine of Bertold will be to choose a new housekeeper. You might consult with Grégoire. Meanwhile," he said, ordering the steward, "have a couple of the maids set to work. I want this room habitable before bedtime."

With respect, Grégoire inclined his head. "Your pardon, monsieur. I took the liberty of employing a female to act as your housekeeper until you see fit to make other arrangements. She had no fear of working here after La Servier died."

"Good. Send up my valet. And one of the maids to oblige Madame Bertold until she can choose her own." Nicolas removed his greatcoat. He threw it across the bed. "Who is the new housekeeper?"

He did not ask what was certainly in my mind: why should a housekeeper fear working here just because Madame Servier died here? Perhaps it was no surprise to him.

Grégoire paused before leaving us. "One of the family you permitted to live on the estate. You were right, monsieur, and I was wrong. They do not seem to be thieves and tricksters, after all."

An ominous beginning, surely!

"Nor ever were," Nicolas said. "I suppose you have hired the gypsy woman, Leocadia, who was Yolande's friend."

He heard me catch my breath and assured me quickly, "She need not stay. But until we can hire a woman from Lyon or Poitiers, or even Paris if you prefer, you will find her an excellent worker."

I said nothing, but I nodded. We could discuss his penchant for gypsies at a more suitable time, preferably when we were alone.

My own boxes, valises, portmanteaux, the endless things we had purchased in Paris, arrived. I sympathized with the footman and the stable boy, who carried bulky weights that seemed astonishing in men so small. Also, their devotion to Nicolas touched me. By the time I had gone up with them to the third story, with its attics and servants' quarters and we stored those trunks belonging to Nicolas and me, we were old friends.

The turret rooms, as they called all these cubicles under the slate roofs, had a wealth of intriguing and even precious household items that must have accumulated for scores of years. I decided to have the lamps, wall brackets, and lusters cleaned, polished, and put in use, but I could hardly set them in place until I had been here longer than a few hours. The same prohibition applied to dozens of beautiful and often comfortable objects, from couches and case clocks to delicate watches and a remarkable little candle clock that might serve well so long as there were no problems with cloudy days and windy nights.

Although I had seen barely half the rooms in this ancient building, I felt that I knew my future home far better than I had when proudly ushered up to view the bedchamber I would share with my husband. Meanwhile I wondered what Nicolas was doing when he left me in the hands of my new guides and went down to settle a mysterious problem about the drains from the kitchen waterpump.

I discovered, to my relief, that the dining room regularly used was on the first story above that high-ceilinged ground floor with its rafters too high even to be called a ceiling. *Roofed* was a better word. But our dining room as well as the grand salon, the music room, and numerous cozy, small salons were all on this first story, one high floor above the pond.

It was Grégoire who pointed out to me the beauties of the pond itself when I came from the attic rooms into the low-roofed corridor. I had walked a few steps ahead of the two workmen and was startled to see the steward's lean, black figure materialize at the far end of the corridor, moving toward me with a deliberation that made me think of ghosts and other such absurd visitors. I am a practical woman, I hope, and I soon recovered from that uneasiness, but his first words were so unhelpful, I could not acquit him of deliberately trying to agitate me.

"There is an excellent view of the pond from the westerly windows, madame. But take care. Those attic stairs are treacherous."

I had been aware of that. They were wooden stairs, badly warped, and if a woman did not constantly watch her footing, it would be easy to catch a heel in the shredded carpeting.

"Yes, " I said. "Very much like our attic stairs at home."

He was persistent. "It was there that Madame Servier's foot became entangled and she tumbled down."

"Ah, but you said she was drunk."

Perhaps Frenchmen did not use the word *drunk* to describe females. He looked at me as if I had uttered some foulness. To hide my discomfort I gave him what must have been a sugary smile. Surprised, he stepped around me, bowed, and began to berate the two workmen for their presence here when they should have been out on what he called "the parapet" burning leaves.

I explained, "I needed them. If there is no time for burning leaves this afternoon, they can always do it tomorrow."

He bowed to punctuate his sarcasm. "Quite so. But not if there is a windy night ahead, madame."

I went down the corridor in regal solitude, but I reflected that it would be just my misfortune to find that he was right. I must stop putting up the backs of these people. Pride might be one thing, but common sense was another.

I had been depressed when we arrived at the celebrated Château Bertold, and even more depressed after examining part of the interior. I could not imagine living here in comfort. Surely it had never been anyone's "home!" But I soon realized that my husband saw it in quite a different light. He seemed happy, relieved of cares, and willing to forget the tumultuous events in Paris.

We dined alone and, surprisingly enough, in Nicolas's own bedchamber before a roaring fire. He explained that I must have my choice of Yolande's dressing room or William's if I liked but that his mother's room adjoined the master bedroom, which was this one, and he wondered if I would like it best.

"We are in my father's bedroom, and the only times I entered were in order to be punished."

"How dreadful! You must have hated it."

"Not at all," he said cheerfully. "I deserved it, you may

be sure. Yolande and I were always in mischief, usually running off to the gypsy camps on the Bertold boundaries of the woods. How do you like the food?"

I had been so sympathetic, picturing him as a mischievous boy about to be thrashed, that I ate without appreciating the flaky white shreds of fish so delicately seasoned and unknown to me. I could not guess what made it so delicious. The beef tenderloin that followed, and the vegetables that came after that, were equally perfect. At home we boiled fresh vegetables every day in summer and autumn, but they had never tasted like this.

"I can't believe this is the same food we eat at home. Incredible!"

"That is because we are at home now, my darling," he reminded me.

Only for the moment, I thought, but did not say so. I liked the wine much better than the Chinon the previous night. Although a dark wine was served, I preferred the pale, sparkling golden wine, which luckily turned out to be a Bertold vintage and tasted much like my favorite Vouvray. Nicolas was particularly pleased, and even Grégoire, who supervised the service of the two maids, looked at me with approval for the first time.

The new housekeeper, Leocadia, as the men called her—not "madame"—was presented to me after dinner. I had been nervous about meeting her and probably showed it. I remembered my recent doings with the Honiger family too well. The woman had a gypsy coloring and those alarming eyes so like Mrs. Honiger's but she wore her graying dark hair neatly brushed back from her intelligent face, and her manner borrowed some of Grégoire's quietness. Her manner was respectful without being servile, and I decided that we would go on excellently together.

The men made no objection when I discussed household matters with Leocadia concerning the airing of linens, the changing of sheets, and the refurbishing of the dressing room that had belonged to Nicolas's mother. It had exquisite high boiseries, cream-and-gold-paneled walls, and a pretty marble mantel and fireplace.

I liked the room very much and decided to use it as my estate office. It was light. It got the morning light like the adjoining master bedchamber. I disliked only one aspect. The most prominent feature to be seen from the two windows was the moat bridge where my brother and his wife had died. Beyond were the thick, dark woods, crowding close against the edge of the pond.

No matter. I would have my desk placed with the windows at my back. Besides, it obviously pleased Nicolas to see how much I liked his mother's room.

When we were alone again, I finally found the chance I had been looking for during the last few hours.

"How long have you known that woman?"

He glanced at the door and shrugged. "Leocadia? Years. There are bands of gypsies coming and going all the time. Yolande and I grew up with them, more or less. In the circumstances we felt that it was the least we could do."

"What circumstances?"

He sighed, got up, and motioned for me to join him. "Come, I want to show you something."

I was puzzled but rose from my chair, letting myself be urged toward the door. I hardly knew what to expect, but I was glad to have this matter explained.

Though it was barely dusk, the corridor felt icy after the warmth in Nicolas's room. There seemed to be leakages everywhere at windows and doors, down staircases, around closed and locked rooms, but I was warmly dressed and much more intrigued by whatever my husband had to tell me.

We went across to the tower steps and down to the hall outside the several salons that opened into each other. The hall was used as a gallery of Bertold ancestors. Nicolas hurried me past pompous ladies, military men, and a few impressive female beauties. The most beautiful of these was certainly the woman Nicolas pointed to.

"My grandmother. My grandfather came upon her and one of their encampments on the woods path to St. Auden. What do you think of her?"

I noticed at once that she had my husband's dark, glowing eyes. Or perhaps it was vice versa. Her mouth, too, resembled my husband's, being generous, full-lipped, sensuous. Curiously enough, I would never have called Nicolas handsome, and yet the face in the portrait was the most wildly beautiful I had ever seen.

No high-nosed, thin-blooded, aristocrat here. Nothing of her clothing was visible but great scarlet earrings shaped like an animal's head, probably a bear, shone through the thick black cloud of her hair. Her lips were the same color, whether by accident of nature or the artist's brush. The color of her face and throat was much deeper than Nicolas's olive hue. She must have been a sensation in Paris among the snobbish aristocrats of the Ancien Régime.

I looked at Nicolas. He was watching me tensely but with a glow of pride. I touched his cheek and lips with my finger. "I don't think I've ever seen anyone more beautiful. You have her eyes."

"Darling, I didn't show you my grandmother to flatter myself by exaggerations, though Yolande had something of her look. But I want you to understand me when I sometimes say I am one of them."

I said quietly, "I know that. Is Leocadia also one of her descendants?"

"I believe so. By another line. One of my grandmother's distant cousins, as I understand it."

We began to stroll past other portraits, none of them possessing anything like the interest of the gypsy Bertold. Nicolas frowned, and I wondered what he could be thinking about. Suddenly he asked, "Will you give me an honest answer if I ask you a direct question?"

It was a curious remark, almost insulting. Surely I had always answered him with honesty. Or had I?

"Yes. By all means."

"Well then, sweetheart—you note that I call you sweetheart—don't you think you owe me a few endearments? I think the score must be something approaching seven hundred and eighty-six to one."

I laughed, but I was deeply touched. "Seven hundred and eighty-six to two, sweetheart." I realized that he wanted a true answer to a question that had never occurred to me before. I could only blame my ancestral customs, my family's ways and rigid habits. We cared for each other in our family, but to display that emotion was a public demonstration of weakness. I must change the habits of a lifetime. I couldn't bear to think that Nicolas might not be aware of my deep love for him.

Still, there were other barriers between us.

We walked through the series of salons, two splendid old oaken doors opening into the next room, and then again at the far end of that room, so that we could see endless open doors before and behind us. It was all very interesting, but his question had troubled me for reasons of my own.

I said finally, "Darling, would you also give me an honest answer?"

"Say on. I promise."

He thought I was flirting, about to say something trivial and perhaps romantic. I hated to disappoint him, but I must know whether he would tell me the truth, especially after discovering the close bond between the gypsy Leocadia and Château Bertold.

"Well, then, was it memories of your grandmother that made you warn the Honigers? You did let them escape after they knocked me unconscious and kidnapped me."

He removed his arm from around me. The lines in his face tightened. Our warm, loving understanding had ended for the moment. Even the stirring tones of his voice changed. He was much too light about such a serious matter. There seemed to be a hint of sarcasm as well.

"As I said, we have a great deal in common."

"Then you admit that you warned them."

"Admit? No. I state it. That boy and his father had nothing whatever to do with your attack. One might as well believe the St. Audens were guilty. And God knows, they were feasting and shopping in London when you were kidnapped!"

That shook me. "You mean to tell me that the St. Audens were in London at that time?"

"Certainly. I met them when I went up to arrange for the export of Bertold Vintage."

I hadn't a single reason to suspect the St. Audens of anything. All the same, anything that linked the château with Ferndene Valley was disquieting.

We walked up one flight of the tower steps toward our bedchamber, each of us busy with tumultuous thoughts. We were about to leave the tower landing and enter our corridor when I heard the beginnings of something very like moaning in the distance, almost as if a female were in agony. It rose to a shriek. I clutched at the stone balustrade, aghast.

"What is it?"

He was amused. "This is a very old building. You might say those are the groans of all the unhappy creatures whose spirits have lingered around these walls for eight hundred years."

"Nicolas, don't!"

"You won't hear it so plainly in the bedroom. It is only the wind howling through a thousand cracks and crevices," he said impatiently. "Grégoire predicted that the wind would come up tonight."

And the leaves hadn't been cleared away from the ground-floor parapet. I told myself that I would be reminded by the steward in some subtle way tomorrow, probably when I found the leaves blowing all over the wretched old building.

I did not find anything amusing in Nicolas's joke about

disembodied spirits. I glanced toward the turret stairs at the far end of the hall and wondered if the spirit of that luckless, drunken housekeeper had joined the howling and screeching of the elements.

CHAPTER TWENTY-ONE

The moaning and shrieking was only lower by comparison in our bedchamber. We still heard it. I was intensely aware of it, but I was relieved by my husband's presence beside me, a confession of need I would never have thought of before I met Nicolas Bertold. I was always intensely proud to boast that I was completely self-sufficient. Since I fell in love, I found myself equally proud to confess that I needed my husband. It was sometimes a delicious bond. At other times, when I realized how little I knew him and how many secrets he kept from me, I was uneasy.

I loved him, but I didn't entirely trust him.

All these things I thought of in the night while I lay close beside Nicolas, even when I was aroused anew by his strong, insistent body.

Everything had been rushed that first day, and so much happened: the "bad-luck" stumble as I stepped out of the coach; the news about the former housekeeper and her gypsy successor; then, at last, the truth about Nicolas's part in the Honigers' escape. I felt I saw the château for the first time the next day.

Nicolas still seemed cross over my questions about the Honigers, and this reaction at once triggered my own. I told myself I was the one who should have been upset. And indeed I was. But he apparently felt that I should trust his motives, no matter what he did. I simply wished he had not tried to keep secret what he had done to aid the gypsy family.

It was also troubling to know that he thought the Honigers had not struck me. Did he perhaps think one of the villagers had done so, or Jeremy or Nanny Pemberton? I almost wished I had some grounds for suspicion of the Vicomte and Vicomtesse de St. Auden. That would have solved everything so nicely.

I waited, hoping Nicolas would inspect the château with me. Grégoire was far from welcome when he appeared, ready to show me the entrails of this gigantic old mastodon of a house. Before he could bring the matter up in some unpleasant way, I asked if he had gotten the leaves burned before the wind came up last night.

"Regrettably not, madame. The master has just taken me to task for failing to have it done. It seems the piles of leaves blew in through several open windows and must be removed now from the music room, the ladies' withdrawing room, and the small blue salon on the ground floor."

"What a pity! Now, about our work today, shall we begin with the kitchen, the stillroom, and the pantry? Unless, of course, they too are covered with leaves."

He thought I was having fun at his expense, as I probably was, and he liked it no better than most of us do. We had not started out at all well in our new relationship. I wished I had not mentioned the business, but it was done now, and we could only make the best of a relationship that we obviously had not sought.

The kitchen and stillroom were surprisingly modern. I suspected that this was due to the insistence of an opinionated little man named Carletti, who bustled around his ancient, stained fireplace with its grate, hanging kettles, and other centuries-old equipment, then rushed to his closed stove, which already showed signs of spilled and burned food from previous meals. All the same, from what I could see of it, and especially from its odor, I knew that Carletti was a treasure. He clearly cared more about his art than about the immaculate (or otherwise) condition of his domain.

One thing relieved me. He may not have gushed with delight at sight of me, but he was not obsequious to Grégoire, either, and upon being presented to me, he remarked to the world at large, "Many thanks. A mistress of the house at last."

I must have looked surprised, because Carletti gave an expressive shrug, adding, "Perfectly true. Not since Madame Bertold, the mother of Monsieur Nicolas."

Leocadia, the new housekeeper, walked out of the stillroom with Grégoire and me, after showing me the way the fresh vegetables and fish were brought in daily during the season, and how meats were kept from spoilage by ice and careful packing in the cold little storage area below the stillroom.

I noted an exchange of glances between the housekeeper and Grégoire, then the steward left me in Leocadia's hands with the explanation, "I will see to the gathering of the leaves again."

I understood that his final word was for my benefit, and we all walked out through a narrow, dark kitchen passage and into the Great Hall where Grégoire disappeared in the dim recesses of its far corner. I had felt guilty over my previous bad manners and tried to thank him for introducing me to the mechanics of running the château, but he walked away before I got two words out.

Leocadia did not watch him leave. I wondered what she was thinking. Her dignified manner did not change, but her eyes were subtly different, with a wistful expression that seemed to obliterate their exotic slant. I looked across the wide, medieval hall to see what had caused this sudden change of mood.

A portrait of two dark faces hung against the stone wall, between tapestries of a savage bear hunt. The frame of the picture was of dark wood, and the portrait also dark. I could not make out the details at this distance and asked Leocadia, "Are they ancestors?"

For the first time she showed me contempt but so subtly that I missed it for a few seconds.

"No, madame. They are Monsieur Nicolas and Mademoiselle Yolande, painted on mademoiselle's sixteenth birthday."

I crossed the room, skirting the long baronial table. I saw a threadbare place in the carpet and luckily avoided catching my heel in it.

Though brother and sister were painted informally, almost as if in gypsy costume, the vibrant, exciting girl bore little resemblance in character to the brooding, powerful face of her older brother. They looked like people who always got their way, she by charm and Nicolas by his authoritative manner. He must have been in his early twenties, but even then his build was impressive, as I judged by his shoulders and the strong column of his throat in that open-necked white shirt. The brother and sister looked so much like gypsies in the portrait that I half expected to see him wearing the earrings of a fierce bandit chief, but he had not gone that far. I thought his eyes were unforgettable in their power as they stared at me.

Yolande wore what appeared to be a gold satin blouse, very wide at the neck and revealing the high swell of her breasts. I could certainly understand William's attraction to her some years later. Jeremy looked like her but more delicate, less lively. Yolande's piquant beauty had matured early, perhaps because she was doomed to die so young.

I winced at the thought.

Leocadia said, "Madame?"

"Forgive me. They are a striking couple, aren't they?"

"I have always thought so." Her voice held depths, throbbing with some emotion, which I took to be devotion. She seemed too old to have grown up with a daughter of the Bertold house. Perhaps she had once been Yolande's maid-servant.

We moved on down the length of the hall and toward the great entry doors. Leocadia pulled open one of the doors, letting in the cheerful morning light. I saw the moat bridge beyond the stone walk that surrounded the château. The sun gleamed off the near abutment, showing fresh timbers and, doubtless, fresh stones as well.

It hit me with dreadful force that these were the signs of William's death and the death of that pretty young woman in the portrait, Yolande with the lively eyes. I stopped in the doorway.

I sensed that the housekeeper was watching me. I wondered what she was thinking. She must remember the tragedy that had occurred here. I turned my head.

I was shocked by her expression. Her heavy eyelids lowered but not quickly enough to conceal the glitter of passion in her eyes. I had no doubt that passion was hatred.

But why against me? What had I done to her or to the dead Yolande Bertold Daviot?

She recovered quickly and seemed her impassive self.

I reminded her, "My brother died there. And Jeremy's mother. I can't help feeling deeply about it." I raised my chin. "But life must go on, you know. William would expect it of us. And Yolande would, as well."

"Yes, madame. Do you wish to cross the bridge and examine the gate house? It is just off the wagon road on the north side. You passed it when you came."

I didn't remember it, but I had been on the south side of the carriage. In any case, I didn't want to cross the bridge at this moment. When the first shock was over and I could look down at those new board-and-stone reinforcements without reopening raw wounds, then I could do so.

"No," I said. "Not this morning. Maybe later in the day.

Show me around the miniature island that the building sits on. I want to get a general impression of the place."

She said nothing. My skirts had swept against hers suddenly in the breeze, and she bent to brush mine off, or else she wanted to brush away the contamination of my touch. I told myself it did not matter. The woman and her feelings meant nothing to me. But I could not lie to myself.

I did care about all these enemies who crowded in upon me unwanted. It was as if they sent their hatred into the air like an evil miasma, trying to stifle me. Worst of all, I didn't know why. They surely didn't blame me for the death of my sister-in-law. And my brother's death had been a greater tragedy to me than to these people.

But I had married Nicolas Bertold, a man some Frenchmen believed was guilty of that tragedy. Possibly that made me as guilty as Nicolas. If that was the case, how could I explain the fact that Grégoire and Leocadia, as well as the valet Perpigny, showed no signs of hating Nicolas? On the contrary, they were devoted to him.

Or seemed to be...

I decided I must have a confidential talk with my husband on a subject we seldom discussed, the double tragedy on the moat bridge.

Meanwhile Leocadia led the way around to the south end of the building while I looked out at the pond on my left, rather than the great, gray fortress walls on my right, which plunged straight down to the bottom of the pond, there being no stone walkway or parapet on the west. The pond, however, was more intriguing, if equally sinister. I saw at once why everyone spoke of the lily pads and the darkness of the water itself. I leaned far over the parapet, holding on with one hand, staring down into those curious black waters.

A row of big sycamores ringed the pond whose south border looked a long way off, a fascinating area. The dense growth might be different from Ferndene Heath, but the desolation was the same and reminded me of home. Somewhere in those woods, between tall sycamores and thick, lighter willows, I saw what appeared to be a white pillar.

I called to Leocadia. "Is there a building on the southwest side of the pond?"

The pond waters glittered under the high sun, and she frowned into the distance. "No, madame. It is what some call a *folie*, a small stone temple, actually. Nothing but pillars and a roof that has been repaired many times through the centuries. It was built by the Romans. There is a stone bench. Nothing more."

"It ought to be very pleasant on a hot day."

She hesitated. "I believe the little grass plot before it is cool and soft in summer. The trees grow very close, however."

"I should think my friend Richard Pemberton would like to paint its location. He used to do landscapes before he took up portraiture."

"Monsieur Pemberton? Yes, I remember." She leaned over the low parapet, looking down at the floating lily pads, then added, apropos of nothing, "It has a privacy that some people prefer."

I was lost for a minute but realized that she must still be referring to the *folie*, though what this had to do with Richard Pemberton, I could not imagine. I wondered if her remark was another of those Grégoire-like hints to unsettle me.

"If the *folie* is so private, I assume that you are about to tell me some ancient mayhem took place there. A twelfth-century murder? Some gory pogrom of Catholic against Huguenot or vice versa?"

Leocadia stared at me and then gave a sudden spurt of laughter, which she quickly stifled with her cupped hand. "Not so, madame. Say . . . love, rather. It has often been used for assignations. That is its purpose." She looked out over the water again at the distant white pillar. "Though whether those assignations led to happiness or misery, or even violence, I could not say."

"No sudden deaths there. Well, that is something."

"Bertold is a very peaceful place, in the general run of things," Leocadia remarked in a chiding voice.

I looked directly at her. "How do you think Monsieur and Madame Daviot died? I would appreciate your honest opinion."

She was taken aback and blinked, no doubt giving herself time to think of some answer that would satisfy me.

"You speak of the young Monsieur Jeremy and what he says he saw from the tower room? A boy of seven. One understands these things. Children often see what they wish to see."

"Wish to see? He could hardly wish to see his parents killed."

"That is true. It is also true that the first plan was for the master to ride to the village over that bridge. Perhaps when Monsieur Daviot and the young madame went instead and the accident occurred, the boy fancied that the master's change of plan was deliberate."

"Or Jeremy was so shocked, he wished his uncle had died instead, and the wish was father to the testimony he gave."

She found that reasonable. She walked slowly back to the point at which the bridge was fastened to the rock base of the château. I followed her, determined to become used to this spot with its painful associations. We studied the reinforcements, which now included iron and steel supports.

She said, "All this, madame, supposes that it was an accident."

Not that old, haunting fear again. I snapped, "Nothing else is possible. We all know that."

"Is it true that the little creature and his wretched nursemaid return to live here?"

"Creature?"

Her mouth tightened. "Have I chosen the improper word? Perhaps it is not the same meaning in your language."

That might be, but she had spoken in French to me. "Perhaps. You must remember, half of this huge estate belongs to my nephew."

"I never forget, madame."

My morning with the housekeeper had proved to be a disquieting time, and I was relieved to join my husband for noon dinner and listen to him talk about the Bertold vineyards. Afterward I reminded him that we must expect Jeremy and Nanny Pemberton within a fortnight. His mind was still on business, and he was puzzled at the way I expressed myself.

"They must come sometime, I suppose, so the sooner the boy becomes used to living here again, the better."

"You don't think it will upset him to live so close to where it all happened?"

He cut another bite of steak and looked at it for an uncomfortably long time. Then, belatedly, he ate the blood-rare bite. With his knife still in his hand he reminded me in an expressionless voice, "When I said he must become used to it, I mean that he will become used to sharing the château with us."

"He shared Daviot House with you."

"Hardly the same thing. Anyway, my nephew had no difficulty living here during the months I was—as we delicately put it—detained. From the reports of the servants here this seemed to give the boy considerable satisfaction."

"Horrible," I murmured. "A terrible mistake, to make you suffer discomfort and disgrace and suspicion when you were innocent."

"Thank you, my love." He was moved by my assurance and covered my hand with his. Then he slapped it briskly. "Now, tell me what you have been doing all morning."

I described my peregrinations with Grégoire and then with Leocadia. Nicolas nodded, seemed satisfied. I thought he was relieved as well.

"Then you are beginning to find your way about your new home? Good. You will grow to love it."

I wondered, but I did not want to discourage him, so I mentioned the positive aspects of the place.

"The kitchen quarters are splendid. Our Hannah Budleigh would be quite jealous, and I like your chef, Monsieur Carletti."

He grinned. "Yes. We all bow respectfully to Carletti. He was once sous-chef in the household of Queen Hortense, Napoleon's stepdaughter."

"And I looked at the lake too. Or, as you people call it, the pond. It's very picturesque. There were some sweetpeas climbing the southeast tower. They looked exactly like the ones we have at home. I loved the portrait of you and Yolande in the Great Hall."

"The robber baron and the gypsy princess."

"Jeer if you like, but it's very handsome. I loved it." I hesitated, then rambled on. "I wondered, though. Are there any portraits of Yolande with William?"

Contrary to my fear, he did not take offense at my implied criticism.

"Haven't you seen any yet? There is an excellent likeness in the Gold Salon across the hall on this floor. It was painted shortly after Jeremy was born. And I believe young Pemberton did some work. He was very smitten with Yolande, you know."

This was news. But there were so many loose threads on this estate that I could scarcely tell what was true and what was merely gossip. Still, one would think Richard Pemberton might have given himself away to me, mentioned Yolande with special affection, perhaps. But no. I hadn't the least idea.

"And then," I went on with more enthusiasm, "the prettiest thing I saw was that Roman pillar down at the south end of the lake. I can't wait to see the *folie*, as Leocadia calls it."

I expected him to be pleased by my praise. It was one of the few things I had been especially thrilled about. But to my surprise he seemed vague about it.

"The old temple? Nothing left there. Just a chilly little

ruin. It catches the crosscurrents of wind in season. Most of our peasants avoid it."

I might have known. "But will you take me there sometime?"

"Sometime. You will appreciate it more in summer."

"Maybe I could walk around the pond myself."

He raised his head. "Not alone. Promise me, sweetheart, that you won't go alone."

"Good heavens! Why not?"

His answer was perfectly sensible. "With the hunting season coming on, some locals jump over the gun, so to speak, and they might mistake you for a deer, sweetheart."

"They already mistook us both for something or other two days ago in the little town near the Indre River, didn't they?"

"You might say that." However, his tone suggested that my own suspicions were right and that the random shot had been something more personal.

I was disappointed over his comments about the *folie*, but I promised, "Very well. I won't go alone."

When we had finished dinner, we crossed the hall into the bright, sunlit Gold Salon which was used for what Nicolas referred to as "small entertainments." The long room had some of the elegance of the Paris house in spite of the fact that the gold portieres and the gilt frames of the portraits were faded from long exposure to the western sunlight.

Nicolas pointed out the painting of William, Yolande, and Jeremy over the mantel, and I agreed that it was impressive. Jeremy was a mere unidentifiable infant in his mother's arms, heavily swaddled in the French fashion, and Yolande herself had a proud, smug air of satisfaction. She looked sophisticated, her hair arranged formally with side puffs and a knot on top of her head. Stuck in the knot was a jeweled comb. Her high neckline and tight silk bodice only accentuated what was visible of her well-rounded bosom.

It was my brother William who puzzled me. He scowled. He must have been very bored by the long sittings. His light hair was brushed back rather than romantically loose about his face, as he so often wore it at home, and his lips were tight and thin. His blue eyes appeared stormy. I knew the signs.

It must have been terrible to have two imperious, ambitious men trying to run an estate like this together. Nicolas would resent a stranger's interference, and William would naturally want the handling of his wife's half of the estate.

The painting made me especially unhappy, and I turned away, wondering.

When Nicolas returned to his work, going over the estate accounts with Grégoire, I walked out to the moat bridge and stood there in the shadow of the great southeast tower, trying ineffectually to communicate with my brother's spirit.

What really happened here, dear William? Let me understand. Why didn't you let me know that you were unhappy (if you were) when you visited me with little Jeremy two years ago?

I was startled by a movement, a flickering of color in the heavily wooded area across the bridge. I backed away from the bridge. I couldn't forget the "stray" shot that just missed us in the Indre River town. Then the figure across the bridge stepped out into the roadway, and I saw Pierre de St. Auden's tall figure. He moved to the bridgehead. He had been shooting and waved his rifle at me. He wore a smart red jacket with an English shot belt and a hat cocked jauntily over one ear. I thought him very handsome there in the sunlight of early afternoon.

"Greetings, Madame Bertold," he called. "I am trespassing on your ground. I would cross to make my apologies, but as you see, I am hardly presentable."

"Never mind," I said on an impulse. "I will join you."

Whatever I might think of his wife, this slim creature was the last man on earth I would suspect of doing me harm, and he might serve me as an escort today, thus helping me to keep my promise to my husband.

I was wearing a Paris wool gown plus a thin pelérine and stiffened skirts, hardly a walking costume, but I went across the bridge to meet the vicomte, anyway, intent on satisfying my curiosity about Leocadia's *folie*.

He came to meet me with every sign of pleasure, bowing over my hand and raising my fingers to his lips.

"This is a delightful surprise." He paused, looked into my eyes, and added with a plaintive little note of humor, "But it is not my irresistible company that brings you here, is it?"

I confessed, "Not entirely, Monsieur le Vicomte."

"Then I must be content with that. What may I do for you, madame?"

I was never one for intrigue, so I blurted out, "You may take me to see the *folie*. My husband doesn't want me to go alone."

He glanced in that direction. From this perspective we could see a bit more of the little temple. Two more pillars, a dark slate roof over the original stone, all within a frame of greenery so dark as to be almost black.

"Yes. A place of enchantment for some." Was I wrong, or had he hesitated before describing it? He added gallantly, "It will be my privilege. Come. Shall we cut through the woods?"

I studied those close-grown stands of trees with their carpet of ivy, the tendrils crisscrossing the ground.

"I think the path around the shore might be easier, even if it is longer."

He smiled. I believe he thought I was intimidated by him. The idea was probably flattering.

"As you say, madame." He bowed again and took my arm.

We started along the edge of the pond, and he began to question me in his pleasant manner. He seemed curious about how I was adjusting to my life in the Bertold world. I was exceedingly positive in my answers.

"You get on surprisingly well with Old Nick," he remarked presently.

"Perhaps love and respect have something to do with it."

"True. But when we heard of this marriage, we feared the worst."

"The worst?" Were they afraid that I had married Nicolas for his estate and his considerable fortune? I said sharply, "I trust you were told that the Daviots are not precisely paupers."

I had shocked him. "No, no, madame. Never. It is nothing of that sort." He scuffed away a shower of leaves that blew across our path. "But we knew you were Daviot's sister, and frankly, it occurred to us that you might have married Nicolas to . . . to avenge Daviot's murder."

Heavy with sarcasm I asked, "And do you think it was murder?"

I expected a too quick denial, something that would subtly manage to cast suspicion.

Instead he said frankly, "None of us are sure. I am rather inclined to believe that it was murder." He held up a hand. "No. Not your husband. You forget, madame. I've known him all my life. He is quite capable of killing, but only by direct action. In defense of something or someone he loves. But never would he tear away bridge supports and hide away somewhere while people drown in a carriage that becomes their coffin."

I had never been more grateful. "Thank you, monsieur. It is good to hear that his closest friends agree with me."

"Then you have no sinister motive in marrying Nick. I shall certainly tell Gabrielle, and incidentally, pay her the thousand livres she wagered that you loved Nick."

So the vicomtesse had believed in my sincerity! I seemed to have underestimated her.

"Will you tell me, monsieur, what you do think happened at the bridge? An accident?"

"No, madame. No accident. As to the rest, I do not know."

We had reached the south end of the pond, and the woods thinned out briefly where a sluggish little stream trickled away into fields and vineyards below. The vicomte helped me over the flat stones that crossed the stream, and almost at once we were locked into the woods again. The woods muffled the sounds of the world outside, but we became aware of tiny scuffling noises among the carpets of leaves. Birds, insects, and field mice scurried about their business.

I looked around uneasily, thinking I heard splashes, as if booted feet had crossed the stream behind us, ignoring the flat stepping-stones. But the vicomte paid no attention. He was pointing out the charms of the miniature temple we saw, stark and white against the dark sycamores.

Sixteen pillars, not all of them erect, formed a square. I saw within the square a stone floor and a stone bench littered with leaves and debris. The wind blew in and out between the pillars. Nicolas had been right. It was cold and uncomfortable this time of day. Earlier in the morning light it might be charming.

I cut into the vicomte's description of the *folie* and its ancient history.

"Monsieur, let us forget the *folie* for a minute. You said that what happened at the bridge was no accident. Why would anyone make it appear that my husband was guilty? Why would people even suspect him, beyond the word of a seven-year-old child who disliked him?"

St. Auden looked surprised. "Did he not tell you, madame? He and your brother quarreled here in the little temple only a day or so before the accident. Nicolas struck your brother so hard, the blow drew blood."

Behind us I heard the deep tones that had never until now been addressed to me in such anger.

"I begin to think I prefer my enemies to my friends. They, at least, don't corrupt my wife."

I saw the vicomte change color. I did not need to look around to see Nicolas behind us.

CHAPTER TWENTY-TWO

I found myself speechless. I was deeply ashamed to be caught by the man I loved in what would sound to him like a furtive betrayal. At the same time certain facts began to penetrate my thoughts. In my mind's eye William lay here bleeding on the hard marble floor, only one day before he suffered again, agonizingly, under the moat bridge.

I told myself that Nicolas must have been driven to such a brutal act as knocking my brother down. But my suspicious, practical mind warned me that he could very easily knock down William or anyone else if his precious Bertold land was threatened. In any case, no one addressed me, nor asked my opinion, so I couldn't even defend myself.

The two men seemed to think the matter lay between them. Pierre de St. Auden recovered his dignity and defended himself. "A pity you didn't hear our entire discussion, my friend. You would not so readily accuse me of corrupting Madame Bertold." He added quietly, "Not that she is so easy to corrupt. You underestimate her."

Nicolas ignored this as he ignored me.

"It never occurred to you, perhaps, that I wished to tell her about her brother in my own time."

"Not when you wait this long, my dear fellow."

I saw my husband's mouth tighten and knew that he disliked an unpleasant truth as much as the next person.

"I did not murder Yolande." He added, almost as an afterthought, "Nor Daviot."

"I know that. Your wife knows it." The vicomte placed a hand on Nicolas's shoulder. "But I am convinced it was no accident. Now, let us have done with this brangle," he added, using the English word. "Tell madame all that you know or suspect. It is always wisest. If your enemy moves again, you may be in no position to tell anyone."

The vicomte bowed to us both and was leaving the little temple when Nicolas echoed, "My enemy?"

"But of course. The accident may never have been meant for Daviot. You may have been the target from the first. *Au 'voir*, my friend. And madame."

I was relieved to discover that the vicomte shared what appeared to be Nicolas's theory. The intended victim of the original crime had been Nicolas himself.

Nicolas ignored his friend's effort to cover their quarrel, but I thought the vicomte deserved some response.

"*Au revoir*, and thank you, Monsieur le Vicomte. Don't forget to pay the vicomtesse a thousand livres."

He nodded and walked away smiling faintly, swinging his rifle.

Out of the corner of my eye I saw Nicolas look at me, doubtless puzzled over my mention of the thousand livres. I said as calmly as I could, "The vicomte kindly agreed to escort me to the little temple. As for the conversation you appear to have overheard, we found we were in agreement about my brother's death." He simply stared at me. I went on, "When I asked how this ghastly suspicion started against you, he told me about your fight with William."

He slapped the nearest pillar with the flat of his hand. I jumped at the sound and was annoyed at myself for doing so. When I looked into his face, I was shaken to find that the anger had gone. He looked sad, perhaps haunted by memories. After an uncomfortable silence he took a long breath.

"There seems to be no end to this business. Now it has involved Pierre. But I wanted to keep you out of it." He offered his hand, but it was only to show the way.

I tried to demonstrate my feelings. "I must be in it, darling. You are my whole life."

"Not quite, my love." It was a denial I couldn't understand. Nor could I reach the emotion that brought that lost look to his face.

I glanced around as we were leaving, side by side but not together.

"You were right. It is cold here. It will be more pleasant in summer. We must come back then."

I wondered if he even heard me. He was frowning up at the blue heavens as they opened above us over the little stream that emptied out of the pond.

"In a month or two we will be seeing the first signs of winter. I used to enjoy winter. I wonder why."

His sister Yolande and my brother had died in January. That would certainly change his view of winter. I said, "Yes, I know."

We said nothing further while we walked back through the woods, over thick carpets of leaves and debris. I knew, even while I denied it to myself, that we had no idea of what was going on in each other's mind.

When he suddenly spoke, I was surprised that he had not yet changed the subject.

"I imagine you will want to know how Daviot happened to end up with a cut lip and a bleeding nose."

It didn't sound nearly so dreadful this way. As a boy, William often came home with a nosebleed, sometimes the result of a fight with Richard Pemberton.

"If you want to tell me," I said. "I think I must explain to you that this would not be the first time William received a bloody nose. Or even a loose tooth. He was always pugnacious, as they say."

He grinned reluctantly, I thought.

"Pugnacious. Only the English would say it." He showed me through a narrow passage between tightly laced trees where we had to stoop to get through. Just as I thought he had forgotten the subject of his quarrel with William, he brought us back to it.

"Your brother felt that Yolande was somehow his inferior. Occasionally it annoyed me."

I could scarcely believe it. "Good heavens, I should think so! Are you certain?"

"Quite certain."

"It seems so unlike William. He was never that sort." I added hopefully, "As a matter of fact, he was very democratic. He had friends among all the farmers of the valley. There were servants he confided in. There was Tad Spindler. William often got him home from the tavern at night."

But though I gave Nicolas several chances, he offered no further explanation.

Nervous and slightly sick, I accepted the fact that he had problems so deep that he could not even confide them to me. I was not one to confide my own deepest thoughts, and I had no right to resent this quality in Nicolas. Still, I believed that if he shared his trouble, it might halve his suffering.

If I still had doubts about William's death and all the mysterious details around it, they were banished into depths so far beneath the surface of my mind that I could tell myself they no longer existed. I was especially warmed by Pierre de St. Auden's agreement that there had been a conspiracy against Nicolas, not against William.

We had very little to say to each other the rest of the afternoon. We were both busy. I spent several hours with Leocadia, going over the problem of refurbishing certain rooms in the château. I decided to concentrate on the most likely public and private apartments, leaving turret rooms and grand but unused salons for later, but of course, there were always those chandeliers that so badly needed cleaning.

I sensed that Leocadia had been close to Yolande Bertold Daviot, so I proceeded carefully when I discussed changes for those rooms Yolande may have furnished. To my surprise she found no fault with the idea of change.

"Mademoiselle Yolande was never interested in household matters. She left them to the meddler."

"Meddler?"

Leocadia hesitated. "I mean to say, Madame Servier, the housekeeper."

"But why a meddler?"

She shrugged. "The woman was always prying. Mademoiselle felt that she was a tale-bearer as well. No privacy, mademoiselle said. And such a gossip! Nothing missed her little eyes." Obviously intending to change the subject, she ran her hand over the inlaid leather edge of the credenza.

"Mademoiselle always disliked these elegant pieces. She preferred the outdoors."

It was somehow unexpected. I supposed that Leocadia might resent my stepping into Yolande's shoes as mistress of the Bertold estates, but her feelings were more closely tied to the facts around Yolande's death. Another odd thing struck me. She never seemed to think of Yolande as a married woman.

I said, "I should think young Madame Daviot would like to stay in this room though, to be near her husband. I mean to say, my brother always preferred to work on estate business in the western light. This was his study, wasn't it?"

"Very true, madame. But mademoiselle—ah, *pardon*, Madame Daviot—did not like this room."

"Or the pretty green room through that doorway?"

"Monsieur Daviot was often in and out of there. So I do not believe—" She broke off, having gotten into difficulties of some sort. She ended lamely, "Madame Yolande did not use these rooms."

I was beginning to accept some very strange ideas. For some reason Yolande avoided William. Secondly, William felt superior to her. This was the most incomprehensible part of the whole story. Though very proud, William was anything but a snobbish person, as I had protested to Nicolas.

From these clues and her previous attitude toward me, I also decided that it was not I Leocadia resented, but my connection with my brother. I assumed this because she was pleasant enough to me until we had come to the moat bridge and discussed the tragedy. Her constant reference to "Mademoiselle" rather than "Madame" Yolande might come from old habit, but there was more. She did not like William, who had lived here, presumably in and out of her company, for eight years. Yet he never mentioned her to me. One would have thought he might, at least, write about her as a troublemaker or incompetent, or think up some other lame excuse for being rid of her.

I could not bear that they should all be so wrong about William. They didn't seem to know him at all.

Leocadia and I went out into the cold, stony Great Hall on the ground floor. There, to my satisfaction, we shared a common goal. She looked up, her oblique eyes narrowing as she considered the huge chandeliers with their hundreds of lusters, each dirtier than the one beside it.

"These should be washed, madame. I mentioned it to Madame Servier, but she said no. Too much work, I believe."

"That's as may be. But you are entirely right. We will make it a first project. Think how dazzling it would be if every luster were clean and shining."

She nodded. Her dark eyes shone. "It would be the first time in my life."

I looked at her. "You have been here all your life?"

"But yes, madame, naturally. Since before—since many years."

We made plans for this undertaking, even though I wondered if we would use the huge medieval hall more than once or twice a year. But it seemed important to me, since every guest who entered the château would be certain to glimpse those candle-gleaming lusters and discover that Château Bertold still held some of its ancient grandeur.

After twenty-four hours of rigid, if polite, formality between Nicolas and me, I was surprised the next afternoon by a visit from the St. Audens. Leocadia and I, with two maids, were busy cleaning the Gold Salon when one of the parlormaids hurried up to the first floor with the announcement of the new arrivals.

Panic-stricken, I tore off the scarf from my touseled head and tried to do the same with my dust-and-water-stained pinafore.

"Show them into . . . into—"

"The Green Salon, madame?" Leocadia suggested in a low voice. She appeared unaffected, but she was brushing herself off with quick, nervous hands.

"Excellent. The Green Salon. And send in a tray of Madeira and some biscuits."

"Pardon, madame, the vicomte drinks cognac or Jerez, what you call sherry. And Madame la Vicomtesse prefers the Bertold white."

In spite of my annoyance, I realized that Leocadia could be of great help in many ways. "Thank you. That will be satisfactory. I'll go and change. Oh—and send someone to notify Monsieur Bertold." I hoped she would not ask me where he was, since I hadn't the slightest idea.

"Very good, madame." We were about to separate in the hall when she suggested, "If you please, I have one of the old estate workers beginning to lower the chandeliers in the Great Hall. Shall I tell him to delay?"

I laughed abruptly. "Yes. In the circumstances, please tell him not to do anything until later."

Leocadia curtsied and left me. I rushed into my dressing room, snatched a Lyon silk visiting suit from the armoire, and tearing off my stained morning dress, I tried to get into the pantalets and petticoats of my new gown. Luckily Leocadia had sent one of the maids, Marie-Clare, to help me dress. Marie-Clare was a pert, lively girl, small but strong. She had been obliging from the first evening and had only two faults: She was an incurable gossip, and she never stopped talking.

She fastened me into the absurd linen-and-lace undergarments, lacing, buttoning, and arranging until I was ready for the rust-gold gown with its stiff, tight Basque jacket. Uncomfortable but flattering, and, as Marie-Clare insisted, "Most correct to wear in the gardens of Paris, madame."

We were not in Paris, nor even in the gardens, but no matter. We smiled together, looking into the long pier glass together. The girl explained her own delight.

"You rescued me, madame. I was told I must help them wash those so-dirty bits of glass in the Great Hall. I am happy to leave it not completed."

"I'm afraid someone must complete it," I reminded her. She wrinkled her piquant nose at me in the mirror, but I only laughed. Let her show her feelings in this easy way. She must still help with the washing of the lusters tonight or tomorrow, the more so, as I expected to work there myself.

In revenge for my reminder about the crystal lusters Marie-Clare watched me walk across the carpet with great dignity, at which point she reminded me, "Best take care not to bend over, madame. These new straps that hold out the skirts will swing and produce a view of the lingerie."

I rolled my eyes but heeded her warning.

I walked down the southwest tower steps slowly, with care, cursing—not for the first time—this abysmally prehistoric way of getting from one floor to another. I kept hoping I would meet my husband before entering the Green Salon, but I did not; so I put the best face on the matter and entered the room, only to find Nicolas standing by the fireplace, with one booted foot on the grate. Opposite him, holding out his slender, aristocratic hands to the small fire, was Pierre de St.

Auden. The vicomtesse had assumed an easy position on the tufted green velvet sofa and, to my surprise, wore an unflattering black taffeta gown with an exceedingly modest crinoline effect.

I admired the way she ignored fashion.

Both St. Audens welcomed me with such sudden, abrupt friendliness that I knew they must have been talking about me.

"*Chérie*, how fresh and full of color you look!" the vicomtesse complimented me in a slightly dubious way, since I had been too hurried to wear any rouge or powder. "Do come and sit by me. Tell me all the changes you intend to make." She patted the sofa beside her.

The vicomte kissed my hand, looking warmly interested in my welfare, and expressed the hope that I was getting to know the huge estate.

But it was Nicolas who pleased me the most. He kissed my forehead and put an arm around me. "Sweetheart, we are friends again, Pierre and I. We have both been duly chastised by each other and agree that you may walk to the *folie* with whomever you choose."

This surprised me and further illuminated the cause of my husband's anger. He obviously had seen me walking around the pond with the vicomte and followed us out of jealousy. The fact that he overheard us talking about him was not the original cause of his anger. This was a fault I could easily condone. I was conscious of some jealousy in my own nature.

"I can't imagine being angry with my husband for long," I told the St. Audens, very conscious of my husband's arm attaching me warmly to his body.

The vicomte offered me one of the little sherry glasses and everyone asked how I liked France, what changes would be made at the château, and if the staff would be enlarged. I told them we all got on splendidly and that the gypsy woman, Leocadia, seemed far more competent than anything I had heard about the late Madame Servier.

"You see," my husband said, pressing me to him, "we have a mistress of Bertold at last."

Gabrielle remarked idly, "God knows Yolande never lived the part."

There was some discomfort. Even I felt it. The vicomte made haste to cover the awkwardness.

"Your talent at running a household of this magnitude is remarkable, Madame Bertold. From what Nicolas says, you have taken it in charge very quickly."

I took pleasure in reminding them, "Thank you, Monsieur le Vicomte, but I have run a household for almost ten years."

"A very talented girl is our Alain," my husband said, and I understood then that my big problem with him in our marriage would not be my absurd, original suspicions of him but his determination to think of me as young, immature. If I loved him enough, and I was convinced that I did, then I must permit him his delusion but not sacrifice my own maturing personality. Rather like walking a tightrope in a village fair, but I thought I could do it.

Perhaps one day, big as he was, he would recognize me as an equal. I was convinced that he needed me, in any case. While they went on making small talk about the housekeeping changes—no one had a kind word for the luckless Madame Servier—I sat on the edge of the sofa. Nicolas had followed me and seated himself on the narrow, uncomfortable arm of the sofa with his arm around me, his hand playing with the bosom of my gown. I was embarrassed by his public attention but certainly did not dislike it.

I asked the St. Audens to remain for a small supper, and they agreed. Outside the windows, the sun had gone down behind the dark bulk of the woods across the pond, and we discussed the pond itself. They all spoke without reserve about the tragedy at the moat bridge, which even the vicomte spoke of as an accident, in spite of the opinion he had shared with Nicolas that it deliberately may have been meant for Nicolas.

When we all got up to study the pond waters lapping at the stony western base of the château, Gabrielle pointed out to me how deep the waters were.

"When I was a girl, I nearly drowned just about there. Remember, Nico? It was the weekend of our betrothal ball, and Pierre was sulking."

The vicomte smiled. "I recall the weekend very well, but it seems to me that I had brought a guest of my own to the ball, that pretty little daughter of the prefect in Chinon."

"Blonde hussy," Gabrielle exclaimed, with a side glance at me. "I was so jealous, I let myself fall into the pond from that spot where the south parapet joins the wall."

Nicolas put in, "And I rescued you, like a fool. Ruined a perfectly good uniform. I should have left the heroics to Pierre."

"Not to me, old friend. I am the worst swimmer in the province."

We all laughed. I do not know what the others were thinking, but I still remember my own little flicker of jealousy. Not only had Nicolas loved Gaby enough to attend a ball celebrating their betrothal, but it was he, and not Pierre de St. Auden, who dove into those ominous black waters to rescue her. To make matters worse in my eyes, they all shared an earlier life that shut me out.

Perhaps the vicomte sensed my discomfort. He suggested shortly afterward, "Are we to see these changes you are putting forth, madame? I, for one, am most intrigued."

The vicomtesse also expressed an interest in any changes that might be made. "Modernize, my dear child. Be rid of these aging signs of, if I may call them, previous reigns. We in France have freed ourselves of Bourbons, Bonapartes, Bourbons again, and at any moment Orléans will go. Surely you may free yourself of all the dusty debris chosen by long-gone Bertolds. I advise you to go into every room, throw out everything. May she not, Nicolas?"

He rubbed my neck with his thumb and forefinger.

"If I object, I plainly see that you will call me Bluebeard and assure my wife that I have mysterious locked chambers here and there."

"So long as you don't have other wives locked in those mysterious chambers," I said tartly.

Everyone laughed, and we adjourned to the hall where, somewhat self-consciously, I pointed out a few changes I had discussed with Leocadia. Gabrielle had some ideas of her own, which I noted, one being the addition of comfortable chairs in the first- and second-story halls.

"To rest in when I drag myself wearily up those impossible steps."

"A worthy objective," I told her.

Nicolas remarked to St. Auden, "Your wife is the laziest female in the province."

"And ever was," the vicomte agreed.

Gabrielle and I exchanged the look common to all wives, which said plainly, "Men!"

We had just reached the ground floor when Grégoire approached Nicolas.

"Monsieur, pardon." His nod included the rest of us. "Your valet just arrived from Paris. He has confidential news from the Tuileries."

Exceedingly curious, we watched Nicolas go off with Grégoire. The vicomte murmured, "Gabrielle sniffs out these things. She believes Orléans is through."

They talked of that poor Citizen King as if he were still the Duke of Orléans, which struck me as a kind of lèse-majesté. I couldn't imagine an Englishman speaking so disrespectfully of our young queen. While they argued about who would follow King Louis-Philippe, whom they persisted in calling Orléans, I led them into what I hoped would be a showpiece of the château someday.

"Think of it," I announced proudly, waving to the Great Hall as we entered. "How splendid it will look when all the chandeliers are dipped in soapy water and every candle is in place! It may even seem warmer in here."

"Anything would help," Gabrielle said, and then we all stood openmouthed, staring up at a stout old man who sat astride a monumentally high ladder, trying to disentangle the center chandelier from its chains and ropes.

I apologized with some embarrassment. "I'm afraid he didn't hear the order to stop working while our guests are here."

"He is a trifle deaf," the vicomte explained. "I recognize Old Henri. He was in the service of the Maréchal Bertold." He waved and called to Henri, but the stout little man up among the crossbeams was busy with his work and merely nodded.

We moved down the length of the room and stopped at the huge baronial table in the center of the hall. There an argument ensued between the St. Audens. The vicomte thought the table most appropriate, and Gabrielle insisted that it was far too heavy.

"It depresses the atmosphere. The hall should be cut up by love seats, sofa tables, taborets, anything to reduce this great emptiness. I swear to you, when I look up and see the enormous height of that ceiling—the roof, rather—I—"

She looked up, then caught her breath so sharply that we stared at her before looking upward at the crossbeam.

"It—it is—" Her face had lost color. Her mouth remained open in horror.

By the time the vicomte and I turned our attention to Old Henri, he was screaming. A chain had slipped out of his hands. The chandelier with all its hundred glass lusters hurtled down upon us.

CHAPTER TWENTY-THREE

Gabrielle seemed frozen with shock. Her husband tugged at her from one side, and I pushed her from the other. She had gripped the edge of the table, and we were still trying to pry her fingers free amid the screams of the old man on the ladder when the huge wheel with its wood-and-metal base and hundreds of bits of glass struck the table, splintering in all directions.

The impact knocked me against a high-backed, heavy "milord" chair that overturned on me and perhaps saved me from most of the glass shards. The vicomte was knocked unconscious by the edge of the outside wheel with its broken, burned candles and what remained of the glass lusters.

Gabrielle was at the center of the disaster, her thick dark hair flowing loose and covered with dust and broken glass. She was still conscious, and it was her dreadful little gasping sounds as she caught her breath that brought me to full consciousness.

Only a minute or two passed, but it seemed like an endless time later when I stumbled to my feet. I found myself so unexpectedly weak, I could scarcely push aside the chair that imprisoned me. I was still trying to reach the vicomtesse when I heard running footsteps, and seconds afterward the big hall was bursting with activity. Strong arms began to lift me from the debris. I heard myself complain fretfully, "...frozen. We couldn't move her."

"Yes, yes, my love," Nicolas murmured, his lips close to my cheek. "She is being helped. We must get you to bed and wrapped up. You must not get cold." I realized that I was shivering. How silly! I thought. It isn't the cold. It's the shock of it.

"The vicomte?"

"He'll come around in a moment. Don't worry, sweetheart." He raised his voice, calling over my head to Leocadia. "How is he?"

"Regaining himself, monsieur. Just a knock on the head."

"Grégoire, have you freed Gabrielle?"

"Yes, monsieur. We have her unpinned now. It is important not to disturb the glass. Luckily her face escaped."

I opened my eyes, squinted at Nicolas. He was pale, his eyes wide and burning with anxiety. There was blood on his cheek.

I cried, "Oh, no! You are bleeding."

"Close your eyes, sweetheart, and try not to move." I suspected then that some of that blood was my own. But the blood on his hands kept seeping out into creases in his palms. He must have reached into a handful of the glass.

I heard murmured questions by the vicomte as he came to consciousness. Louder, authoritative voices cut through scurrying, rattling noises as the servants removed the injured pair from the debris. It seemed to me that above all I heard the grating, crackling sound of wooden sabots trampling on broken glass.

Nicolas said "Thank you" to someone and placed a delicate wineglass at my lips. I wanted to refuse whatever I was being offered, but Nicolas said persuasively, "Drink it for me, sweetheart. Just a drop or two of laudanum in water."

I did not approve of laudanum or opium or anything that

might cloud my brain, but I was too tired and confused to argue, so I drank.

I found myself loosely wrapped in a blanket. Then, with the greatest care, my husband lifted me high out of the debris. The laudanum in water worked rapidly, and I retained only a blurred memory of being moved.

Much later I awoke in the ancient bed with its heavy velvet curtains pushed back so that I might see the comforting lamplight on the candle stand and, across the room, the rising moon above the easterly woods. I would not like to have awakened tonight in the dark, I decided.

Having turned my head to look out the window, I discovered that my left arm and my left ankle were wrapped.

"I may as well be a mummy," I muttered to myself.

I was startled and momentarily alarmed when something moved in the shadows on the other side of the bed. With difficulty I turned in that direction. Nicolas stepped into the light. He looked tired, but his smile was warm and vital.

"You sound better, sweetheart."

He flexed the muscles in his shoulders and balled his fingers into fists, then released their tension.

"I am perfectly all right. But you look dreadful," I said frankly. I remembered how sensitive he was to endearments and added, "Darling . . . bend over."

He bent over me. I raised up with a groan or two and kissed him. As uncomfortable as both our bodies might be, we lingered over that kiss. When I finally fell back, he said brusquely, "Move."

As fully dressed as he was, he settled himself on top of the covers, lying back on the pillows beside me. After a few blissful moments, during which our tired bodies relaxed, I asked, "How are the St. Audens?"

"Pierre is little the worse for it. He's been hit harder by a cognac bottle in an Algerian estaminet. Poor Gaby is suffering, but thank God her face isn't marred! She could never have survived that. She is badly cut about the neck. One shard of glass cut through her clothing. Her right hip. And countless cuts and scratches. Also, a very large bump on the back of her head. Luckily she has more of that bushy hair than she will ever need."

A little embarrassed by my own frankness, I confessed, "I've been praying for her."

"My sweet." His lips touched my temple.

I couldn't bear to have him think me sentimental. I was anything but that.

"No, darling. I prayed because it was my fault. I insisted on having those stupid chandeliers cleaned."

He contradicted me. "Poor Gaby has herself to blame. She says she froze with fear—as she puts it. Neither you nor Pierre could have gotten her away in time. Old Henri saw it that way as well. He accepts the blame; says he had just freed the two ends of the chain, and then it fell through those rheumatic fingers of his."

"He must feel dreadful."

"No. Mostly worried. He thinks he will be turned off. God knows what would happen if I did let him go. He would starve to death."

That worried me too. "But you mustn't. He was doing the best he could. Please, Nicolas."

He pretended to be indignant. "You think I am a monster? The man was born here. He dies here. We'll find some way that he can be useful. Meanwhile neither Pierre nor I think Gaby should be moved until those cuts begin to mend. How do you feel about having visitors for a few days?"

"Certainly. We get on very well. I like them."

There was a tiny but significant pause.

"Especially Pierre."

"Don't talk nonsense. Especially both of them."

He raised up and studied my face while he leaned on one elbow. "You are able to snap back. You must be feeling more yourself. Shall I order up supper to fatten those wan cheeks?"

"I've never been wan in my life. Thin, maybe. But never wan."

Eventually Leocadia, herself, brought up a tray containing a broth with diced vegetables from the Bertold gardens and Forcing House, plus spiced wine and an absurdly elaborate, fresh-baked cherry tart. I had never tasted anything more delicious than the vegetables in their broth and admitted freely, "I'm afraid that in our valley we overcook our meat and vegetables. I must take lessons from Monsieur Carletti."

But here Nicolas interrupted to inform me, "Don't give the credit for this meal to Carletti. It was Leocadia who prepared it."

"Not the tart," Leocadia said dryly.

I thanked her with all my heart, and I thought her frigidly correct manner thawed a little. I did not retain her goodwill, however, when I went on to ask if our guests were feeling better.

"Monsieur le Vicomte goes very well, I believe, madame. Naturally he is concerned for the vicomtesse."

"And the vicomtesse?"

"I cannot say, madame. I did not wait upon the lady."

She curtsied and left the room, ignoring the thanks I offered nervously. I puzzled over her attitude for a minute.

Nicolas must have been watching me. He put out a hand, his knuckles against my cheek.

"What is it, sweetheart? Upset? You feel warm."

"No, no. I'm ever so much better. You were right. It was the food I needed."

"Not me?" It was whimsically asked, but I felt that there might be a certain amount of feeling in the question.

I ran a finger over his nose and lips. "You first, darling. Then the broth. Actually, I frowned over something else. It occurs to me that Leocadia doesn't like Gabrielle." He started to say something, but I rushed on. "Nicolas, she also didn't like my brother. Is there some connection?"

I knew he was hiding something. He answered too quickly,

too loudly. "Nothing could be further from the truth. Leocadia simply takes likes and dislikes to people. God knows why. Pay no attention to her. She does her job, but if you had rather—"

Alarmed at the injustice to Leocadia, I interrupted, "I go on very well with her. I want her to remain. I was just curious."

"You are the mistress of this house. Not Leocadia or Gaby or Queen Marie-Amélie. Or myself. If you want to keep her, she stays."

"Good." But I had a feeling that he knew my answer.

We kissed briskly, hugged each other, and he went away to find out what the St. Audens needed. I eventually went back to sleep.

Nicolas never did come to bed. He had sent to Boisville for a physician who was home on vacation from Tours and apparently much trusted by the Bertolds and the St. Audens. There was an understandable panic over the disaster in the Great Hall and, afterward, visits to several sickrooms. I missed my husband, but I knew how much must be done.

Then, too, I slept most of the time, which was just as well, because I ached in every bone and muscle, as I had weeks ago after being struck by the gypsies. Or, as Nicolas insisted, "my unknown assailants." It had not been a lucky year for me, except, of course, for the most important act of my life, marrying Nicolas.

Knowing all this, I found myself curiously uneasy when I awoke alone at four in the morning and found the room dark, with only the faintest light from the late-night sky to tell me the difference between the objects in the room, and the sky so oppressive beyond those long windows. A night bird, huge and black with one while breast feather, peered in at me once before flying away.

After trying to close my eyes and not think of my surroundings, which had seen so many sinister goings-on during the last eight hundred years, I decided to get up and close the drapes. Nicolas had meant well in trying to keep me from feeling shut into a tomb, but those night birds and the wide sky with its sensation that God or someone was watching me proved too much.

I got out of bed shakily and with great difficulty. My ankle almost collapsed under me. I doubt if the glass cuts were deep, but my body had reacted badly to the whole accident. Eventually, gritting my teeth and clutching the furniture like a wretched invalid, I got to the first window, found the cords, and then closed the drapes. The second was about to follow, but at this close vantage point the whole horizon seemed to be filled with those great, dark trees that bordered the pond. From them I looked down at the moat bridge, its fresh wood and the stone abutments gleaming in the light from the now western moon, which had trickled around the corners of the château.

I wondered for the hundredth time what really had happened there.

Closing the drapes, I moved to the last window and saw lights moving rapidly through the woods toward that bridge. Horses' hooves became audible. Had the doctor only just arrived? He must be very late. I hoped the vicomtesse had not suffered all this time.

The closed carriage, hardly larger than a gig, appeared behind a hard-breathing horse who trotted onto the moat bridge. In spite of the two carriage lights, I could only make out the black outlines of carriage and horse. When the carriage pulled up before the ironbound doors far below my windows, I could no longer see anything but the glow of the carriage lamp on one side.

I pushed the window open and tried to listen, but the voices below were muffled and the wind had risen, causing plaintive, mournful sighs as it passed through the woods across the bridge. I waited a few minutes, wondering, but the night air chilled me. I drew in the window, closed the drapes, and felt my way back to the bed, stubbing my toe on the footstool.

After a timeless period during which I tossed and turned, wincing at what this did to my bandaged arm and ankle, I went back to sleep.

I was awakened late in the morning by the opening and closing of the hall door. I called out. "Is it you, darling?"

No one answered. I sat up groaning, as though my bones were twice their age. Indeed they felt like it. My nerves began to betray the rising fear I had experienced in the night. I sat there shaking a little, waiting. There wasn't another sound until I heard a whispered command. "Now!"

A second later something quick and agile climbed onto my bed. Before I could cry out, I was smothered in hugs by my nephew, Jeremy.

I was so relieved and so glad to see him, I splashed tears over his tousled, dark head. Squeezing me hard, he felt me wince and drew back.

"Oh, I am sorry, Aunt Alain. Uncle said I must be very careful of you. Are you really sick? You never were before."

"Nor am I now, dear." I held him off and examined him, especially his face. "You look radiant. Evidently Nanny was wrong. England agreed with you."

Guiltily he looked toward the door. "It was coming back home to my wonderful château that did it. As soon as we walked off the little sailboat at Calais, it was exciting. It even smelled like France."

I knew from Jeremy's behavior that Nanny Pemberton had been listening at the door. I called to her, "Come in, Nanny. Don't hang about in doorways. Did you like the smell of France?"

Nanny bustled in, looking somewhat harassed. "I never listen at doors, Miss Alain, as you very well know. And as to the smell of France, let me tell you, this nose sniffed out some mighty pretty doings when we came through Paris. Even in Calais I noticed it. Dreadful talk among the people. All about their precious Prince Louis-Napoleon. He was imprisoned for years by the French king, you know."

"Yes. I know. His name was against him. And maybe his ambition."

"He has been living near London since his escape. And now they want him to come back and be president of the French Republic. Did you ever?"

"What! They already have a king. I ought to know. I met him."

Jeremy chimed in. "They said bad things about him. Everybody says his friends kill people and don't get their heads cut off for it."

I looked at Nanny. She agreed. "Quite true, my dear. His Majesty is in serious difficulties. But if you will forgive me, this is far less important than what we see here. I was never so shocked."

"We wanted to come in and see you right away," Jeremy told me with pride, adding resentfully, "He wouldn't let us."

Nanny explained. "Monsieur Nicolas looked in on you several times and made us wait to see you."

My first reaction was to resent Nicolas's high-handed ways, but I told myself that this was done to protect me, and of course, I was aware that he'd never liked the nurse-governess. He regarded her, with some justification, as a gossip and a troublemaker. He must have discovered very soon what I had always known, that William and William's son were first in her affections. All others were secondary.

"How long have you waited to see me?"

Nanny stifled a yawn. She was not above demonstrating points without saying so. "Only since four, I believe. We slept a little in the carriage. It wasn't too rough until we reached that appalling, bumpy road through the Bertold Woods."

I began to laugh, remembering my ridiculous imaginary fears in the night. That winded horse and the little black carriage had carried nothing more terrifying than these two loved ones. When Nanny showed signs of hurt feelings, I explained the reason for my amusement. Her scant, graying eyebrows went up, and after an awkward moment during which she and Jeremy looked at each other, she said, "Yes. I suppose we did arrive somewhat precipitously. And perhaps it is just as well. We found things most inhospitable when we passed through the village. Several stones were thrown at our horse after we stopped to rest her and get a sweet bun for Jeremy. He has been of great help, I must tell you. Half the time he handled the reins himself."

"Nanny helped," Jeremy confessed.

Although I was concerned, I didn't want either of them to know how unpopular Nicolas had been since the death of his sister and William. But my caution was useless.

Jeremy confided, "It's Uncle Nicolas. Everybody thinks he killed Father and Maman." He added in a rush, "I told the baker it wasn't true, didn't I, Nanny?"

"You certainly did, my lamb." Nanny had been giving me what we used to call her "eagle eye," and she said now, "My dear Miss Alain, if ever a body needed sustenance, you do. I'm going down to the kitchen and prepare something healthful to start you out all right and tight."

She was already on her way when I realized the havoc she might cause in Monsieur Carletti's domain. I called after her anxiously. "Nanny, don't disturb the chef. He is a skilled cook, but he has temperament."

"Temperament!" She sniffed from the hall. "I'll temperament him if he offers me any of his Frenchified airs." I heard her small feet chattering along the hall and knew that Nanny was one of the hazards of life that could not be prevented, like typhoons and earthquakes.

Jeremy was examining my bandages with great interest.

"The lights fell down on you, Uncle Nicolas said. Excuse me, Aunt, but you do look dreadfully . . . dreadful, wrapped up like that."

"Thank you," I said gravely. "However, I feel much better. Where is Richard Pemberton? Why did he let you travel all this way alone?"

"He didn't. Not exactly. He rode here with your doctor, and we came after. They went before us. Richard said they were the advance recon—recon—"

"Reconnaisance. I don't remember seeing a doctor."

"He said Uncle Nicolas bandaged you proper. His name is Oliver. Monsieur Oliver. He just gave you more laudanum." Jeremy looked around the sunlit room and then lowered his voice to a whisper. "The vicomte said something funny when I was in the hall. He didn't know I heard."

"Well, what was it?"

"He thinks somebody wants to kill him or his pretty wife. Or you."

I sat up again, very fast, anxious to put to rest such a sinister idea.

"That is absurd. It was an accident. Anyone but a fool knows that."

Jeremy scratched his head. "That's what Uncle Nicolas said. But the vicomte said, 'Henri will—.' I knew Old Henri by the cracked, funny old voice. Was that the one who did it? Old Henri?"

"Yes, yes. Do go on. The vicomte said what?"

"That Old Henri knows more than he is saying. Do you believe that?"

"No, I don't. It's the greatest piece of nonsense I ever heard. I saw it happen. It was a plain and simple accident."

Jeremy shrugged. He had the absolute certainty of children who repeat something without knowing whether it may be true or not.

"That's what he said. And Uncle Nicolas was angry. He didn't like it even a little bit."

"Nor do I."

I had to get up, to stop this idiotic speculation by St. Auden and disastrously repeated by Jeremy.

My nephew panicked when he saw me put one foot over the side of the bed and feel for the footstool. He ran out in the hall and called to Nanny, but it was Nicolas who came.

He heard his nephew's anxious complaint that I wasn't "behaving" and came in to demand in mock-official tones, "What is this? Revolt in the ranks? Who do you think you are, my love? Jeanne d'Arc?"

Jeremy giggled at the picture of his bandaged and mummified aunt as the great Joan, but I explained reasonably, "I am perfectly all right, except for a few cuts, and if I don't begin to move around soon, I will be as stiff as a poker."

Nicolas agreed that if I felt that belligerent, I should certainly be permitted to get up. He rang for Marie-Clare, sent Jeremy to join Nanny, remained to help me bathe in the huge hip bath carried up the tower steps, and then offered unwanted aid when Marie-Clare managed very skillfully to dress me.

I felt more myself once I was clean, dressed, and on my feet. When we were about to leave the room, I reminded Nicolas of his gossiping guests.

"The vicomte has been saying that the chandelier affair was no accident."

"Rubbish!" he snapped, surprising me by his sudden burst of anger. "No such thing."

"I know. And we must stop his talking like this, carrying such tales. Small wonder that Nanny and Jeremy were stoned by villagers as they came through the village."

"Stoned? I heard nothing of that." He was still cross. "It's all the work of that troublemaking Pemberton. He is playing the busybody at this minute in the Great Hall. If I thought he would break his fool neck, I would let him get up on Old Henri's ladder, as he is dying to do."

"To examine the chain?"

"What else? How he thinks a man Henri's age could saw through steel is beyond me. It was a perfectly simple accident. The chain slipped through Henri's hands. Nothing simpler. If I had known he was put to that job, I would have vetoed it."

"It is my fault. Mine and Leocadia's. We knew he was working up there."

"Anyway, sweetheart, it is all over now, and it won't be repeated, so you may breathe easy."

Quite true—if chandeliers were the only threat. Then I hurriedly changed the direction of my thoughts.

CHAPTER TWENTY-FOUR

Nicolas was surprised and secretly pleased, I think, when I did not rush down to greet Richard. I knew what to expect of my girlhood friend and companion, and I was much more anxious to see how the St. Audens were feeling.

They were in adjoining bedrooms across and down the hall from our own bedroom. Their rooms were more modern, with few heavy furnishings of oak and velvet. The rooms were cheerful, and Gabrielle, though justifiably fretful, seemed to enjoy this break in their lives.

I considered myself fairly mummified, but it was nothing to Gabrielle's condition. The back of her head was cushioned by a heavy, moist bandage, and she had to lie with her head sideways, which bothered her somewhat. Her neck was wrapped, and I was shocked to see that bloodstains had seeped through. She claimed in a rueful way that her worst problem was a word I did not understand. Nicolas translated it as her hip. Her contagious grin told me the word she had used was more coarse and descriptive. A thin shard of glass had stabbed her there.

Nicolas said she was lucky that she had been stabbed in

the stoutest portion of her anatomy, but she made an absurd face at that and insisted that only champagne would soothe her shattered nerves. With my good hand I rang for one of the kitchen staff, and Gabrielle held out her own good hand.

"Dear Alain, what an excellent creature you are!"

I accepted that and her hand as a compliment. Gabrielle rambled on with a light but sinister tone that did nothing to ease my basic uneasiness over this ancient house.

"Nico, what do you intend to do about your ghosts who arrange all these accidents?"

"Ghosts?" he echoed, amused. "Henri's age and palsied hands are perfectly natural, I assure you."

"All the same, I hope we won't see him and his palsied hands next time I visit you."

"You will see Henri wherever I place him."

I thought it might have been polite and in keeping with his promise to me, if he had said, "Wherever my wife places him."

But in spite of his remark to me, this was his house, not mine. I must often have referred to "my" farms in Dorset; yet the minute I married Nicolas, they became his property by law.

I had more reason to note this matter of property when I talked with the vicomte a short time later.

He was sitting by his window, reading a week-old *Moniteur* from Paris and put the newspaper aside to get up and greet me. I hastily banished manners, ordering him not to move and disturb that crack he had received on the head. He reseated himself with signs of relief. Obviously he still suffered from a bad headache.

I apologized again for what had happened, and he waved aside my responsibility.

"If you please, madame, we will not discuss this foolishness. You have behaved with exquisite tact. Another bride in your place would have run screaming from the château by this time. Nicolas has had his difficulties. There is no doubt of it, but your trust is admirable."

I reminded him, "You, yourself, believe that these frightful happenings are not my husband's fault."

While my heart beat all too rapidly, I waited for his answer. Why did he hesitate now?

"Very true in one sense. Still, one wonders if my friend, perhaps unconsciously, attracts these strange happenings. I'll wager that Old Henri may know more than he seems to know."

"I tell you, it was an accident!" I fumbled for reasons, though the truth was self-evident to me. "Why would anyone wish to kill you or the vicomtesse or me? Perhaps you have enemies, monsieur, but no one would profit by my death." I thought that would silence him, and I was shocked when he presented an answer.

"One person would profit by your death, madame. Your husband becomes the owner of very valuable farming property in your native Britain."

"Legally he has control over it now. Aside from that, he is a very rich man."

The vicomte smoothed the plush padding on the arm of his chair. "This is true. We know it, you and I. But if Nicolas had spent a fortune on his defense in the deaths of the Daviots, and if he has lost money on crops and vineyards and a dozen other investments, then he would need your estate." Before I could intervene angrily, he added, "Or if he has sacrificed his fortune to save His Majesty's throne."

It was much more likely. The thought only increased my anger.

"These are all lies. How can you claim to be his friend?"

"Because I analyze all possibilities. I do not say that these things are true," he reminded me quietly. "I say that these are weapons against my friend, in a sense. Someone has thought of this. We must do likewise."

"To turn me against my husband? If so, he has failed."

I hoped he understood that this flat statement was directed

against him. I left the room and went down to see Richard. I dreaded to meet him, knowing that he, too, would talk against Nicolas. While I was uncertain whether St. Auden was still my husband's friend or a very subtle enemy, I did not doubt Richard's motives. He had been Nicolas Bertold's enemy before I ever met Nicolas.

I found Richard browbeating the three maids, including Marie-Clare, in the middle of a strangely denuded Great Hall. From what I heard as I entered, he had just demanded the "truth" from a trembling and frightened young parlormaid who assured him, while sniffing back the tears, "But I didn't, monsieur. He never discussed it with me at all. The old man just took the ladder and came in here. I was in the entry."

"When the chandelier fell?"

"No, no, monsieur. Before anything happened. Then I went to the housekeeper's sitting room to—to ask about dusting the m-music room."

The poor girl looked like a terrified bird, and I was about to interfere when Marie-Clare began to chatter. She was not a girl to be crushed by a man as attractive as Richard Pemberton, even when Richard was being particularly obnoxious.

"Oh, but Monsieur Pemb'ton, I came by Old Henri shortly before the big crash. To me—I have excellent eyes, no?—he was very suspicious."

It was all Richard needed. "Suspicious. Yes. I mean to say, how?"

"But it is so plain, monsieur. Henri is old. That is true, yet he is still a man. He wishes that I should be his—you understand? His mistress. This old man. It is to laugh."

I wanted to laugh at Richard's expression myself. I don't think he had ever been so embarrassed. Nor did it help matters when one of the browbeaten parlormaids giggled. He reddened so visibly, I thought it best to intercede when he began angrily, "Now see here—"

"Good day, Richard," I hailed him, distracting his attention from the girls. With a brief curtsy to me each of them scuttled out.

It was hard to be cross with Richard over his officiousness when it all appeared to be performed on my behalf and he was so glad to see me.

"My dear Alain!" He took my unbandaged hand and kissed it, then he kissed my cheek. "I was never more shocked! But you need not look so sad. I mean to see that the culprit confesses. We will discover who is in back of this."

"In the first place, I am not sad. I am cross. What do you mean by quizzing our servants as though you were the master here?"

He seemed genuinely bewildered.

"But, Alain, you have been attacked. Hurt. Surely you want the man punished. And the person who hired—or ordered him—to do this thing."

I was thoroughly disgusted. "Richard, for the hundredth time nobody ordered the old man to drop the chandelier. It just happened. Haven't you ever had an accident, let something slip through your fingers?"

He shook his head, not in answer to my question, as I knew, but in total disbelief at my blindness. He tried to banish unpleasant feelings between us.

"Come, then, can't we be friends, as we used to be?"

I agreed at once, relieved to be on good terms again and to have finished with all this deeply troubling talk about "deliberate" accidents.

Things went very well during the next twenty-four hours. Richard was polite and deferential to Gabrielle, and she flirted with him. He was reasonably civil to Nicolas, who seemed to care very little about his attitude, one way or the other. So much had to be done about the château that he was busy from early morning until the late supper we all shared in the main dining salon, the formality of which I found depressing.

It seemed that Richard and the Vicomte de St. Auden had much in common, both being readers and somewhat intellectual. Intellect had always been a subject of contention between Richard and William, who was a man of his hands, not his brain. I often felt that Richard might profit from whatever he learned in books by getting along better with his fellow men, which seemed to be my poor brother's failing, but Richard did very little better. Perhaps it was not in his curriculum. He usually managed to annoy me within five minutes of our meeting, though I knew he meant well.

Nanny and Jeremy spent most of the daylight hours showing me around the estate. This was very pleasant, but it was not like being with Nicolas. I accused Nanny only half in jest, of trying to separate me from my husband. We had been walking through the woods far west of the pond, and stopped to rest Jeremy, who was beginning to make wheezing noises in his chest. He worried us in spite of his indignant insistence that he felt quite fit.

Nanny made me uncomfortable by not smiling at my words.

"Well, my dear, he is not so very much in love with you now, is he?"

"What on earth do you mean?" It was bad enough, but there was worse to come. Jeremy eyed me in the same way. He had straddled a broken tree limb and was scraping away dry needles from the earth between his feet. His big eyes were full of concern. I always marveled that he had so little of his father's Anglo-Saxon looks and so much of his mother's dark beauty. He reached out and touched my skirts.

"Aunt Alain, he is a bad man."

"Has he been bad to you?" I asked it lightly, more lightly than I felt, for I knew at once that he referred to his uncle.

He did not look away as another child might have done. He stared directly at me, and I wondered why there was something about his eyes that made me shiver. A curious resemblance to something in the past. A portrait of his mother, perhaps. But why should I fear that dark gaze? Nicolas had dark eyes, and I didn't fear him. No. There was something different about Jeremy and about Yolande, his mother. A primeval darkness.

Nanny put in nervously, "He is only a child, Miss Alain. The poor lamb doesn't know how to answer you."

Jeremy cleared his throat. He sounded hoarse, older.

"I do too. I heard people whispering last night. They think somebody tried to kill Aunt Alain. Just like Father and Maman. I know who it is. And they let him go before."

I could hardly get the words out.

"You don't know anything of the sort. How dare you!"

But still he kept on while Nanny made little hush-hush sounds.

"It's true. I started to like him again, but that was before he tried to kill you. And you love him more than you love me. It's not fair."

For the first time in my life I realized what I owed to a child of my blood, a child orphaned and alone except for Nanny. I felt the pain of his loneliness like a deep, aching hunger. I swallowed hard and reached out to him.

"My lamb, he had nothing to do with it. I swear to you, it was an accident. I saw it myself. Anyway, I love nobody better than you."

He hesitated. His pride prevented his surrender for a minute. Then he went into my arms, sniffing and blinking back "unmanly tears," while Nanny accompanied our tears with her own, copiously shed.

Afterward, as we made our way through the woods, the late-afternoon sun gradually blotted out by storm clouds, I caught both my nephew and Nanny exchanging glances that told me they wondered where we were going in this purposeful manner. I explained when I thought they had endured enough uncertainty.

"We are heading toward the pond and then around to the coach house. Leocadia says that those rooms opening off the northwest tower are over the carriageway. I want to talk to Henri. Most of the household sleeps there."

"But that's the horrid old man who tried to kill you!" Nanny gasped.

"That old man was disentangling a pair of chains and ropes when one chain slipped through his hands. That is all."

"Well, I never! Why, you must be mad to take such a chance, Miss Alain."

Jeremy, whose hand was in mine, suggested thoughtfully, "Maybe he will tell us who told him to do that."

"Paid him, like as not."

"Nanny, for heaven's sake!"

"Anyway," Jeremy reminded us cheerfully, "we're going with you, Aunt Alain. He won't dare hurt you when we're all there, will he, Nanny?"

Nanny was not nearly so keen to beard the old man, but she grunted and subsided.

We had some difficulty finding our way back to the pond. I foolishly counted on either of my companions to know the way, but it was clear that they, too, were somewhat confused. Nanny fussed and excused Jeremy, taking all the blame to herself, reaping the usual reward of martyrs. She annoyed me, and Jeremy paid her little heed. He seemed to be worried about other matters he kept to himself.

Every time the breeze rustled through the tightly laced trees, or a red squirrel darted across our makeshift path, Jeremy jumped. He seemed to cough more, and that worried me, for fear that his lungs might be adversely affected amid all this dust and debris of summer, but Nanny reassured me on that score at least.

"We came upon those horrid gypsies in just such woods as these. The poor lamb never liked them. They hovered too much. Master William was furious. He wouldn't let them near the poor lamb."

"Why?" I wanted to know. "William got on reasonably well with gypsies in our valley. You remember, Nanny."

"Yes, but of course, this was quite a different thing. Naturally, he resented—" She turned her foot on a twig, and we all stopped while she rubbed her ankle.

I persisted. "Why, Nanny? What was so different about the gypsies here?"

Jeremy was watching Nanny, but it seemed clear that her mind was on her ankle.

"I do hope I haven't sprained anything. Dear me, how provoking!" She felt the oppressive silence and dismissed the subject of gypsies impatiently. "Because they were French gypsies, my dear. Master William was quite chauvinistic, you know."

Jeremy was about to ask a question when I heard a heavy series of crackling sounds through the underbrush that separated us from the pond waters. I gestured Jeremy to silence. Nanny caught her breath. I don't know what she expected to see. I was certainly unprepared for the huge brown bear that lumbered across the path ahead of us.

I had heard that it was best in such circumstances not to move. I obeyed this rule as did Jeremy, but Nanny gave out a stifled scream and the creature turned. The fur about his neck was like a great ruff, making him look even more imposing. His features were deceptively harmless, big, clumsy, almost friendly. But the eyes, set deep in that powerful frame, seemed to glitter in my overcharged imagination.

He turned and padded toward us. I felt Jeremy shiver. I shoved him behind me where he pressed close to my spreading skirts. Common sense should have told me that the bear's owners would be near, but common sense fled when he stopped within a few yards of us and, with deliberation, rose up on his hind legs. Nanny screamed. Jeremy began to cough, and I felt as though I had been turned to ice. I had Jeremy still behind me, but Nanny kept wringing her hands, praying aloud.

I pulled my wits together and in my loudest, sternest voice I yelled: "Down!"

Just to be doubly sure, I shouted the command in French,

but those paws waving in the air still looked bigger than anything I had ever seen.

As though this were not bad enough, something bright moved through the trees behind the bear and caught my eye. Gaudy yellow satin with a pink velvet blouse and jerkin, all of which looked familiar to me.

The gypsy woman was Zilla Honiger.

CHAPTER TWENTY-FIVE

I very nearly forgot my fear of the big furred creature who towered over me, swaying as if he girded his loins for the strike. Those claws looked far more deadly at this close range. But it was anger that caught me by the throat.

How dare Nicolas bring these people to his estate after they had knocked me on the head and kidnapped me! This was worse than his original crime in warning them and helping them to escape the country.

Mentally I pulled myself together.

"Mrs. Honiger, will you please call off your pet before I have him shot?"

Though she gave us her usual toothy grin, her eyes narrowed. Like her bear, they glittered with what I assumed must be hatred. That emotion was mutual.

"You afraid of poor Yvgeny? He is friendly soul. Yvgeny, come."

The bear dropped on all fours to sniff out the sugar lump in her palm, but I thought he gave us a reluctant glance. Doubtless he would have preferred salty flesh to a small lump of sweetness.

"What are you doing here on Bertold property?" I asked her, not mincing words.

Nanny began to recover, once Yvgeny lumbered back to his owner. She nipped at my sleeve.

"I know that—that person. She is the one who hounded Jeremy and me in the village that day."

"I remember. Mrs. Honiger, you and your family are not wanted on Bertold land. Pack up your things, including that creature, and be off this property before sunrise or I will have the local prefect notified."

Mrs. Honiger shrugged. Tiny bells tinkled somewhere on her still voluptuous body. They must be sewn to the back hem of her jerkin. Her smile remained.

"You say. But the master, he says we may visit our cousins."

I had a sinking feeling that she was probably right.

"Who are your cousins?"

"The housekeeper, Leocadia, she is the cousin of my husband. And, madame, let me remind you, Leocadia holds a place very special in the house; isn't it so?"

"No more than any other housekeeper," I told her, and deliberately walked around her in the path, maneuvering myself between Jeremy and the bear, who eyed us with his head cocked on one side, as if he debated whether to eat us after his first course or his second.

I was pleased that Jeremy ventured out from behind my skirts and tried to present himself as my protector while we passed the animal. Nanny followed timorously to the accompaniment of Mrs. Honiger's laughter. It was a harsh, metallic sound that made me grit my teeth. But my quarrel was with Nicolas, not with the impudent gypsy woman.

Luckily Jeremy made out the dark pond waters, within a minute's walk, and we were soon on our way back to the château, whose slat-covered pepperpot towers loomed up against the bleak northeastern sky. I dreaded the approaching conflict with Nicolas, but something must be done. It had been insensitive of him to let that woman and her family establish themselves again under my nose, and I felt that insensitivity was the mildest face I could put on the matter.

By the time we reached the château, however, he had gone off to Boisville, leaving a message for me that read:

> Sweetheart,
>
> Pierre and I are off to talk the local Jacquerie out of setting up a guillotine, or worse, for His Majesty, poor fellow. We suspect a few livres, properly distributed, may do the trick. Pierre thinks a dinner for the village worthies might sweeten the bribe. We will try this invitation as well.
>
> Returning home before dark for a late dinner, but you and Gaby and the boy should not wait for us. Enjoy yourself. Getting lost in the towers and turret rooms used to be my favorite game when I was Jeremy's age. But see that you don't break that neck I am so fond of.
>
> Until I enfold you again, my love,
>
> Nicolas

Obviously curious, Nanny asked me, "Was it anything important, my dear?"

Embarrassed to tell her that in spite of my anger I also wanted to kiss this great black scrawl of a letter, I said, "Nothing in particular. Monsieur Bertold and the vicomte have gone to town. They will return before dark for a late dinner."

"Very well. Jeremy and I will go to our rooms long before." Jeremy groaned, but she explained, "They may want to talk politics to your aunt, and you know how dreary that is for you. Shall I tell the housekeeper about the late dinner?"

"No. I'll have a few words to say to her, in any case. I'm going now to visit Old Henri."

Jeremy said with great conviction, "We'll go too. Then he can't drop any chandeliers and things."

I didn't see any reason why it would be unsafe for Jeremy and Nanny to accompany me. On the contrary, it might serve a good purpose. They would hear for themselves that the episode had been an accident.

Nanny and Jeremy also showed me the way to the servants' sleeping quarters, around the eastern front of the building, into the northeast tower whose base was the carriage house. This had once been a root cellar, and something else exceedingly unpleasant.

With a naïveté that disgusts me now, I remarked on the rusty iron rings in the wall and the water seeping up between the broken stones of the floor.

"What was this place before the Bertolds stored their carriages here? I am happy to see that they don't house the carriage horses or the dogs here."

Jeremy was shocked. "It's half mine, and I'd never let animals live in a torture chamber. They're nice and warm and fed in the stalls behind the tower steps over there."

A torture chamber. I might have known.

They led me to the door, obscurely tucked into one corner of this delightful torture chamber.

We began the tiresome climb up to one of those turret rooms used by the man called Old Henri. I looked through each chilly aperture on the way up, wondering that people could live eight hundred years in this condition without ever taking shortcuts to their destination.

Breathless, I stopped finally and saw that my nephew was also breathing hard. It seemed ridiculous that he should have to go farther. Nanny fussed over him as always but insisted that he could go on because he wanted to so much. But I stopped in one of the embrasures and drew him to the open air. He took several long breaths of the thick, misty air and then refused to stay behind. "If you are going, I must go. I am the only man here. It is my place."

I hugged him, and we went on.

"Madame Servier used to sleep in the rooms in the main part of the château, opposite these walls," Nanny explained.

"She saw a lot," Jeremy put in.

Nanny agreed in a disgruntled way. "She used to give Master Jeremy sweetmeats when she knew they did not agree with him. And she was forever spying. She could see the whole area of the pond."

"My room has almost this view," Jeremy reminded me.

"I know, dear."

I still wondered how he could have noted all the details that were described in his testimony against his uncle. Perhaps this was one reason why his testimony had been discounted.

I was interested in the "spying" of the dead woman, however, and just before we reached Henri's door, I asked Nanny, "What was Madame Servier curious about? Did she spy on everyone?"

Nanny was brushing a dust stain off Jeremy's jacket and surprised that I found the late housekeeper an interesting subject. She said caustically, "Everything was fodder to her. One day when I was scolding her about the wretched handling of Master Jeremy's food, she informed me, as bold as brass, 'I know what I know. There's many a secret here. Take Monsieur William and Madame Gabrielle.'"

I stared at her in the dusk of the ancient stone passage, chilled by the implications in that.

"You don't mean there was anything between my brother and the vicomtesse?"

Nanny took umbrage at once. I had insulted the person she loved best in all the world. Even her own son was aware that William had always been first in her affections.

"Miss Alain! Master William was never unfaithful to his wife. Not once, I'd swear to it."

"Well, then."

Her mouth tightened. "There were provocations, heaven knows. The gravest provocation. Who could blame him if he passed the time of day with a pretty woman? We had best knock, Miss Alain. It is chilly up here, and we shouldn't like Master Jeremy to take cold, should we?"

"What provocation?"

I could see that Jeremy's presence inhibited her, but I was determined to have the truth later. Jeremy insisted on knocking, and when the warped old door opened, Henri saw only Jeremy standing there for an instant.

"Come in, young master. Come to call on Old Henri, have you? Ay. There's a caring young gentleman. Like his uncle, he cares about Old Henri."

We two women appeared then, in the light from the deep window embrasure. Small panes of glass protected him from too many drafts but the tiny room was made a little warmer by a portable stove that burned wood and some smoky stuff like peat. The old man bowed to Nanny and me, a courtly bow that seemed to be a remnant of past glories.

"I am brewing coffee, Madame Bertold. Madame Pemb'ton. May I offer you a cup?" He pointed to the kettle on top of the heating stove and started to bring down two tiny china cups from a shelf beside the rosary at the head of his sleeping cot. I refused with thanks. The gesture was charming, but coffee beans cost money. Then, too, I was not used to drinking the vile stuff, which was stewing away as we talked. I always said Frenchmen had iron stomachs.

Henri proved my theory when he boasted, "Monsieur Nicolas, he drank with me just before he rode off to Boisville. He is very fond of my coffee. Especially when it is sufficiently black."

"My husband was here to see you?"

"But yes, madame. We chatted of the old days. He brought me more coffee beans. I crush them myself. They are stronger so."

Jeremy was peering into the thick black liquid and wondering, "Does it taste sweet, like chocolate?"

"Indeed, yes, little master, when honey is added."

Nanny hustled him away from the coffee, and he soon

became enthralled with the view from the window embrasure. While Nanny picked up the cap he had dropped and then joined him at the window, I questioned Henri.

"Please forgive me, but I was curious to know how the chandelier happened to fall."

He looked apprehensive. His small features somehow gained added dignity in that wrinkled facade.

"I have explained very carefully to Monsieur Nicolas. It was these hands, where the pain comes. Then it goes. Like that. The chains, they were tangled. I freed them. Just when I free them, they run through the fingers."

"I understand. And you told my husband precisely how it occurred. I think that should be sufficient. You have been very kind."

"No, madame. Pardon. It is your kindness. You refuse to have me removed from this house where I was born. But others, they whisper. Point to me. They say it may be that I was paid to do that bad thing. But I would never do such wickedness. Madame la Vicomtesse is my friend since I was sous-chef for the old Madame Bertold."

"The vicomtesse is charming." I felt that Nanny was listening. I added, "She and my brother were always good friends, I believe."

He started. I could not mistake his reaction. He evaded my eyes. "That is true, madame. Monsieur William was not always happy here and Madame Gabrielle tried to make things easier."

"I am sure his wife tried to make him happy here."

"But, yes. Little Mademoiselle Yolande, she was an angel. A mischievous angel. It was not her fault."

More mystery. I had been assuming that any gossip about William and Gabrielle occurred because his wife drove him to—whatever he had done. Why else would his relationship to the vicomtesse be excused by "provocation"? Whose provocation, if his wife was an angel? Surely Nicolas had not provided the provocation. I did not know what to think now.

Perhaps I am easily duped, but I believed this old man. I felt sincerity and dignity in him, these qualities so important in my family's teaching.

Henri cleared his throat. "Now, if you will please excuse me, madame, I must go to relieve the gate man. It is my new post, outside the gate house across the moat bridge."

"I beg your pardon, I should not have kept you. Good fortune at your new post. I hope it is a pleasant one."

I shook his hand. He looked a little surprised but gave me a flickering smile and bowed the three of us out.

We made our way out of the tower and around the front of the château toward the forbidding main doors. Just before we entered, we saw Richard Pemberton and the Vicomtesse de St. Auden leaning over the parapet and pointing to the moat bridge as they talked. I did not hear them, but it was obvious that they must be discussing the accident to William and Yolande, if accident it was.

I called to Gabrielle. "I am delighted to see you up, madame." I added truthfully, "You look wonderful."

"Many thanks, *chérie*."

Gabrielle was still bandaged, but most of her face was visible, lively and piquant as ever. When she turned to us, I saw that she was still unable to walk without help, thanks to the painful hip wound. Richard, on the contrary, looked tense and harassed.

"Time to give me the benefit of those gentle arms," she teased. She confided to us, "I intend to arouse Pierre's jealousy by one means or another."

It was a curious, joking end to a scene at the moat bridge that looked much more like an animated discussion of the tragedy.

At a nod from Gabrielle, Richard lifted her. Followed by the rest of us, he marched into the house while she teased him about her weight.

"I do not envy my poor son," Nanny muttered when the

invalid had disappeared up the tower steps in Richard's arms. "Flirtation, indeed. She is a heartbreaker, that one."

I was anxious to discuss the problem of William's relations with Gabrielle but Jeremy was tired, and when we took him up to his room, he pleased me by asking if I would continue to give him the chess lessons we had begun before Nanny and Richard had arrived home from France.

When I went back downstairs to see how the dinner was progressing, I found it necessary to soothe Chef Carletti. He tore his few remaining hairs and vowed that the dinner would be ruined, which I doubted. By this time it was near sunset, the hour when Nicolas and the vicomte would be returning from town. I looked out the front windows of the Great Hall, saw nothing but the trees across the bridge, swaying in the late-afternoon breeze.

Hearing the creak of old timbers under the same windy onslaught, I glanced around behind me, and then up at the rafters where the chains still dangled. The missing chandelier made me think of a gaping mouth with a tooth gone. The other two chandeliers looked sturdy enough, but in my imagination I could hear again that grinding, screeching noise and, at last, the sickening crunch of glass.

I was nervous enough to jump when I heard the slippery voice of the steward, Grégoire, behind me.

"It would appear to be safe, madame."

"I devoutly hope so." All the same, I shifted my position, moving into the embrasure where the small, leaded panes badly cut down the light.

"Madame, if you are watching for Monsieur Bertold, I thought you would like to know that I saw the two gentlemen riding along the High Road past the Bertold vineyards some minutes ago." He saw my surprise and explained, "From the turret room on the northeast tower it is possible to see a bit of the road across the estate. There is a break in the heavy foliage just there. The gentlemen should be crossing the bridge in the next few minutes."

I was pleased and even touched by his kindness in telling me.

"Thank you, Grégoire. I'll walk out and meet them."

He bowed, turned away, then stopped. It was the first time I had known him to be hesitant with me.

"The road is quite safe, madame. But I would not advise crossing through the woods until it is settled just where the gypsy wagon will be staked. These people occasionally have wild animals they use for their performances."

"I know," I said dryly. "I've already met Yvgeny."

He looked puzzled, then understood. "Ah. The dancing bear. The Honigers purchased him from our own gypsies. They say he is harmless." He added after a second's hesitation, "But perhaps unpredictable."

"Exactly my sentiments. I'll stay out of the woods. By the way, I believe the man they call Henri has been assigned to keep the gate."

Since Grégoire had been in the high turret of the northeast tower, he must have passed Henri's room to do so. Perhaps he had given the old man his change of position. Evidently not, for Grégoire's tone was cold.

"I believe so. Not through my suggestion, however. I regard the accident in the Great Hall as inexcusable."

When he was gone, I started out the front doors to the bridge but was stopped by my new maid, Marie-Clare. She offered me one of my older shawls against the late-afternoon breeze. I thanked her and went across the bridge, trying not to think about what happened here less than a year ago.

The wind freshened and began to blow my billowing skirts around me. I was almost sorry I had come, except that I wanted very much to be with Nicolas. I told myself that later, when the time was right, I would question him about Zilla Honiger. Not now.

I suppose I must have been deeply troubled by recent events, and Nicolas seemed like my only haven, the strong protector I had never needed before.

Perhaps if I broached the subject of the gypsies in a quiet way, making it clear that they must go, he would agree without causing a rupture between us. Secondly, I must have an answer to the riddle of what had come between William and his wife. These were matters that must be settled in spite of my love for Nicolas, or even in spite of my need for him. I could not continue to live here as a privileged guest, surrounded by both enemies and mystery.

The undergrowth grew close on the dusty, pebbled road. It should be cut back. Best not mention that at once, however. More important matters came first. I must move slowly in domestic problems, not let him and the household think I wished to interfere in a matter outside my own province.

Even so, I sensed that when I did confront Nicolas, we would have a serious quarrel, and I dreaded it.

After several minutes I made out the miniature pepperpot tower of the gate house, a stone building about a story and a half high. Situated amid heavy foliage on the north side of the road, it was easy to miss except when the sunlight filtered through the tangled greenery overhead. Smoke rose in little black puffs from one of the chimneys, and I wondered if Old Henri was having trouble starting a fire.

The barricade across the road ahead of me hardly merited the word *gate*. It consisted of three joined boards and a lock and hasp. Currently it swung wide, unfastened. Henri must have unlocked it and then gone back to the gate house without fastening it open. Perhaps he went back to keep warm. But the gate should be fastened, not swinging back and forth this way.

I didn't want the poor fellow to get into more trouble, so I reached for the gate and walked with it toward the post to which it should be fastened. Henri had dropped a bundle of rags near the post. I decided he must be busy housecleaning, making the gate house habitable for his daytime use.

Bringing the gate around, I almost stepped on the rags before I made out a man's wooden sabot. Here in the dusk, beyond the sunset glow, it looked disembodied, as I might expect of a shoe that had been thrown away.

I reached down and felt over the wooden surface, but to my horror, instead of the padding within the shoe, I felt an old knit stocking that covered human flesh.

I let the gate swing wide. I knelt in the dust and traced the body from the frail, bony leg to the breeches and then the bare hand. Exceedingly cold. But still, I told myself, he could be unconscious. I ran my fingers over his face, first gently, then with firmness, almost kneading the flesh, calling to him.

With fingers that shook badly I unfastened his jacket, then an underjerkin and his homespun shirt. When I felt for his heartbeat, I could not be sure. My common sense told me that there was no reaction. I could find no signs of blood. No wound. So if he was dead, it must be from natural causes, probably the exertion of trying to open the gate.

I felt as sorry as if I had known him for years. Just when he was about to take a new post that made him happy, he must die.

The prophecy made by Nicolas had been fulfilled: Old Henri was born on Bertold land, and he would die on it. But was it exertion that had killed him?

CHAPTER TWENTY-SIX

I got to my feet, hearing hoofbeats.

Exceedingly nervous, I ran out in the road and got hold of the swinging gate, dragging it over beside the dead man and fastening it open. In the distance I made out a stir of dust and desperately hoped that the horsemen were Nicholas and St. Auden.

I did not want them to ride past me, so I went out into the road again, waving my shawl over my head at the two men as they came into my view. They were both excellent horsemen, but as I might have expected, the vicomte drew up easily, gently, in plenty of time. Nicolas stopped with a suddenness that alarmed me, but not his big black stallion. That animal skidded to a halt, barely puffing. He knew his master. Nicolas was more upset than the horse.

"Good God, sweetheart! We might have trampled you. Never run out in the road like that."

He leaned down, pulled me to him, and under the vicomte's amused gaze, he kissed me so hard and so warmly that he lifted me off my feet in the circle of one arm.

As soon as I could, I cried shakily, "He's dead. Old Henri. Over there."

The vicomte dismounted, leading his horse to the bundle of rags. Nicolas leapt down beside me and went to Henri. Neither man said anything. They examined Henri in a professional manner, emotionless but thorough. They looked up at the same time while I watched them, rubbing my cold hands nervously.

The vicomte shook his head. "There seems to be no question. The man is dead. Do you recall him when we were boys? Every time we went exploring in the woods, Old Henri—or was it young Monsieur Henri then?—sneaked a bundle of food to us."

"Monsieur Henri. So he did. Gaby used to swear that he was no older than we were . . . so here he is. Poor devil. He seemed perfectly healthy this morning when we talked to him."

The vicomte studied the pallid features of the dead man. "Curious. No signs of pain. One would think a heart attack or apoplexy would leave some signs. Gaby and I were beside the bed when my father died of apoplexy. My father looked tortured in those last minutes. But you must remember."

"I remember. You and I had just come in from a hunt. I rode to Boisville for the surgeon. He arrived too late."

Both men studied Henri's face and throat and then his hands. I was surprised that they could see even in this gray dusk.

The vicomte was still puzzled. "He looks as though he were asleep. Remember how that thieving steward of yours looked? The one before Grégoire? When he died, he looked like this. Calm. Absolutely serene. But, of course—"

"Of course, that fellow had just taken an overdose of laudanum," Nicolas finished for him.

I stood there shivering, not entirely from cold. I could not mistake the long, thoughtful look the two men exchanged. The implication was terrible.

"Is there some way we can find out?" I asked, mentally cursing the way my voice wavered.

Nobody answered. Nicolas took off his greatcoat. The two men wrapped Henri in the coat and carried him through the trees, avoiding clumps of leaves, twigs, and various late-summer refuse. I had to take more care. My skirts caught on every branch, and I could scarcely see the ground, but none of this was important at the moment. All I could think of were the implications.

If Henri had taken laudanum, it must have been an accidental overdose. He was certainly happy about his new post an hour ago when I talked to him. As for his taking the drug in order to sleep or cure a headache, this was improbable. Henri was dedicated to his work. I felt that he would never take medicine of that sort until he had completed his day's tasks.

The door to the gate house was wide open. The two men carried Henri in and carefully laid him on the threadbare sofa in the main room. A smoky fire had been started in the grate across the room. It was badly smothered by an excess of twigs and trash Henri had piled on. He must have intended to come back immediately after opening the gate, in order to stir up the fire.

I could do nothing that would not interfere with the two men, so I found a piece of cloth he had folded many times and obviously used to wrap around his hands when he touched the handle of a hot kettle. I put this under his head as gently as possible. I saw Nicolas look at me and apologized, "I know he cannot feel it, but even so—"

"He knows, sweetheart."

His expression was gentle. I thought that if those who hounded him could see him now, they would be ashamed of their suspicions.

Nicolas and Pierre did several strange things then, wandering over the room, examining the fire grate, the floor, the little gateleg table with many scratches and a kettle I remembered.

I said, "He was boiling coffee in that pan today."

The vicomte examined the pan. "Nico, he has been drinking this. There are several drops on the floor. The cup is on the taboret by the door. Do you think anyone might be able to tell from this pan what he drank?"

Nicolas shook the kettle. "Still almost a cupful left. I'll take it to Tours."

"Not Tours!" I protested. "That would take forever."

The vicomte patted my shoulder in consolation. "Not forever, madame. We could make the trip and return tomorrow afternoon." Nicolas started to object, reminding the vicomte of his recent injuries, but the vicomte added quickly, "We should go together. To demonstrate solidarity."

To show that someone believed in Nicolas, whatever the suspicions might be, I thought.

The vicomte went on. "Nicolas will be returning as rapidly as possible. There are all those guests to accommodate at the dinner in two days. And that will take planning."

Something else to be alarmed over. A small matter compared to Henri's death, but still nerve-racking. "Then, we are to entertain?" I could picture more disasters like those soirees and receptions in Paris, but it was evident from the attitude of the two men that the dinner for provincial acquaintances had been planned with a purpose in mind. Nicolas's note to me called it a bribe. They hoped to soften the volatile feelings of those antiroyal groups currently active in the province.

Nicolas understood the tone of my question. He reminded me gently, "You will be of enormous help to us, sweetheart. These people are only waiting for a friendly act from the king's side. Pierre and I have already paved the way with money and what the mayor of Tours calls 'good works.' In two days' time, when we hold the dinner, the word will have gotten around."

I only hoped the wrong word would not travel concerning Old Henri's death. Servants' gossip, spread to these dinner guests through their own servants, could be twisted against my husband and prove disastrous. It seemed to me as I took time to consider the matter that Henri had died of natural causes.

"Do you really believe that there is some question about the cause of his death?" I asked them, hoping to hear a negative.

"Probably not, madame," the vicomte said too casually. "But it is best to know. Otherwise, history may repeat itself." He looked quickly at Nicolas and then away.

I asked with as much calm as I could muster, "Is that how it was with William and Yolande?"

The vicomte nodded. Nicolas explained. "We believed it to be a simple, terrible accident. Jehan Fidel helped me work on the bridge. He sometimes acted as second coachman. William must have demanded to be driven to St. Auden when I delayed my own trip into the village. William could be insistent, so Jehan agreed to take him. Then, for some reason, Yolande went along. The bridge should have held, even so."

"It was an accident," I insisted.

The vicomte said, "There may have been another detail. The log that you and Jehan Fidel placed as a reinforcement. There were marks in the fresh sand and mortar, footprints, as though the log had been shoved over the edge. But no one paid any attention until too late."

"Any person might have done that," Nicolas put in. "It required no particular effort. Even a heavy stick used as a lever might have shoved the log away, but neither I nor Jehan Fidel had any reason to believe that such a thing would happen. Some weeks later, when Pierre brought up the matter in my defense, no one remembered the marks, and I was his sole witness."

I began to understand bits and pieces.

"That was when Jeremy reported what he thought he had seen weeks earlier, when his parents died. Why did he wait so long to testify?"

The vicomte poured the black, boiled coffee from the pan into a small, lidded iron pot.

"It is my opinion that the boy was inspired in stages. So many painful moments. The shock of the event itself. The funeral. The talk by everyone. More and more gossip. Everyone knew about the quarrels between Nicolas and Daviot. It was the wearing down of the child's real views, his true knowledge."

Nicolas agreed. "With Old Nanny sobbing every hour, and in a stupor on other occasions, there was that wretched housekeeper, Madame Servier, hinting at everything under the sun. An incurable rattle. Leocadia and I tried to care for the boy, but he disliked Leocadia and hated me. Small wonder that the poor little fellow blamed me. He had to blame someone."

I could only say, "I'm sorry." I was desperately sorry, for both Nicolas and Jeremy.

The vicomte said, "Forgive me, madame, but I myself have witnessed some of the causes of this dissent between my friend and his nephew."

"No." Nicolas shook his head, evidently to silence the vicomte while he finished wrapping Henri in the greatcoat he had taken off. It was too long for the little man and served as a temporary shroud.

"It is true," St. Auden added on a firm note. "The boy's father took a violent prejudice against Nicolas and even against Yolande."

There it was again. The mysterious animosity of my brother. I said, "William was never quite so unreasonable when he lived at home. Please tell me—" But I did not like to pursue the matter while the Vicomte de St. Auden was present.

Leaving the vicomte to guard the body, Nicolas insisted on setting me up on his stallion and walking back with me to the château. The stallion objected to my skirts, but we managed. At the front door Nicolas lifted me down and went on to find the coachman we all called Grenadier.

By the time I reached my dressing room to change for dinner, I heard the rattle of harness and wheels crossing the bridge. Looking out, I saw Nicolas at the reins of the old tumbril with Grenadier stroking his long mustache beside Nicolas. This tumbril would carry the remains of Old Henri along with the little iron pot of boiled coffee.

I still hadn't mentioned the two matters uppermost in my mind, and I was more apprehensive than ever of an explosion between us. Was I reliving William's experience with Yolande?

I told myself we all wanted to know the truth about Henri's death, but I didn't. Not then. I wanted to go on in ignorance and trust, without these deadly suspicions.

It was Marie-Clare, naturally, from whom I heard the first rumors in the late evening when I was preparing for bed. It had been a silent, uncomfortable dinner, served hours after its normal time with Nanny sitting at table with us, and nervous Jeremy sneezing and insisting he was well, and Richard murmuring, "Something in the air. I don't like it. Where the devil did Bertold ride off to in such a hurry?"

"I've told you before. He and the vicomte rode to Tours to see about arrangements for the dinner in two nights."

Nanny was puzzled. "I thought they went to Tours this morning."

"Very true. But they forgot something." It was not a very brilliant excuse but the only one I could think of.

I had less trouble with Gabrielle, whom I visited before retiring. The wound to her hip kept her from sitting at the table, and she was spread out languidly on a chiase lounge eating chocolates. Almost every time I saw her I marveled that Nicolas could have married anyone else. Even in dishabille she looked stunningly beautiful. Her vivid coloring and the way her stiff crimson-and-gold skirts spread around her reminded me of a peacock I once saw worked on a fire screen.

"Well, *chérie*! I don't envy you that dinner those wretched boys are determined to give for their king. And not much of a king when it comes to that." She beckoned to me with one finger.

I came to her thinking she wanted to confide something. And so she did, but it was a political secret.

She winked before whispering, "Do not let it go beyond this room, but frankly, at heart, I am a Bonapartist. All this nonsense about the stupid Orléans. His father's vote sent Louis the Sixteenth to the guillotine, you know." She sat up. "Now, as for me, I had rather give my fortune to that young Bonaparte prince, Louis-Napoleon. He cares about the people. And he is a nephew of the Great Napoleon."

"Yes," I said. "I met the young prince once in London. I believe he is sincere, and immensely popular."

"So, instead, we must entertain what Pierre calls the worthies." She sighed mightily. "I will do what I can to help you, but that isn't much, I'm afraid."

"Never mind. It may take their minds off—" I stopped only just in time. I wished her a good night and went back down to the housekeeper's room.

Leocadia was her usual calm, contained self, but as I might have expected, we found Chef Carletti in a panic. He walked up and down the stillroom hammering his fists on shelves as he passed. He could not obtain enough fish. The beef would never satisfy. The vegetables must be obtained at once, preferably yesterday. The ices, the soups, the fruits, the patisseries—impossible so soon!

"Only you could manage," I assured him. "When my husband mentioned the importance of the dinner, I said, 'Only Monsieur Carletti. No one else can do this impossible thing.'" I clasped my hands. "Oh, Monsieur Carletti, was I wrong?"

Carletti rose superbly to the occasion. "Madame, your trust was not placed in vain. You may count upon Carletti."

When Leocadia and I left him, I saw her smile for the first time.

"Long ago I worked for Monsieur Bertold's grandmother, madame. She was the last of the great ladies at the château. You are like her."

I accepted this as the rare compliment it was.

"Thank you. I hope someday I will be what you say. But what is your opinion? Can we manage the dinner? Good heavens! I forgot to ask how many guests and whether they will remain the night. We can hardly furnish guest rooms for all of them."

She was her efficient, unemotional self again.

"Unlikely that they will all remain. They know there are pourboires to pay, the little gifts for the Bertold servants who attend them, and most cannot afford it. They will go at the end of the evening."

I had not thought of this as a reason why they could not stay the night. "I must say, you relieve me. How many, do you think?"

"Well then." The shrug was very French. "It is unlikely that twenty will remain. That is ten rooms. We have them. I will go to work at once."

I could scarcely believe that we had ten apartments ready for overnight guests, plus those for the St. Audens, Nanny, Jeremy, Nicolas, and me.

"I trust you may be right."

I said good night and went into my dressing room where I felt the loneliness that surrounded me without Nicolas.

But Marie-Clare was present, ready to help me remove my clothing and hair ornaments and shower my shoulders with water when I sat in the big hip bath.

"What a pity, madame!" she murmured as she poured over me pitchers of water that had been reheated under my direction at the low-burning fire in the hearth.

By this time I knew all the signs that Marie-Clare was aching to tell me some bit of fresh gossip. She repeated her line about "a pity," and though I was annoyed, I encouraged her tiredly.

"Yes, yes. I am sure it is."

"These gossips, they are wicked."

"I could not agree more."

But she did not accept this barb. When I was bundling

myself in robes and letting down my hair before the fire, the girl went on chattering.

"Merely because Old Henri died. After all is said, the man was old. Why should he not die? If I were so ancient, I would not want to live. What is there left in life for him?"

"I've no doubt you will feel differently when you reach his age."

Completely oblivious to my tone, she began to brush my hair. "They do say Old Henri's death is what's to be expected." I did not react, and she added, "Because of the chandelier and all."

I sat up quickly. She had a strand of my hair in her hand, and my own action made me wince.

She apologized at the same time that I said, "I'm sorry. My fault."

"I understand, madame. It is a horrid thing to think of."

"What is?"

She was all innocence. Perhaps her innocence was genuine. "That the old man was killed before he could tell who ordered him to drop the chandelier. Nonsense, I say."

"Who dares to spread such lies?"

She waved the brush airily. "Everyone. I mean to say, it spreads as if by magic."

"And we know who spreads it, don't we? By just such gossip as you have spread tonight."

She protested, "I only repeated what was told to me, madame. I would never spread lies that I've made out of my own head."

I looked hard at her reflection in the mirror, catching her eyes, which dodged my gaze in a nervous way.

"I happen to know Henri died of a heart attack brought on by the exertion of swinging the gate open against the afternoon wind," I told her.

I almost smiled at the disappointment in her face. She was uncharacteristically subdued during the next few minutes. When she said good night and left me, I wondered how long it would be before my own version of Henri's death traveled through this big household, not to mention our guests.

The next day, wherever I went in the château, I was aware of conversations cut off or abruptly changed; of whispers when I was at the opposite end of a large salon; gossip and speculation everywhere. I worked a great deal with Leocadia, and one time I asked her directly, "Is there any way to stop all this gossiping about Henri?"

"About Henri, madame?"

It was a curious counterquestion. I asked myself what else would be the subject of gossip at a time like this. "About Henri's heart attack."

She said, "I find, madame, that there will always be gossip. Mademoiselle Yolande used to laugh about it. That, of course, was in her girlhood."

Why "of course"?

But Leocadia was not a woman given to gossip, and eventually I let the matter drop. I determined more strongly than ever to have the matter settled when Nicolas returned.

We were still hard at work, dealing with endless problems, when Nicolas arrived home. He left the vicomte at his own estate to settle various crop problems that had arisen in his absence, and it looked to me as though this was the ideal moment to discuss my problems with Nicolas.

I met him in the entry hall on the ground floor. No one could have looked less like the Mistress of Bertold. My hair was covered by a bright kerchief I had found on the top shelf of the armoire in my dressing room, and I was wearing a faded pinafore over one of my oldest gowns. I wasn't surprised when Nicolas laughed before he embraced me and we kissed.

"Now you see the true Alain Bertold," I reminded him.

He said at once, "I prefer it. It is just how I saw you for the first time. My love, you can't imagine how close you came to being seized up and thrown into my bed that night."

"*My* bed," I reminded him. "You were in my house." A

thought occurred to me then. "It is your house now. As your wife in law, I am your chattel. Daviot Farms belong to you."

He teased, "Are you sorry? If I were to die tonight, half of Bertold and all of Daviot Farms would be yours."

"Dreadful thought! Don't say it." I felt a cold whisper of fear, a superstitious feeling that if we made these statements aloud, the devil might somehow make them come true. It made me less anxious than ever to quarrel with Nicolas, yet it could not be avoided. I would be wandering blindly through my life here if I did not know the answers to my questions. I told the two footmen who had been helping me, "I will return soon. You may finish moving in the long tables."

One of the footmen rolled his eyes, and a parlormaid, hearing my words, giggled but returned to her dusting.

Nicolas locked my arm in his as we walked up the steps. "You cannot bear to be apart from me. Confess it."

If I did not watch my emotions, I would soon be back where I had been, awed by this man's overpowering attraction. I would let myself become a passive talking doll, with no knowledge of life around me beyond that which my master kindly offered.

Nevertheless, because I did love him so much that his slightest touch excited me, I kissed his cheek, and we went along in what he probably thought was perfect amity.

He said casually, "Louis Millet, the king's prosecutor, will be a guest here tomorrow night. At that time he brings the final verdict on that coffee."

I, too, pretended indifference.

I remember passing a heavy-framed landscape in a shadowed part of the upper hall and noticing it for the first time. It was a woods subject with fog gathering in little puffs between the slender tree trunks. Among those trees was a brown figure in furs. I stopped Nicolas and looked closer, only to discover that the furred man was a dancing bear, rearing on his hind legs.

"The symbol of our house," Nicolas reminded me.

It also gave me the opportunity to speak to him about the gypsies. When we went into the bedchamber that we shared, Perpigny, his little valet, was waiting for him with his dinner clothes laid across the bed. The valet attempted to bow me out as usual, but Nicolas made my conscience trouble me more than ever when he laughed and dismissed the man.

"I don't need you, my friend. I have my wife."

Perpigny seemed curious. He took an inordinate time getting to the door and then spent a couple of minutes examining and trying the latch, as though he found something wrong with it. Nicolas said finally, "You may go, Perpigny."

He could hardly ignore that and, bowing again, closed the door, leaving us alone. As Nicolas had often done in the past, he demonstrated that, in some ways, he could read my mind.

"Now, tell me all about it, and we'll have the fellow's head off by sunup. Whoever he may be."

He took off my bright blue-and-green challis scarf and pulled the pins out of my hair. Then he ran his hands through the falling, disheveled strands until his palms caressed my cheekbones. It was hard to resist that.

"Tell me, sweetheart. Don't be afraid. I won't eat you."

I wasn't afraid of him but of myself. I looked up into his eyes, tremendously aware of his touch, the excitement of him. Wasn't it better to postpone this confrontation?

I licked my dry lips, and he looked as if he would kiss me. I closed my eyes.

"Nicolas—"

"Darling—"

"Nicolas, darling, you remember the people who struck me on the head and carried me off in that tinkers' wagon?"

I could sense the alertness about him. He was changing, on guard. I opened my eyes.

He said evenly, "I remember that Pemberton found you in the Honiger wagon, yes. They said they hadn't done it. They had no idea how you got there."

"Naturally. What else could they say?"

His rough, warm hands slipped off my flesh. My cheeks felt cool and naked without his touch.

"And?" How crisp and official that sounded!

"They are here on the Bertold estate. They have one of those supposedly tame bears. His name is Yvgeny."

"The bear?" He sounded amused. To me there was nothing amusing about these gypsies.

"Of course, the bear!

"They say you gave them permission to stay here. These people who kidnapped me—" I drew a deep breath and went on. "That knock on the head was no love tap. And yet you let them come back into our lives."

I could see that he was trying hard to be patient. No doubt he had seldom found it necessary to be patient in his whole life.

"I have assured you many times that they did not hit you on the head."

"Then who did? And why was I put in that wagon?"

He hesitated, then said quietly, "I don't know. Honiger and the boys are as anxious to find out the truth as I am."

On a deep note of irony I asked, "Is that why they are here?"

"Partly." He ignored my tone. It was obvious to me that he believed what he said. Incredibly enough, he thought the Honigers were innocent. I changed my own manner. I had been too abrupt, too inflexible, like William. I tried again.

"Darling, if I told you that they terrify Jeremy and me, could you send them away?"

A long, painful silence followed. I knew for the first time what people meant when they used the expression "My heart sank."

"You refuse?"

He reached for my hand. I avoided him. He said, "Sweetheart, as God is my judge, no gypsy will hurt you or Jeremy."

"Does that include Zilla Honiger and the bear?"

"Yes. It does. Zilla's manner is unfortunate, but she has

never hurt anyone. As for the bear, he has roamed these woods for years. He may be alarming to see, but he is simply playful. Ask the children of the estate. Yvgeny has been their playmate since he was a cub. I didn't know the name, but I do know the bear, believe me."

"He has sharp claws. He stood as tall as I am. Taller."

"My people carry sugar lumps. Yvgeny thought you would give him sugar." Watching me intently, he added in the surprisingly gentle way that I always found irresistible, "I will see to it that Yvgeny never roams free around these woods if he frightens you so much. The Honigers have bought him, in any case. They need him as part of their performance."

I felt ashamed that a tame animal had alarmed me so much, but the basic problem remained.

"Nicolas, why must these gypsies remain here at all?" I saw that rigid look again and thought, He chooses them. . . . Pain made it difficult for me to speak.

"In a choice between your wife and these vile gypsies, who might have killed me, you choose the gypsies."

This time he would not let me go. He shook me a little, as one shakes a child.

"I do not choose them, sweetheart. In a sense they chose me. Long ago."

"Is that why you came to Ferndene Heath? You knew the Honigers were there, didn't you?"

He shook me. "I did not. I met them for the first time, and quite by accident, when I went walking on the heath. As for their relationship to Leocadia's family, all gypsies are related, in a sense."

"You warned these vicious criminals, and then you sent them here to safety."

"They were innocent!"

I looked hard at him. "I don't believe you. You are loyal to them because of your gypsy grandmother."

"I am loyal to them because Yolande's mother was Leocadia."

He must have known how this would shock me. William and I had been reared in a household where deception and lies were the ultimate crimes, more terrible than murder.

William. My God! Did he know that his precious, aristocratic beauty was the daughter of a gypsy woman who was related to the murderous Honigers? William was more proud than I, by far. Such knowledge must have been devastating.

I backed away from Nicolas, sickened by this chain of lies, first against William and now about to destroy my life, as it had destroyed my brother.

I heard his voice. "Alain, I would like to explain to—"

I didn't look back. I had so much to think about, so many lies to weigh against the one truth I had not doubted until this moment: that he loved me in a special and wonderful way.

He had loved his dead sister and his family, his housekeeper, Leocadia, who was his little sister's mother. He loved the Honigers, who had kidnapped and might have killed me. He loved the St. Audens.

He hadn't loved me enough to tell me any of the truth, and he must love Jeremy even less.

The worst of all these disclosures came later. I had returned to work on the plans for the political dinner. This might well become my only important contribution to Château Bertold if I left Nicolas.

Dreadfully depressed, I caught a glimpse of my face in the mirrored frame of a sixteenth-century portrait and was shocked by my passing resemblance to William. That mirrored face reminded me suddenly of the change that had come over William while he was here at Bertold.

I understood it at last. He must have been torn, as I was now. He must have stayed here, hating everyone who lied to him but wanting to protect his child's inheritance and, perhaps, to stay close by his child. Certainly Jeremy had been devoted to William. There was a very real tie between them. William would be afraid that he would lose Jeremy as well as the chance to protect him from his mother and the Bertold influence, such as it was.

Did he go on loving Yolande in spite of her illegitimacy and her lies, as I would go on loving Nicolas, even if I left him?

He was in the big, dour library on the ground floor when the footmen and I went in to arrange piquet tables for some of the elderly male guests after the dinner. He had poured himself a glass of brandy and was about to drink when we entered. He said abruptly, "Leave that!"

The youths left abruptly. I was surprised. He had never used that harsh tone in my presence. I started to leave but he snapped, "Not you."

The door closed behind the footmen. A few steps and Nicolas would be between me and the door. He was much too big to argue with.

I was quiet and expressionless, hiding the turmoil within. "Yes, Nicolas?"

CHAPTER TWENTY-SEVEN

He made a sweeping gesture toward the sideboard. "To bring out more honesty, what shall it be? Sherry? Port? An excellent Bordeaux? Or our own Bertold red?" He looked at his glass. "This is cognac. Not your sort, I would say. May I suggest a Red Chinon?" He smiled. "You liked that pretty golden Vouvray, as I recall on a happier occasion."

"Vouvray, please."

He found the bottle of the local white wine more easily than I would expect. I was relieved to think that he had not gotten drunk. Every man I knew—William, Richard, my father—all of them had drunk too much at one time or another.

He offered me the glass. I took it, careful to keep my hand steady. I felt that his own masterful nature and the fact that he had been older than his sister and his childhood playmates gave him this manner of schoolmaster or even a parent, ordering others around. At this minute he put me strongly in mind of my father, watching me as a hawk watches a bird, ready to swoop down.

I took a long swallow of the wine, cleared my throat, and asked, "What was it you wanted to say?"

Somewhat taken aback by my own manner, he seemed to change his mind about whatever he intended to say.

"Does it matter to you so much that my sister was half"—he stopped, correcting himself—"more than half gypsy? Are you so deeply mired in your little island prejudice that you think no one is worthy to mate with an Anglo-Saxon?"

He had misunderstood me. I denied the accusation indignantly. "Never. I knew you had gypsy blood. I took pride in it. I would have been happy to see your gypsy blood in our children." Although he smiled, I read something else in his eyes, a pain that I did not want to see. I hurried on. "It is the lies I cannot forgive. Surely that was what happened in William's case."

"Oh, no." He set his glass down and went to the window. I wondered what he was actually thinking as he stood with his back to me. "Your precious William discovered the truth some weeks after Jeremy was born. He overheard Leocadia and Yolande talking. Simple as that. I had no idea that his prejudices ran so deep. He never forgave any of us. Some time later he began flirtations with village girls, purely to humiliate Yolande. He tried to turn Jeremy from his own mother. I don't think he succeeded, but he certainly twisted that unfortunate child against me."

It sounded like William. I could be more charitable about my brother than Nicolas could be. I believed William's hatred was not caused by Anglo-Saxon prejudice, but rather by his bitterness at the lies that surrounded him.

"So many lies." I repeated my thought aloud, hoping in some way that he would have an answer that denied all these deceptions the Bertolds had practiced on us.

His voice was quiet, almost conversational, indicating that he no longer cared or that he cared so much, he had schooled himself to conceal his true feelings.

"I wanted you. I thought, with time, that you could learn to forgive the deception. That seems to have been a mistake."

"Everyone in France seems to know, even Old Henri and Nanny Pemberton."

This time there was no mistaking the bitter edge to his words. "Yes. William saw to that."

"Does Jeremy know?"

The question, or its answer, puzzled him.

"I don't know. I think the boy must know something. There are times when I am certain he wishes me dead."

"Very possibly. But it was a child's wish, unreal," I said. "He doesn't mean it. He almost learned to like you in Dorset."

He turned with the wry smile that had so little humor in it.

"Oh, he means it, right enough. I've seen the hatred in those big eyes. Such innocent brown eyes! But I believe a child's hatred can match that of a man any day. I think a child may be capable of anything."

"Horrible."

"I find it so."

He deliberately misread my comment. I had meant that it was horrible to be so cynical about a child.

Feeling desolate and alone at this fresh example of his savage nature, I set down the glass and started to the door. Before I reached it, he had his hand on the latch. I looked at him, saying nothing. Indeed, there was nothing I could think of to say. I felt too sick at the end of my great romantic dream. When there was danger everywhere around Jeremy, his uncle actually expressed a belief in that child's villainy!

"Does the fact that I love you, that I need you, count for nothing?"

I managed to remind him, "You have your family and your estate. You love me as a kind of . . . adjunct." I had scarcely opened the door when the flat of his hand slammed it shut. For the first time in our acquaintance I found him an insuperable barrier.

"Listen to me!"

In other circumstances his grim face could have made me uneasy, but I was feeling very grim myself.

"What can you tell me? More family secrets? Nicolas, we have never understood each other. It may be too late now. I'll play hostess to your political friends. Don't concern yourself on that score. But after . . . I don't know."

"Don't play games with me." How often he had held my shoulders in a tight, warm grip this way, and always I was aroused to heights of passion at his touch. It would take so little to surrender now.

I was sure he knew it.

"No game, love," I murmured sadly. "No game at all."

"Don't lie. You say you hate a lie. You love me."

His hands traveled over my throat, lingering on either side of my neck. I could not move my head when he brushed my lips with his, and then his lips clung to mine. He must have felt me trembling. His kiss held a furious passion I had never known before, and for a few seconds I could make no protest.

He let me go so unexpectedly, I fell against the door. To complete my humiliation it was his arm that held me erect.

I did not trust the glitter in his eyes as he reminded me, "You love me, and I think I've proved that I love you. I tell you now that I want you more than I want this estate, or the family honor, or anything else under heaven. Remember that."

He opened the door and bowed me out.

As I recall it now, jumbled in my mind with the greater pain to come, I went about my work that evening in something of a daze.

For a few hours I hated Leocadia, remembering what trouble her people had brought to my family, if not to the Bertolds. But honesty prevailed eventually, and when I said good night to her, thanking her for her great help, I added on a sudden wave of understanding, "My husband told me about your daughter." Her eyelids flickered, but she said nothing. I went on more rapidly, unsure of her reaction. "It must have been very painful for you. Was pressure used to make you give up your own child?"

"No, madame." She was surprisingly calm. "I did not love the Maréchal Bertold, but I pitied him and madame. It was the idea of madame herself. The maréchal was a man with a man's needs, his desires. Madame, his wife, became an invalid early in their marriage, after the birth of Monsieur Nicolas. It would be a great thing for a child of mine to become a Bertold. I was glad. Madame and I went to Montecatini, in Italy, until after the birth. But these secrets become the property of others eventually. There were several here at Bertold who came to know of it. Not through me."

"I'm sure of that. You never felt . . . embittered about it?"

"Bitter? No, madame. I am now the housekeeper here. None of my family ever went so far with your race."

I was ashamed to pursue the sad, ugly story. My sympathies were with this self-contained gypsy woman. And with young Yolande, too. None of this was her fault. If only William could have seen that!

"I beg your pardon." But she had left me wildly curious, and I said, "Did Madame Bertold ever come to resent the child?"

"Madame told me in Montecatini that she had produced a son, the heir to Bertold. No more could be expected of her. Of course, she could not know that the maréchal would divide the property between his daughter and his son."

"It must have been dreadful for you, to give up your child so easily."

Leocadia looked at me. "Easily? But yes. Imagine, madame, her future as the illegitimate child of a servant girl. Thank you, madame. I see that you can imagine. But as the heiress to the Maréchal Bertold—"

"I understand," I managed to insist. "Yes. I see. And he would not marry you after his wife's death?"

Her quick, sharp laugh was my answer. "The Maréchal Bertold, madame? You know him very little. He was like his son physically, of great sensual attraction. But otherwise, no. Monsieur Nicolas is of good heart. Like his mother. The maréchal was not of good heart."

I remembered that Nicolas's grandmother had been a gypsy and asked, "Was the grandmother related to you?"

Leocadia smiled. "When I said you were like the *grand-mère* of Monsieur Nicolas, I meant to say, the mother of his mother. She came here after Monsieur Nicolas was born. No, madame. You are not like the old maréchal's gypsy mother."

Embarrassed at having forgotten the complimentary comparison, I thanked her, apologized for my curiosity, and went up to the room that was my dressing room and study. I would sleep there tonight.

I did not hear a sound in the big bedchamber adjoining my room, so I supposed that Nicolas must have slept elsewhere that night, probably in his library. I dreaded seeing him in the morning; as a matter of fact, I got very little sleep that night.

Marie-Clare surprised me in the morning by her confidential inquiries about Richard Pemberton, of all people.

"Why?" I asked as I drank my chocolate and pretended to nibble at the toasted sweet cakes. "He is very handsome, I will allow."

Her golden eyes rolled mischievously. "Well enough, madame. But he has promised to paint me in oils, and every time I seek him out, he is so very busy."

"Painting?"

"Admiring the age of the château."

"What? He has seen it hundreds of times."

"That is what I thought, madame. And then, to spend all his time on the top floor, among the old servants' quarters. So dusty. What things of admiration does he search for there in the two rooms of Madame Servier, who fell down the stairs?"

"I remember." It was very odd. I set down my cup and pushed aside my tray. "I think Richard and I must have a little talk. He is treating Bertold as if it were his own private domain."

While she helped me to dress, Marie-Clare said with smug satisfaction, "It may be that Monsieur Pemb'ton will spend more time on my portrait now."

"Maybe," I agreed, but I wondered if the business of the portrait was a ruse to keep the girl's goodwill, since she was so clearly a gossip.

I went to the end of the hall and up the narrow staircase that, along with liquor, had contributed to the death of the previous housekeeper. I could see how it might have happened. The staircase was almost vertical, and there were no protective balustrades or railings. The area was not as light as it might be.

We must arrange for lamps and a balustrade.

But it might no longer be my concern. By this time next week I could be back in the valley, alone, my dream of romance ended.

This was the attic floor with its many slanting roofs and leaded windows, but it had its own charm of sorts. I looked into each room. Impossible not to think of how these cubicles could be redecorated, made livable, used for one purpose or other.

But I could no longer believe anything Nicolas told me, including the real reason for his quarrel with William. How bitterly he must have hated William for spurning and humiliating his sister! I pushed open a window on the westerly face of the building and caught glimpses of the white marble *folie* at the lower end of the pond. It seemed to me that I saw at last why Nicolas had been so angry when he'd caught William and Gaby together. William must have insulted Yolande, and insulted her over her birth. It was his greatest weapon. Such a thing would have put Nicolas into a killing rage.

And William had died the next day.

I closed the window. I hated my own growing suspicions.

I found Richard Pemberton in the sitting room of Madame Servier's little apartment. He was kneeling on a threadbare rug, scrambling through a sewing basket. Around him was a fine assortment of threads, patches, needle cases, buttons, and other objects of interest to a seamstress.

"What on earth are you doing?" I demanded.

He dropped the sewing basket. While I watched him he collected objects that rolled all over the floor. He further angered me by his flat challenge.

"Someone must do it. Once Bertold was released for lack of direct evidence, everyone assumed that he had been found not guilty. Even my mother reminds me that he may be innocent." He stared at me. "Alain, no one ever looks for evidence anymore."

"And I assume you are."

He waved to the scene around him. The few objects of furniture, a rickety old oaken table, a chair with the cushions badly worn, a number of shelves containing bric-a-brac, from miniature china cups to aged pattern dolls, had been rearranged. He must have examined every item in the room.

"Not so far, but I have barely begun."

Entering into the spirit of this in spite of myself, I asked, "What are you searching for?"

"Proof, my dear Alain. You see, I don't believe Madame Servier died by accident. Not after the way Old Henri died so suddenly of a heart attack."

I dropped the needle case into his hand. "Murdered, of course. May one ask why?"

"Because they discovered something about the murderer." He was sickeningly triumphant. "Someone ordered or forced or paid Henri to drop that chandelier on you."

"Why?" I tried to give this a casual sound.

"To gain control of Daviot Farms, among other reasons."

"He already controls them, as my husband. It is the law."

Richard tapped my hand with his long forefinger. "You see? The name leapt to your mind. Nicolas Bertold."

I hated him for that. I drew back. "Get out of here. I don't want you here. If you must see Nanny, see her somewhere else, but not where I can see you."

He was aghast. "Alain, you don't mean that! We have been friends since you were born. At least, let me prove that—" He stopped, tried again. "Let me prove that I am right. This woman may have known or seen something about William's death. That girl of yours, Marie-Clare, she let drop the remark that Madame Servier expected a small inheritance. Said it would continue for her lifetime."

"Ridiculous." I sat down suddenly.

"No doubt. But it was all I could think of, to look through her things. If she did know something and was bleeding someone in this house, she would be a fool not to make some note of it, to hold over his—that person's—head."

"Ridiculous." I realized that I was repeating myself and got up. I went to the door thinking that I would forbid him to go on with his investigation, like one of those Bow Street Runners of London, whose adventures had enthralled me when I was a child. Then I asked myself what it was that I feared.

Was I so afraid of my husband's guilt?

To prove that I was not, I said, "Waste your time if you choose, but don't expect anyone to believe you."

I marched out, caught my skirts in the door, tore them free, and walked into Nicolas in the hall. It was difficult to make out his expression in these dim quarters, but his manner was forbidding and his voice light with derision.

"Not surveying your domain, by any chance?"

I explained awkwardly. "My maid said Richard was prowling around these rooms. I thought I would remind him not to—to take anything that doesn't belong to him."

"We couldn't have that, could we?" He seemed to feel he owed me an explanation as well. "Leocadia tells me she has had the rooms at the south end cleaned and prepared for the servants they will be bringing with them."

"That was lucky. It never occurred to me."

I could not bring myself to turn away from him. We walked along the hall, peering into different rooms, even making a small joke about the sparkling condition of the rooms that apparently were cleaned and made habitable by Leocadia.

I felt ashamed that I had not been responsible for these good works, the talent and knowledge of a woman whose daughter had recently died as a result of either accident or murder.

As for Nicolas and me, we were excessively polite and even friendly, but never personal. It is possible that if we had been alone, we might have made our peace and understood each other, but even this seemed impossible to me, surrounded as I was by so many shocking events and suspicions, all with ties to my husband.

I felt guilty, myself, whenever I thought of Richard Pemberton up in that attic room looking for evidence against Nicolas. But whatever the evidence, I must know. At least, I owed that to my dead brother. And a part of me still believed that Richard might find evidence implicating someone else. This thought, which grew stronger as the day wore on, brightened my spirits.

Nanny Pemberton had caught Jeremy's sniffles and, bless her, insisted over and over that she did not wish to make trouble for the household and was quite ready to help in any way possible. Fortunately her help was not needed, but her condition proved worrisome. She seemed lethargic and not too aware of things around her. Her face was more heated than it should have been.

I visited her several times before the guests arrived. To my surprise on one occasion I found Nicolas straddling a bedstool opposite Nanny, who was huddled in a big armchair looking as if she understood only half of what he said. His attempts at conversation produced little success. He left immediately upon my entrance.

Without any real humor I remarked to Nanny, "I'm afraid I sent him out of here."

"My dear, you haven't quarreled? All newlyweds quarrel, you know. Even your sainted parents."

That made me laugh. "My parents were anything but saints. Papa married Mama for her ancestors, and Mama married Papa for all those lovely land and bond investments."

She roused herself to chide me.

"Miss Alain, I don't like to hear you so cynical."

"What did you talk about with Monsieur Bertold?"

She had begun to nod. Worried, I repeated my question a little louder.

She opened her eyes in startled apology. "Monsieur was curious about young Jeremy. He asked questions about the poor lamb. Why this, why that? Did I notice such minute things about him? A child Jeremy's age. Dear me! I've yawned again. I do beg your pardon."

She fumbled for her handkerchief and buried her nose in it briefly. Then she asked me how Jeremy was doing at this minute.

I told her that I had found Jeremy half an hour ago, in a temper because he wanted to go out on the grounds in spite of his cold and was confined to the house.

"It is big enough, heaven knows," I finished.

She said, "Poor lamb," and then, after another yawn, "I wish I might see him and occupy his mind. He shouldn't be alone."

I assured her that one of the young parlormaids was with him, and at the moment they were playing hide-and-seek in the southwest tower.

"But he musn't run or breathe dust. It makes him cough."

I promised faithfully that I had given these orders to both the parlormaid and Jeremy. Then I pursued the matter of Nicolas's visit.

"What, in particular, did my husband want to know about Jeremy?"

Nanny sneezed and apologized. "I didn't quite understand. Such odd little things! Like how often I left him alone. As though I would, except when necessary."

I wondered and worried. "But has Jeremy been alone very much? I know I am usually busy on the farm business. Jeremy often went with me during those months when you were separated from him, and he made friends among the farmers' children. But here at Bertold there are few children. I haven't seen any."

"Jeremy is very mature for his age, Miss Alain." Nanny thought this over. "But how lonely he must have been, poor lamb."

There seemed to be nothing more that Nicolas had discussed with Nanny. It was a peculiar little episode, and I wondered what was in back of it.

I went to see Jeremy afterward, but I'm afraid he was sulking because he couldn't go outside and walk in the wind. When I asked him to come down and play host with Nicolas and me, he refused that too.

"After all, it is partly your house, so these are your guests, dear."

His young lip stuck out in a stubborn way I couldn't mistake. "It's not part mine. It's half mine. But I don't want to go. I want to walk outside, down to—through the woods. I have to." He sneezed.

"Tomorrow. You'll feel better tomorrow."

It was no use. He was as stubborn as William. I kissed him, receiving no response, and turned him over to the parlormaid who, with youthful exuberance, coaxed him out of the sullens while I watched in the doorway.

I went on with my work, my thoughts chaotic, combining the problems of Nicolas and those of Jeremy.

In mid-afternoon when I greeted the first of our guests I welcomed the presence of my husband beside me, with only the tiny red ribbon of the Legion of Honor on his lapel to relieve the stark splendor of his figure in black and white.

He watched me a good deal, but since I was not certain of my own feelings about our future, I avoided his eyes.

I wore for the first time the resplendent blue-green changeable taffeta with my own grandmother's diamond parure and earrings. After our greeting of the first arrivals went well, I found myself quite at home with these people who were so like my own acquaintances, country squires, farm owners, and gentry. But for their language and slightly shorter stature, they might have been my Dorset neighbors.

They were curious about me. I could scarcely blame them. But with it all they seemed to accept me. It was disconcerting, however, to see them glance at Nicolas furtively when they thought we were not aware. Were they thinking about the events in which he had been so closely involved less than a year ago?

I closed my mind to this, but the idea recurred several times during that hour of reception.

I decided that eventually even the Great Hall would be comfortably filled. Meanwhile we escorted our last guests into the big Receiving Salon to meet those neighbors they had probably gossiped with informally only the day before in Tours and Boisville and Chinon.

We were about to go in to dinner when the procureur du roi, Louis Millet, arrived very late. He was discharged from his carriage at the château doors with his furtive-looking little wife. Then the carriage and team circled in a small space before the building and headed back across the moat bridge to the big guest stables near the gate house. This had been repeated with other teams and with the surprising number of individual horses their riders had turned over to grooms and stable boys.

But the arrival of the king's prosecutor held a special tension for Nicolas and me. I wondered if he was as anxious as I to learn what Monsieur Millet's investigation had disclosed. Madame Millet nipped at the sleeve of my gown as we entered the Receiving Salon. She confided in a voice disconcertingly deep for such a little woman, "My dear Madame Bertold, we must forgive the gentlemen if they linger behind us. Business matters, you know. About the coffee your husband and the vicomte left with Monsieur Millet and the prefect."

Pretending a calm I did not feel, I was casual. "Then you are acquainted with the whole affair."

"But yes, Madame. It is not difficult to hear such matters when my husband and the prefect of police discuss them in the next room. The test was made as usual, on an animal. The prefect had an aging hound, very crippled. He fed it the coffee. The beast went peacefully to sleep and did not wake."

"Laudanum."

"Precisely."

I felt sick with dread.

CHAPTER TWENTY-EIGHT

Conquering my fears with an effort, I waved the big, mirrored fan with its gold sticks.

"Thank heaven the truth is known. Poor Henri. I suppose he hated being demoted to gate man. He had worked in the house so long."

A little frown made wrinkles appear between the lady's close-set eyes. She had clearly expected some spectacular reaction from me.

"Er—yes. Very probably. But I do believe I see the Vicomtesse de St. Auden on that lovely old sofa. I must pay my respects. What a sad accident that was! Not exactly unexpected, of course."

I bristled. "What do you mean?"

"Such an unlucky house, I've always thought! Oh, Madame la Vicomtesse, do not stir yourself. We cannot have you suffering new outrages."

As the woman took her hand Gaby looked over the woman's head to wink at me.

"Suffering seems to be our lot these days, under the Orléans rule."

Of all times to insult the Royal House, just when her

husband and Nicolas were trying to rebuild the king's popularity! But it was so like the vicomtesse that I could only shake my head at her and smile.

I couldn't guess how the evidence affected Monsieur Millet. His round, jovial face was unchanged. He was joking with Nicolas when they entered the salon, but I knew my husband's moods well enough by this time to guess that despite his smile and his exchange of sallies with various other guests, he was troubled.

When I assumed we would be dining within the half hour, I slipped out and went up to see if I could persuade Jeremy to eat some of the delicacies that were brought to his room. He was still in his sullen mood and refused the tray Leocadia brought, but the succulent roast chicken won him over when the baked carp and vegetables, and even the pâtés completely failed.

After seating himself at the inlaid leather chess table and unfolding his napkin in a very casual, throwaway fashion, Jeremy made it clear to me that I was still in his bad books for not letting him walk out in the woods at four in the afternoon.

"Could I have 'Cadia here to talk to me while I eat?"

I looked at the housekeeper. Her cool reserve did not change, but I thought her black eyes softened.

I said, "I know you have a great deal to do. Would you mind?"

"If you say, madame."

In spite of her words, I knew she was enormously pleased. It must be heartbreaking to see her grandchild reared before her eyes and to be relegated to a position as servant in her daughter's house. Even Nicolas failed to see how embittered she must be.

A sudden stab of fear or presentiment made me hesitate when I was leaving. It was wildly cruel to believe that she would harm her own grandchild. Still, it would be wise to have no doubts whatever. I tried the door to Nanny's room.

It was locked on Jeremy's side. But Nanny could use the relaxation. I looked into her room, found her taking chicken broth, tea, and several pieces of bread broken off a narrow baguette. She dipped the bread first into the broth, then the tea, and finally popped it into her mouth, chewing contentedly.

Marie-Clare stood up and moved back at my entrance. Obviously she and Nanny had been gossiping.

Nanny looked up, beamed at me, and assured me in a hoarse voice, "Bread dipped into tea. Sheer heaven, my dear, when one's throat is raw. How is the little party going along?"

"Moderately well. I wonder if I might borrow Marie-Clare to sit with Jeremy until it is over."

Nanny's hands fluttered in panic at the thought of her charge, who might be alone. "I should go myself, not ask this child to spend hours with the dear boy."

"Don't be ridiculous. Stay right there and please stay well wrapped. Marie-Clare may have an afternoon off tomorrow."

"Oh, madame," Marie-Clare assured me. "I will keep the little monsieur company and never let him be lonely. I will talk and talk."

I sighed and murmured to Nanny, "I was afraid of that."

No matter. With two people to watch over Jeremy and each other, I would be more relieved.

I went back down to our dinner guests, meeting Richard Pemberton and the Vicomte de St. Auden in the hall outside the Reception Salon. I seemed to have interrupted an argument between them. They stopped arguing and bowed to each other with rigid politeness. Then the vicomte excused himself, explaining to me, "If you will forgive me, my wife finds her elaborate clothing a trifle cool for this fall night. I will fetch down a shawl."

The décolletage of Gabrielle's crimson-and-black-brocaded gown was truly spectacular, so I wasn't surprised at this news. I wished him luck, and when he had gone, I asked Richard what on earth the sharp words had been about.

"As you may have surmised, Alain, that popinjay constantly defends his friend. According to him, Bertold can do no wrong. In my loyalty to you and Jeremy I may have gone too far, but—"

"I must say, I prefer his loyalty to yours. No one gave you leave to defend me and my nephew against my husband."

Smarting under my reproof, he tried to arouse my curiosity. "Don't you even want to know what I found up in that dead housekeeper's rooms?"

"No, I don't." A footman was about to open the salon doors for me, but I stepped back after an instant to demand, "Well, what did you find?"

He tried not to be smug. "Notes under her carpet." While I exploded at the idea of his turning up the underside of a carpet, he showed me a sheet of creamy Bertold notepaper, rather frayed around the edges. "Figures. Here. 'Received ten livres. Promised more later upon my persuasion.' And below it: 'Received two livres. Persuasion effective.' What do you make of that?"

I made many unpleasant things of it, but I lied angrily, "Someone owed her money. That is clear."

"And the constant talk of persuasion?"

"To make him"—I hesitated—"or her pay a debt."

Richard remained firmly triumphant on the subject of his spying. "I believe there are more notes. I simply haven't found them yet. They may be under the bedroom carpet. This was in the sitting room."

I tried to be indifferent. "You haven't found anything direct. This might refer to a hundred people."

"But the French don't usually have carpeted bedrooms. Maybe this woman always kept notes of her secret dealings there."

I waved him away. I didn't want to hear any more.

A young footman, promoted today from a lackey and general help, opened the doors proudly, and I went in, not a moment too soon. Everyone was ready for dinner.

With Monsieur Millet, the most honored guest, I led the sparkling throng of women with their partners, many in uniforms from Napoleonic days, across the entry to the Great Hall. I suspect there was a deal of gossip about the broken chandelier, but Grégoire and Leocadia had decorated the empty space with fragrant boughs and other foliage from the Bertold woods, and the remaining two chandeliers shone with a dazzling glow, now that they were cleaned and polished.

There were gasps all around, and Nicolas nodded congratulations to me from the second of two tables occupying the center length of the room. The clatter of voices and of chairs being scuffed over the floor mingled with the clink of silver and shining glassware. Through all this happy confusion my thoughts reverted to the words blazoned on my brain: "Promised more later upon my persuasion . . . persuasion effective. . . ."

How fortunate for her victim that Madame Servier took a tumble down that steep flight of stairs! But as for Nicolas being that victim (and murderer?)—preposterous! The amounts of money were too small, among other excellent reasons.

There was a great deal of talk about "that worthy fellow, King Louis-Philippe, a truly bourgeois ruler with the common touch," and Nicolas proposed a toast to His Majesty. We all rose and drank to the king. We were just seating ourselves—accompanied by the much-magnified rustle of silk, taffeta, and satin gowns—when Grégoire left his place at the head of the innumerable servants attending us. He spoke to a young lackey who had just stuck his head in from the entry hall. Grégoire came back to Nicolas and whispered something, pointing with his hand, in its immaculate white glove, to the entry hall beyond.

His break with manners and protocol was extraordinary. More puzzling, we all saw Nicolas get up from his seat between Madame Millet and the vicomtesse. Having made a brief apology inaudible to anyone at my table, he strode to the doors, which opened as if by magic. Two footmen in the entry hall bowed. One pointed to something out of sight of the diners, who were probably as consumed with curiosity as I was.

A minute later we all heard an ear-piercing shriek, followed by Jeremy's wild, broken protests.

"You can't make me. I have to know. I have to!" He was coughing now, and I got up so fast, I overturned my chair. Jeremy kept protesting through whatever low-voiced warning Nicolas gave him. "You just want to keep me from knowing you killed the old man."

Horrified, I managed to retain my common sense long enough to tell our guests, "Our poor nephew is being very naughty. I'm afraid we have indulged him a trifle. He is not well, as you may have heard. Please excuse me. We will calm him. Children are a godsend, but they can be provoking at times, as we all know." My smile was fixed and toothy, I am sure, but at least my words had produced sympathetic and knowing nods from the many parents present. Meanwhile the sounds in the entry hall came through to us, appallingly clear.

"I won't be carried. I want to go by myself. You just don't want me to find out."

I picked up my skirts and hurried out.

Reaching the stunned footmen, I signaled them to close the doors and saw Nicolas, Grégoire, and Jeremy in the archway to the southwest tower steps. Nicolas had lifted the struggling boy off the floor while Grégoire picked up the heavy hunting jacket and one boot Jeremy had dropped. Jeremy evidently wore the jacket over his long nightgown, whose hem had by this time picked up all the dust and leaves blown into the deep window embrasures over the tower steps.

"What on earth is the trouble?" I asked Nicolas, who had subdued Jeremy's arms but was having difficulty with those drumming legs.

"God knows! Something about sneaking out into the woods.

It will be dark in an hour. I can't understand what he wants out there."

I lost patience even though the boy's frantic conduct worried me.

"That is ridiculous. He was terrified in the woods the other day, and that was broad daylight."

"Well, I don't pretend to understand what goes on in his mind. It must be his father's influence, reaching out of the grave. It would be exactly like Daviot."

"Don't!"

Nicolas didn't answer me. He had Jeremy securely pinned against his body now and carried him up the tower steps while I followed behind, not understanding any of this except that Jeremy's hatred of his uncle went far deeper than I had expected. I was also angry that both Leocadia and Marie-Clare had failed me. We found Leocadia in the upper hall, looking into various rooms for Jeremy. She was relieved when she saw Nicolas and his burden.

"The vicomte could not find his wife's shawl. I was only gone a minute or two. Monsieur Jeremy promised faithfully not to move."

"And Marie-Clare?"

She shrugged. "A lackey of good appearance came by and told her he had set a dinner tray in Madame Pemberton's room. She could not resist that." Leocadia's eyes widened. She looked from me to Nicolas and then behind him to someone else. I, on the contrary, felt a deep sense of alarm when I saw that the king's prosecutor, Monsieur Millet, had followed us up the steps.

Surely he didn't take Jeremy's childish ravings seriously!

Much as I disliked the ever perfect Grégoire, I admired him now for his careful handling of the prosecutor.

"*Monsieur le Procureur*, may I assist Your Excellency? These towers and halls make it difficult to find one's way."

Like most people, Millet was intimidated by the elegant steward, and he turned away.

"If I can be of assistance, I have two children of my own. Two daughters. I am more or less familiar with childish tantrums." He hadn't quite reached the tower steps before he looked around. His small, shrewd eyes wandered too casually from Nicolas and the now sullen Jeremy to me and, lastly, to Leocadia. He seemed to have no interest in Grégoire.

"I might be able to talk with the boy when he is sufficiently calmed down. Perhaps I could reassure him."

Nicolas ignored this, which I felt was a mistake.

"Open the boy's door, if you please, Leocadia."

Jeremy protested, "I'm not your boy, Uncle Nicolas. Let me down."

I gave the prosecutor my most ingratiating smile. "Perhaps, monsieur, you might have a suggestion about calming my nephew's nerves. What do you do when your daughters throw tantrums?"

While Nicolas took Jeremy into his room and dropped him on the thick, comfortable mattress, Millet answered me and, at the same time, sauntered toward Jeremy's room.

"Actually, I resort to the methods advocated by our surgeon. If it is night, a drop or two of laudanum. But in the circumstances perhaps Bertold hesitates. I can appreciate his delicacy about such a treatment."

Nicolas said stiffly, "I've no objection. He may take whatever he will not refuse. I am no surgeon. Nor am I a parent when it comes to that."

Millet chuckled. "No. One may readily see that. Perhaps I may help in some way?"

Nicolas moved away from the bed. He did not approach me. We were still in that state of nonbelligerence, which suggests that much hostility remained.

Monsieur Millet looked around. "You do have a bottle of laudanum? It requires a very carefully administered dose of drops. A single drop can serve its purpose."

"There must be some hereabouts." All this talk about laudanum made me nervous. I wondered when someone would mention the death of Old Henri again.

Grégoire reminded the room in general, "Pardon, messieurs, and madame. I believe the Vicomtesse de St. Auden has a bottle of liquefied laudanum. The vicomte brought it to her on the day after the accident in the Great Hall."

"That should serve," Millet agreed, and Grégoire started away.

My husband probably shared my worry that Gaby would want to know all the details. He suggested, "You had better ask the vicomte privately."

"Yes, monsieur. I had that intention."

It was impossible to outguess Grégoire.

He returned within minutes with the vicomte. The little bottle he carried looked almost full.

Jeremy stared at us all in turn. He was obviously terrified, and my heart went out to him. "I won't take it from Uncle Nicolas."

Everyone looked at me, and for one painful moment I caught the doubt in Jeremy's eyes. I found what I considered the perfect solution. I turned to Monsieur Millet.

"Perhaps Your Excellency will be so good as to count out a drop or two in water?"

"Of course. Very like my daughters at home." He suited the actions to the words as he reassured Jeremy. "I don't believe you have met my daughters, young monsieur. You would like them. They are very jolly creatures, and pretty, though you may think that is a father's boast."

"My father said I was clever." Jeremy drank while I put my palm under the bottom of the glass so he would not have to hold it. His hands were unsteady in his nervousness.

"Indeed, young monsieur. And clever you are," Millet congratulated him. He still held the bottle and looked around. "With your permission, Monsieur le Vicomte, we will lock this up."

He motioned to Nicolas, and they left the room. Presently

I heard the door of an old armoire in the linen room creak open and shut. I went to the hall and heard the snap of the lock. Millet came out ahead of Nicolas, tossing the huge armoire key in his hand.

"There. Now you all should sleep soundly tonight. Monsieur Bertold has suggested that I keep the key for the moment, as I shall be staying the night. By morning things will look much more cheerful to the young monsieur." He beamed at us, quite as if he hadn't just hinted that one of us might poison that helpless child.

I saw that the vicomte had joined Nicolas, and the two men exchanged low-voiced comments. While the king's prosecutor stood by Jeremy's bed, pointing out how safe the boy was, I asked Leocadia to find Marie-Clare for me. As soon as we could decently end this disastrous dinner and send most of our guests on their way, I would change to something comfortable and spend the night in Jeremy's room.

I told Jeremy this when the others drifted out into the hall, exchanging tales about frightened children.

"It is plain to me," Millet said, "that all the gossip about Old Henri's death has preyed on the boy's mind. However"—he chuckled in his jovial way—"see that you do not have another laudanum suicide. That would be a trifle hard to explain, even to me."

The vicomte smiled politely, but Nicolas was not amused. Grégoire led the way down the tower steps. Over his shoulder the king's prosecutor called to me: "Best lock the child in until you can join him, madame."

"Yes. I shall." I sat down on the edge of Jeremy's bed and took his thin fingers in mine. "Are you feeling better?"

"I am now." He motioned toward the hall. "Now that they're gone. That man, the vicomte, he should watch his wife. I saw her kiss Father one day in the *folie*."

"Was that when your uncle caught them?" I asked. It was bad enough that it should happen at all, but that Jeremy should see it . . . !

"Father hit at Uncle Nicolas but he missed him, and Uncle Nicolas hit him so hard that Father's lip bled. And the next day he killed Father, because Father was going off to—to talk to Madame Gaby. I heard Father say that he could get sympathy there, and Mama screamed and said not to leave her. She said they still loved each other."

"What did Will—your father—say then?" I felt like a traitor to William's memory, but I must know every detail, to understand better.

Jeremy looked down at our hands, which were locked together.

"He said—he said that she was a gypsy beggar and that her father and Uncle Nicolas had lied to him in the beginning."

I closed my eyes. Jeremy shook my fingers.

"Aunt Alain, he didn't mean it. What lies could they have told about Mama? I never understood that. Father was just angry because Mama was on Uncle's side when they quarreled."

And so William had rushed off in a pique, Yolande hurrying behind him, and both had gone to their deaths. It was a gesture typical of William with his quick temper, pride, and long resentments.

I said, "Now think carefully, dear. An hour before the bridge gave way, you said you saw your uncle slip out a big log, a bridge support, so the bridge would give way. How could you see it from the high turret room? It was very high."

"But I had my spyglass, like sailors use. It's still there."

"Everyone says your uncle originally intended to go to Boisville. Why, then, would he push away that supporting log?"

He seemed puzzled. After a minute he reminded me triumphantly, "He changed his mind about going. Maybe when he was fixing the bridge."

Monsieur Millet had been right. Jeremy was a clever boy. He had reasoned out all the details.

Still, I had a curious and disquieting thought as I locked

his door and went down the steps to playact the efficient hostess.

Jeremy had not seemed nearly as sure of his facts when he first described for me the events of that ghastly day last winter. It must be that he had dwelled on them so long in his thoughts that they now seemed much clearer.

The dinner had proceeded with unexpected success during our absence. When the Vicomte de St. Auden and the king's prosecutor joined Nicolas in small talk about the whims and temper tantrums of children, they had done much to assuage the gossip, though I knew that the whole region would be full of the story tomorrow.

More fuel added in this vicious, if accidental, campaign against my husband!

I remember nothing of the conversations at that dinner, or even the food we ate. I am told that my manner was a trifle distant but that Nicolas Bertold's grandmother had just such a manner, and no one found it odd. I discovered later that the squab in champagne was a success. The carp was not overcooked, and the turnips were prepared *à l'anglaise* with a type of white sauce that proved to be successful because of some secret ingredient, unknown to me.

I do remember one whispered bit of "humor" from the lady who sat at the king's prosecutor's right. "Let us hope the secret ingredient was not laudanum."

The king's prosecutor very kindly pretended that he had not heard.

By the time we reached the fruits, cheeses, and champagne, not necessarily in that order, I was frantic to know what Monsieur Millet thought about Jeremy's outburst. But even when he thanked me charmingly for "a memorable evening," I could not read his thoughts. Adding to my apprehension, I saw how the Vicomte de St. Auden kept watching him, looking puzzled. Not a happy sign.

The party was ended at last. Nicolas and I left the entry hall together, following the departure of the last slightly tipsy horseman. The guests remaining over had gone to their rooms, all except Gabrielle, outside the room assigned to the St. Audens. She had been carried there by a young politician from Tours who persisted in the notion that he belonged in this bedchamber with her.

Before Nicolas and I could interfere, passing the matter off as a joke, the door opened and the vicomte came out. He was politeness itself.

"Pardon, monsieur. I believe the lady in your arms is my wife."

The young man grinned, mumbled apologies, and, with great panache, poured Gabrielle into her husband's arms. He then bowed to us and sauntered down the hall to his own room.

Nicolas said unexpectedly, "I had hoped our relationship would be like that."

"If you mean tonight, you know I must sit up with Jeremy." How much I would rather be with my husband! But a husband I trusted completely and would trust again, after we had uncovered all this appalling mystery that surrounded us.

He spoke my worst suspicions aloud. He was harsh, angry, and hurt. I could not blame him. "You don't really trust me, do you? That boy has convinced you that I murdered my own sister, just to kill your brother. That I poisoned a kind old man who had been a friend since my childhood. Now you believe that I would murder my nephew, the only blood relation left to me."

"Hush! Someone will hear you."

He seemed to care very little, just as he was indifferent to those who once heard his quarrels with William. His eyes burned with the passion of his feelings that must have been building all night. He reached for me. I reacted instinctively against that look in his eyes, backing away.

It was then that he hustled me into our bedchamber. In his bitterness at my lack of faith, he thought to shame me by forcing me to strip myself for his bitter pleasure. But when he made love, some of our despair gave us renewed passion, and even as we thought we acted in hate, our love burned us with its violence.

Afterward, when he saw that nothing of my suspicions had changed, he cursed me in his despair.

"By God, I wish I had never met the Daviots, any of them! Your brother or that accursed boy or you. You may rot in hell for all it concerns me."

When I left our bedchamber, I crossed the hall to Jeremy's room, rather shakily, still overcome by tremors from those moments in bed with Nicolas. Then I heard another sound: the careful closing of a door near the northwest tower steps. That would be Monsieur and Madame Millets' room. This eavesdropping seemed to put a suitable period to the most ghastly and the most memorable night of my life, and perhaps of Nicolas's life as well.

I unlocked the door of Jeremy's room. He was sitting up in bed, hugging his arms as if he were chilled, although the fire on the hearth gave off a pleasant warmth. I reached for Jeremy. He drew back. I felt horribly rejected, and then I remembered the moment with Nicolas.

But this had a happier ending. Jeremy sat up on his knees. "Aunt Alain?"

We put our arms around each other and hugged hard. It made the evening seem just a little less grim.

Since his mood had softened, I wanted to mention Nicolas, but in spite of his gentleness and need for love, I could sense the deep reserve within. Something told me to wait. While we sat there thinking deep thoughts, a loud chain of sneezes next door disturbed us.

We looked at each other guiltily.

"I forgot," Jeremy whispered. "Nanny always says good night to me. Could you go and tell her that I said I'm sorry she's sick?"

"If you promise to lie down and go right to sleep."

"That's easy. I am sleepy."

I went into Nanny's room. I found her breathing stertorously in bed, her face hidden behind a big handkerchief. She peeked around the cloth at me, then struggled to sit up.

"Miss Alain! I do beg pardon. Just when you need me, I've let this silly thing beat me. Well, I won't. The poor lamb needs me."

"No, he doesn't. Nanny, you are behaving very badly. Now lie down. I'll fetch you up a hot posset. Or brandy."

Her handkerchief wavered. "Now, my dear. I do not believe in spirits, except under unusual circumstances. The important thing is that Master Jeremy is safe. But I don't know when I've been so tired in every bone. Just not worth a farthing. It's this stupid cold."

"Jeremy is perfectly safe, and we must get you on your feet. Good Lord! You are as bad as Jeremy. Forever worrying. Both of you get to sleep. At once."

Nanny's smile flickered. "Easier to make an old lady sleep than an active young boy." She took the handkerchief I gave her and began to wipe her eyes. "Do tell me, how did the dinner go? My boy Richard hasn't been to see me yet. Too busy. Always too busy. But tell me, was the dinner a grand success?"

"Huge."

"And all the Frenchies, have they turned back to that nice king? He carries an umbrella, you know. Like anyone."

"Not when I saw him. The weather was bright, and he carried a walking stick."

"Dear me. Not an umbrella?" She moved her head anxiously on the pillow. "Can you trust the person with Jeremy now?"

"No one is with him. I locked the door." But I started across the room guiltily. At the door I remembered my message. "Jeremy says good night. And so do I, dear Nanny."

She waved the handkerchief and blew a kiss. "Tomorrow I shall be on my feet. You will see."

"No rush."

Before returning to Jeremy, I stopped in my sitting room, poured water from the carafe into a pewter cup, and satisfied my thirst for the moment with dull, lukewarm water.

Out in the hall I had scarcely closed the door when I was startled to see Nicolas with his hand on the door latch of Jeremy's room. He still had that forbidding look that told me nothing had changed. If he had gotten into Jeremy's room with another key, it was clear that Jeremy continued to react badly to his presence. If not, then he must resent the locked door.

He told me brusquely, "This is all nonsense, you know. Several of us have keys to every room."

"Yes. I guessed as much." I tried to smile. "But locks impress prefects and prosecutors." I could see, however, that he did not find this humorous.

"I'll make it easier for you. And the king's prosecutor."

His hand dropped from the latch. He walked away, passing me with no indication that anything of our once passionate love remained.

I unlocked the door.

The bed candle on one of the twin stands near Jeremy's head flickered as a gust of air entered with me from the hall. I closed and locked the door as silently as possible and settled myself in the armchair I had drawn up beside the bed. Jeremy did not stir. The drop or two of laudanum administered to him earlier by Monsieur Millet must have done its work at last.

I tried to close my eyes and rest, but perversely enough, I felt wide-awake, so tense that even my fingers shook. It might be the wines at dinner, in part, but I knew the real cause was worry. I could not bring myself to believe Nicolas might be responsible for the events that had occurred recently, but I could not dismiss them, either.

Was it possible I went on loving Nicolas in spite of my suspicions? Perhaps. But I could not risk Jeremy's safety. As I watched him, he turned over restlessly, thrusting his hand out, his fingers closing around the glass that stood beside his water carafe on the opposite bedstand.

Remembering my own monumental thirst after that salty dinner, I whispered, "Are you thirsty, dear?"

He grunted, shook his head, and curled into a ball, returning to his deep sleep.

I sat there thinking over the events of the last few days, always coming to Richard Pemberton's curious discoveries. Richard could be lying for some sinister reason, but what that reason might be, I couldn't imagine.

This was certainly not the way to get rest. I resettled myself, sighed, and wished I had brought in my own water carafe. I looked at the hall door, dreading that drafty darkness lit only by blowing oil lamps at the two ends of the hall.

Across Jeremy's bed was his water carafe on the twin stand. I got up, walked around the bed, and carefully removed Jeremy's fingers from the glass. Then I reached for the carafe, poured and drank the water. For the moment my thirst was quenched. I settled back again and closed my eyes.

My sleep was filled with demons.

The next time I opened my eyes, the sun was pouring in. It must be mid-morning. But the demons had not finished with me, pulling at me, shaking me, forcing my head over a silver basin, walking my limp body up and down. . . .

Nicolas urged me to make the effort. Effort to what? "Just walk, sweetheart. I'll hold you. Left foot, right foot."

Other voices kept quizzing me. Most persistent was that wretched king's prosecutor, Monsieur Millet.

"Water," I managed to whisper finally. "From Jeremy's carafe. Thirsty."

Monsieur Millet's round blue eyes closed briefly. When he opened them, he was looking over my body at Nicolas, whose strong arms held me up.

"It was meant for the boy, monsieur. I think we have heard

enough. Will you put yourself in readiness, Monsieur Bertold? And you, the steward, please to accompany him."

I knew then. My worst nightmare had come true. Nicolas was being arrested. And this time the king would not dare to rescue him.

CHAPTER TWENTY-NINE

I tried to protest, to show them how wrong they were. I remember that it was difficult to get the words out. My tongue seemed dry, my mouth was dry, and everyone refused to understand my efforts.

It was enough to drive one mad.

Someone held me, a man with strong, restraining arms. Richard Pemberton. As for Nicolas, he had left me. I saw the door close behind him and his "warder," Grégoire. No one had a word to say in Nicolas's behalf until the Vicomte de St. Auden came into Jeremy's crowded room.

He looked at me with a gentle reassurance I appreciated before he said to Monsieur Millet, "You are wrong, you know. This is all contrived by an enemy of Nicolas Bertold. Bertold is meant to be the legal victim."

"Excuse me, Monsieur le Vicomte. I, myself, witnessed a bitter quarrel between Madame and Monsieur Bertold. Some little time later I also saw, by merest chance, that Monsieur Bertold was at the door of young monsieur's room." The king's prosecutor was gentle but unshakable.

"He didn't go in," I reminded him fiercely. But he ignored my words as those of some foolish, drugged female.

"Preposterous. The plot from the beginning has been against my friend," the vicomte added.

"Then why is his nephew always threatened, monsieur?"

"That proves the untruth of all the rest. Nicolas would never poison a child. And certainly not Madame Bertold, for all your snooping and spying. They are very much in love."

The king's prosecutor did not raise his voice at this insult. What he said sounded even more terrible in that quiet, reasonable voice.

"But I am afraid that you do not pursue the matter to its ultimate conclusion, monsieur. To all intents it was young Monsieur Daviot who was poisoned tonight. In the normal course of time young monsieur would have drunk from that carafe."

"I thought you said his wife was his target. Be consistent, Monsieur le Procureur."

They were both so exquisitely polite, it sickened me. As for Jeremy, he had been crying silently. He sniffed and looked at the vicomte.

"Nobody would kill Aunt Alain, not even Uncle Nicolas. It was me, don't you see? I'm the one they—"

"Your uncle loves you," I managed to get out hoarsely. "He wouldn't do that dreadful thing."

The vicomte said, "I quite agree. I'll go along with Your Excellency and my friend."

"So long as you make no interference, monsieur."

My head ached excruciatingly and gave me difficulty when I started to get up. I heard myself crying, "I want to go to him. Where is he?"

Richard Pemberton caught and held me while I struggled. He hadn't said a word, but I saw his face, shocked and determined. Opinionated as always, I thought.

I must have been ridiculously weak, unlike myself. I remembered very little for some time, perhaps an hour. I am told that Nicolas kissed me before he went away with the king's prosecutor and the vicomte.

I awoke in the bedchamber I shared with Nicolas. The sound of hoofbeats pounding over the moat bridge aroused me. I knew at once what had happened earlier. All those horrible charges, and Nicolas going away with Monsieur Millet. I had to get to Tours and help him in some way.

Out in the hall I heard Nanny Pemberton sneezing and blowing her nose. I called to her, and she tiptoed in, as though I were on my deathbed.

"My dear, your husband worries about you. He acted most peculiarly. He didn't want the vicomte to go with them. He wanted him to stay with you. Even that boy of mine acts strange. Galloping off as though—"

"Richard has gone?" I had to rush to get ready. It would be very like that impossible man to rush off with that ridiculous evidence of his. Anything to cause fresh trouble for Nicolas.

"I'm sure he didn't mean to disturb me," Nanny chattered on, pushing my crumpled dinner gown over to one side and sitting down. "He leaned over my bed and asked if I was asleep. How absurd, because, of course, if I was asleep, I could not answer him intelligently. I thought he would fuss, the way he usually does, so I said nothing. Then he just went away. All that racketing about. Where is he off to?"

"I've no idea. To the gate house, probably." To find more evidence? Or further. It seemed most unlikely that he would ride clear to town. "How was he dressed?"

"In a jacket. No. A kind of jerkin. Not at all substantial, should it come on to rain, as it often does here, you know."

Unlikely, then, that he had gone far. I laced myself into my corset, pulled over my head the first day gown I found in the big cupboard, and stepped into a pair of sturdy morocco slippers.

Nanny shook her head. She was on a different subject. "What was so shocking, I thought, was that impudent prosecutor looking into cupboards and finding a laudanum bottle. They say it was nearly empty. No one I ever heard of found laudanum or any other medication in a—what they call an armoire."

"Obviously everyone in Jeremy's room knew about it." I shared her distaste for Monsieur Millet, however. "It was the king's prosecutor who accompanied Nicolas when they locked the medicine away."

"My saints, Miss Alain! Can it be the king's prosecutor who tried to poison my lamb? He poisoned you by mistake?"

Even I had to laugh at that. "I can think of no conceivable reason." I had decided that I must know where Richard was going and what he was up to, if he didn't intend to go far.

I sent Nanny back to her bedroom and told her to ring for tea and whatever would calm her agitated spirits at her abrupt treatment by her son. Snatching up a shawl, I made my way, a trifle dizzily, up the steep flight of steps to the turret floor. The rooms of the dead housekeeper were some short distance down the narrow corridor. I tried the sitting room door and found the woman's remaining property in a haphazard condition as before, but some effort had been made to replace the furniture and the sofa cushions. The backs of the cushions were ripped, but someone, presumably Richard, had set them up again in the armchair and on an old love seat whose legs looked unsteady.

The carpet was smoothed back in place, and except for the edges, which were puckered up, it looked undisturbed.

I glanced around and thought of Richard's boast. He had found nothing directly incriminating against Nicolas on that sheet of figures the housekeeper kept in her sitting room, but the last time he discussed it with me, he hoped to find something in the small, narrow bedroom that opened off the sitting room.

I lowered the latch and opened the bedroom door. A tall, black pillar barred my way.

I was so startled, I cried out. Leocadia stood facing me, within an arm's length. For a few seconds she did not move.

It took me that long to pull myself together. She inclined her head with some slight trace of respect.

"Forgive me, madame. I must see to Monsieur Jeremy."

I conquered my shock with an effort.

"Why are you up here?"

The black brows arched in surprise. "But to inspect these rooms, madame. I am giving orders for the cleaning. Nearly all the guests have gone."

"Yes. I suppose they went while I was sick."

"Exactly, madame. *Pardon.*"

She passed me and went toward the outer door. I called after her.

"Did someone sleep here last night?"

"It would seem so. It is in a bad state. I believe Monsieur Pemberton spent some time here yesterday, and again this morning."

I glanced at her hands. They were empty. Unless she had hidden something in the bosom of her close-fitting black-and-white gown, she seemed to have taken nothing out.

But then, how could she? I was positive that it had been some new discovery that sent Richard galloping off pell-mell for God knows what purpose.

"Have I your leave, madame?"

"Yes, yes. You may go. Thank you."

When I heard the door close, I stepped into Madame Servier's bedroom and, finding a ladder-back chair close at hand, jammed it under the latch. Then I turned around and studied the austere little room. The bed coverlet was scrambled in a heap, and the mattress seemed to be set a trifle crookedly. I turned it over. This, too, showed knife cuts. Obviously Richard had searched here for more of the housekeeper's jotted figures.

I found nothing significant until I reached around to replace the coverlet and knocked one of the housekeeper's gowns off its wall peg. I picked up the black gown and decided that it hung too heavily for the material. I shook it, thought it had been weighted down, like many expensive gowns, in order to make them hang better. That could hardly be the case with Madame Servier's clothing. I felt along the seams. In the hem I touched what I had no doubt were coins.

With a little effort I tore the first threads of the hem and took out a dozen gold coins, one after the other. The largest was a twenty-franc piece. Most of them bore the profile of Louis Eighteenth or Charles the Tenth. One shiny five-franc coin showed the profile of the present "King of the French," as he styled himself.

The curious thing was not the discovery. Richard and I had known for a day or two that the woman was extracting money through "persuasion" when she died, but such small sums were incongruous. It is true that the quarterly rental of a room in Paris might cost no more than a couple of these coins, and many delicious meals could be obtained for one of them, but I had always thought that such vile bargains as Madame Servier practiced would involve hundreds of guineas.

I suppose the crime lay in the act itself, not in the payment.

The gown had dropped on the carpet. I started to pick it up and noticed that the carpet itself had been shifted. Contrary to my first thought, nothing was hidden under the edge. At a previous time, however, some form of spirits had been spilled on the carpet, which stuck to the wooden flooring in one patch. I pulled hard at the carpet in that place and found that torn strips of white paper, very like the Bertold stationery, stuck to the floor.

I tore off bits of paper that contained nothing but partial figures blurred by that long-ago wine stain. Again, in the old-fashioned way, they were listed in livres. Whatever else was listed opposite these figures had been torn away and carried off by Richard Pemberton, I did not doubt.

I got to my feet, realizing that Richard had not missed anything.

A cloud crossed the sun, shadowing the room for an instant. I went to the window, remembering suddenly that from this view I could see a small area where the estate road and the High Road joined. If I waited, perhaps I would see the coach that carried Nicolas and the others.

At the end of that ride, with all that was known against Nicolas, the guillotine might be waiting.

Don't think of it, I told myself. Something will be—must be—done.

My fingers closed over a tubular object in the deep-set recess. I tapped it absently on the little leaded panes, then examined the long tube for the first time. A naval spyglass. How like our spying housekeeper, the late Madame Servier! Small wonder that nothing escaped her.

I put the spyglass to my eye and studied the distant High Road. Nothing in sight. I brought the glass down to the moat bridge below. The low stone-and-wooden supports gleamed in the sun.

Something flashed at the periphery of my vision. While I stood there, puzzled, I saw a small figure, heavily bundled in an outsize hunting jacket, dart across the bridge and then stop on the other side, breathing heavily. I thought for a minute that Jeremy was headed toward the main estate road and perhaps the gate house, but he turned and headed south along the bank of the pond.

Where on earth was he going alone? And why?

I leaned out the window. He was concealed from my view now, between the sycamores ringing the pond, and the willows and lily pads that crowded the murky water near the shore.

He had wanted to go into the woods yesterday evening and failed. He seemed to have gotten away from surveillance now. I knew I must go after him. It was very possible that he had the key to all our disasters.

But beyond the far end of the pond, where the runoff trailed down into a distant valley, I saw curls of smoke and the upper half of a chimney above the trees. The tinker's wagon of the

Honiger family had a chimney like that. Surely Jeremy wasn't hurrying to meet those people who had frightened him in England.

I closed the window in a great hurry and got out of the room so fast, my forehead gave me a nagging reminder of my earlier laudanum-induced headache. No matter. I had to know where he was going and what he was up to.

In the front of the building the air revived me. The autumn breeze carried with it the smell of wood smoke and crisp, drying foliage. I crossed the bridge, answering my dead brother's insidious, if silent, accusations by closing my mind to them.

I began to run along beside the pond. A red squirrel scampered across the path, stopped beyond my reach where he sat up on his bushy tail and peered my way. The day around us was serenely beautiful with all its many shades of green and gold, scarlet and tan.

I was soon beyond the squirrel and enveloped in a stand of trees so thick that I could no longer see the château when I looked behind me. I thought I must come up with Jeremy soon, but that was not my immediate plan. Without giving him enough personal attention his parents, his uncle, and I had all indulged Jeremy, and nothing but tragedy came of it. From the first moment I should have guessed that he was hiding some terrible knowledge. Because of his physical problem, we had never made him face the consequences of his childish mischief.

Although William and I had been reared with a swat across the backsides when we behaved badly, I would never suggest corporeal punishment for Jeremy, but he should have been punished in other ways, sent to his room when disobedient, deprived of one of his endless gifts for a brief time. And above all, we adults must be ready to give him our own time now. That should be our first priority . . . when Nicolas and Jeremy and I were a family again.

I reached the little runoff stream and stopped to catch my

breath. My head ached excruciatingly. I stood there in the shadow of a clump of willows, aware of a gentle nudging around my shoes. I looked down. Several lily pads crowded against me and stuck to my stockings in a way that made me sick at their touch. They were like chill fingers reaching out of that black water. I heard myself gasp, but luckily the sound was almost inaudible.

Seconds later I heard Jeremy's shrill young voice.

"You walked so fast, I had to run. Didn't you want me to find it?"

I swung around, wondering where he could be hiding. Then I saw the marble pillars of the little *folie* a hundred yards above the stream, half concealed by sycamores and the cedar grove. More important, I must know who had met him there in the *folie*. I moved carefully, watching every step I took. I did not dare to reveal my presence by the snap of a twig or the crunch of leaves and needles underfoot.

At last, only a sycamore stood between me and the near portals of the crumbling little Greek temple. Jeremy coughed and pulled up his shirt collar. With his free hand he held out a small amber vial. Considering our recent dealings, I assumed that the bottle contained laudanum.

Jeremy shook the bottle. He was deeply troubled and agitated. "See? He never gave it to Old Henri like you said. It's been here all the time." His mouth trembled. My heart went out to him. He went on. "I felt so bad when they arrested him. It wasn't fair. And you never said that Aunt Alain would take it. That was bad. It hurt her. If I'd been awake, it wouldn't have happened. I wouldn't have let anybody drink that. You said nobody would."

I was breathless with anxiety to see his companion, who was somewhere in the back of the *folie*, probably at the stone bench between me and two of the pillars.

Jeremy's companion answered then and shook my own confident little world forever.

"Now, my lamb, never forget. I saw what happened after

that wicked man assaulted my William. My poor boy was covered with blood from your uncle's brutality. His lips were bleeding, I tell you. My William was lied to from the beginning, deceived by your mother and her family."

Nanny Pemberton had been Jeremy's guardian, his foster parent, forming his opinions, his beliefs, his brain, even catering to his illness and his whims. She had been his constant companion from birth. From the beginning it had been the fault of his careless, selfish parents, and later, his selfish aunt and uncle, with this appalling result. How deeply had she involved Jeremy in her crimes?

The old woman, in her mad devotion to my brother, must have instilled in Jeremy every ounce of her own jealousy and resentment against Nicolas. It was Nicolas who ran the Bertold properties, though William, as Yolande's husband, doubtless thought he had an equal right. It was Nicolas who had helped perpetuate the lie about Yolande's parentage. She was not the daughter of an ancient family but the bastard child of a gypsy servant. It was Nicolas who had struck Nanny's beloved William, spilling blood and later "threatening" him, as we had all heard, thanks to Nanny.

All of this poison was instilled in Jeremy from his birth, including William's own bitter jealousy and resentment.

I was sick at heart to discover how little I had ever understood Nanny, my lifelong friend and companion.

Jeremy stamped his foot. "You almost killed Aunt Alain. You tell me how Mama deceived Father, or don't you say that again! I won't listen."

Nanny protested. "I can't say it, my lamb. It's a grown-up secret. But it is very bad. The worst thing anyone can say about another grown-up."

But Jeremy looked down at the vial in his hand and shook his head. "The worst was killing Father and Mama like that. If I had really seen it, like you did, I'd have yelled and made Uncle Nicolas stop pulling that log out. . . . You should have done that when you saw him doing such a bad thing, Nanny."

I heard the pain of loss in his voice, and I wanted to hold Jeremy close, to comfort him. It was clear to me now that Jeremy had not actually seen Nicolas commit the act that killed William and his wife. Nanny had been the real witness, if witness she was. Then why should she persuade Jeremy to make the report to the police?

Because her violent prejudice against Nicolas Bertold was too well known. Her evidence would be suspect. But no one could imagine that Jeremy was guilty of such a complex lie. Small wonder that the eyewitness evidence came so many weeks after the so-called crime. It must have taken Nanny a long time to convince Jeremy that he alone could punish his "murderous uncle." Loneliness and her constant obsession might do it to him.

Nanny, I thought, still with that sick feeling of loss, we never knew you at all.

Nanny reached for the vial, but Jeremy held it behind him. I could see her face plainly now, her features working. Despite the awful crime of twisting that boy's mind and feelings, she suffered pain over it as well.

"You don't understand, Jeremy. I didn't know what it meant when I saw your uncle drag that log away. Not until after the thing happened. Then I understood." She pulled herself together and smiled; the warm, dear smile that had always seemed so motherly to me. "There, there, my lamb. It's all over now. That wicked man will pay for what he did to your mother and to my William."

I noticed that Jeremy was backing away from her, moving very slowly down the slope toward the sycamore where I stood. Beyond was the edge of the pond where the thick lily pads floated gently back and forth. I decided I could not wait. Much as Nanny loved Jeremy, she might be capable of doing him harm. But when Jeremy questioned her, I waited.

"In Old Henri's room that day, I saw you when Aunt Alain and Henry were talking. You picked up the cap I dropped."

"Yes, dear, and mighty careless of you it was. Your kind aunt had knitted that for you."

"Nanny, you put your hand over Old Henri's kettle."

Nanny seemed vague, but I knew that she was alert.

"Perhaps I did. I don't recall."

Jeremy cried out in a sad, wise voice, painfully old for a child. "Oh, Nanny, did you put something in the kettle? Then it wasn't Uncle that poisoned him?"

Nanny reacted with shock. "You forget, your uncle visited Henri that day as well. Who else could have given him that laudanum? Why should I do it, just to put another nail in that wicked man's coffin?" She took a step toward him. Seeing this, I steeled myself to get between them. Nanny was still protesting when I moved. "What a shameful thing to say! As though your old Nanny would do a thing like that."

"Wouldn't you, Nanny?" I asked, moving out in front of my nephew.

Of the two it was Nanny who recovered first. Jeremy panicked, crying to me, "Don't, Auntie, please. Go away. We've been so bad. You don't know. *Please*." Bless him. He was afraid Nanny would hurt me, but I knew from what I had overheard that Jeremy, himself, was merely a tool in Nanny's plan to destroy Nicolas Bertold.

Nanny understood him as well, and in spite of everything, her feelings were hurt. She reached out to touch him, but I pushed him behind me. Tears welled up in her pale eyes.

"Miss Alain, tell the child. I would as soon hurt my boy Richard as touch you or that poor lamb in anger."

"I know it, Nanny. Let's go home. Jeremy shouldn't have been running so far from the château. The Honigers are camped nearby."

"Gypsy schemers," Nanny murmured. "You remember what they did to you, Miss Alain. They did it for Master Nicolas."

I did not ask her why "Master Nicolas" would wish them to kidnap me. She was running on with her specious excuses.

"But you are right. I never should have let Jeremy go so

far today. Come along, dear." She reached for Jeremy's hand. Unfortunately the last few minutes had crystallized certain doubts that must have begun for Jeremy when he realized that I had been poisoned last night.

He tugged at my fingers. "Aunt Alain, could you go and see the man that took Uncle Nicolas away? You go and tell him . . . please."

We must be very careful. I wasn't afraid of Nanny. But I didn't want to be forced to use violence to protect ourselves from this old woman who had been my second mother.

"Later, Jeremy. Nanny and I want to go home and—and talk."

"Yes, my lamb," Nanny put in. "Your dear aunt will understand when I explain why we did it." She broke off as we started back down the little slope, walking carefully on the slippery needles. "Jeremy, take care."

Reverting to her earlier remark, I tried to be as understanding as possible.

"Nanny, I quarreled with Nicolas last night. I must say, he deserves to be punished. Let them think he killed Old Henri. And—and William. I know you didn't mean to kill our William." I hoped to bring out the truth, but it was hard to calmly discuss the monstrous things I now suspected.

Young as he was, Jeremy understood what I was doing. He clutched my hand tightly. I sensed that he was staring at me, but I could not go on with this terrible pretense and look at him, so I avoided that searching gaze.

Nanny sounded a little wild. "It was that wicked man who did it. He changed his mind and didn't go to the village; so there it was. A trap for him, but my William fell into it. Nicolas Bertold caused Master William to die, as truly as if he himself had dragged that log away."

Jeremy made a plaintive, animal sound, and I pinched his hand in warning.

"You are remarkable, Nanny. Such a heavy log! Even moving it a foot or two must have been a tremendous effort."

"But that was easy. The four-horse team was waiting on the—" She became aware of Jeremy staring at her, his eyes wide with horror.

To divert her attention I said hurriedly, "Poor Jeremy doesn't understand how some things must be done. We had better talk later."

Perhaps she knew me too well. Nanny seemed to have lost interest in the subject. She murmured, "How cold it is for September! Might I borrow your shawl, Miss Alain?"

"I'm sorry. This bodice is very thin. I came out in a hurry. Then, too, Nanny, your cold seems to be quite cured, doesn't it?"

I felt all the cruelty of my refusal and the reminder of what was probably a masquerade of illness on her part, but I thought her old-fashioned pelisse was warm enough. There may have been another more sinister notion in her head when she hoped my hands would be busy with the shawl.

Nanny pulled her pelisse up around her throat. She looked so hurt, I could scarcely believe that she was guilty of these hideous tricks against us, culminating in murder. I steeled myself against pity. She had proven all too dangerous.

I felt Jeremy's body stiffen with tension. In spite of myself I looked around to see what made him stare. Lumbering up the bank of the little runoff stream was the gypsy bear Yvgeny. In that quick glance I got of him before he could attract Nanny's attention, I thought the creature appeared bored but more powerful than ever. Then Nanny turned abruptly. She didn't seem aware of the creature, perhaps because at that moment a black bird flew off the pond lilies and southward until it was lost in the hazy sky.

Then Jeremy screamed, "No! No! Don't!" At the same moment I felt a terrific pressure against my shoulder, throwing me off-balance. I knew even as I slipped down over a carpet of fallen needles that Nanny had hurled her body against me with all her strength.

As I scrambled to regain my balance I cried to Jeremy, "Run!"

I heard Nanny's indignant order. "Wait, lamb. Wait for Nanny." But I could not see them. I could only hear his yells, which were punctuated by coughing and panic-stricken cries. The world of treetops, sunlight, and willows spun around me as my fingers lost their grip on the slippery willows.

I felt the cold shock of the pond waters close about my feet, then around the hems of my clothing. My attempts to swim were hampered by my many skirts. As they soaked rapidly, oozing stirred-up mud, they dragged me down beneath the black surface of the pond.

CHAPTER THIRTY

With a furious effort I pushed myself up toward the surface, dragging my infernal skirts that tangled around my legs and tried in every way to pull me back into the murky depths. I got my head above the surface only just in time. My lungs felt as though they would burst in another second.

Dragging those petticoats and outer skirts behind me, I began to swim to the near shore. I hadn't swum since my childhood when William loaned me his breeches and shirt, out of sight of Nanny, of course. She would have been frightfully upset. As though my thinking of her conjured up the demon, she knelt on the shore, and just when I groped for a bush growing low on the embankment, she began to beat me about the head with a dead tree limb.

The limb itself would not have been so painful, but several of its sharp twigs jabbed at me like knives. I cried, "Nanny, it's Alain. Your own Alain . . . Nanny?"

Even squinting to avoid those poisonous jabs, I could see her sorrowing face. I did not doubt that she suffered, but with William's death her whole thinking appeared to have centered on one thought, to avenge him and obtain the entire Bertold estate for William's child.

"Don't fight me!" she commanded with harsh and desperate force. "You won't take him away from me like the Bertolds did. William was my boy, like Richard. There! You won't—"

Flinching at the stab of a sharp twig, I fell back into the waters, dragged down by my sodden skirts. Whatever else she cried to me was drowned by a loud, clapping sound that reverberated across the pond. Dazed, I tried to surface again but became entangled in lily roots that curled around me like serpents. In the waters over my head the light was cut off by a roof of lily pads. I fought wildly to free myself from those twining, curling roots.

When I clawed my way upward, the lily pads proved a ghastly barrier to the air above. One of my arms managed to work its way out into the air. I waved that arm frantically.

The pressure was too much. Coughing, swallowing the chill water, and inhaling in spite of myself, I knew I was going under for the last time. I remember thinking, Let them discover the truth. For Nicolas. And for Jeremy. . . .

A violent jerking on my wrist and arm aroused me. I found myself drawn up painfully by one arm, through the black waters, dragging strings of lily roots with me, into the blessed air. Curiously enough, it was when I could breathe again that I began to choke and cough. In the process of drowning I had lost the ability to feel the death that crept into my lungs.

The first thing I saw when I was yanked ashore and dragged up over the reeds was the evil, grinning face of Zilla Honiger. The second was her companion and familiar, the big brown bear, Yvgeny. He stuck his snout into my face, and I drew back. More gentle hands than Mrs. Honiger's took me from her and from the curious animal. In a daze I looked around, saw the two boys, Demian and Josef, staring at me, their sisters looking over their shoulders in great interest.

Demian's anxious voice woke me to the violent scene that

had been enacted there. "You are safe now, Miss Alain. The old witch can't hurt you."

I looked at Zilla Honiger questioningly.

No one took offense that I should instantly accuse the woman who had saved my life. Zilla's grin broadened. Her two canine teeth glistened in the sunlight. Demian hurried to correct my misapprehension.

"The old lady who teaches. Father saw her across the pond. We all heard the little boy screaming for help. Father made a clean shot. Into the shoulder, it was. She is lying over in the grass. Father is trying to revive her."

Poor, twisted Nanny. I raised my head with an effort, trying to see her. She looked very frail, a small bundle of bones. She did not move. I said, "Help me to my feet. I must find my nephew."

"No, no, mistress. He is safe." Demian tried to stop me, but by leaning on his slim body, I pulled myself up. Seeing that there was no help for my obstinacy, Demian took my arm, and I began to stumble along, still coughing up the pond waters I had apparently swallowed.

"Where is he?"

"Very smart boy. He ran toward the château calling for help. Very loud, he was."

Josef took my other arm. "Not to the château. On the estate road. He heard horses and a carriage. You hear them?"

I heard them now, quite near, the hoofbeats and then, in the distance, the jingle of a harness. Was it possible that Nicolas and Monsieur Millet had returned? A miracle. I began to run. The boys begged me to "be easy."

By the time the heavy, wooded area parted briefly and we could see the walls of the château, a horseman reined up at the moat bridge. It was Nicolas, still dressed very correctly in frock coat and neat trousers, as befitted a gentleman appearing for a prosecutor's examination. His hat must have fallen off somewhere on the fast ride that winded the big black stallion. Before him in the saddle there appeared to be a large bundle.

Leocadia and a stable boy rushed across the bridge. The stable boy took the horse in charge, but to me the most astonishing sight of all was the "bundle" Nicolas set down on the bridge in Leocadia's arms. It proved to be Jeremy. An instant later Nicolas raced toward me with Jeremy valiantly following after.

I broke away from the boys and ran also, crying in a senseless way. "You are free? A miracle, sweetheart."

Against the strong, warm haven of his body, I kept hugging him and repeating a great deal of nonsense about miracles.

He raised my chin with two fingers while he corrected me. "The miracle is that you called me 'sweetheart' without being prompted."

Then we kissed each other with a violence and passion that seemed to make up for all the recent hours of our estrangement.

All around us there must have been excitement and activity. The carriage and team of Monsieur Millet pulled up just short of the bridge, and Richard Pemberton burst out, rushing past us along the edge of the pond. Perhaps he guessed what had happened to his mother.

Grégoire and Leocadia gave Monsieur Millet the greeting and attention he obviously expected. Nicolas and I became aware at last that Jeremy was tugging on my sodden skirts. His voice was very small.

"Could I see if Nanny hurts bad?"

"Yes. Of course, you may."

He hesitated. "She was very bad. She made me bad too. She said Uncle Nicolas killed my father and Mama. But he didn't."

I thrilled to the understanding in Nicolas's deep voice when he assured the boy, "No, Jeremy. I didn't kill your father. Or poison Old Henri, who was my friend. And I didn't try to poison you with laudanum last night."

Jeremy scoffed, "Oh, I know that. Nanny made me promise not to drink from that glass. This morning I was supposed to say, 'It tastes funny.' Then they would know Uncle tried to poison me. She said you should be punished for your wickedness, Uncle Nicolas. Only—you weren't wicked, after all."

He started along the path after Richard Pemberton, stopped, and explained to Nicolas, "I thought about it a lot this morning. That's why I went to find the poison bottle. Nanny hid it in the little temple. Nanny was the only one that knew where we put it. And then I found it upside down, not the way I saw her put it there the first time. And I thought about her in Henri's room."

He hesitated, wondering, I suppose, if he really wanted to face Nanny. Then he went on along the path.

Arm in arm, Nicolas and I followed more slowly. "Why did they hide the laudanum in the first place?" I asked Nicolas.

He shook his head. "Probably Nanny didn't want anyone to know how much was used around her. The less she had contact with, the more easily she could turn suspicion to those who handled it. I know she pretended to object when the doctor ordered laudanum for Jeremy."

"So you were forced to give him the dosage yourself."

I think Nanny's deviousness troubled me most. No one could ever really follow the tortuous processes of her mind. Her hatred of Nicolas must have grown more virulent every time she thought William was bested in one of his eternal arguments with Nicolas.

By the time we reached the huddled little group on the grass beneath the trees, the Honigers had stepped back. Josef was holding Yvgeny on a leash, and Mr. Honiger was holding his rifle behind him in the hope that Richard could not see it.

Nicolas gave the Honigers a heartfelt "Thank you, my friends." His voice was quiet, but Richard heard it and looked up. Nanny's head lay resting on his knee. One of his hands covered her cheek. I was touched when he spoke.

"I know you did not mean to kill her."

Honiger touched his stocking cap in respectful salute. "True, Monsieur. It was her arm. She was beating Madame with a stick." Richard winced, but Honiger added, "I meant only to stop that arm. The lady is dead, then?"

Jeremy touched Nanny's curled fingers in a tentative way.

Richard nodded. "Shock, I suppose. Perhaps," he admitted painfully, "it is better this way. She was not herself. My mother was ever a gentle woman. It is only that she loved too well."

"May the heavens preserve us from such love," Zilla Honiger remarked in her guttural way, and for once in my life I agreed with her.

I dreaded the painful discussion to come. I was still afraid of the king's prosecutor's view of these events. Who could believe that a slight old female had committed staggering crimes with only one object in mind, to destroy Nicolas Bertold?

"Richard will certainly defend her," I pointed out while we waited for Monsieur Millet. The king's prosecutor was being divested of his greatcoat and hat once again and being served a hot, spiced brandy before facing us. I could only hope that the brandy gentled his spirit, so to speak, and he could admit the truth, with only the evidence of a prejudiced woman (myself) and a boy barely eight years old.

For some reason Nicolas was not afraid. I still didn't understand how he had been permitted to return to the château, what Richard Pemberton had to do with it, and why Monsieur Millet was treating Nicolas like a host and not a suspect prisoner. Nicolas further surprised me by his unexpected warmth when he spoke of Richard.

"He wants to see you, sweetheart. I told him I would leave you alone."

"He has been against you from the start," I reminded him.

"But when the choice came, he was a man of honor. God knows what it cost him!"

Richard must have been waiting in the hall. Nicolas went out, gestured to him, and as he had promised, left us alone. In his black frockcoat and holding his black beaver hat, he looked much older than his years. When he took my hand, I kissed him softly on the cheek. He started to say, "I thought it was—I had no idea that Mother—"

I cut him short. "None of us knew. She was sick, Richard. It began long ago. You know how she favored William, over me, and even over you. Something in his nature seemed to need her. You were self-sufficient. So was I. So she clung to William."

He shook his head. "I should have known. All of us thought the bridge collapse was an accident until Mother began to talk about the quarrels and Bertold's 'threats' against William, as she saw it. Then there was Jeremy parroting everything she told him. My God! I believed his story. I thought he had actually seen his uncle loosen that log. And then, to read exactly how Mother managed it—I became physically sick, Alain. I sat there on the side of Madame Servier's bed, asking myself if I could betray my own mother. I tried to tell myself that it was all a lie conjured up by this Servier woman. But I knew better. Everything fit."

"I understand."

"But I couldn't let an innocent man die. They wouldn't execute my— They would see that she was mad. So I rode off to stop that carriage." He hesitated. "I will tell you frankly, I don't like Bertold. Never did. But an injustice was done and I had to right it. It's the English way, you know."

"It was very noble of you."

Dear Richard! A trifle pompous, certainly insular, but an honest man.

After an awkward hesitation between us he shook hands with me, and I walked with him to the double doors. Just as he was leaving, he made a poignant little remark I would not soon forget.

"I sometimes wish Mother had cared as much for me as for William."

He bowed to Nicolas, who took his hand warmly.

"You did a courageous thing, Pemberton. I wish we might have been friends."

Richard said nothing but walked rapidly away.

It was all very sad and mysterious. But I had Nicolas back, and this time I would fight like a tigress if they tried to accuse him again.

Monsieur Millet arrived in the little Gold Salon with a businesslike step that alarmed me, but I was soon put at ease by his manner to Nicolas. They shook hands like old comrades. He motioned us to take seats opposite him by the sunny window when he had been royally seated in a gilt throne chair that was usually reserved for such dignitaries as the king and his sons.

"Bertold, I believe we have untangled this dangerous web. Among others, your nephew has been useful."

I said anxiously, "He should not have been questioned so soon. He is very upset over Nanny—over Mrs. Pemberton's death."

He held up an imperious hand. "One considers these things, madame. But the little monsieur visited me in my room. A brave lad, despite his fears of that gypsy band. He tells me, incidentally, that his feelings toward the Honiger family have undergone some slight changes. I thought you would like to know."

"I'm glad," Nicolas said.

The king's prosecutor agreed. "I understand that this nurse, Madame Pemberton, warned him that they would murder him. It seems she had a great abhorrence toward them."

Because of the lie about Yolande's legitimacy, I thought, but said nothing.

He turned directly to me. "The woman confessed her crimes to you, madame?"

"She explained and excused them. Jeremy saw her poison the kettle in which Old Henri was boiling his coffee, but he didn't understand at the time. Perhaps it never occurred to him."

Monsieur Millet nodded. "An act of pure and simple spite, to give credence to the gossip she spread that Henri carried out his master's orders in dropping that chandelier. A twisted mind indeed."

Nicolas began to walk up and down. "The fall of that old chandelier was an accident. Gossiping servants must have carried that absurd story."

The king's prosecutor agreed. "Your maid, madame, this Marie-Clare, she tells me she first heard the gossip from Madame Pemberton. Then, when Henri died, the story caught fire, as she knew it would. Because of the death of the old man, this madwoman pointed a finger at Bertold. It led the way to what was to be the climax, the false attempt to poison the young monsieur and implicate Monsieur Bertold."

Nicolas said, "Hatred can do terrible things. I have seen it in war."

"This time," Millet contradicted him, "it was love. I made no doubt that when that baby—your brother, madame—was put into her arms, she began to love him even better than her own boy. These things happen. Natures are different. Perhaps this William was of a nature more attractive to her."

I asked abruptly, "Why did you permit Nicolas to return home, monsieur? Did Richard have something to do with it? He told me of something he found in Madame Servier's possessions."

The king's prosecutor exchanged a quick nod with Nicolas.

"Monsieur Pemberton indeed, madame. It seems he was prowling the attics and servants' bedrooms, searching, as he admits, for evidence against my friend here. Instead he found what seems to be genuine evidence against his mother. It must have cost him a great deal when he took one of Bertold's mounts and rode out to save Bertold from arrest. But he should not have left his mother unguarded."

I shook my head. I understood.

"She told me he stopped by. Richard thought his mother was asleep. Poor man. We were all so wrong about her."

I thought of the gypsies who had saved my life. And then I remembered that night at the Ferndene fair. Nanny knew that if she implicated the Honigers, she would involve their friend and protector, Nicolas Bertold. With Nanny dead I would probably never be able to prove that it was Nanny who struck me and left me in the gypsy wagon. She must have been driven to that desperate act when she saw I was falling in love with the devil of her nightmares.

She had even used the accidental breaking of the rein on the pony cart to her advantage. She may well have cut it later to make it appear deliberate, an act traceable to Nicolas and his gypsy friends.

The king's prosecutor showed us several crumpled, wine-stained sheets of Bertold stationery. The edges were ragged, undoubtedly where Richard had torn them off the floor.

"To answer your question, madame, these appear to be the records of the Servier woman's sharp dealings. She saw a kitchen apprentice steal a silver spoon. A coachman drunk. That sort of thing. Each time they paid for her knowledge. Perhaps only a few sou. Or several francs. Read for yourself, madame, these pages about Madame Pemberton."

I took them up. Like the others I had seen in Madame Servier's room, they were written in a positive hand. But these were a trifle blurred by the wine stains. Still, they were clear enough.

> To the Procureur du Roi:
>
> I have held these notes until I felt it the right time to disclose the matter to you. A case for you: L'Anglaise, Pemberton. One must describe the act. It

is safer, should La Pemberton threaten me. With the child's spyglass I saw her today.

The team was waiting for the carriage. Monsieur Bertold, having repaired the bridge with Jehan-Fidele, intended a visit to town. La Pemberton studied the situation. Then she looped the reins of the bay mare around the log monsieur had placed to strengthen the bridge. She prodded the horse in the hindquarters. The mare leapt forward. La Pemberton then removed the reins. The log was partially free, not noticeable unless one were suspicious, as I am. She went into the house. She appeared nervous, as she should be.

I puzzled much over this curious thing she did. But then, later, the English monsieur and Mademoiselle Yolande were killed, and Jehan as well. But it was Monsieur Bertold who had been expected to cross that bridge. And me, I understood then.

This was the end of the note to "Monsieur le Procureur du Roi, Tours, Indre et Loire."

I took up the next sheet and read what I supposed would not be sent to the king's prosecutor, since it clearly involved Madame Servier's efforts to bleed the criminal.

I spoke with great politeness to La Pemberton, describing what I had seen. She was agitated. She paid me five livres. It was all she had, or so she said. But later, when she lied to the procureur du roi and pretended that young Monsieur Jeremy had seen the log removed—then I knew she would find more money. I mentioned her son as provider . . .

L'Anglaise produced ten livres. She is like a well I can visit when I have a thirst.

> Another little drink from the Pemberton well. Three livres.
>
> Nothing. If I do not receive my petit *pourboire* by the week's end, I will send the note to the police. One must have honesty in one's dealings.

"Are there more?" I asked, for the back of the page was blank.

Monsieur Millet smiled grimly. "Several, dealing with local acquaintances. As you see, Madame Servier had no time to send me the note containing the story of the Englishwoman's crime. It would be my guess that the last entry was made shortly before Madame Servier's unfortunate accident on the staircase."

I shuddered and gave him the pages. We looked at each other—Nicolas, Monsieur Millet and I. Nicolas closed his eyes. I knew he felt what I did, the horror of Nanny's life, blindly devoted to one person she had reared from infancy and believed omnipotent. Then he went to France and discovered that he was not omnipotent. Every hurt he either suffered or provoked, she felt it more deeply.

I saw the king's prosecutor's expression change. He looked vaguely uncomfortable. Nicolas and I followed his gaze and saw Jeremy looking very small, framed in the doorway by two gilt-paneled doors. Leocadia stood behind him, expressionless as usual.

I held out my arms, and Jeremy ran to me. After a little hesitation he hugged me so hard that I protested laughingly. With his face pressed hard against my bosom he pleaded, "I got lonesome."

"I know, dear. But you'll never be lonesome again. Will he?" I looked at Nicolas who reached out and tousled Jeremy's hair.

"Never. Well, Nephew, you liked riding before me on the horse, didn't you? What you shall have is your very own pony cart, where you won't be close enough to cough and sneeze."

"I'd love that. Thank you, Uncle." He added shyly, "I'm glad you aren't what Nanny said. 'Cadia told me Nanny was wrong, only I didn't believe her. Nanny said the gypsies would cut me up with knives because they hated Father. But I know that's not true. Because 'Cadia wouldn't do things like that."

"No, Monsieur Jeremy. I would not do that."

As usual, Leocadia showed none of her feelings. I began to suspect that only Jeremy saw the warm, human side of her. She addressed the rest of us.

"Monsieur and Madame de St. Auden are waiting in the Great Hall. The vicomte has told Madame of your meeting with Monsieur Pemberton on the road."

Nicolas groaned. "We should never have let him go home. I haven't even had a moment alone with my wife."

I welcomed the jovial king's prosecutor's acceptance of the problem. "Young monsieur, you and I will play host to these charming guests."

Jeremy was thrilled to play host and took the arm he offered. In the doorway Monsieur Millet reminded us, "Tomorrow we will visit the prefecture, and you and young monsieur will make the statements. We may count upon Monsieur Pemberton as well."

He went out, telling Jeremy how important he would be when he made his statement. Leocadia moved out behind them with all her accustomed dignity.

I said, "We must tell Jeremy who Leocadia really is."

"Soon. But we have other matters to cover first."

He swung me around so suddenly that I almost lost my balance. Though I laughed, he silenced my mouth with his own, hotly conquering any amusement I might have expressed.

I had never surrendered to my own desires quite so willingly.